LOVE IN STRANGE PLACES

YOU CAN RUN, BUT YOU CAN'T HIDE FROM LOVE

The timeless love stories from
True Romance and True Love live on.

Edited by Barbara Weller,
Cynthia Cleveland and Nancy Cushing-Jones

A BROADLIT BOOK

BroadLit

October 2012

Published by

BroadLit ®
14011 Ventura Blvd.
Suite 206 E
Sherman Oaks, CA 91423

ISBN 978-0-9859596-6-1

Produced in the United States of America.

Visit us online at www.TruLOVEstories.com

This collection is dedicated to all of you who are looking for true love or have already found it.

Love in Strange Places

You Can Run, But You Can't Hide from Love

Table Of Contents

Introduction

What is the perfect place to find true love? Most likely it's not a question you've pondered, and yet you probably do have a pretty clear idea of the scenario. You'll meet your man in a gorgeously romantic setting while you're looking your best and feeling on top of your game.

Certainly you don't think of finding true love in your kitchen at the end of a terrible day at work, or when you're a passenger in a semi-truck being driven by a handsome stud -- *and* you're vomiting because you're pregnant with another man's baby! And yet, IT happens. You can stumble into true love in the most decidedly unromantic places and under some pretty shocking conditions– as you are about to discover through the stories in this collection.

True love – thank goodness! -- has also been found when you decide to literally escape from a twisted "love" -- such as a stalker's crazed obsession or a father's incestuous possession. The genuine love these women eventually found was all the more glorious when juxtaposed against the terror of their past.

Then there's the failure of merely good-enough love, which can lead you to despair of ever finding true love. To protect your fragile heart, you might play mind games by telling yourself that you don't care about true love or that you *aren't* looking for it or that you don't need it to be happy. You will read stories here, however, where that ruse eventually just didn't hold up in the face of a beckoning true love. Ultimately you have to risk shedding your defenses – and the disappointments of your romantic past – in order to slip into true love.

So if you enjoy asking couples, "How did you two meet?" be prepared for a wild ride of answers to that question in these stories. Spoiler Alert: True love is going to find you no matter how down and dirty you look or feel about yourself, how unglamorous the setting, how traumatic your past or present is. True love, as it turns out, writes a new story for every couple.

SAVED BY A TRUCK-DRIVIN' STUD
He was the only thing that stood between my baby and me and utter despair

"Hey, there, Kelli," Luke Jameson called as he walked into the gas station. Long-legged and broad, his twice-a-month visit was usually a highpoint in my life. But that day, even Luke's shy friendliness represented only yet another shame-provoking poke at my own stupidity.

"Hey yourself, Luke," I said. Leaning against the bathroom door, I jerked my hand to my mouth as a second wave of nausea churned my stomach and bolted like lightning up my throat. I raced back into the rest room just in the nick of time.

A few disgusting noises and gut-ripping heaves later and the illness settled, leaving me weak and weary yet again. For a moment, I simply palmed my forehead, my elbow on the chipped toilet seat. Tears gathered in my eyes and total wretchedness flooded throughout my system. How could I have been so dumb, so careless, so totally infatuated?

"Kelli?" Luke's questioning voice sounded from behind me. I felt his hesitant, but strong, hand on my back. "You okay, sugar?"

He offered me a wet paper towel, then gently massaged my shoulders, smoothing the wayward hair away from my eyes. Humiliated to be found in such an unattractive state, I struggled to stand and flushed the revolting mess down the toilet.

"I'm okay, Luke, thanks. But you shouldn't be in the ladies' room, you know."

"Well," he chuckled, peering hard into my face, "I figured at five o'clock in the mornin' the ladies' room wouldn't be exactly crowded with females. Besides, you looked pretty green when you came rushing in here. Are you okay, Kelli? Maybe you'd better go on home. There's a lot of that old flu going 'round, and you don't want to get any sicker than you ought to be."

Luke's genuine worry added to my disgrace. I pushed around him, washing my hands and face. Though I wouldn't have wished my current plight upon my worst enemy, I couldn't fight the maternal urge to be as germ-free as possible. Clean and tidy, my hormonal imbalance calmed for the day, I studied myself in the mirror.

How could I have been so foolish?

"Kelli?"

Again, Luke touched my arm, his expression puzzled and alarmed. At twenty-five, Luke was eight years my senior. Yet despite the tough, lonely life he led as an interstate truck driver, he had managed to retain his boyish charm. Luke Jameson was an old-fashioned softy.

In the six months I'd known him through my job as an early-morning cashier at the truck stop, he'd been a steady, personable customer. He always had a self-effacing smile, a kind word, and a stray, abandoned animal tucked under his arm. The local humane society shuddered when Luke came into town! And while Luke was well-built and carried himself on a sturdy stride, he was not a particularly handsome man or gifted conversationalist.

Inwardly, I snorted. I'd fallen for a good-looking, fast-talking guy and come up alone, miserable, and pregnant. When my boyfriend found out about the baby, he'd merely scowled, and told me to get an abortion. When I refused and begged him to marry me instead, he'd casually said, "No way" and deserted me like one of Luke's doomed puppies.

My parents hadn't behaved much better than my creepy boyfriend. With five children of their own, they didn't exactly welcome another mouth to feed. They'd been disappointed that their supposed golden child had ruined her youth on a hot-blooded man and motherhood.

Like my lover, Mom and Dad had given me a heinous ultimatum: Have an abortion and go back to school, or take my troubles and stand on my own two feet.

It had been bad enough that the father of my baby had forsaken me, but to be left high and dry by my own family was an embarrassing, shabby degradation.

"Kelli?"

The squeak of the bathroom door and Luke's peeping presence snapped me out of my woeful reverie once more. I sighed.

"What is it, Luke?"

"I'm having engine problems with the rig. Do you mind if I drive it around back, check it out?"

"Go ahead, Luke," I said.

I glanced at my watch. Five-fifteen in the morning. The cook wasn't in yet and I was in serious need of food. I was sure that the late-night cook was in the back catching up on some sleep.

Since I'd become pregnant, my morning sickness was followed by an urgent, almost painful hunger. Looking at Luke, I realized that he must be hungry, too.

"Before you start work, how about a little breakfast? I'm not much in the kitchen, but I can scrabble a mean omelet and fry up some tasty bacon."

He shot me such a quizzical look that I had to laugh.

"How can you be hungry after all that vomiting, little lady?"

"Just lucky, I guess!" I chuckled cynically, and patted my slightly curved tummy. "You hungry or not?"

"Yeah, sounds good."

Twenty minutes later, I laid a full plate in front of him, and began digging greedily into my own food. Glutton-like and simply famished as only a pregnant girl can be, I hardly noticed the weird, silent stares of my breakfast partner. I was halfway through my meal when Luke leaned forward, a baffled question about to escape his lips.

"Are you pregnant, Kelli?"

Luke's on-the-mark query startled me. I had been so engrossed by my feeding frenzy that I'd nearly forgotten an explanation for my appetite.

I glanced up at Luke mid-bite, then self-consciously, my eyes batted shut.

Although I didn't know Luke all that well, I hated to see the condescending expression I knew my answer would evoke. For some unknown reason, I could not bare that "how could you have been so stupid" smirk from Luke. Still, he was no nincompoop, and he'd obviously pinpointed my ailment.

"Yes, Luke, I am pregnant."

A quaint smile lifted his lips and he reached across the table, covering my hand with his. Luke appeared almost misty as his eyes ranged up and down my body, his fingers flexed sentimentally over mine. "Congratulations, Kelli. You must be so happy!"

Speechless, I felt my jaw drop and my eyes widen. Although only my doctor, parents, and disinterested lover knew of my with-child situation, nobody, not one solitary person, had treated this like a jubilant celebration.

"Your husband must be very proud." Luke glowed, a curious tinge of envy brightened his eyes.

"I'm not married, Luke," I whispered guiltily, expecting him to let go of my hand and harden his heart against me like everyone else had.

But once again, he amazed me. Instead of attacking my lack of character or spurning my slatternly behavior, he only nodded, his grin still intact. "Nevertheless, a baby is always reason to rejoice. They renew our hope in tomorrow."

A guttural sneer puckered my mouth. Luke's statement had brought a fresh crop of pain to my voice. "Maybe to some people, Luke. But according to my baby's father, my folks, and even my doctor—this baby is a tragedy. A horrible mistake that will burden my life, destroy my future, and make me an old maid before my time."

Totally astonished, Luke inhaled harshly. "Even the father thinks this way?"

"*Especially* the father!"

Luke whistled quietly. "And, the guy doesn't want to marry you, sugar?"

"No, he says a baby is too much responsibility. He thinks it would interfere too much with his plans."

"Seems he should have thought of that before—" Luke stopped abruptly. Since he was too nice a gentleman to voice his most honest thoughts, I supplied the coarse words for him.

"Guess I should have thought about it, too. After all, even in this enlightened day and age, girls still get stuck with the toughest decisions."

He shrugged, his customary good-humored grin easing his taut features. "That's all water under the bridge now, Kelli. Do you love him?"

"I don't know. I know I did once upon a time. But when he was so brutal about the baby and all—I just don't know. Guess that really makes me a piece of trash, a real—"

Luke's hand stiffened on mine and he lifted my chin with an unsparing index finger. Intense sincerity warmed his plain features and deepened his voice. "What that makes you, Kelli, is an inquisitive, inexperienced seventeen-year-old girl who, unfortunately, confused love with desire and passion. You aren't in an easy position, there are no definite answers, but it isn't the end of the world, you know."

"Your optimism is admirable, Luke, but not very realistic to me right now."

He grunted, frowning in mock indignation. "On the contrary, Kelli. Optimism can always improve realism. I know your folks aren't pleased, but what do they think about your condition?"

I felt my hands begin to tremble at the mere thought of my parents. "Oh, they're as bad as my boyfriend. They don't want me to get married, either. They want me to get an abortion and forget about this terrible fiasco."

Luke cocked his head in pensive thought. "Makes sense, Kelli. Remember, your mom and dad are in shock just like you are. More importantly, however, *you* are *their* baby. They love you and are looking out for your best interests."

Up until that second, I'd never thought about that point before. What Luke had said was true. I was their baby, and they only wanted what was best for me—for all my brothers and sisters. Mom and Dad had invested their entire adult lives in raising us kids. They understood the consequences of my sexual conduct. They also recognized what lay ahead for my baby and me. Mom and Dad had known much more than me.

Still, I wasn't convinced, and couldn't quite grasp the ramifications of it all. Then, once again, Luke startled me with another unexpected question.

"And what do *you* want to do? What will make Kelli happy?" he asked solemnly. His relentless concern for my feelings, my wishes, got to me.

Since I'd learned about my pregnancy, no one had even thought to ask me what I wanted, wondered what *I* thought best. And while they all believed in the "my body, my choice" scenario, they'd neglected to consult me. Not that it would have mattered any.

"I don't know, Luke. I really don't know. It seems each way I turn, people are hammering me with accusations, telling me what I must do. My boyfriend has left me, my folks and I quarrel constantly— bitter, ugly, loudmouthed battles where no one listens to anyone. I'm continuously torn, always in an uproar. I come up with lots of questions, but not many answers. Between my throwing up and my emotional state, I can't think straight anymore. I cry all the time, too. It's as though I got pregnant and my brain went out the window alongside my virtue!"

"Don't run yourself down, Kelli. Yes, you made a mistake. But, aside from marrying a man who doesn't love you or having an abortion before you're ready, you do have other options."

"Yeah," I lamented, whimpering my secret fear, "I can always kill myself. That'd put an end to everything and all my problems would instantly be solved!"

Suddenly, I burst into tears and boohooed like a tiny baby myself. I covered my face and hung my head. I'd never felt so alone, so swallowed by despair.

Visions of pill-popping unconsciousness, bloody razors, and fiery car crashes obliterated my common sense and brought a chilly, eerie peace to my pounding heart. They were half-baked schemes, yet nonetheless potent.

But before anything could really take root or lodge too indelibly within my soul, powerful arms engulfed me; a steady, solid heartbeat pulsated beneath my tearstained cheek. "It's okay, Kelli, everything will be all right. Don't cry. I know your life has hit a horrifying glitch, but it isn't that black, it isn't that hopeless. Suicide is definitely not an option."

Luke's soothing voice and gentle cradling surrounded me and somehow eased my heart.

As Luke pulled me to his lap, rocked me and stroked my hair, I continued to sob, and mourn the burden of my impulsive sins. Somehow, despite the fact that we were barely acquaintances, unrelated and from two different worlds, I was comforted, and felt worthy of someone's affectionate embrace. Luke dried my eyes. He gave me an encouraging wink.

"What you need most, I think," he contemplated out loud, "is a chance to think things through. Rationally, calmly—without outside interruptions. How far along are you, Kelli?"

"The doctor says I'm six weeks."

"Then you still have time. You don't have to do anything right this minute."

"No, but I'll have to do something very soon."

Luke sat absently petting my hair, staring out the window. By the time my school-hour replacement had come in, Luke had reached a decision of his own.

"Look, Kelli, I know that this will all sound kind of bizarre, but it's the best I can do on short notice." He grinned. "I want to help you. And I think I know a way to do that."

"That's decent of you, Luke." I laid a grateful hand on his arm. "But you aren't the one in trouble—"

"No, *you* are. And you're my friend. Let me help you."

"Just like you help those stray animals? You've got such a soft heart."

"Most people would say I've got a soft *head!*" He laughed with his characteristic self-reproach, then added a serious, "I like you, Kelli. I like you a lot. I have since I started this route. And, just for the record, you aren't a stray, just a mite lost."

"Thanks, Luke, I truly appreciate your concern. Still, though, I don't know what you could do to help me through this predicament. I don't know how anyone could."

"You need time to think, plan your immediate and long-term future. And, you need a quiet, safe place in which to do it. With your mom and dad so angry, your boyfriend so uncaring, you won't find the space you need here."

I couldn't dispute Luke's logic. The constant upheaval in my personal life kept me dizzy and in an uproar. It wasn't good for me, and I shuddered to think of what all this rigamarole was doing to the tiny, innocent fetus swimming around inside me.

But I didn't know what Luke planned to do about it. He took a short, steadying breath, then gazed deep into my eyes.

"Finish this haul with me, Kelli. If all goes well—which it should— we can make the round trip from here to Michigan, unload, reload, and be back in two weeks. That should give you plenty enough time to truly know what you want to do about the baby."

"Oh, I don't know, Luke!" If he'd suggested that we sprout wings and fly to the moon, I couldn't have been more stunned. I blurted out the first thing that came to mind. "I've never been out of Indiana before!"

"Good, then you can have a pleasant vacation, to boot."

"I hardly think that after the mess I've created, I deserve a vacation. Besides, you run on a fixed timetable, Luke. Between my morning sickness and frequent bathroom stops, I'll just slow you down."

"No, you won't. At any rate, I'm ahead of schedule this trip."

"Oh, I don't know—"

"Listen, Kell. The cab of a big rig like mine is comfortable, roomy, and infinitely quiet. You'll find lots of time to think. And I promise," he symbolically crossed his heart, "that you will be absolutely safe. I'll be with you every second. And though we'll be side by side in the truck, I won't infringe upon your privacy. There's a little bunk in the back where you can nap anytime. You'll see, it'll be great."

"But I have no money—"

"You won't need any."

"I've got to eat."

"Ah," he said. "How much can a little thing like you eat?"

I gave him a skeptical smirk, then nodded toward my empty plate. Not only had I scraped it clean, but I'd wolfed Luke's bacon and toast, as well. "Since I've been pregnant, I've developed a hollow leg! And I have to fill it up at least three times a day."

"Well," he shrugged, grimacing comically, "I'll start a tab that you can pay after everything is straightened out."

Despite the turmoil that raged within my soul, a few pertinent things did stand out. I had a tough choice to make, and I didn't want to bungle it with a pressured, snap decision. A decision that, no matter what course I selected, would haunt me forever—mold the rest of my life. I'd already made one major error, and I couldn't afford a second, perhaps more traumatic, one. Nevertheless, to run off with a virtual stranger. . . .

"We hardly know each other, Luke. We're merely a couple of ships passing in the night."

"That's not true, Kelli." Luke appeared somewhat taken aback, hurt even, by my feelings. "During the past six months, I've made this Michigan run a dozen times. I'm so predictable and methodical that I always stop at the same truck plazas along the way. Each place is loaded with colorful characters and friendly waitresses. I see them so often that they become like family. But this place is my favorite— homelike. Why? Because of a sweet girl named Kelli."

"Why, Luke!" I patted his reddened cheek. Luke rolled his eyes, embarrassed.

"Solo truck driving is a lonely profession. I could use some company. Come on, Kelli. What have you got to lose?"

"My parents will kill me . . . I'll miss two weeks of school," I said, defeated. "Of course, my reputation is already in tatters."

"Hey, now." Luke stiffened, his expression stern and foreboding. "None of that 'let's beat up on Kelli' routine. Everybody stumbles, everybody falls facedown sometimes. But that doesn't make them bad people. It just makes them human. You've had some rotten breaks, some lousy luck. Now, it's time to lick your wounds and plot your next line of action. The separation from your folks might give them a necessary period of adjustment, too. Come with me, Kelli; let me help you help yourself."

Not unlike my earlier bout of morning sickness, my body was a whirlwind of thoughts and feelings. But I felt Luke's outstretched hand too welcoming and sincere to refuse. Although his reason for rescuing me remained a mystery, I didn't push him. I just accepted.

"Okay, Luke. What time do you want to blow this pop stand?"

"That's my girl!" He winked at my giddy joke. "We'll leave as soon as possible."

"Half an hour?" I suggested.

"Great! I'll have the truck all warmed up and ready to roll." He smiled.

I stood, prepared to leave, when Luke clutched my hand, his eyes full of concern. "Kelli, maybe I should go with you, you know, speak to your parents. They'll be worried—"

"They'll be at work and won't even miss me until after six o'clock tonight. I'll leave a note for them."

"Still, Kelli, you really should—"

"It'll be okay. Now, Luke, you've got to trust me!"

Feeling like some kind of common criminal, I trumped up a lie to tell my boss, then scurried home to pack a bag. I was glad no one was there. I didn't want to face them in person.

The letter I left was cryptic and brief. I merely assured them that I was with a dependable friend and would return in a few days. I grabbed my vitamins and iron pills, and hurried back to meet Luke.

Surprisingly, once we hit the highway and crossed the state line, I felt as though a thousand-pound weight had been lifted from my shoulders. The ironclad band that had seemed to constrict my chest suddenly loosened. I lowered my window and took in a fresh breath of air. Of course, Luke saw my relaxed posture and smiled at me.

"Freedom!" He nodded in understanding. "Exactly the reason I love being a trucker."

Funny how we don't realize things. I'd been under so much stress, suffered so many restless nights, that I slept for the better part of the next two days. Luke didn't mind, as he said he made better road time. But after I caught up on my sleep, and the tension drifted away, I found the passing sights fascinating. My morning sickness abated, though I continued to eat like a horse. This was a constant source of amusement for my traveling partner.

But as always, his jokes were lightly aimed, more silly than judgmental. And despite the unorthodox trappings of the semi's constraints, I felt at home—safe, secure, and pampered. I had originally presumed that Luke viewed me as just another stray creature, a needy case. Yet, as the miles whizzed by, he genuinely seemed to enjoy my company.

Luke showed me off at truck stops with a proud demeanor and a boastful smile. Although my pregnancy was still a secret to the outside world, for all intents and purposes, Luke acted as if the baby developing deep inside my body was his, a growing symbol of his love and devotion. Luke catered to my every whim, and looked out for my well-being as no one ever had before. We were inseparable, and oddly content to be so.

It was a peculiar scene, but again, I didn't question his deeds too profoundly. I just accepted his kindness with a thankful heart and prized my momentary respite.

By the time we'd reached Luke's home base in Detroit, we still had not discussed my future. Luke had not divulged any new options, nor suggested any further propositions. Furthermore, I still had not figured out what to do. Yet, I felt calmer, more capable, and finally in control. It was my life, my choice, and I alone who should determine my destiny. Thanks to Luke, that much was assured.

To my additional astonishment, Luke took me home to meet his family. Naturally, he didn't mention my being with child—nor did he mention my dropping out of school, or how I'd ran away from home. They didn't even seem to notice the difference in our ages.

His siblings were a curious array of blondes, brunettes, and one little redhead. Luke and one brother were well over six feet tall, while the rest of the boys looked dwarfish beside them. It struck me as curious, but of course, it would have been impolite to actually speak about it.

Regardless of their physical disassociation, however, they, up to and including Luke's parents, shared a uniquely streamlined philosophy: Any friend of Luke's was a friend of theirs. They welcomed me with open arms. In fact, they treated me like some long-lost cousin—or the girl who had stolen Luke's heart.

Three days later, when we headed back for the return trip, I sincerely regretted having to leave. But, I knew that I had to go home and face the music. Once more, the dilemma loomed in front of me. Yet, this time, I was backed by Luke's steady regard and his family's easygoing manner. I was ready to meet the challenges squarely and logically.

"Did you notice anything remarkable about my brothers and sisters?" Luke asked conversationally after lunch one day.

"Well," I hedged diplomatically, "they were a great bunch, so friendly, and they genuinely seemed to like each other."

"Anything else?" He glanced at me, a huge grin on his face. His expression was so mischievous that I wondered what he was getting at. Since we'd become so close in this tiny window of time, I shrugged and told him the truth.

"They sure are a rainbow of hair colors and heights. That seemed a bit extraordinary to me."

"Yeah." Luke laughed, glancing at me out of the corner of his eye. "They are an eclectic group! Didn't you wonder why?"

"Quit playing games with me, Luke Jameson!" I swatted his shoulder with frisky camaraderie. "What are you trying to tell me?"

"We're all adopted. Some of us from infancy—the younger ones were foster children."

"That explains why you're always rescuing homeless cats and woebegone dogs." I paused a second and tacked on a bemused, "And pregnant teen misfits."

"Hey," Luke said as he turned from the wheel and tweaked my chin, "none of that 'misfit' stuff, remember?"

"Yeah, yeah, I remember." I blushed and ducked from his earnest expression. "So, why did you want me to meet them? I mean, they were all great and I am glad I got to know them. But, why take a stranger home to meet the family?"

"Well, you are hardly a stranger to me, Kelli. We've known each other for months." He hesitated as if he'd like to say more, then quickly changed his mind. "I thought if you met them, saw how well they all turned out, it might show you that other option."

He took my hand, squeezing it gently. Although his eyes never left the road, his voice dropped to a husky, pensive rasp. "If you don't feel comfortable having an abortion, Kelli, you could go on with your pregnancy, have the baby, then give it up for adoption."

Slowly, his words began to sink in and my mouth hit the floorboard. Adoption. I'd never thought of it. I stared at him and blinked.

"It isn't that I'm against abortion," he assured me quickly.

"No, me either. In fact, in some cases, I think it's the best for everyone involved. But, while I believe in a woman's right, unlike everybody else in my family, I'm not sure it's the right choice for me. And the 'right choice' is what it's all about."

"Exactly, Kelli."

"Yes." I shook my head sadly; tears blurred my eyes. "I'm the one who has to live with my decision—now and forever."

An icy chill darted through me and I shivered. The baby would have to live or die with my decision, as well. Furthermore, this baby that floated around inside of me was not to blame for my mistakes. Yet, to raise it alone, to be cast out by my family—adrift, uneducated, and condemned to a life of endless poverty and deprivation was no life for it, either. But adoption. . . .

"Through adoption, Kelli," Luke cut into my reverie, his voice far away, but crystal clear, "you could have the baby, then give it to a loving couple who can't make a child of their own. In a sense, you could turn this tragedy into a miracle for someone."

"But, Luke," I began, staring hard into his face, "even if I give the baby up, and it ultimately has a wonderful life with some other worthy couple, won't it eventually wonder about me? Question why I did what I did?"

He took a deep breath, then shrugged thoughtfully. "I can only speak for myself. But, as an adopted kid, I have often daydreamed about my biological parents. Sometimes, I study my face and body in the mirror and contemplate whether I look like them, act them, or even think like them. Sometimes, I walk down a busy street and search for them—especially when I was younger. But, I've come to realize that they did what they thought best. Whatever their reason was, I need to accept it."

"Do you hate them, Luke?" I asked, my voice a hoarse, emotional whisper.

"Hate them? No. Mostly, I'm just glad to be alive. Of course, if I'd been aborted, I'd probably never know the difference."

Again I gazed unseeing, through the wide, high-up window. The wheels of the truck hummed a lullaby-like melody while my reflection in the window stared back at me. Objective and vulnerable, my single consummate dread surfaced, and I could no longer hide from its sickening truth.

"Perhaps you wouldn't have known the difference, Luke," I reaffirmed, "but your birth mother would have. Just like I will."

Unthinkingly, my hand moved to my belly, and I systematically rubbed the half-shaped bundle of cells sailing within. No matter what I did, no matter how I handled this "surprise" calamity, I would always know, would always question my decision. Therefore, I realized that in the final analysis, my only genuine choice was to pick the alternative that would trouble my heart the least.

From across the semi's cab, Luke leaned slightly toward me. Tenderly, he, too, massaged my swollen curve. Like always, his smile was merciful and benevolent.

"Whatever you decide, Kelli, I'll support you and do all I can to make it easier. All I ask is that you search your soul, make sure that your choice is the right one for you, Kelli. Make this decision for yourself."

The rest of our trip passed by in a haze of silent miles and profoundly intense self-scrutiny. I worried about everything from money to my folks, from that moment to my deathbed. But mostly, I worried about the baby.

When we reached the city limits of my hometown, Luke automatically pulled off the highway and parked the rig behind the gas station where I'd worked. I looked at him. My inner turmoil was gone; my soul was at peace. I'd made my decision.

"I'll go with adoption, Luke. Just tell me where to start and I won't bother you again."

A tremendous sigh of relief blew from his lungs as he took my hand and raised it to his lips. Lovingly, he kissed my knuckles, his expression warm and compassionate.

"Although it wouldn't have changed how I feel about you, Kelli, on behalf of adopted kids everywhere, I'm grateful and thank you for making this impossible choice. But just as importantly, you are not now, nor will you ever be, a bother to me. I'm fond of you, Kelli, more fond than you know. I have been since the beginning of this incredible adventure, and even beforehand. I was sincere when I said that I would do all I can for you—"

"That is so sweet and so just like you, Luke." My voice wobbled and my never-far-from-the-surface tears threatened to undo my fledgling maturity. "But none of this is your affair, certainly not your fault. You've already gone above and beyond friendship. Surpassed duty—"

"Sssh. . . ." Luke pressed a chivalrous finger to my lips, and bumped my nose with his. "Don't say any more. Just give me a big hug and then I'll take you home. Together, we'll explain to your folks where we've been."

"That's unnecessary," I said, although the prospect of seeing my parents—by myself and unprotected—filled me with unqualified panic and misgiving.

Another pseudo-serious warning and Luke gathered me close to his heart. He warmed my icy fear with his firm, self-confident embrace. The safe, homey thud of his heart soothed me. Like always when in his arms, wrapped in his gracious attention, I felt safe, sure. My baby did, too. With the pure hope of a child, I wished I could stay swathed in his sureness forever.

Wriggling nearer still, I spread my hand over his shoulder, pressed my breasts to his ribs. I looked up at him.

For a moment, I stared into his dark eyes, hoping that my heartfelt gratitude could be conveyed by this guileless gesture. My fingertips fluttered to his lips, then traced the intimate fullness of his mouth. His eyes softened and he bent his head to return my gaze. The scratchy roughness of Luke's chin on my cheek seemed to stir my sensitivities in a brand-new way.

As if in slow motion, our lips touched. The light and airy pressure was a gossamer promise of things to come. Despite my pregnancy, in Luke's eyes, I felt virginal, clean, and unsoiled—a pristine lady in white. Once again, I basked in his tenderness. It was a rebirth I had no right to feel.

Starry-eyed and flushed, my body coursed with the most feminine of yearnings. I felt sensual sensations I'd never experienced before, not even with the father of my baby. I felt faint, fevered, and completely unprepared for the gruff rumble of Luke's rigid ouster. Though his features retained a trace of his more kindly demeanor, the determined set of his once-pliable mouth shocked me back to reality, centered me on the task at hand—facing my folks.

My folks. The mere thought of them sent a chill up my spine and weakened my knees.

With Luke's reliable bulk bolstering my sagging spirit, I handed my parents my decision, and girded myself for their virtuous reprimand. But true to Luke's prediction, they were more happy to see me return safe and sound, than they were at my hard-won decision. They didn't mind the adoption plan and allowed me back into the house.

Before he left on his turnaround haul to Michigan, Luke accompanied me to a local women's clinic, and held my hand through the embarrassing question-and-answer counseling, patiently reading dog-eared magazines while I underwent my physical examination.

The clinic proved a godsend of help and reassurance. They even hooked me up with a sympathetic doctor and a reputable adoption agency.

As my gloom gave way to springtime blossoms, the weeks passed in supercharged emotions. Although I'd left him high and dry, my boss welcomed me back without dissension. My high school had more to say, though, and they were infinitely hesitant to permit me back to class.

Still, once they learned that I would not "brag" about my condition, and I assured them that I would not "show" before graduation, they capitulated, and reluctantly let me finish out my senior year.

My ex-boyfriend had absolutely no interest in our baby. He avoided me like the plague. But somehow, I didn't care. Indeed, I was glad to be rid of him—an immature, selfish little boy.

Through it all, I had one unvarying, uncompromising champion in my corner: Luke Jameson.

Luke called me every night, and sent me postcards from random truck stops. Every two weeks, he came through town and took me out to dinner and a movie. Luke listened to my troubles, and stroked the burgeoning roundness of my belly as though the being inside was an object of phenomenal delight. Luke giggled like a first-time father every time an errant foot or fidgety fist nudged his loving hand.

Despite our closeness and obvious physical attraction toward one another, by mutual, unspoken agreement, we did not fool around sexually. We never kissed or touched again, but we did constantly hold hands. Our emotional bonds grew more personal, but our physical relationship stayed strictly platonic.

Since I intended to give the baby up for adoption, I struggled to remain unattached to my little bundle, which I frequently referred to as "the fetus." Nonetheless, some things are easier said than done.

As my belly protruded, bounced around, and ruined my sleep, I couldn't help but talk to it. Late at night and early in the morning, I told it my life story, and dreamed aloud its prospects with some loving, caring family. My hands became a safeguarding shield around it's shifting, kicking orbit. With all my might and no-nonsense logic, I endeavored not to love it. I desperately tried not to think of my unborn child's postpartum future.

As my due date grew nearer, winding down to a last few days, I was surprised to see Luke in a pickup truck, instead of his usual eighteen-wheeler. He wasn't scheduled to arrive for days. I was, however, immeasurably joyous to see him. But I'd never felt larger, more uncomfortable, or more unlovable. The baby had been too quiet and my back ached fiercely.

Luke jumped out of the cab and winked at me. His eyes roamed up and down my huge torso like I was the most beautiful woman in the world. I almost cried, but then, I was always near to tears, it seemed.

"How can you look at me and be so proud, Luke?" I waddled toward him and gave him a pudgy-faced grimace. "I'm a water balloon about to pop!"

"Oh, I love water balloons. They're so darned squishy and soft and bright and cheerful. Besides, Kelli—you are *glowing*. Simply radiant, sugar."

I rolled my eyes and sighed at his playful assessment while Luke made his customary acknowledgment of the baby. Gently, he patted my oversized stomach, and held a sunny conversation with my belly.

Not unlike me, Luke enjoyed talking to my tummy and usually explained his latest trip and any excitement he'd had along the way. Not only did his one-sided chats entertain me, but his carefree dialogue seemed to affect the baby. It responded to Luke's voice with a muffled squiggle and an amniotic gurgle.

"What are you doing here, now, Luke?"

He shrugged bashfully. "I took my vacation. I wanted to be here with you when the baby comes."

"Who knows when the baby will be born?" I groused, weary of being pregnant, terrified of the childbirth ahead, and profoundly relieved to have him with me.

"I'd say soon. You hungry?"

"No," I admitted, amazed that I hadn't been all day. "Just tired and swollen. My feet hurt and my back is *killing* me."

Luke's grin widened hopefully. "Really?"

As if on cue, another spasm shifted the load within me and a sharp cramp shot through my torso. I stumbled, caught by Luke's steadying embrace.

Alarmed and leery, I straightened, only to feel the almost soothing sensation of something warm oozing inside, then staining my maternity pants. I gasped and looked up into Luke's eyes.

"Maybe we'd better put off lunch until after we call the doctor," Luke said panting, his arms tight around me. He held me strong against his chest.

"Good idea," I chuckled, then was hit by another savage jab.

For the next ten hours, Luke never left my side. He sponged my sweating face, watched the bleeping monitors, and didn't even notice the ragged welts my fingernails had clawed onto the backs of his hands. When the baby braced itself against my lungs and wrung out the air within them, Luke drew a breath for us all, and loosened my labor with his tranquilizing voice.

When at last the delivery-time came, they draped a concealing sheet to separate me from the happenings below. Luke held my hand and braved the curtained sheet.

Through his eyes, I watched the birth of my baby. As I bore down for a last, tooth-grinding push, Luke gasped, and shared the life-freeing cramp with me. His mouth formed an awestruck circle and moisture glistened in his eyes.

Seconds ticked by, and time hung suspended in that breathless heartbeat. Then, my baby sputtered toward independent life with a shrill cry.

Helpless and fragile, the newborn's voice grew stronger, more determined, until its scream was boisterous. And with each life-reaffirming squall, I gripped Luke's hand, choking back my own bittersweet tears.

"Is it okay, Luke? Is my baby all right?"

"Oh, Kelli," he twisted, eyes brimming with emotion. "She's beautiful. She's perfect."

"Can I see her? Can I touch her?" I sobbed, squeezing his hand with all my frail, drug-induced power.

"Better not, honey," the nurse interceded, blocking what little view I may have sneaked.

"Oh, please!" I beseeched her, but my pleas fell on deaf ears.

Fortunately, Luke was not as sensible. With a puckered smile on his lips, he leaned away from me and reached toward my baby.

Although I could not see my baby, the instant Luke made contact with her, I felt her in my entire being. I could almost feel Luke's strong hand caressing her. His hand tightened on mine and his face beamed with unadulterated joy. Luke stroked her little body, and whispered sweet phrases against her ear. Soon, her angry cries hiccuped away.

"Oh!" Luke chortled, his tone thick, muffled by a wistful throb. "Her skin feels like wet velvet, her eyes are blue. Little, precious blue orbs! She looks like you, Kelli. Ten little fingers, ten little toes. She's just the most precious little angel I've ever seen!"

I struggled to sit up and tear away the sheet that kept me from my baby. However, the entire hospital seemed to know of my adoptive decision, and the burly nurse grabbed my shoulders gently and pinned me back down.

"It's better you don't look, Kelli," she murmured. Though I begged her to free me, she shook her head and pressed me to the bed. In my weak-limbed condition, I could not fight her. All I could do was grieve, and taste the sour, regretful tears that dripped down my face.

Looking again at Luke, my utter misery must have broken his heart. His face contorted and I saw wetness collect in the corners of his eyes. For one quick moment, he turned back toward the baby, his finger tracing her delicate, soft mouth. Luke kissed her forehead and breathed in her newborn scent. With paternal-like reluctance, he stepped away from the child, then moved to stand beside me.

With his lips to my forehead, his fingertips on my lips, he gave me my baby's kiss.

A primal, bestial sob ripped from my deepest being, my heart shattered into a million, blood-dipped shards. Luke caught me to his chest, and bore the heartbreaking torrent of my dying soul.

After some scuffled footsteps and muted orders, my baby was gone—spirited away, torn from my body, withheld from my sight, and completely erased from my life.

I continued to struggle and scream. Even Luke's tight hug could not placate me. Even my hero, Luke, could not diminish the sorrow that swallowed me whole.

"It's okay, Kelli," Luke wept, his tears mingled with mine. "It's okay, you are doing the right thing."

But before I could tell him he was wrong, explain how deeply in love I was with my unseen child, another compassionate nurse bustled at my IV, pumping yet another dulling drug into my veins. Blackness swirled around me as conscious thought drifted away.

I've no idea how long I slept. It could have been an eternity, or a timid half-second. Nevertheless, when I awoke, my entire body throbbed. My hospital pillow was saturated, yet my eyes were puffy and dry. On my bedside table stood a stack of official papers—papers that, once signed, would seal my baby's fate forever. I couldn't stand the thought of her receiving some other mother's love. . . .

I wrestled to an upright position and saw Luke sitting in a chair at the foot of the bed. When he realized that I was awake, he offered a gallant, but vacuous, smile.

"How are you feeling, Kelli?"

"Like I was hit by your semi!" I managed a feeble grin, then felt the blurring of tears. I wondered if I would ever stop crying.

"Your folks came by."

"Did they see the baby?"

"No."

A deafening silence seemed to smother the room and I shuffled the papers, pushing them farther away from me. Of course, Luke noticed and picked them up with trembling hands.

"You haven't signed them yet, sugar."

"I love my baby and I want what's best for her. But. . . ." My voice cracked and I just couldn't continue.

Luke patted my hand and pulled his chair close to my side. For a time, he just hung his head, studying the floor. At last he looked at me, wiping a tear from my cheek.

"I love her, too, Kelli. I have since—I don't know when. The nurse was right, though, I shouldn't have touched her. I shouldn't have stared into her eyes or kissed her tiny forehead." His voice broke; his face blanched ominously. "In my heart, I'm sure that giving her to a good family is best for her. With babies so scarce and in demand, no doubt, she'll go to a wonderful family with plenty of money. She'll have everything a kid could ever want or need. Orthodontia, college, ballet lessons—"

"A pony," I added. I tried with all my soul to mollify my broken heart with the glorious picture he was painting. I crossed my fingers and prayed like never before. Despite my best efforts, however, it didn't work.

Apparently, Luke wasn't buying it, either. With a single, callous sneer, he decimated any hope I had for giving my baby away.

"No, she'll never have a pony. Her new parents will live in the city where she can't have one!"

"Luke!" I blinked, my bottom lip quivered.

Mindless to my bewildered plea, he was building steam, working himself up into a belligerent, heart-wrenching fury. "No pony, ever. Not only that, but that darling, precious baby will be damned to a lifetime of wondering who her biological parents were and why they didn't love her enough to keep her! She'll always imagine that there is something wrong with her, something that made her so detestable that they had to give her away—hand her off to strangers!"

"Luke!" Again, my own precarious sentimentalities took a backseat to his inconsolable ranting. Now, it was I who had to comfort him. "But look at your family, Luke. Your folks love you, and your brothers and sisters *adore* you. You've been happy, Luke. You know you've had a good life, despite being adopted."

"That's true," he agreed heartily. "But I've wasted years wondering why. Why didn't my real mom and dad want me? I've spent so much time wondering what was wrong with me that prevented them from keeping me."

"But there *is* nothing wrong with you. I suspect your birth mother may have been just like me: a reckless girl, old enough to conceive, but too young to raise you herself. No doubt, Luke, your mother made the best of a bad situation. Just like I'm trying to do. You've got to believe that."

"In here, Kelli." Luke tapped his head. "I know you are right." Then, he stabbed a self-castigating finger into his chest. "But here, I always wonder. Your baby doesn't have to do that, not ever. I have another option for her—for *us*. One I thought of before, but didn't have the guts to present to you."

He picked up the papers that littered my table and heaved a great sigh. Placing my baby's birth certificate on top of everything, Luke's voice lowered, his eyes penetrating mine. His knuckles whitened as they seized the rail of my bed.

"I know ours has not been a traditional, romantic courtship, Kelli. I also know that there are eight years between us. But what I feel for you is genuine and lasting. What I feel for your baby is unquestionable and lifelong. We've been through so much, your baby feels like mine. Marry me, Kelli. Let me claim fatherhood to your little girl. I love her, and I love you even more."

My mouth hung open and I couldn't speak. As he waited for my answer, he found a pen and began writing in the baby's legal birth papers.

Under *Mother*, he wrote my name, hyphenating my last name with his. Beneath *Father*, and though he knew the truth, he wrote his own name. Once the deception was made, he bit his lip and gave me a quavering look.

"Say, yes, Kelli. Say yes and I can have a justice of the peace here this afternoon. As soon as you and the baby are ready, we can drive down to Michigan and live in a mobile home behind my folks' place. Just temporarily," he amended hastily, "until we can afford a home of our own. Someday, when the baby is older, we can explain the truth to her, and, God willing, to her little brothers and sisters."

Although his proposal seemed haphazard on the surface, deep in my heart, I knew it was not. He'd thought this "option" out meticulously. It was Luke's nature, part of what made me feel so anchored, so safe, when I was near him.

And despite the cautious fluttering of my own heart, I was not too uncertain, either. For, in truth, I'd spent more time with Luke, understood the workings of his mind and soul, far better than I did my baby's father—a man whose face I could hardly recall, a man I had never loved and could never love, now that I'd been so touched by Luke.

I took Luke's hand, kissed its palm, then cupped it to my cheek. Impulsively, his fingertips dried the tears from my face.

"You don't have to twist my arm, Luke. I love my baby and I want to keep her with me, be her mom. And, despite the goofy relationship we've had, I, too, have grown to love you and feel as if she is your child, as well. Maybe that's because you have, from the very start, acted like her father. Yes, I'd be most happy and proud to marry you, Luke Jameson."

Such a flood of relief and absolute joy wreathed his face—and mine, too. For the first time since I'd discovered I was pregnant, I knew without a grain of doubt that I had made the correct choice, finally done a complete right.

I grinned up at him.

A heartbeat later, Luke eased down the bed rail and carefully sat on the edge of my hospital bed.

With a tenderness and generosity I had come to cherish in him, he wrapped his arms around me, let his adoration caress away my every hurt. Our tentative kiss soon deepened and made honeyed promises for our future ahead. We giggled and dreamed, and then tore the adoption papers into a million shreds. Hand in hand, we ambled toward the nursery to say hello to "our" baby daughter. . . .

I cannot describe the sheer, sweet fulfillment that holding her close and touching her tiny features gave me that first time. I doubt any mother could. I only know that it was the single greatest blessing of my existence, and ultimately became worth every trauma and emotion I'd wrestled with.

Although marrying Luke, keeping my baby, and moving to Michigan was my saving grace, I know that it would not have worked for every teenage mother. Not every man is as forgiving and compassionate as my husband is; not every man is as devoted and good. Nonetheless, through perseverance, dedication, and unselfish love, Luke and I have forged a strong, lyrical union. Our daughter, Sabrina, is at its center, the sunshine of our lives.

We've been married three years now and have recently moved into a little brick bungalow on the outskirts of Lansing. Luke's family members are regular guests and they are enchanted by their granddaughter. Even my parents have yielded and visit on occasion. Ours is a bountiful life.

In a few weeks, on my twenty-first birthday, Luke and I are leaving Sabrina with his folks while we spend our honeymoon in Aruba. There, if my good luck prevails, I should be able to come by his twenty-ninth birthday gift—we are hoping for a boy this time. Not that it really matters; we just want another beautiful collaboration to love and cherish. THE END

THE LADY-KILLER AND THE MAN-EATER
They were the perfect match— if they could only stand the heat!

Brendan and I split up—again—two days before the auditions for *Oklahoma* at Heaven's Hollow Community Theatre. I'd been trying to terminate this relationship for the past three weeks, but he kept pleading with me to continue going out with him, and I kept stupidly agreeing. This latest get-it-over-with conversation was not the most scintillating discussion I've ever had.

Let's be honest: It was trite.

"Belinda, what's with you? We've been dating for two months. I didn't even know there was anything wrong and you turn around and dump me just in time for auditions for a show bound to have lots of guys in it. What's the matter?"

"Brendan. We have never been exclusive. We went out. We had a good time. I'm not ready for anything else. We've been in the process of breaking up for three weeks now. Get a grip."

"Please, Belinda. Just one more chance? Have I done something wrong?"

"No. Look, I'm just not great at long-term."

I looked at his miserable face and relented, slightly.

"I mean, it's not like we're never going to see each other again. You know Corky's gonna cast you in the show. We'll be at rehearsals together. Okay?"

I knew it wasn't going anywhere. Brendan was a wimp who let me do anything I pleased. There's something about a man begging that's a serious turnoff for me.

I'm not proud of what is undoubtedly a lacking in my character, but I find weak men *boring*. Neanderthal Man isn't my ideal, either, but I at *least* want someone who won't give in on every issue with me. After all, I'm not right *all* of the time, much as I might pretend to be!

And so, Brendan joined the list of last year's castoffs, which included Jeremy, Todd, Fenton, and Rick.

Jeremy: Mr. "Marry me, Belinda, or we're through."

"I don't think so, Jeremy—I've known you for a whopping two weeks."

Todd: "My mother's not going to be pleased with me dating a dancer."

"Fine, Todd. Date your mother."

Fenton: "But, Belinda, the enormity of this issue is life shattering! This legislation has to pass! By the way, I don't think Chow and Chat is the best restaurant to be eating at. Didn't I see a report on Channel 7 about them? No, wait—that was the report Fox News did about the congressman who's in league with the meat packing industry."

"Aargh! Enough with the politics and debates, Fenton! Let's have one evening that doesn't resemble a documentary or a commentary!"

Rick: "Why do you laugh, Belinda? What's so funny about a man dressed up as a shark ringing apartment doors and hissing, 'Land Shark' at the people inside?"

"Rick, Rick, you gorgeous, blond, steely-blue-eyed, muscles-to-rival-Arnold, stud muffin. Why do you possess not an ounce of humor, along with not an ounce of fat? Does one cancel out the other? How can you watch originals of *Saturday Night Live* with Bill Murray, Chevy Chase, et al and not crack a smile? 'Bye, Rick."

Now, it actually felt nice to be unattached. I figured I might stay in that state for a while, actually.

At least a day or two longer.

As I sat waiting my turn to sing at the auditions, though, I found that I was musing about Rick, wondering if the old *I Love Lucy* tapes my mom had made the week she had insomnia might help him learn how to smile. Imagining his mouth muscles twitching as much as his biceps was making me a little weak in the knees. Alas, my daydreams were rudely interrupted by the heated conversation coming from a couple standing in the aisle two rows down from me.

She was a knockout. The kind of face and body I've always wanted—and would never have without ten years of plastic surgery and implants and a meat cleaver. Maybe five-one, with perfect blond curls, crystal blue eyes, a turned-up nose—she was a porcelain doll. My exact opposite. I'm five-nine, with straight brown hair and hazel eyes, and a jazz dancer's body—basically, straight up and down.

The man she was arguing with reminded me a lot of my Irish setter, named Kooky for obvious reasons. He—the man, not the dog—looked familiar. He was well over six feet tall, with arms and legs that looked like they weren't following where the rest of the body was leading. He had light brown hair and freckles splattered over a crooked nose. He was wearing an obnoxiously loud, yellow, Hawaiian-print shirt that clashed with his hair, faded jeans, and tan Hush Puppies with holes in the toes. The man's sense of style was apparently rooted in comfort.

He and the mannequin were arguing. At least, she was. He didn't even really appear to be listening to her. The attitude between them was, to one who'd been there, that of breaker with breakee at the beginning of the breakup. He was definitely the breaker. Her whole posture oozed: *I'll do anything for you.* As her voice grew louder, I quickly realized that all of my observations had been correct.

"Finn! This is just not fair! We've been seeing each other for two months now, and I never knew there were any problems and now you want to just call it quits? Just in time for a show with a lot of female dancers in it, I notice!"

"Heidi, I never said we were exclusive. I also never led you to believe that there was anything serious going on on my part. I was never looking for a committed relationship; you know I've been trying to call a halt to this for the past three weeks. We had fun, though, so let's not get carried away, okay? We'll still see each other through this show. You know Corky's gonna cast everybody here, so we'll both be in it, no matter what."

I couldn't help it. I started to chuckle—loudly. What had this guy done—taped my last conversation with Brendan? While not

Memorex, it was awfully close to an exact representation.

Heidi and Finn turned toward me when I started laughing. She glared. He grinned. The minute those white teeth flashed, I could see what Heidi was finding so attractive about this lanky puppy dog. Big green eyes danced with sheer wickedness. His expression was that of a very young angel caught smoking pot outside the Pearly Gates with an equally young devil!

Finn and I exchanged a glance only understood by two people who've just dumped their respective partners. I winked at him. He winked back.

"Belinda? Yo! Come onstage. You're up."

Corky, the director, was waving at me from the orchestra pit under the stage. I'd done three shows with Corky since moving here last year. He was maybe five-three—on a good day—with the face of a leprechaun, and the body of a tiny boxer. He'd had some sort of close relationship with the theatre's set designer, Newman, since they'd met in college. He and Newman loved to go out and drink a few brews and sing at Kareoke bars with their casts, but they were known for being completely professional and amazingly strict during rehearsals. I respected their talent; they respected mine. Of course, they also took great delight in teasing me about the fact that I'd gone through two boyfriends during the run of *Pippin*, my last show with them. They'd even started calling me "Man-eater" after male number two—I believe that was Fenton—finally fell by the wayside.

I slid carefully by the battling duo in the aisle on my way to the stage. I could feel Finn's warm eyes on me the whole time. I could also feel Heidi's. Hers were the icy darts piercing a hole between my shoulder blades.

The casting notice specified that Corky wanted those songs actually sung by the characters in *Oklahoma!*. I'd chosen "I Cain't Say No!" as my audition piece. I was going after the part of Ado Annie—it's her big number, and I do it well. My roommate, Tessa, says it's because I agree wholeheartedly with the underlying philosophy of the song—being as fickle as possible and dating a multitude of men. I disagree.

"It's a great song for me to sing because it's in a dancer's key. Not too high, not too low. Just right."

Tessa had handed me my dance bag and car keys, and shooed me out of the huge house we share, calling out in a high-pitched cheer:

"Good luck, Man-eater!"

Great roommate. If Rick had been gifted with even *half* her sense of humor, he and I might've been honeymooning in Barbados by now.

Owen, the musical director for this production of *Oklahoma!* was doing double duty as the audition accompanist. He and I had worked together on two of the shows I'd done at Heaven's Hollow, and I was very comfortable with him at the ivories. Nonetheless, I felt a twinge of nerves as I handed him my music, took a deep breath, faced the audience of show hopefuls, and started to sing. A little voice inside of me was telling me to do my best for that freckle-faced Casanova still standing in the aisle.

About midway through the first sixteen measures of the song, I just went ahead and aimed my words right at him. He was grinning widely, and his soon-to-be ex-girlfriend was scowling like she'd just bitten into a very rotten egg. I couldn't help noticing that Brendan was now seated in the audience, as well. He was scowling like he'd just swallowed that very same rotten egg.

Song sung, I cheerfully acknowledged the applause from the crowd of waiting hopefuls, and began to walk back to my seat, preparing to pass the couple once again.

"Nice job! I have a feeling you're gonna make one heck of an audacious Ado Annie!"

A big hand had gently touched my arm. I felt an unaccustomed tingle.

"Why, thank you, sir! What part are you auditioning for?"

"Will Parker, Ado Annie's love match."

Sparkling green eyes peered into my hazels. Held. I covered confusion with sarcasm.

"Well, how nice to see that you actually know the show! So, you think you'll get Will Parker? Can you dance?"

"Can I dance! Lady, be prepared for the Astaire of the twenty-first century! Finn Doran, at your service."

He was extremely cocky for a slightly homely, too-tall lug.

I adore cockiness.

"Belinda Montague."

"I know. I saw you dance when they did *Pippin* here in December. You were spectacular."

"Thanks! Hmm. Finn Doran. Where do I know you from?"

Before Mr. Doran could respond, Heidi's whiny voice sputtered behind my ear, "Excuse me, Ms. Montague, but you've interrupted a very private conversation between Finn and myself. Do you mind? And, by the way, there are other people auditioning for Ado Annie, so I wouldn't start the congratulations just yet."

Finn's face wore a look of surprise. "Who's stupid enough to audition for that role? Belinda's just too perfect."

Heidi's cheeks flushed a rosy color that had nothing to do with blush. "Well, me, for instance."

"I thought you were auditioning for Laurey."

"I was. I changed my mind."

"No offense, Heidi, but you're a soprano, not an alto, and Ado Annie's songs are kind of low for you."

"I can do both! Anyway, Will Parker kisses Ado Annie in this show and there's no way you're getting anywhere *near* anyone but me! And as for you, Ms. Montague, I think I mentioned that I was having a talk here, and I don't need you around."

I was standing below the pair in the aisle, so Heidi's face was thrust inches away from mine. Well, I like my space, and I *don't* like jealous females. I bowed graciously, raised up my right hand in a "Hey, back off, I'm outta here" wave, smiled slightly sardonically at Finn, and plopped quickly back down in my seat to watch the rest of the auditions.

I was looking forward to seeing what Finn Doran could do with a song. If it was anything like his ability to charm offstage, we were surely in for a treat. Though I was *not* looking forward to working with Heidi in *any* capacity.

Corky called Finn's name just then, and I watched his rangy form stride to the stage. He gave his music to Owen, faced the audience, grinned widely, and began to sing "Kansas City," Will Parker's wonderful number from act one.

There was nothing extraordinary about his voice, but Finn had a stage presence that drew the eye. I noticed everybody in the theatre had stopped digging through their bags for sheet music, whispering to neighbors, and stretching in corners, to listen to him. He'd even apparently asked Owen to include a portion of the dance break for his audition. And when Finn started to move, those legs and arms of his that looked impossibly long offstage came together perfectly to create a picture of sheer grace and energy.

"Gwen, look! That's Finn Doran! Remember him from *Hair* last fall?"

Bingo! The conversation behind me, plus Finn's dancing onstage, helped me place where I'd seen him before. He'd been in the chorus of *Hair*, wigged beyond recognition with a long, black curly mop. There was no disguising that energy and talent, though. Watching him, I couldn't imagine anyone else playing the role of Will Parker—here, or at any other theatre in the country. The applause, whooping, and hollering that greeted the end of his audition convinced me that the rest of the crowd felt the same way. The two girls behind me squealed louder than the rest, and then one of them whispered:

"They call him Lady-killer. I heard he's dumped more women than most men have ever dated! Did you know that he. . . ."

Her voice dropped too low for me to catch the rest, even though I was unashamedly trying to eavesdrop.

Finn left the stage, and started sauntering up the aisle at the same time that Corky was calling out: "Heidi Larsen." She and Finn passed each other coming and going. She never said a word to him.

Finn took a seat several rows down from me, turned, and waved at me. I gave him a high-five sign, then quickly buried my nose in some sheet music. Heidi took the stage.

If she hadn't been so tacky to me earlier, I would've felt really sorry for her. It was obvious that her relationship with the big charmer was at an end. If she'd had any sense, she'd have made plans to travel to London or Paris for the summer—

Anywhere but *Oklahoma!*

The moment she started to sing, I just wanted to cringe with embarrassment for her. Midway through the pain of hearing her struggle with "I Cain't Say No," Corky stopped her and asked if she'd prepared something more appropriate for her range, letting her know that she could try one of Laurey's songs.

I couldn't figure out why she wasn't doing that in the first place. Laurey's the lead female character in *Oklahoma!*. If I'd been born a soprano, it's the part I'd have tried out for. Apparently, though, Heidi was just determined to try and torpedo me, her supposed new rival. She finally sang "Out of My Dreams," from Act II. It was better than her first attempt, but there was no way I could see Corky casting her in a principal role. She just didn't have it. No presence, no real sound. Just a cute little girl onstage.

Polite, insincere applause followed her audition. She stormed down the aisle, grabbed her bag from Finn, and stomped out of the theatre. He followed, albeit, with obvious reluctance. He gave me a thumbs-up sign as he passed, and then leaned over.

"See you at the first rehearsal—Annie."

"Looking forward to it—Will."

That rehearsal was scheduled for two days later. I stood outside the theatre, early, reading the casting results. I already knew that I was playing Ado Annie. Jennie, the stage manager, had called the day before. I scanned the list.

Much of the cast I'd worked with in previous shows. Stephen was playing Curly, the male lead. Colleen was Laurey. I'd predicted that that role would be locked up long before Heidi had ever even attempted to sing. Colleen was incredible—beautiful voice, beautiful girl, amazing actress. She'd also been in the December production of *Pippin*, and she and I'd gotten to be friends. I might have a reputation for discarding men after three months—tops—kind of like mascara, but I'm very careful not to infringe on another girl's territory, so I haven't alienated *all* the women I know.

I continued to read the list. There it was: Will Parker—Finn Doran. No surprise, but nice to see, anyway. The other romantic interest for my show character was the Persian peddler—Ali Hakim. I scanned down and saw a name I wasn't familiar with: Red Arrow Chekhov. Wow. A real mouthful. Then, I saw Heidi's name listed among the chorus. Brendan's was there, as well. Corky, the director, came by as I was reading the list.

"Hey, Belinda! I'm glad we'll be working together again! I can't *wait* to see what you do with this character!"

I hugged him. "Hey, thanks for casting me!"

Newman came up to both of us. "Belinda, my love, my sweet! Have you had a chance to meet your Will Parker yet?"

"Yes, Newman, I have. Looks like a great dancer, sings well—I'm really looking forward to working with him!"

Newman chuckled. "I'm looking forward to the fireworks when the man-eater and the lady-killer get together!"

Suddenly, Finn appeared from behind the door of the theatre. "Did I hear my name mentioned?"

Corky shook his hand to greet him. "Strictly speaking, Finn, Newman didn't say your name. All he said was lady-killer. Guilty conscience?"

Both Corky and Newman were doubled over with laughter. I looked at them. I looked at Finn.

"Do they know something we don't?"

"Beats me. Hey, wanna grab a hamburger before rehearsal?"

"Sure. We'll let Tweedledee and Tweedledum hold their sides till we get back."

Finn and I walked to his car. The whole way, I could hear our director and his partner howling. As mature adults, we chose to ignore their silliness and pretend that our notoriety for breaking hearts hadn't been the cause for their side-splitting humor. We drove to the nearest fast-food joint and managed to keep our conversation geared only to the show schedule. We got back in plenty of time for rehearsal and carefully sat far away from each other for the initial read-through of the script.

I didn't really see much of Finn the first few days of rehearsal. The cast was primarily working on music, and since we each had solos, we were called in at different times. But once Corky started directing scenes, things changed. When I wasn't needed onstage, I hung out in a little corner in the back of the theatre under the light booth. Red Arrow Chekhov, the actor playing Ali Hakim, was usually up there with me.

Mr. Chekhov was, to put it bluntly, a *hunk*. His ancestry had been amazingly pure Cherokee up until his mother married Igor Chekhov, from the former Republic of Czechoslovakia. Little Deer and Igor christened their firstborn son Red Arrow, eventually sending this bronzed skin, blue-eyed, chiseled-jawed, muscular heartthrob out into a world of susceptible females.

"Call me Red," was the first comment he made to the cast. We did.

Ado Annie and Ali Hakim are together quite a bit in *Oklahoma!*, so Red and I spent a lot of time running lines with each other, talking probably more than we should have. For some reason, we had immediately established a kind of brother/sister relationship. I was glad. He was being chased by every female—and some of the males—in the chorus, and I was fending off my own share of advances from the guy playing Jud, the dancer playing Curly in the "Dream Ballet," and, of course, Brendan, the ex, who was still moping. It was restful to have at least one relationship with a man that didn't include sexual tension.

Gradually, though, Finn began to join us more and more in our corner. We all tried to stay professional, going over lines with each other, wandering into the lobby to practice dance steps, but that rapidly disintegrated, since all three of us were quick studies and serious talkers with too much extra time on our hands. We'd chatter nonstop until Corky would call from onstage, requesting one or all of us. Finn, Red, and Belinda were quickly becoming good friends. Finn and Belinda were quickly becoming interested in each other. Still, Finn and Belinda were not ready to admit it. So teasing became our flirtation ritual.

"So, Belinda, you're looking a trifle tired this evening. Partying too much last night?"

"I'll have you know that I've been a very good girl. I'm teaching for the Junior League summer drama program. I have twenty fifteen-year-olds trying to learn to tap all at once at eight in the morning five days a week. They're wearing me down! And what's *your* excuse for those dark circles under your eyes?"

"You try defending underage delinquents on charges of every kind of drug possession and joyriding offense known to man and see if *you* don't develop instant crow's-feet." I'd heard that Finn worked in the public defenders office. This verified it.

"Hey, Finn—be nice to those kids. I bet I teach half of 'em during the year at the Academy! No. Wait. Come to think of it, sic the prosecutors on 'em!"

"What do you teach?"

"Dance. Since it's a chi chi private school, the little dears have their choice of artistic disciplines, and many future terrorists have decided that ballet must be an easy 'A', so they all sign up. But I'm being too cynical. I actually do have some really special students."

"And I have some really special car thieves and pushers! There are times when I wish I'd listened to my mother and flown airplanes. Much safer!"

We'd grin at each other. Then I'd go back to running lines with Red, who'd be following this exchange with great interest, and Finn would go off to warm up his long limbs for a dance number. Until the next topic.

"So, Finn—I hear you've been dating Shawna."

"You are *so* far behind the times, Belinda. Shawna was last week. This week it's Melanie."

"You're good. We've only been in rehearsals two weeks."

He bowed, then leaned over and kissed my hand. "You're no slouch yourself. I hear you and Robby went out two nights running last week."

"Old news. It's over."

We gazed admiringly at each other. Two of a kind. Red looked at us with amazement.

"You two are incredible. Have either of you ever sustained a romantic relationship for longer than two months—ever?"

Finn looked at me. I looked at him. We both looked at Red.

"Go ahead."

Finn was being gentlemanly with the ladies first bit. I wrinkled my nose at him.

"I believe I managed to keep a young man around for a year once. Of course, that was grade school, and he liked to come over and play baseball with my brothers. Does that count?"

Red and Finn shook their heads. Red wagged his finger at me.

"We're talking adulthood here, Belinda. Sorry. Okay, Finn, your turn."

"Five months. But she left to take a job in London, so who knows how long it might've lasted?"

I shook my head. "I'm not buying the London bit, Finn. Plenty of people have conducted successful, long-term, long-distance relationships."

Finn grinned. "Well, come to think of it—we *were* on the verge of that last good-bye about a month before she left." He turned to Red. "Let's face it, Chekhov, Ms. Montague and I are not known for stability in our love lives. So, everybody going dancing Saturday night at this new disco club? Belinda? You up for checking this place out and giving it our stamp of approval?"

"Already planning on it. I even raided my mother's closet for vintage Seventies disco dresses. I found a sexy black number that'll knock those plaid socks off your feet." I couldn't believe he was *actually* wearing plaid socks with red sneakers. I couldn't believe anyone actually *made* plaid socks these days! I also couldn't resist a tiny jab at the lady-killer.

"So—how's Heidi? I hear she fell during the chorus rehearsal for *Farmer and Cowman*."

Finn smiled sweetly at me. "Well, according to Heidi in one of her fourteen daily phone calls to me, she's in terrible pain. I suggested that she rest at home when we all go dancing this weekend, but she immediately said she was sure she'd be in perfect shape by then! And how's Brendan? I hear he had a virus."

I smiled sweetly back. "A case of poison ivy, actually. It should render him inoperable for about a week. Untouchable, too!"

I liked Finn more and more. He and I shared a sarcastic sense of humor, enjoyed the same movies, books, shows, and foods. We'd argue over politics, and we both loved to dance. We'd really become good friends in the three weeks we'd been in rehearsals.

The nightspot Finn had referred to was Taste of the Seventies, a Seventies, disco-style dance bar. A bunch of us had been waiting all week to let loose at what promised to be the hottest new club in town. First, though, we had to survive a very long rehearsal. Saturday's posted schedule included two hours of dance, two hours of music, and four hours of scene staging.

One of those scenes was the very funny, very intense kiss between Ado Annie and Will Parker. It's known as the "Oklahoma Hello!" and I've seen it done several ways on stage, and onscreen in the 1955 movie version. Generally, Will grabs Ado Annie, throws one leg over one side of her, tilts her down like a slant board, and then lays a big, sloppy smooch on the enthralled vixen.

I was really looking forward to it.

The vocal and dance rehearsals went well. Even though I consider myself a dancer first and an actress/singer second, the part I was playing didn't call for a lot of dance, so I got to watch the others rehearse the "Dream Ballet." Heidi was in that number. She danced like she sang—without feeling. Brendan was also trying to master the intricacies of the choreography without much success—and without getting touched in any areas afflicted with poison ivy. It was not a pretty sight.

Finally, at about three in the afternoon, Corky began to work the kissing scene. I think the entire cast was waiting to see the sparks fly. The "Oklahoma Hello!" comes right after Ado Annie's been kissed by Ali Hakim in the "Persian Good-bye!"

First kissed by Red, then by Finn—

No wonder every girl there had wanted the role!

We began the "Persian Good-bye." Red dropped little kisses from my wrist to my shoulder, finally ending in a very nice one on the lips. But it was very much a stage kiss—enjoyable, to say the least—but not a lightning rod of electrical current.

Then it was time for the "Oklahoma Hello!." Finn and I recited our lines. Then he threw me into the diagonal pose, tossed one of those long legs across me, and held me firmly in his capable arms. When his lips met mine, I swear I heard an explosion rock the back of the theatre. I also heard Corky talking into his headphones, but I ignored his voice. So did Finn. We stayed locked in position. Finally, I heard Corky yelling.

"Hey, you two! Newman's just informed me that one of the air conditioners has blown! Talk about generating heat! Keep it up and our G-rated show will turn into a triple X! This is just the 'Hello!' okay? It's not the 'Hello, let's get it on!' "

Finn released me. We looked deep into each other's eyes. I could fall hard for this man; I knew it, and it didn't make me happy. I was the "man-eater," after all. I wasn't *about* to get involved with a "lady-killer."

After Saturday's strenuous rehearsal, we headed straight over to Taste of the Seventies—nothing like a little more dancing to help you let off steam! Dubbing Red and Newman as the designated drivers for the evening—they didn't drink, anyway—ten of us squeezed into two cars and took off. Nobody seemed to own a car larger than a Volkswagen bug. Even Finn, at six-feet-five, drove a Mazda Miata!

We arrived at Taste of the Seventies at about ten-thirty, just as things were really starting to move. We paid, strolled in, and then stared, numbly frozen in place by the sight of the ugliest décor I'd seen outside of a New York City graffiti-filled subway car. Green and yellow neon paint; posters of John Travolta, Donna Summer, and the Village People tacked onto the walls. A deejay booth painted purple with an orange banner over it proclaiming "Dr. Heat" held two huge turntables and a gentleman who looked like he'd been sent by central casting after shooting *Saturday Night Fever*! A final touch was the mirror ball hanging over the ceiling. It was all delightfully tacky.

Dr. Heat was playing some great songs. My parents had brought me up on every kind of music imaginable, from Verdi to Van Morrison, from Glenn Miller to Steve Miller, and from Tchaikovsky to the

Trammps. The songs blaring from the deejay's perch were more than familiar to me; my mom had taught me how to dance to Gloria Gaynor's, "I Will Survive." I loved this stuff!

Apparently, Finn loved it, too. While the rest of the *Oklahoma!* crowd found a table and ordered a round of beers, he grabbed my hand and rushed me onto the dance floor. Donna Summer's, "I Feel Love" was setting that mirror ball spinning. I was soon spinning, as well. Mom would've been proud.

Finn twirled me under his arm, making our own little private circle as I happily turned and turned and turned. We started adding high kicks and floor splits and lifts, egged on by our cheering castmates, who were toasting us from the table. Except for Brendan and Heidi—I'd yet to see that girl crack a smile, and was fairly certain that my performance gyrating to early disco with Finn wasn't going to help. Brendan just looked morose, as always. Of course, with little red, itchy blotches covering his face and arms, I could understand why!

Finn and I danced nonstop for the next fifty minutes or so. It was so nice to dance with someone who really knew what he was doing, could lead, be outrageous, and was big and strong enough not to drop me when I was balancing somewhere between the top of his head and the bottom of the ceiling!

The Seventies had delivered some superb fast dance music. People forget that the era also produced some really nice ballads. Taste of the Seventies had remembered. After the marathon of sweating and spinning, the deejay started playing "With You I'm Born Again," sung by Billy Preston and Syreeta. It's a gorgeous song—a gorgeous *slow* song. Finn pulled me toward him then, and for the first time since we'd been dancing, we were able to focus totally on each other. We just melted together, both of us singing softly along with the music. I could feel his breath on my cheek, his arms firmly encircling me. I rested my head against his chest and felt strangely, powerfully secure.

When we finally got back to the table, Corky and Newman were in hysterics.

"I told you—I told you! It's too perfect! 'Lady-killer and Man-eater.' It was only a matter of time before they got together. Any bets on who'll survive?"

Red immediately tossed a twenty on the table. "Belinda will have his scalp hanging over her mantle within the month."

Colleen laughed. "Belinda's good, but no offense—I've worked with Finn and seen him break more hearts than he has freckles!"

Finn and I looked at each other. What a way to start a romance! If that's even what we were doing.

Finn whispered in my ear: "Want to make 'em all eat their words?"

I stared up at him. "And just what does that mean?"

He took my hand and led me toward the bar, which surprisingly, seemed to be the only place not completely noisy or crowded. Finn ordered a couple of margaritas. He turned back to me and grinned.

"First, that's an extremely enticing little outfit you're wearing. I'm surprised another air conditioner hasn't exploded."

"Like it?"

"More than words can say."

"Well, thank you. All compliments are gratefully accepted."

"That said, I've been thinking."

Finn wasn't one to waste words. One acclamation over the dress, then right to the point.

"The entire cast is going to know that there's something going on between us before we've even had a first date. Right?"

"You got it. They're a very nosy group. And, let's face it—neither of us has been winning any 'Commitment of the Year' awards lately! 'Bets on survival!' Are we *that* bad? Wait—don't answer that!"

"I'll tell you what, Miss Belinda Montague—how about we show them all and turn our friendship into the most passionate affair this group—heck, this *town*—has ever seen?"

I squinted at him suspiciously. "Mr. Doran, are you propositioning me?"

"Yes, indeed."

I smiled sweetly. "Well, don't look now, but I'm turning you down. I may be the 'Mad-Man-Eater' of the Heaven's Hollow Community Theatre, but contrary to popular opinion, my mattress is not a bed-and-breakfast for every stud trying to carve a notch on his unbuckled belt!"

Finn burst into laughter. "To be honest, Belinda Montague, I'd rather have you in my life for the next forty or fifty years just getting to know you, than in my bed for one night—hellaciously exciting as that would doubtlessly be. I realize you don't believe that, but I think it's going to be fun spending the next fifty years trying to convince you. Starting with this."

Then he gently cupped my chin in his hand, and leaned down. Soft, generous lips met mine. I could vaguely hear music blasting and the bartender cheering. It didn't matter. We were alone and together in our shared feelings.

When we'd kissed that afternoon while rehearsing the "Oklahoma Hello!" I'd felt every nerve in my body tingling, but we'd both been in character then as Will and Ado Annie. I hadn't wanted Finn to know how he was really affecting me.

But *this* kiss was clearly Finn and Belinda. And when we parted, I stared into those roguish, blue, Irish eyes, and for the first time, I saw something very serious, and very real. I'd never felt so happy. And I was sure that he knew it. So I tried to play it lightly.

"So, Mr. Doran, we talkin' the 'R' word here?"

"If the 'R' word is Relationship and not Racquetball, then I'd give that a definite 'maybe'!"

We headed back to the table holding our drinks. I poked him in the ribs with my free hand.

"All those bets on which one of us will dump the other first! However are we going to resolve the gambling crisis?"

Finn gave me a very long look. Then he grinned—a slow, ultimately mischievous grin.

We deposited our drinks at the table. Finn excused himself and walked over to Dr. Heat's perch above the crowd. About thirty seconds later, I heard the good doctor make an announcement.

"We've had a dedication here, gang. It's not strictly disco, but it's a great dance song, and you know I love dedications. So, going out to Belinda from Finn, here's the Hall and Oates classic from the Eighties—'Man-eater'!"

Our entire table started screaming.

I turned twelve shades of red.

Then Finn bowed to me from the deejay's booth, crossed over, and led me out onto the dance floor once again. Just before we started to dance, he whispered:

"You win. Hands down. No contest."

A fifty-year run with this man would never be enough. THE END

UP AND DOWN ON A ROLLER COASTER:
I rode for free!

The back of my neck crawled as the silky hairs stood up. My skin prickled electrically. Had there been clouds in the sky, I would've been certain that I was about to be struck by lightning. But the stars sparkled clearly in the heavens above, and a warm August breeze caressed my cheek.

I was strolling aimlessly through the traveling carnival that was in town for the week, letting my mind wander just as aimlessly. Then that intense, otherworldly feeling came over me again, and I sensed someone's eyes on my back. The sensation pulled at me until I turned slowly around and felt my gaze drawn upward to the entry gate of the "Mystifying, Terrifying Death Machine!"

There, leaning back casually against a gatepost, was a slender, well-built man who looked to be in his mid-twenties, his black eyes sparkling as he grinned down at me. It was a smug, knowing grin, like he knew he possessed an uncommon force of will that could actually exert control over others, and I'd just responded exactly as he'd commanded me to.

I felt myself drawn to him in a strange, undeniable way that frightened me more than just a little. But some power outside of myself held sway over me. I walked slowly to him, not even aware of my feet moving. I couldn't pry my eyes from his hypnotic gaze. As I approached him, he reached out toward me, summoning, and my hand, of its own accord, placed itself in his.

His expression remained unchanged as he ushered me into one of the cars beside him. He lowered the bar and locked me in place without a word.

Suddenly, I felt the car lurch forward. The movement jerked me back to my senses.

I was in the Death Machine—and I hated roller coasters!

My stomach jumped up into my throat as the bottom dropped out from under me and I plummeted downward. All the terror from childhood dreams of falling through space clutched at me.

How in the world had I gotten into this?

Moments later as the train ground to a halt back at the platform, I was too drained to get out of the car by myself. My knees shook when I tried to move. The man, still with his knowing grin, reached for me. He put a hand around each of my shoulders and lifted me effortlessly to my feet. As I stumbled out of the car, I fell helplessly against him. His arms enclosed me—strong, sure arms. The scent of him filled my head—stirring, and yet, indefinable—mysterious and teasing.

It made me think of exotic, unknown places where I might've lived had I been born into another existence, far from the boring small town in which I'd spent my entire life—in which four generations of my family had lived their entire lives. My nice, safe, incredibly boring town. Why, in this town, people knew who you'd marry before you'd even figured it out yourself. They knew almost from the day you were born. Life here was laid out before me like a seamless, endless carpet, continuing on smoothly, predictably, until it reached the end of my time on earth.

"Oh, I . . . I'm sorry," I apologized as I leaned against him, my head still spinning.

"We shut down at one in the morning. Meet me here," he whispered in my ear, so softly, I wasn't sure he'd really said it.

I pulled back, startled, and peered into his face. His eyes bored into me as I regained my equilibrium and stood alone.

"One in the morning," he said again. Then he turned me away from him and propelled me down the exit steps as new riders crowded onto the platform.

I looked at my watch. It was a few minutes before midnight.

Don't be ridiculous, I thought to myself. *You shouldn't even consider meeting a strange man like that!* I'd been daring enough to come wander around the carnival alone when none of my friends were available, but I wasn't a fool.

Yet, as the night wore on, I found myself unable to leave. The image of his eyes kept forcing itself into my consciousness. And each time it did, I felt that strange, undeniable pull.

Well, I thought, *you came looking for something new, an adventure. Now it's dangling right in front of you. Do you want to spend the rest of your life remembering that when the one opportunity you ever had for an adventure came along, you just passed right on by—too chicken to even check it out?*

As the lights on the various rides began to blink out, I was still at the carnival, still wandering indecisively around. And when I finally looked up, I found that I'd wandered right back to the Death Machine. There, on the platform, stood the black-eyed man. As he turned from unloading the last riders, his gaze rested once more on me—that "knowing" gaze.

He motioned me up onto the platform. I found myself climbing the steps almost against my will. He hit a switch and the lights blinked off, leaving me disoriented in the darkness until I felt his hand on my shoulder. It was warm, firm, strong—constraining, somehow. I stood beside him for a while, in silence, until there was no one left that I could see. Then he climbed into the last car on the roller coaster and reached for me. I hesitated, and then followed him into the car. From nowhere, another man appeared on the platform, and as the gate closed on our car, he pressed the start button and then disappeared.

I tensed as the sudden movement of the roller coaster sent a shiver of fear through me. The black-eyed man put his arms around me and pulled me tight against him. Then, with one hand, he tipped my chin up and pressed his lips gently, softly, against mine. I couldn't stop myself from responding. His lips pulsed against mine. His tongue sought entrance, stirring my passion.

My heart lurched as his hand caressed my bare belly beneath my knit shirt, then cupped my breast. An unbidden hunger began to consume me just as the roller coaster topped the first big climb and plummeted over the edge.

My pulse pounded in my ears as the force of the car rounding a sharp curve flung me harder against him and he lifted me to straddle his lap. All I could do was hang onto him for dear life. I hadn't bargained on this!

But from somewhere deep inside of me, a wild, heated passion that I'd never before experienced, arose. I was aware of nothing but motion—the motion of the ride as we circled again and again, and the undulating, pulsing rhythm of plain, raw sex.

I don't know how, but the roller coaster ride finally ended. There was nobody in sight as he lifted me from the car and onto the platform. I was in a daze; I'd never done anything like that before in my life! I just wasn't that kind of girl; as it was, I'd only had sex with two other men in my life—in serious relationships. The last time had been nearly a year ago.

"Come this afternoon, around two," he murmured in my ear. "I'll meet you right here."

"I . . . I can't!" I cried involuntarily.

"Why not?"

"I . . . I don't even know you—"

"My name's Rebel," he said. "Now you know me."

He tilted my head up and looked deep into my eyes. The bit of light from the street lamp, several yards away, was swallowed up by the bottomless blackness of his eyes. I felt pulled into those depths. As he tenderly kissed my lips, I knew I could do nothing but follow his bidding.

Later, I lay in bed in the darkness of my upstairs room, gazing out the curtained window at the full moon shining down on the rooftops and yards, streets and pathways of my little town. I could feel the sameness, the unchangeable stability of the town and its inhabitants—the core of its existence. It felt permanent, right—the very fabric from which came my wonderful family . . . myself.

And yet all that couldn't calm the stirring I felt inside of me. I shivered, thinking about what I'd just done . . . what I would do again, as surely as I drew breath. Something "outside" had taken hold of me. Something that scared me, thrilled me, and drew me to it nonetheless.

The next day, I lingered just out of sight, around the corner of a building, until two-thirty. My gesture of independence—showing him he couldn't really control me. However, even from there, he had a magnetic effect on me.

He was something to look at, all right—six feet tall; dark brown hair streaked from the sun that tended to fall in his eyes when he bent his head; a small nose, lush lips, and those midnight-black eyes. He had no shirt on, and his dark, deeply tanned skin shone from sweat and the sun as his muscles rippled.

Even as I peeked around the corner, watching him, a woman waltzed up to him and began what was obviously a flirtation. I didn't know her; she wasn't from around here. When he actually stopped his inspection work and began to talk with her, I couldn't help myself. I popped out and strolled casually up to the Death Machine. His eyes were on me even as he talked to the other woman. She moved her head, trying to catch his gaze, and then, when that failed, she turned and saw me standing about ten feet away. His eyes twinkled and that knowing grin spread over his handsome face. The woman looked flustered, then angry, but she gave up, turned on her heels, and stalked off, leaving me to face my temptation.

"Hi," he murmured, the grin never leaving his face.

"Hi, yourself," I answered.

"Didn't know if you were going to show," he said.

"I thought about it," I said.

"And?"

"And . . . well, I don't know. I've never done anything like this before. I've never done anything like. . . ." I couldn't quite say "last night," but I could feel the color creeping up my neck into my face as I thought about it. Rebel laughed, then looked at me for a long moment.

"I didn't think you had," he said with a look of satisfaction on his face. "Want a beer?"

"Okay," I said. "But what about the Death Machine? Aren't you supposed to be working?"

He pointed to a man climbing along the roller coaster tracks high overhead. "Naw, Earl's got it. I've got some free time, anyway. C'mon."

I followed him to a long "gooseneck" trailer parked on the back edge of the fairgrounds. He unlocked the door and climbed in. I followed. I was surprised by the roominess of the place. Rebel opened the small refrigerator and fetched two beers, opening them, then passing one to me as I stood, trying not to be too obvious in my curiosity.

"Thanks," I said.

"Ever seen one of these before?" he asked, motioning around the room.

"Not up close. It's nice."

"Makes for decent living quarters on the road," he said, shrugging. "Anyway, beats a motel room every night." As he talked, he watched me in a level, appraising way. It made me a bit uncomfortable. Suddenly, it occurred to me that I didn't know this guy at all. For all practical purposes, he was a complete stranger to me.

Clutching the beer, I edged toward the door. He was leaning against the kitchen sink counter opposite the door, one leg crossed over the other, sipping his beer. As I inched toward the door and reached for the handle, he grinned.

"A little nervous, aren't you? What do you think I might do? Make love to you again? But, why would you be nervous about that?" He cocked his head sideways and winked at me.

I was dumbfounded. I could feel my face getting redder. In my consternation, I looked at the floor, not knowing what to say or do.

Just then, he leaned forward and his hand shot out, grabbing my wrist. Startled, I tried to jerk away, but his grasp was too strong. He held me motionless, looking deeply into my eyes. I felt weak—too weak to fight. At that moment, he could've done anything he wanted to me. But all he did was pull me to him and press his lips tenderly to mine as he released me. The gesture took my breath away.

Then, before I knew what had happened, he was out the door, standing there, holding it open for me to leave. I stepped out, confused. He closed the door behind us and began strolling back toward the midway. As I walked beside him, I could feel the heat building between us. We were almost touching, yet not. I wanted to reach out and wrap my arms around him, but something stopped me. It was as though he'd put up a barrier between us. No matter how much I wanted him, I couldn't touch him. Only he could break the barrier.

Then we were back at the roller coaster. He waved to Earl and picked up his tools. I stood mute, not knowing what to do or say.

"See you tonight at one," he said matter-of-factly, then turned and climbed up onto the entry platform.

I felt dismissed. And angry. He surely had his nerve, assuming that I'd be there when he said, at his beck and call.

"You don't even know my name!" I shouted at his back.

"Yes, I do, Mindy." He turned his head and smiled wickedly at me.

How did he know?

I hadn't told him.

At least—I didn't think that I had.

I whirled around and left. It was all I could do to keep from running out the gate.

As the clock on my nightstand ticked away the hours and minutes, I remained determined that I would not go to the carnival that night. My friends, Kelly and Michelle, had called, wanting me to go with a group of our friends from work. I'd turned them down, pleading a headache, but knowing it was truly because I wanted to eliminate the temptation of seeing Rebel again. I didn't *dare* tell anyone about my encounter.

Yet, as I lay on my bed watching television, through my open window, I could hear snatches of carnival music wafting over the summer night breeze. Unbidden, the memory of his body against mine, the pressure of his lips, the sweetness of his kisses—all of it began to creep around the edges of my mind. My breath began to come in ragged gasps as the feelings took over.

Then the memory of walking so close, but not being able to touch him, insinuated itself. He'd awakened something in me that I hadn't known was there. No one and nothing in this town had ever had that effect on me before—and probably never would. And soon, Rebel would be gone, and all my chances for those feelings would be gone with him. It was more than I could bear. The clock said twelve-twenty-seven.

I could just make it.

Plagued by indecision, I dressed slowly, thinking that if I was late, maybe he'd be gone. Then it would be over. Out of my hands. I knew I needed to be saved from myself. But the clothes I pulled on were a miniskirt and a cropped top—hardly an outfit to discourage a man. My desire was working hard against me.

I glanced at the clock again. Twelve-fifty-five. Suddenly, a shot of adrenaline surged through me. I had to hurry! I raced down the stairs and out the door, not bothering to leave a note for my parents. There was no time.

Breathless, I straightened my hair and walked around the corner of the main fair building toward the Death Machine. The overhead lights and most of the lights on the rides and game booths were out; I saw no one I knew from town.

Good, I thought. That'd only be more of a complication than I could cope with just then.

The roller coaster lights were out and I couldn't see anyone around. I stood in the dark at the base of the entry ramp, feeling a tremendous letdown.

But how could I be so disappointed over not seeing someone who was nothing but a stranger to me?

Suddenly, there was movement in the shadows. Someone grabbed me, an arm around my waist, and a hand clamped over my mouth as I started to scream. I felt myself pressed tightly, yet gently, against a strong, firm body.

He twirled me around to face him, still pressing me tightly against him. Then a familiar scent reached my nose, just as warm, lush lips covered mine in a passionate kiss. I pulled back slightly and peered through the darkness at the black eyes I yearned for. He kissed me again, then led me to a blanket beneath the scaffolding. I glanced around.

"Rebel, not here," I protested.

"Why not?"

"Someone might see us!"

"They couldn't see much, and besides, they wouldn't know who it was," he replied, undeterred. "Come on—it excites you, doesn't it? Knowing what we're getting away with?"

But I didn't have time to reply . . . he was slipping my top off over my head even as he lowered me to the blanket.

Perhaps it was the thrill of the forbidden; perhaps it was that I'd found the perfect lover. Whatever it was, I was completely caught up in it. Rebel's muscles flexed as he lowered himself onto me. I wrapped my legs around his narrow, powerful waist and lost myself to passion. There was no future, there was no past; there was only now—now and Rebel, and this feeling.

Later, as we lay side by side, looking up through the scaffolding at the moon and stars, he said quietly, "Stay with me tonight."

"What?" I asked.

He turned his face toward me. "Stay with me tonight," he repeated.

"Oh, but—I can't! No one knows where I am." I blurted it out before I thought, then added hastily, "And I have to work tomorrow."

He lay on his back in silence, looking up at the heavens. Something in his brooding silence tugged at my heartstrings. I raised up on one elbow and caressed his cheek tenderly.

"Rebel, I can't stay tonight. Really. It's not that I don't want to . . . but I have a job I have to be at by eight in the morning. And I couldn't explain to my parents why I was coming in just to change for work."

"You couldn't just tell them that you'd been with me?" he asked, with a sudden edge to his voice.

"Well . . . they'd want to know all about you. And what could I say? What do I even *know* about you?"

He pushed my arm away and rolled over, reaching for his jeans. He sat up with his back to me, pulling them on. "What do you need to know about me?" He spat it out, like I'd just insulted him horribly. "You wanna know if I'm an ax murderer? You think something like that about me?"

"No!" I cried, confused and upset. "No, I don't think anything like that! But, Rebel—I don't even know if . . . well . . . if you're married!"

At that, he turned and gave me a long, level look. "If that mattered to you, then why are you here?"

My mouth dropped open. I could think of nothing to say. Because he had a point—a very good point: If that mattered to me, why was I here? Questions began to crowd my brain. What on earth was I doing? Sneaking around, having wild sex with a man I didn't even know—a man who spent his life, for all I knew, roaming the country, seducing women in every town.

We dressed in silence. Rebel jerked the blanket up from the ground, rolling it into a manageable mound, then struck out toward his trailer, leaving me to find my way out on my own.

The next day was Friday. All day at work, one thought kept haunting me: The carnival would be gone on Sunday. Rebel would be gone . . . forever. My life would be back … normal. By four-thirty, I knew what I had to do.

When I got home, I told my parents that I was going to the fair with Kelly and Michelle, who shared an apartment, and would spend the night with them at their place. Then I threw a change of clothes into a duffel bag and left.

I left the bag in my car when I reached the fairgrounds, got out, and headed for the Death Machine, my stomach turning flips. The turmoil I felt is indescribable. I was going on blind faith, after all. For all intents and purposes, I was placing my life in the hands of a stranger. But I had to find out—was Rebel someone I couldn't, shouldn't, let go? Was he worth the upheaval in my life?

As I approached him, Rebel glanced up at me. Then, wordlessly, he continued with his work, adjusting a bolt on the machine. The invisible barrier was up again—I could feel it. I just stood there, patiently, and eventually, he looked at me again.

"What are you doing here?"

"I had to see you. Does the offer—does it still stand?"

"What offer?"

"The offer to stay the night," I said softly.

He looked at the ground, then back up at me—a long, assessing look. I began to feel even uneasier as I wondered what was going through his mind.

"You're not afraid someone will find out?" he asked pointedly, the edge still there.

"No. I want to be with you," I said, hoping my uncertainty didn't show. "I—I want to know you better." It slipped out before I thought.

"Oh. Still not sure about what you've gotten yourself into, huh? Well, you don't need to worry, cuz you're not in anything. I'll be out of here in two days, and then you can go back to your regular little existence and forget you ever knew me."

"I don't think so," I said quietly.

"You don't think what?"

"I don't think I'll ever be able to forget you," I said.

He hesitated a moment, then reached a hand out to me. I took it and he pulled me to him. And there, in broad daylight, where anyone in the world could see, he kissed me long and hard, and held me tight.

That night, I wandered around the fair, stopping by the Death Machine every so often, though Rebel was so busy he had little time to talk. Friday night, the fair was jam-packed with people. It seemed like just about everyone I knew was there. I can't deny it; it made me uncomfortable. There was something furtive about my connection to Rebel, something I couldn't quite pull out and deal with. At this point, I wasn't ready for anyone from town to find out about Rebel and me. Mentally, I chided myself. After all, this was exactly what he'd been talking about. But it wasn't shame I felt, exactly, when I saw someone I knew as I was standing next to Rebel during one of the infrequent lulls at the roller coaster. I didn't know what it was. I hoped that by tomorrow, though, I'd have it figured out. Tomorrow would be my last chance.

As I wandered through the crowd, that thought kept repeating itself over and over again in my mind . . . tomorrow would be my last chance.

But, suppose I did get it all worked out in my head. Then what? Would I talk Rebel into quitting the carnival? Would he consider settling down in our little town and becoming a regular citizen? Would he be the same person I'd fallen for if he made that change?

As the carnival lights blinked out that night, the surge of passion I felt watching Rebel as he shut down the Death Machine pushed all other thoughts from my head. I burned for him, and tonight, I knew I wouldn't be rushing to get home. Tonight would tell the tale.

I couldn't wait to have his hands on me. The lights went out then, and as he finished locking up, I pressed myself against his back. I heard him catch his breath. Then his head rolled back, eyes closed, as his hands reached back and found my thighs. I swayed gently against him. His hands slid under my miniskirt. My arms were wrapped around him, my hands caressing his muscular chest. Then my hands moved downward, down to that special place that told me how much he wanted me. Rebel moaned lowly, then turned and clasped me to him. As he bent to kiss me, he slid down onto the roller coaster entry ramp, pulling me astride him. He slid my panties off, and then handed me a condom.

"You do it," he said huskily.

There we were, where anyone might see, only the darkness to hide us, and I didn't care. As I rolled the sheath onto him, I could feel my excitement building to an uncontrollable pitch. Our coupling there on the entrance to the Death Machine was even more passionate than before. I hadn't known these depths were in me. I couldn't imagine ever giving him up.

When it was over, and we'd caught our breath, Rebel helped me to my feet. He slid his arm possessively around me and led the way to his trailer. He stopped me just outside the door and made me close my eyes and wait while he went inside. I felt light-headed. I'd surrendered myself to whatever the night would bring.

Rebel popped out of the door and came to me, looping an arm around my waist and holding my hand as he ushered me into his place. When I opened my eyes, a warm glow enveloped me. Rebel must've placed fifty candles around the small room. The couch was made out into a double bed, on which he'd spread luxurious, black silken sheets. Cool jazz emanated from speakers in all four corners.

As a tenor sax wailed seductively into the night, Rebel lifted me in his arms and placed me gently on the bed. Then, with a mock flourish and a wicked grin, he produced two wineglasses and a bottle of wine. As I lounged on the bed, sipping my wine, he opened the refrigerator and removed a platter containing a wedge of cheese, crackers, smoked oysters, and olives and carefully placed the platter on the bed beside me.

"I'm all sweaty. I'm gonna jump in the shower. Care to join me?" he asked.

I hesitated momentarily, but a duet shower sounded very good. "Sure," I said.

What came next at first astonished me, then felt wonderfully sexy. Rebel picked up two towels, took me by the hand, and led me outside.

"Where are we going?" I asked.

"You'll see," was all he said.

Then he led me around behind the trailer to a wooden platform with a large, circular rod overhead supporting a shower curtain that encompassed it, and a large, plastic container overhead. He shed his clothes, piling them on a nearby yard chair, and reached to slip my top off over my head.

"What's this?" I asked, a bit unsure about what, exactly, was going on.

"The shower," he answered, a mischievous grin teasing at the corners of his mouth.

"What?"

"You said you wanted a shower . . . well, get naked, then. This is it. Come on in."

With that, he parted the shower curtain and entered the platform, pulling me in after him. As I quickly shed my clothes and tossed them onto the chair, he turned some handles, and suddenly, wonderfully hot water cascaded over us.

"How do you get hot water out here?" I asked, laughing in

wonderment.

"Solar heat," he said. "I have a portable panel set up just over there." He motioned with his head.

It was the most sensuous shower I've ever had. We lathered each other's bodies with our hands, caressing, stroking gently. Then, as the hot water cleansed us, Rebel embraced me tenderly, planting kisses all over my body.

Refreshed and relaxed, we lounged on the bed afterward, wrapped in towels, and dug into the snacks he'd prepared for us. As we worked on the second bottle of wine, he lay on his side, looking at me silently. A wistful, almost sad look came into his dark eyes. As I reached out to him, he took me into his arms. Every nerve ending in my body seemed more alive than ever before. He caressed me, held me tight, and made soft, tender love to me. I slept a deep, peaceful sleep in his arms that night.

Hours later, I woke to find him propped on his side, facing me, those black pools of his eyes reflecting the warmth of the morning sun, a sweet smile on his lips. The chirp of grasshoppers in their summer assault on the nearby fields accented the laziness I felt as I stretched out on the silken sheets. Just then, at that moment, my world was perfect. I wanted nothing more than to lie there in the summer morning and not have to move even a toe. I smiled at Rebel, then lazily closed my eyes again. His fingers traced paths up and down my body like feathers on the wind. I felt the passion begin to build inside me. Then, once again, we made love tenderly, lovingly, completely.

"I'm not married," he said, out of the blue, as we lay in each other's arms afterward. There was a palpable silence. Then, very lowly, he said, "But the truth is, I almost was... once."

"What happened?" I asked.

There followed a long pause, and then he said, "She left me," and offered nothing more. His life was still a complete mystery to me, but the things I felt in his arms couldn't, wouldn't, be denied.

Finally, hunger pangs reminded me that we had other human needs to tend. "If you'll go get my bag out of my car, I'll see what I can put together for breakfast," I said, though I would have preferred to lie there naked with Rebel all day long.

I pulled on one of his T-shirts and began to rummage through the small refrigerator and the cabinets in search of breakfast fixings. To my surprise, he had eggs and sausage, biscuits, coffee, and jam—even some scallions to chop into the eggs as I scrambled them. We ate, and I set about cleaning up afterward.

Rebel sat in his chair and watched me, a strange, unreadable look on his face. Then he got up and left—without a word, without a kiss, without a gesture of any kind. He just left. The invisible barrier had slammed back into place. I had no idea why. I killed as much time as I could in the trailer, but as a couple of hours passed with nothing from Rebel, an uncomfortable, restless feeling overcame me.

Had I been dismissed?

Was our time together already over?

Something clutched at my heart. Not knowing what else to do, I took my bag and headed for my car.

But my path took me to the roller coaster, instead. As I shielded my eyes from the sun and peered skyward, I spotted Rebel up high on the scaffolding, intent on his work.

"Rebel, I'll be back tonight," I called out to him.

But he didn't respond, simply kept on working.

Had he heard me? I couldn't tell. Did he want me to come back? I couldn't tell that, either, but I did know I felt like a fool just hanging around there like a stray dog hoping for a handout. I could feel the eyes of the other carnival workers on me. What did they know? Did Rebel do this in every town they worked?

My parents were, blessedly, gone when I got home. They'd left a note saying that they wouldn't be back until late. I felt relief at not having the possibility of questions being asked that I didn't want to, or couldn't, answer. I'd managed to fairly well block those things from my own mind, but I knew I was skating on thin ice.

As I busied myself doing my week's laundry, niggling doubts and questions kept bobbing to the surface of my conscious mind, threatening to crack through my defenses. I avoided asking myself if I'd completely lost my mind. Had this been happening to a friend of mine, I know I would've sworn she should be locked away for her own protection.

By six that evening, though, I could hold out no longer. I packed my bag again, already knowing that I would stay the night with Rebel . . . if he'd have me. I wanted him so very badly; my self-control had almost completely disappeared when it came to him. I got in my car and headed for the fairgrounds, stopping to pick up hamburgers, fries, and shakes for both of us. I'd already figured out that he could seldom find the time to get anything for supper when he was working, and hoped this might serve as a peace-offering icebreaker—anything to get through that wall of his.

When I arrived at the fairgrounds, I took my bag to Rebel's trailer, stashed it beside the steps, then headed for the Death Machine, hamburgers, fries, and shakes in hand. I lingered at a bit of a distance, watching him, feeling the surge of emotion he inspired in me.

As I watched, the woman I recognized from the other day went up to him, wrapped her arms around him, and hugged him tightly. He looked down at her and smiled. My heart froze. They both looked at their watches, talked briefly, and then she left. Just then, there was a juicy thud as I dropped the bag of burgers, fries, and shakes. I was so crestfallen, I could barely think straight.

Then, I did, for me, an incredible thing. I lost any semblance of self-respect and lurked about the fair all night, spying on Rebel. I was obsessed with uncovering his secrets. I had to know if I was just a momentary diversion for him, one of countless gullible women he'd seduced over the years, or did I actually mean something to him? I just had to know!

The woman came back to talk with Rebel twice more during the night. I burned to know what was going on between them. The minutes dragged by until, finally, one o'clock arrived. I stood in the shadows and watched as he shut down the roller coaster. He sat in the dark afterward beside the platform and drank a beer.

Eventually, the place was empty, except for Rebel . . . and me. Slowly, he got up, looked around as if he were expecting someone, then headed to his trailer. I followed at a safe distance, keeping to the shadows. Sure enough, as he approached his trailer, that woman appeared, and hugged him again. They talked, heatedly, and then she left. Rebel sat alone in a lawn chair beside the trailer for what seemed like hours.

Then, just as he started up the steps to go inside, he spotted my bag. He picked it up, then turned to look around. I felt like a complete fool; I didn't know what to do, so I simply walked up to him. Even in the dim light, his black eyes burned. They burned a hole in me.

Without a word, he turned, my bag in his hand, unlocked the door, and went in. Hesitantly, I followed.

The moment I was inside, he dropped my bag and glared at me, his fists clenched. Then he grabbed me tightly and kissed me long and hard. I felt myself land heavily on the bed, and then he was on top of me. He tore at my clothes, ripping my blouse open as his mouth devoured me. He tore at my panties, then was inside me roughly, pounding at me. I was in shock. I had never experienced anything like it. At first I was frightened, then angry, then, suddenly, a tremendous passion took hold of me, and I was lost again in the passion of our union.

"Don't leave me," he whispered breathlessly against my ear as he lay heavily on top of me, spent.

At that moment, I felt myself so bonded to him, I could no more have left him than if we'd been conjoined twins. Logic and reason had no place in my heart or in my brain.

And yet there was something pulling at the corners of my mind— the smallest of doubts. Even as I basked in the glory of our lovemaking, a small voice, like a rumble of distant thunder, said: *But what do you really know of him?*

I swam to consciousness through a crushing headache. The light from the sun beating down at an angle onto the trailer skylight, hurt my eyes. I had been dreaming. I was on a train, rumbling down the tracks to an unknown destination. In the dream, I was naked, and I kept trying to tell the conductor that I had to go back, that I wasn't ready; my clothing—everything that was mine was behind us—getting farther and farther behind with each click of the wheels on the tracks.

But the conductor never heard me.

I lay in the bed, my head throbbing, a nasty, wooly taste in my mouth. Where was Rebel? Suddenly, it registered in my brain that I was, indeed, in motion. The trailer was moving rapidly . . . somewhere.

Frightened, I leapt from the bed and lurched to a window. Through the mini-blinds, I could see roadside passing at a high rate of speed. There was nothing but open country beyond that. I stumbled to the front of the trailer and peered out. It was hooked up to Rebel's tandem truck, barreling down the highway.

I rushed to the door and tried to open it.

Locked!

I tried to unlock it. It was secured from the outside!

I flew to a front window and opened it, screaming out, "Help! Let me out of here!" over and over. The wind whistled against the screen, the only answer to my pleas.

I sat on the bed and pulled on my clothes. I was terrified. What was going on? Where was I? Where was Rebel? My head swam from the pain and confusion. I looked at my watch: It was almost four in the afternoon. How had I been so soundly asleep that I wasn't wakened by all the activity and noise it must've taken to load up the trailer and get on the road?

The taste in my mouth . . . I'd noticed a bitter taste to the wine that Rebel had given me last night.

Suddenly, it dawned on me: There had been something in the wine. Something to knock me out. I couldn't even remember going to sleep.

I was being kidnapped.

I stayed at a window, watching, all afternoon and into the night, trying to catch a clue as to our location. Rebel was sticking to back roads. By the time I'd wakened, we must've already been a couple of hundred miles from my town, and I could only guess from the angle of the sunset, as to the direction we were traveling.

Finally, at two in the morning, we stopped. I sat on the bed and looked at the door.

The handle moved. I heard the lock click back. Then the door opened and Rebel climbed in. As I watched the door behind him, he stood very still, blocking any access I might have to escape, and looked me in the eye. There was defiance in his expression. Defiance and determination. But there was also a vulnerability—a questioning look in those black, depthless eyes.

What was I going to do?

"What's going on, Rebel?" I demanded.

He stood there silently for what seemed an eternity, then turned and locked the door behind him, pocketing the key. He moved to the kitchen and began pulling out the makings of a meal. He didn't speak, didn't look at me—just set about dumping the contents of a can into a pot and putting it on the stove.

I was terrified. What was going on in his head? What did he intend to do with me?

He fixed two plates of food and placed them on the table. "Eat," was all he said.

"I can't!" I cried.

"Up to you," he said, then went silently about eating his meal.

"Rebel, what's going on?" I tried to make my voice sound reasonable and friendly.

He didn't reply, simply cleaned up the kitchen area, then removed his clothes and climbed into bed.

"What's going on? What are you doing with me?" I screamed as I leapt onto the bed and pounded my fists against his bare, solid chest.

He grasped both my wrists and held me immobile. He held me like that for a long moment, then, still silent, pulled me into his arms and imprisoned me in his embrace. When he fell asleep, I tried to get away from him, but he roused and tightened his hold on me until I quit struggling and finally drifted off into a fitful, feverish sleep.

I dreamed we were making warm, tender love. My heart was filled with love and happiness.

Suddenly, I became aware that it was not a dream. I awakened in Rebel's strong arms, moving in perfect rhythm with him as a moan of pleasure escaped my lips.

Once more, I was helpless against him.

When I awoke the next morning, we were already on the road. Rebel had gotten up, locking the door behind him once again, and driven us away.

I peered out the window. There was no clue as to where we were. This time, we stopped at noon. As I looked out the windows, I could see that we were pulled off at a tree-shaded rest stop somewhere. But there were no other cars or trucks around, only those whizzing past on the highway.

Once again, Rebel entered the trailer and locked the door behind him. As he set about preparing sandwiches for the two of us, I tried to talk to him.

"What is it?" I implored, but he remained silent, turning his head away.

"Rebel . . . what? Tell me—please!" I pressed.

"Nothing." The word came choked out of him.

"What?"

"Nothing." He hesitated, and then, "It's just . . . I don't want this to end." He turned to face me with an expression of such vulnerability and defensiveness on his face, it told me more than words ever could.

I could hurt him in ways that would not heal. He was as helpless against me as I was against him.

Just then, there was a loud rapping on the door. Rebel, as startled as I was, opened the door and looked out. There seemed to be no one there. He opened the door wider and leaned out. Suddenly, a hand reached around the back of his neck and jerked him outside.

There, guns drawn, were two highway patrolmen. One had knocked Rebel's feet out from under him, and now had him spread-eagled, facedown on the road, his right arm twisted behind him, handcuffed. The other patrolman was peering cautiously inside the trailer. Then he looked at me.

"Are you Mindy Erlichson?" he asked me.

"Yes! How did you find me?" I cried.

It seemed that several people who knew me had seen me with Rebel at the fair. Then my car had been found deserted at the fairground parking lot after the carnival had pulled out. It hadn't taken much detective work to put the pieces together.

We were taken to the jail in the nearest town and held separately. Late that night, my parents rushed into the room where I was being held, crying and reaching for me. I was more or less in a state of shock. I didn't know what to tell the police or my parents. I didn't really even know what I felt.

But I refused to press charges. I just couldn't. I simply got in the car with my parents and went back to my quiet, safe little town. I felt nothing, just sort of numb.

Now, as I look out the window at the passing landscape, I know I'm going to have to check the map again. I pull to the side of the road and do just that. Then, through my open car window, I hear bits and snatches of carnival music drifting on the autumn air. I can nearly smell the peppers and onions grilling with the big sausages in the concession booth.

Three months' worth of letters, deeply revealing letters, from Rebel lie in a neat, ribbon-tied stack on the front seat next to me. My bags are safe in the trunk, and my clothes hang in their garment bags in the backseat. I flip the left turn signal as I move back onto the little-traveled, rural, two-lane highway. I'm somewhere in Kentucky, far away from my little hometown, and I'll soon be home. THE END

MR. MECHANIC, I NEED SOME *BODY* WORK!

The mechanic spoke over the phone in a calm voice—the kind of voice you're supposed to use on an hysterical person. My car had gone into the shop for a routine physical, but the mechanic had found the auto equivalent of heart failure.

"We can fix the problems, Ms. Redford, but. . . ."

"But what?"

Was I supposed to fill in the blank? I wasn't normally so snippy—at least, not openly—but I had a bad feeling about this conversation.

"But you have an old car, and there's a lot that needs fixing." He sounded unwavering.

I rolled my eyes and tapped my toe. *Boy, this guy is sharp. Next, he's going to tell me it has four wheels and a missing hood ornament.*

"So, what's wrong with it?" A pin-sized headache started behind my eyes.

He proceeded to give me a detailed diagnosis of my car's current diseased state. He used words like *damaged head, leaky valve,* and *terminal.* I wondered if I'd taken the car to a hospital instead of a garage. As he spoke, my hearing vanished, my vision blurred. I could see only dollar signs.

"You see, once the gasket starts to fail, the oil leaks through. . . ."

"Did I hear you say, *costly?*" I interrupted. He'd sneaked that word in somewhere.

"Well, yes, I'm afraid so." He sounded so sorry for me that I wanted to smack him.

"As in hundreds?"

No immediate answer. I did, however, hear a long, slow exhalation of breath.

"More than hundreds?" I crossed my fingers, hoping he'd lie to me.

"Umm, a lot more, ma'am."

I felt sick. I sat down hard in the metal chair by the pay phone in the break room. I yanked off my nylon hair net.

What a rotten day.

Another deep breath came through on the other end of the phone. "This is a very sick car, ma'am, and from the looks of things, it has been for some time."

Did I mistake the slight scolding tone of his voice? How would *I* know if the car had been sick for a long time? I work in a bread factory, not an auto plant. So long as it kicks on when I turn the key and rolls forward when I push the gas pedal, it's fine by me.

"Look, all I wanted was a tune-up."

"Yeah, but there's blue smoke pouring out the back. You know, you really ought to—"

"Can't you just put it back together and I'll drive it till the engine falls out?" I began to panic. I couldn't afford a new car—or even a heavily repaired one. "Look, I hate to point this out to you, but the car was running when I came in. I didn't *push* it in."

The trio of Coke-swilling bakers at a nearby table silently applauded me and mouthed: *You go, girl!*

The mechanic didn't say anything.

I glanced at the clock over the door. Five more minutes of break time.

"Excuse me, are you still there? Mr. Mechanic?"

I knew I sounded sarcastic, but I didn't care. All my life, I'd kowtowed to everyone, held my tongue when I wanted to stick it out, did what I was told, followed everyone else's rules. Well, no more. I wasn't going to be pushed around by a greedy mechanic who probably indulged himself in manicures and pedicures at my expense. Besides, I'd never seen this guy face-to-face; I could say whatever I wanted.

The customer is always right.

Right?

"Look, I can put the car back together, Ms. Redford, but I thought you'd at *least* want to fix the problems."

There it was again—that sly, scolding tone.

"Well, you thought wrong. I'm not a problem-solver. I'm a get-byer."

I cringed. Get-byer? I sounded like a nutcase. I turned my back on the gawking bakers who slapped their knees and held their jiggling bellies. My headache moved from my eyes to the top of my scalp.

Why had I taken my car to this place in the first place? There was a perfectly disreputable Gordon's Garage not two blocks from my apartment. I'd been there several times, and Gordon had never said one word about the blue smoke and terminal oil hemorrhage.

But noooooo, I had to listen to the machinists at the bakery.

"Eastwood is the best," they'd unanimously advised. "You can drop it off, and then walk right across the street to work. And by the end of the day, you've got a brand-new car. They even vacuum the interior and wash the windows."

When I'd dropped the car off, I'd thought the mechanics charging in and out of the office looked strange. Their jumpsuits were clean. Their hair was clean. Even their *language* was clean. The way I looked at it, any self-respecting mechanic had grease under his fingernails and grunge on his face. But these guys all wore those tight, rubber gloves that surgeons and septic tank repairman wear.

"What was your estimate again?" I stared down at the worn soles of my shoes.

"About two thousand dollars."

Two thousand? My lungs collapsed.

No!

This couldn't be happening.

Not now.

Not when I was so close.

I had two thousand dollars, but I wouldn't touch it. Not even to fix my own heart, much less my car's. It'd taken me a whole year to save that much for the college classes I wanted to take; I wasn't about to squander that nest egg on an oil leak.

"Ms. Redford?"

I stared at the receiver, trying to connect the dots of the mechanic's face.

What did he look like?

I couldn't remember, other than clean. Like all the others.

"Let me think about it," I said finally.

"Take your time."

Take my time? I didn't *have* time. And right then, I captured him in my memory: the short blond one with the artificially tanned skin. The one who'd stood in the office and shown off his brand-new gold watch.

"I'll bet you have all kinds of time," I shot back. "And money, too."

"I beg your pardon?"

"Look, I'm twenty-three years old and I haven't started college yet. Unlike you, I don't have all the time in the world. It's not *your* savings account being sucked out of the bank. It's not *your* future evaporating. It's not *your* time wasted."

"Ms. Redford. . . ."

I sat up straighter in the chair, one hand on my hip. "I just want you to know that I intend to get a second opinion, and if I find out that you're ripping me off so you can buy yourself a new gold watch, or a power boat, or a Harley Davidson, then I'll do everything I can to put you out of business. Do I make myself clear, Mr. Mechanic?"

"Yep. Perfectly."

I slammed the receiver down so hard, it fell off the cradle and swung like a man on a noose. I stood up. Several people in the room clapped and whistled, but most of them laughed. My face started to burn. As I marched out, I heard one of the bakers say, "I ain't never heard her say 'boo' before. She sure let fly on that poor bugger!"

Great. Now I'd be the talk of the dough boys.

Loaves and loaves of white bread cruised by on a conveyor belt. Identical. Every loaf the same.

I shuddered. *Oh, God, that's me. One more loaf. Do I make myself clear, Mr. Mechanic? That comment will be my distinguishing mark. Oh, brother.*

I grabbed my time card. Okay, so what if I'd acted like a darned fool? There're worse things.

Yeah, and I'd done them all.

"What're you looking so woozy about, Redford?" my supervisor barked as I punched back in.

"I've just discovered that I'm a fool."

"Oh, yeah?" She shook her head. "Well, better to know it than not. And get your hair net on while you're at it."

I headed back to my production line, and with every step, I told myself not to fall for the mechanic's smooth voice and quiet certainty. After all, I wasn't about to bankroll his next trip to Hawaii; I had *plans* for that money. Next semester: MS Dos 101.

Then I groaned inwardly. Who was I kidding? Without a car, I couldn't *get* to the college, anyway. I'd have to take two buses from the bakery—three, if I detoured home first.

I felt the sting of tears in my eyes, but I refused to cry. *Bag bread and don't think,* I ordered myself.

After work, I trudged to the corner to wait for the number twenty-one bus. At least I wouldn't have to stand in the dark, since I'd finally racked up enough seniority to snag the day shift. Only took me five years. But who'd have thought I'd still be working at this dead-end job?

A summer stint after high school—which was what it'd started out as. And then I got a credit card, and then another, and another, and before I knew it, I was chained to my factory job just to pay off my debts.

And what did I have to show for all that debt?

Memories of mediocre restaurants and smoky bars. Of meaningless dates with shallow men—men who I knew simply as Steve or John or Tom—first names only. I swore I'd never again date a man whose last name I didn't know. None of the Bobs, Bills, or Bens had been worth the interest I was paying them now, that's for sure.

Which brought up another hot topic.

"Those greedy banks ought to be shut down!"

I quickly glanced around to see if anyone had heard my unexpected outburst. Nope. Just the bus sign I leaned up against. Get a loan for a newer car when you've had five years of steady employment? Not a chance. Too much debt already. How 'bout a credit card, instead?

Jerks.

Offering a kid right out of high school a $700 credit line when she doesn't even make that much money a *month* is purely criminal. If I had the money, I'd stop them.

Well, you can afford a thirty-three-cent stamp on a letter to your congressman, I reminded myself. And you could have pitched those credit card offers when they came in the mail.

But who can pass up 2.5% on the good life? Especially when you've never *had* the good life. And when ten of those banks offer you 2.5% . . . well, it's downright irresistible. Of course, now the good life was costing me 18%—and there *was* no good life.

No dates.

No clubs.

Just interest payments.

I hated all men. Bankers, especially.

And now mechanics.

It's not that I didn't want a social life. It's just that I attracted men who wanted my credit cards more than they wanted me. A sleaze magnet—that's what my own mother called me. She thought I deserved better, though—something along the lines of a king or, at the very least, a crown prince.

So, I'd stopped dating. Six months ago. And, truth be told, I felt happier. I figured I should start a support group: Men Anonymous. Anyway, at twenty-three, I had plenty of time to find someone who really *did* like me. Me—the woman who read poetry, listened to jazz, who wanted to learn karate, and take guitar lessons.

A teenager strolled by just then, moving in that half-dance/half-strut walk of his generation, his head jutting back and forth like a chicken's. He paused after he passed me and lifted his nose. He looked around and sniffed. A brief smile crossed his face, changing his expression from grim to glad.

This happened a lot. No one ever even considered that the aroma of freshly baked bread might be coming from me. I'd gotten so used to the smell, it made me rather sick. But I never tired of seeing the nostalgic, wistful, hungry expression that crossed a person's face after just one waft. At least my dead-end job did something good for *other* people. Made them think of happier times. Put smiles on their faces. But that wasn't *me*. *I* hadn't done that. No, I wanted to do *something* that put smiles on faces.

Well, you certainly opened your big, fat mouth today and stuffed your foot in it. You did that, all right!

More and more people arrived at the bus stop. The clouds turned darker. The wind picked up. Rain fell, polka-dotting my white uniform. A collective groan sounded from the crowd as the bus pulled up, already full of passengers. I boarded and pushed and shoved my way through the aisle, keeping my gaze on the floor, on the hiking boots, cowboy boots, and galoshes. I settled my clog-clad feet in an empty spot between the scuffed wing tips and the Air Jordans, and held onto the metal bar overhead. The man next to me smelled like wet wool and gasoline. I turned into another pocket of air. The bus growled forward.

"Excuse me," a voice below my elbow sounded. "Would you like my seat?"

I looked down at a pair of deep brown eyes. Black, rain-slicked hair; straight nose; delicate, yet manly, features; full lips. About my age. No, creases at the corners of his eyes—a little older, then. Instinctively, I looked at his left hand.

No wedding ring.

The man smiled, revealing straight, white teeth.

"Oh, I'm fine, thanks." I glanced away. My face felt hot. No one had ever offered me a seat on the bus before. That type of gallantry went to silver-haired ladies or dyed platinum blondes, not mousy, brunette factory workers.

The bus jerked to a halt and I wobbled sideways toward him. He placed his hands on either side of my waist before I could tumble into his lap.

"Oh! I'm so sorry."

He grinned. "Happens all the time."

Not to me, it doesn't. Whoa, girl. Remember: You're a sleaze magnet. And he's riding a bus, not driving a Mercedes. He probably smells the debit card in your purse.

Fortunately, the credit cards were in my freezer, frozen inside Tupperware containers. Still, out of the corner of my eye, I watched his chest rise and fall under his navy blue jacket, the kind of jacket worn by the machinists who worked at the bakery. *Anthony* was embroidered across the left pocket. He sat with his hands on his lean thighs, his knees dropped open, one leg bouncing slightly, as if keeping time to a song. I wondered what kind of music he listened to.

He cocked his head and smiled up at me. "You're the Nissan, aren't you?"

"What?" It was the strangest pickup line I'd ever heard.

"The red Nissan Sentra with the peeling roof?"

I swallowed hard. A creepy tingle tiptoed down my back. "That's my car you're describing. Why?"

He slid out of the seat and stood up next to me. A scowling, pinched-face woman who smelled of baby powder quickly slithered into his spot. He grabbed hold of the bar overhead. His hand touched mine. He studied me with an expression that lived someplace between curious and amused.

"What do you know about my car?" I demanded.

He pointed to the embroidery over the other pocket on his jacket. *Eastwood Garage*, it read.

I closed my eyes. "Oh, crud."

The urge to flee made my legs wobble. But with every stop, the bus filled up with more smelly bodies, causing us to have to press closer and closer together. There was absolutely no way for me to get away from Anthony of Eastwood Garage.

Well, he stood at least six inches taller than I did, so at least I didn't have to look him in the eye. I stared at his embroidered name and cursed my big, fat mouth for getting me into this mess. Suddenly, my mother's voice sounded above the chatter on the bus: *What goes around, comes around.*

Now what was I supposed to say? Oh, sorry for verbally abusing you on the phone today?

Wait a minute, though—

This couldn't be the same guy I'd yelled at; I'd already decided that it'd been the tanned blond. Besides, Anthony's deep voice didn't sound anything like that smooth Mr. Mechanic I'd unloaded on in the break room.

I squared my shoulders, set my feet farther apart to stay steady, and tried to look blasé.

"How did you know the Nissan's mine?"

He shrugged. "I saw you come in with it. I was in the office."

Whew. I offered up a small prayer of thanks to the God of Close Calls. So, he must've been one of the surgical nurses running back and forth from the operating room. One of the ultra-clean ones. I studied his long fingers, the nails cut evenly across. My shoulders relaxed.

"Worked there long?"

"Couple of years."

I pressed back against the gasoline-smelling fellow until I could lift my head to see Anthony's face. A gorgeous face. Not Hollywood gorgeous, of course, but one with clear skin, the shadow of a dark, thick beard, and a faint red flush over the cheeks. He had inquisitive, bright eyes, and the longest eyelashes I'd ever seen on a man.

"Did you look it over? My car, I mean?"

"A little." He seemed utterly relaxed. Not at all bothered by the heaving of the bus, whereas it was all I could do to stay upright. "I mostly looked over the mechanic's report."

I grunted. "I didn't much like that guy—the mechanic, I mean."

"Really?" He frowned. "Why not?"

"I don't know. His attitude, I guess. He's not very skilled in customer service."

A half-smile formed on Anthony's face. "I'll be sure to pass along your feedback to him."

"Oh, I already passed it along."

I kicked at a piece of hardened bubble gum stuck to the bus floor. Anthony moved closer to let a woman wearing some sort of horse liniment grab an empty seat. He smelled like Dove soap. Yummy.

"I suppose you're going to tell me that the guy's a really good mechanic."

He shrugged. "Good as anyone."

I held up a hand in surrender. "Okay, okay. So, Mr. Mechanic says my car needs more than a tune-up."

"And are you going to fix it?"

Staring at his mouth, I said, "I don't know. If you were me, would you let Eastwood Garage fix your car? I mean, you must know the real story."

His expression turned thoughtful, as if he was truly considering my question. I liked that.

"If I had a car, yeah."

I frowned. "A mechanic who doesn't own a car?"

One black eyebrow rose. "Do you have a bread machine at home?"

I saluted. He dipped his chin A gracious winner. I liked that, too. I must've been smiling a lot, because my lips ached.

"So, how did you know I work in a bread factory?"

He reached over and plucked the nylon hair net off my head.

"Oh, my God."

My hands flew to my mashed mop. He grinned. I wanted to keel over right then and there. Truth was, I'd gotten so used to wearing that hair net, I never felt it anymore.

Yeah, and he's been laughing at you this whole bus ride, you dumb do-do!

"I like your hair."

"Yeah? Well, you could've told me about the hair net sooner." I ran my fingers through the mess, freeing the curls.

"I thought it might be some kind of fashion statement."

I tried to stay embarrassed, but the absurdity of the remark made me grin. "Yeah, that's me—a walking fashion statement. So how come you don't drive?"

"I like the bus." He handed me the hair net. "You never know who you'll meet."

"Freaks, usually." I stuffed the net in my pocket.

He laughed. "Actually, I have a '65 MG, but it's in about four hundred pieces in my garage at home. I've been trying to restore it for three years now."

"You won't take that long on my car, will you?"

Several passengers pushed past us at the next stop, leaving more breathing room and a couple of single vacant seats. Neither of us moved to take them. I could feel his gaze on me. I knew it was a pleasant gaze, too. He liked me. I could feel it. And I liked him, too.

"So, you must enjoy being a mechanic." The bus started off again. I kept my focus on the hollow at his throat. I liked hearing him speak. He had one of those soothing voices that you hear on late-night jazz radio.

He shrugged. "It supports my addiction."

My head jerked up. Addiction? Well, of course he *would* have a sleazy side. Didn't I like him, after all? A guaranteed sleaze indicator. But—*addiction*? Well, he certainly was frank about it!

His mouth turned upward in a grin, as if he knew where my thoughts had gone. "Music," he said.

"Huh?"

"Music's my addiction. I play bass in a jazz club."

Idiot, I scolded myself. "Oh. What club?"

"The Basement on Fifth."

"You're kidding? I used to go there all the time!" I strained to remember any of the bass players' faces. Couldn't. Back then, I was always too busy signing credit card receipts. "What nights do you play?"

"Thursday through Sunday. But we're working on an album, too." His whole face lit up; his eyes shone.

"Wow, that's great! I love jazz."

"I know." At my surprised look, he shrugged. "I saw your cassette tapes in the Nissan."

Another spontaneous cringe. Those tapes were strewn all over the passenger side floor. Most of the cases were cracked, and I'd rewound so many of them with a pencil that their sound quality was shot.

"You don't go to the club anymore?" he asked.

"Can't afford it." No point in going into detail about how much I hated all men. "I've been saving up for school."

That caught his interest. I could tell from the way he tilted his chin again.

Careful. You're starting to memorize his mannerisms.

"What are you studying?"

"Nothing yet." I tried to swallow back the bitterness I felt about spending my hard-earned college money on car repairs. "But I was hoping to start taking computer classes at the community college next term."

"Computers?" It was more of a surprise statement than a question—like he expected me to study something more flamboyant. "Good field. Lots of jobs."

"Uh-huh."

We fell into an awkward silence. I glanced around. The bus windows had fogged up from all the hot human air. The fluorescent lights had kicked on, giving everyone a bluish complexion. I sneaked a look at his face. He looked down at the floor, his eyebrows drawn together.

"You could come with me for free," he said then.

"To school?"

"To the club." He lifted his head and grinned that gorgeous grin. "I wouldn't want you to have to give up music because of money."

I stared into his eyes, searching for the sleaze. Couldn't find it. His expression was warm and sincere. Truthful. No one had ever offered me anything for free. No, the way I looked at it—anything offered for free would only end up costing me a bundle.

"No cover?" I asked. "How?"

"You can carry my bass into the club."

Slave labor. I should've known. "So, if I'm your bass caddy, can you get me a discount at the garage, too?"

He threw back his head and laughed. A deep, warm laugh. The momentary awkward silence had passed. "Free cover and a discount, too? Hmmm, I'll have to check with the boss."

"I'll bet the guy who owns the place is a real fat cat. Probably smacked his lips and rubbed his hands together the minute I rattled in."

Anthony shook his head. "Not exactly."

I lifted an eyebrow.

"There is no 'guy' who owns the garage." He leaned up against a metal pole and crossed his arms over his chest. "Used to be, and he was a bit of a fat cat, but he died and left the shop to his kid. The kid wasn't much of a businessman, though. He didn't want the responsibility of the place, so he sold the garage to the mechanics."

"It's like a co-op, then."

"Uh-huh."

"And you're a partner?"

"Yep."

The bus jerked to a stop and I swayed. He didn't. How could he stand there so balanced? If I weren't hanging onto the overhead bar, I'd be draped over somebody's lap by now. I shifted my weight and noticed the scowling, baby-powder woman staring at me. Suddenly, she smiled and nodded toward Anthony. She winked. I quickly looked away. Oh, jeez, what if he'd *seen*?

"I don't think Mr. Mechanic meant to make you feel bad." Anthony's gaze rested somewhere over my right shoulder. He sounded apologetic. "Was he rude?"

"No."

He shifted his gaze to meet mine. "Then what bugged you so much?"

"Well..." Right. So what exactly *had* bugged me? My voice ratcheted up a few notches. "Well, he insinuated that my car's condition was all my fault—like I obviously hadn't maintained it or something. And just how would he know that? I mean, I've had the oil changed. I drive carefully. I don't ride the brake. Once in awhile, I even put premium gas in it."

His expression grew thoughtful "You know, a mechanic's like a dentist. Your dentist always knows if you're flossing regularly, or if you've just given your gums a quick fix the week before an appointment. Mechanics can tell the same things about your car by just looking at the engine."

I bit my lip. Crud. Then he must know that I'd just had the oil changed at one of those drive-through lube joints so it wouldn't look like tar when I took it in. You'd think I'd have learned something from my dad, the original, every-three-months oil-changer.

Dentist, huh?

I fumed again.

"You know, that's another thing: Since when do mechanics use the same vocabulary as heart surgeons?"

Anthony scratched the side of his face. That crooked smile still lingered on his lips. It made me want to smile back. "Well, there are similarities," he said. "Hearts and engines both have valves."

Mrs. Baby Powder leaned closer, her ear turned upward in the direction of my mouth.

I looked at Anthony. He looked at me. My heart started to pound. To my ears, it sounded much like the noises my Nissan's engine had been making as of late.

"He made me think I'd let my car go to ruin!" I burst out.

Anthony took a deep breath "Well, did you?"

"Yes, damn it!"

The bus shuddered to another halt; more passengers scuttled off. Tears formed in my eyes, and I suddenly realized why I was really upset. And it had nothing to do with Mr. Mechanic or the two thousand dollars. "The truth is, I haven't done squat to that poor car since I inherited it from my dad. He'd croak—well, actually, he's already dead—but if he were still alive today, he'd have a fit if he ever saw the current state of his precious automobile." I took a deep breath and tried not to let loose with a full flow of tears. "And by the way, I *do* floss my teeth regularly, so don't give me that dental analogy again." I noticed then that several passengers were staring at me.

Anthony grinned. "You live up to your hair."

"Uncontrolled?"

"Fiery." He laid a hand on my shoulder. "Look, I think you should fix the car. There's a lot that's right with it."

My lower lip started to tremble. "Yeah. And there's that little, two-thousand-dollar problem."

He squeezed my shoulder and then let go. "We'll work out a payment plan."

I gazed at his hand resting against his leg, wishing it were back on my body. "Look—if it's more than twenty bucks a month, I can't afford it."

"Then twenty it is."

My jaw dropped. "Are you serious? Just like that? But you don't even know me. How do you know I'm good for it?"

"I know where you work, remember?"

The bus ground to another halt, the air breaks letting out a long, exhausted sigh. "Last stop!" the driver yelled.

"Oh my God!" I frantically tried to see out the foggy windows. "I missed my stop!"

"Me, too." Unlike the fiery, uncontrolled woman beside him, Anthony didn't look in the least bit upset about it. "We passed it when you were confessing to flossing your teeth."

"So why didn't you get off?"

"I've got nothing better to do. Anyway, it's the band's night off."

I started to follow the throng of passengers filing off the bus. Anthony and I were the last of the stragglers. Then suddenly, he turned around and blocked the aisle.

"Have dinner with me." He smiled, and I noticed he had the faint hint of a dimple. "We can talk about your car, if you'd like."

My breath shortened. "I—I'd rather talk about jazz."

He dipped his head to my level. "Is that a yes, then?"

"I guess it is."

He moved to one side of the aisle to let me pass.

I hesitated. "Who's paying?"

He laughed. "I'd offer, but you'd call me a chauvinist. How about we go Dutch?"

I held out my hand. He took it.

"Deal."

Out on the street, the rain fell in a soft mist. Anthony offered me his arm, and we huddled close together as we walked. Music and laughter from several busy restaurants floated out onto the night-time street, along with the smells of delicious food.

This isn't a date, I told myself. *It's a business dinner. You'll discuss your car, and his music.*

Then again . . . maybe it *was* a date. . . .

So much for Men Anonymous.

I let go of his arm and stopped in the middle of the sidewalk, facing him.

"What's your last name?" At least I'd remembered one vow: No more first-name dates.

"Eastwood."

Eastwood? I swallowed hard.

"As in—the fat cat's son?"

" 'Fraid so."

He actually looked embarrassed.

I should've known.

I bit my lip and pretended to scrutinize the people dressed in overcoats, carrying briefcases, who scurried past us. Eyes down, shoulders hunched, cell phones glued to their ears. Probably walking the same route as yesterday and the day before.

Loaves of bread.

All of them.

I could fall in step with them and disappear down the street.

Anthony reached for my hand.

I took a step backward.

We stood in the middle of the sidewalk, in the rain, and stared at one another. I could feel my hair curling into ridiculous ringlets as the rain now fell in earnest. I knew he was waiting for me to say something, do something. I didn't want to ask, but I had to.

"You're Mr. Mechanic, huh?"

In two steps, he stood in my airspace. Taking my hand, he said, "Ms. Redford, I'm Anthony Eastwood, jazz musician, car mechanic. I've just met the most fiery, sharp, spirited woman on bus number twenty-one, and I'm dying to have dinner with her. She's suddenly reminded me that there's life beyond my MG and my music. But there are some things that will forever be a mystery, and the true identity of Mr.

Mechanic is one of them."

Then he brought my hand up to his lips, keeping his focus on my eyes. It was the most electrifying kiss I'd ever felt.

Warm breath.

Soft lips.

Firm grip.

"Have dinner with me, Ms. Redford. Please."

I should've turned tail and run. Any other self-respecting, big-mouthed fool would have—but his brown eyes held me fixed.

Fiery?

Sharp?

Spirited?

Suddenly, I burst out laughing. "This has been the most rotten day of my life!" I shouted.

He grinned. "It's been the best day of mine."

Then he wrapped his arms around my waist and hugged me.

What else could I do?

I hugged him back. THE END

LOOKING FOR MR. RELATIONSHIP
I didn't think I'd have any luck in a singles' bar, until . . .

"Feelings, nothing more than feelings. I wish I'd never met you. I'll never love again..."

An eerie feeling came over me as the words of the song and their haunting melody reached me over the background noise of the room. Why did that darn song always make me feel as if it were trying to tell me something?

For two years, I'd heard that song at every function I'd attended since my divorce. I certainly intended to love again, though I doubted if my presence in the bar that night would expedite my plans in any way.

Once again, I looked around at my surroundings, pretending a nonchalance that I didn't feel. Dim lighting, smoke so thick I'd have to wash my clothes and hair when I got home, pre-recorded music, a dance floor, and intimate tables meant to hold no more than three occupants. Though this place had a bit more class than others I'd seen, it was nothing more than a place for men and women to come together to drink, dance, and meet each other. The men were often married, looking for an easy pickup, or just some company for the night. It was definitely *not* a place where you'd find everlasting love and happiness.

Only, I didn't drink more than socially, I didn't want to date anyone who drank more than I did, I was rarely asked to dance, and I'd never met anyone worth seeing again once I left the establishment.

Honestly, my sole reason for being there that Friday night was as a favor to a friend. Colleen, newly divorced, had asked me to come with her. Unlike me, though, she'd hardly been back to the table since we'd arrived that night, her long blond hair attracting the men like flies to honey.

The last time I'd been in one of these places was a year ago. It hadn't taken me long to realize that I was a washout in this setting. It wasn't that I was ugly or unkempt. In fact, I'd been told by many that I was even pretty, with my nice figure, emerald green eyes, and even features. I was wearing a green jersey dress that night that clung to me in all the right places. What I lacked was self-confidence, that indefinable charisma that makes some people just stand out in any crowd. As usual, I spent the evening wishing that I hadn't come.

Oh, I'd danced a few times. But the men had been total losers, like the one I'd just purposely ditched. He was so drunk that he could hardly stand up straight and his breath smelled like a hundred proof. Ugh. I only hoped he wouldn't find me again.

"Would you like to dance?" said a soft male voice suddenly behind me.

Startled by the unexpected request, I turned to stare into the turquoise eyes of a man I'd noticed earlier. Something about him had caught my eye when he walked in, casually dressed in a loose, Hawaiian-print shirt and tan denims. I'd been unobtrusively watching him before, but hadn't seen him approaching. Now, it was a pleasant surprise.

"Sure," I said, standing.

I followed him out onto the dance floor, observing the breadth of his wide shoulders in front of me. We passed Colleen on the way, who gave me a knowing smile—one that said she approved of this guy. I smiled back, communicating non-verbally my pleasure with this turn of events.

Taking our places on the already crowded dance floor, we assumed the usual dancing stance. Gratefully, I noticed that he didn't hold me too close. I'd learned the hard way that some men use a dance floor to essentially molest a woman in public. As we swayed to the music, I felt delightfully small next to this guy. We fit well together, him being only three or so inches taller than my own, five-feet-seven frame. The song finished all too soon, though, and we separated.

Suddenly, I felt awkward. Should I walk away, or wait for him to ask me to dance again? I glanced at him, waiting for his cue.

"Let's wait for the next song," he said. During the lull that followed, he asked, "What's your name?"

"Molly. Molly Bright." I smiled. "And yours?"

"Lars Svensen."

"Glad to meet you, Lars."

Now what do I say?

I blurted out the first thing that entered my mind. "Are you Swedish?"

"Norwegian, actually—on my father's side. My mother's of the Heinz 57 variety, though, so I guess you could say I'm a mixed breed."

I smiled brightly as a song with a faster beat started. As soon as we began to dance again, though, I groaned inwardly. Lars was not a good fast dancer; his movements were stilted, and he barely kept to the beat. I steeled myself to endure the next few minutes.

Lars shouted over the music, "Are you intellectually curious?"

"What did you say?" Prior to this question, our conversation had been the usual mundane, boring stuff that strangers who've just met ask each other. But no one had ever asked me if I was "intellectually curious" before.

Whatever did he mean?

"I asked you," Lars repeated, "if you consider yourself to be intellectually curious."

Assuming he wanted a positive response, I shrugged. "Yeah—I mean, I guess I am." After all, I prided myself on my intelligence, and I enjoyed learning about new things.

Lars nodded, apparently satisfied. A few moments later, he spoke again. "Have you seen *Aliens Among Us*?"

"No." Not being a science fiction aficionado, I'd no intention of seeing the newly released movie.

"Would you like to see it with me?" Lars asked.

My mind spun. Had I heard him correctly? The man knew nothing about me except my name, and he'd just asked me out on a date.

For microseconds, I debated it, and then came to my decision. Something about this man was drawing me in, despite his lousy dancing, and a movie date seemed like a safe way to get to know him better.

I smiled. "Yes, I would."

Lars seemed relieved. His answering smile displayed his even, white teeth, which were very nice to look at. "Great. Is next Friday all right with you?"

"Sure," I said, my trepidation over my rash decision quickly overshadowed by my delight. It was flattering to have someone I was attracted to also be attracted to me.

When the music changed, Lars said, "Let's sit this one out."

At my nod, he took my elbow and steered me over to an empty table for two on the side of the room. His hand felt warm and comfortable on my bare arm.

"Would you like a drink?" he asked.

"Yes, thank you."

He signaled for a waitress. When she arrived, she leaned down and Lars spoke to her. The decibel level in the room prevented me from hearing his order. When the waitress turned to me, I ordered my usual, a vodka collins.

The waitress left, and I turned back to Lars. Since I'd already committed myself to going out with him, a virtual stranger, I figured it would be wise to learn more about the man. During my two years of single parenthood, I'd formed a mental checklist of what I wanted in a relationship. I had no intention of wasting my time dating men when I saw no future in the relationships. My plans included finding another husband—one who'd love my son—and having a second child with him. A palm reader had once told me that I'd have two children, both of the same sex, and I intended to prove her right. At thirty, though, I often felt like I didn't have a lot of time to waste.

So, I began with the most important question of all:

"You are single, aren't you?"

Lars put his left hand on the table, displaying his unadorned ring finger.

"Yes."

He seemed bemused. Since many men don't wear rings, anyway, the lack of one meant nothing. So, for now, I'd have to take his word for it. If he was lying to me, I knew the truth would show up sooner or later, anyway. I'd become adept at reading all the signs.

"Have you ever been married?" I needed the answer to this one as a lead-in to my next, biggie question.

"Once."

"How long have you been divorced?" I'd found it took a man at least a year to get over a marriage. Prior to that, they were still hung up on the ex-wife.

"Four years. What about you?"

"I've been divorced for almost two years." I took a deep breath. "Do you have any children?"

"No."

Good, I thought, feeling hopeful. It wasn't that I'd *mind* if he had children and had to pay child support, but I figured that his lack of children meant that he'd probably want one in the future.

Then he added: "I like my life unencumbered."

Taken aback, I asked, "Why?"

"Because I want to travel, use my sailboat to see the world."

"You own a sailboat?"

He nodded. "I live on it, as a matter of fact. Built it myself from scratch. Unlike most boats, it's made of ferro-cement. It's not completed yet, so all of my free time and money goes into The Persephone."

I knew nothing about sailboats or sailing, but the idea of living on a boat seemed unique to me. I wouldn't mind seeing the world someday, either, but not until my son was older.

Should I tell him that I had a child? I decided to wait. He'd said that the boat wasn't completed yet, so he wouldn't be leaving on his round-the-world trip anytime soon.

Then the waitress came with our drinks, temporarily stopping my flow of questions.

"Where do you keep your boat?" I asked when she left.

"On a mooring in the downtown harbor. The boat's attached to two buoys about a hundred feet from shore, so I have to row out to it. It's a little lonely, and I don't have a telephone, but I enjoy the peace and tranquility."

Peace and tranquility? It'd been a long time since I'd experienced either one of those. Living with an active two-year-old made those particular phenomena very rare in my life.

"How old are you?" I asked.

"Thirty-two."

Perfect. Older than me, but not by much.

"What do you do for a living?" I asked next.

"I'm an engineer. Listen," he said, grinning, "it would expedite things if you'd give me the application to fill out myself."

"I'm sorry," I mumbled, blushing miserably. I stared at my drink as I fingered the frost on the glass. "It's just that I hate all of the small talk that goes along with trying to get to know someone, so I like to get it over with as soon as possible."

"It's okay," he said, his voice reassuring.

I looked up in time to see his warm smile and the twinkle in his lovely eyes.

"Ask anything you want. It's obvious that you're looking for a relationship. The truth is, I am, too."

And would he still be interested when he found out that I was "encumbered?" Only time would tell. So I might as well plow on.

"Do you smoke?"

"Nope."

"Neither do I. What about drinking? I mean, I know this is a bar, but—"

"Here. Taste this," Lars interrupted, handing me his tall glass filled with a yellow liquid.

I took a tentative sip. I don't know what I'd expected, but it seemed to be plain orange juice, and nothing but.

"Orange juice?"

He nodded. "I found out early on that I don't like the way I feel under the influence."

Neither did I. Suddenly, I felt guilty for my drink; I'd only ordered it to "fit in." Clearly, Lars was more confident than I was.

"Now it's your turn," he said.

"Sure," I told him. "What would you like to know?"

Lars shook his head. "Nothing. I want to show you something." He stood. "Now, stand in front of me."

Curious, I complied.

"Raise your right arm like this," he said, demonstrating. He held his arm stiffly out in front of him at a ninety-degree angle.

I did as he asked. He held my hand, put his other hand on my upper arm, and said, "Now take a sip of your drink, and hold it in your mouth without swallowing. Try not to let me push your arm down."

My arm sank like a stone under Lars's gentle pressure. Laughing, I asked, "How did you do that?"

He handed me his orange juice. "Take a sip of this, and I'll try again."

I sipped. That time, my arm didn't budge.

"What is this? Some sort of magic?"

"It's called kinesiology. It's a way of testing one's inner self to see if something's good for you, or if you're allergic to it."

As a nurse of many years, this hocus-pocus was completely foreign to me. The way I looked at it, one tested for allergies by injecting a small bit of the substance under the person's skin and waiting to see if a welt appeared. Lars's little experiment, however, had been enlightening.

"How did you learn about this? Didn't you tell me that you're an engineer?"

He chuckled. "I'm taking a class. It's called, 'Touch for Health.' " He reached for a packet of sugar from the bowl on the table. "I want to try one more thing." He ripped open the packet and held it by my mouth. "Let me sprinkle some on your tongue."

He tried to lower my arm a third time. It held firm.

"That's funny," he muttered, frowning. "Try me."

He sprinkled some on his own tongue, and I put my hand on his outstretched arm and pushed. Amazingly, his hand went down easily, despite the fact that I knew he was far stronger than I was.

"You're playing with me," I said, grinning.

He shook his head. "I'm not. Most people are weak when tested with sugar."

"Then I guess I'm not average," I quipped, and sat down. Actually, I thought I was pretty darn *near* average. Lars was the one who was unusual. What would he surprise me with next?

"Have you ever heard of volitional science?"

Now, I'd taken my share of science classes, but that one was new to me. "Nope. What is it?" I put my elbows on the table and propped my head up on my clasped hands, eager for his explanation.

"It's the science of choice. I'm taking a class called V-50. When I finish the course, I'll no longer live in flatland."

"Where will you live."

"In space, of course."

I laughed. Studying Lars's face, I saw warmth, friendliness, and intelligence reflected there. He was watching for my reaction, and I suddenly knew that he wasn't joking. Then I remembered the first question he'd asked me, and realized the truth. He was a man who was "intellectually curious," certainly a different breed of man than I'd ever met in a bar before, or anyplace else, for that matter.

My curiosity piqued, I said, "Tell me more about this course."

He smiled broadly. "I'm glad you asked. Are you familiar with the libertarian party, or Milton Friedman, the economist?"

I shook my head.

"They both advocate less government control and lower taxes. The general public is in the habit of letting the government take care of many of its needs—things like education, highways, law enforcement, and the military."

"Wait a minute," I said. "That's what we pay taxes for. We can't pay for those things individually; we need to put our money together."

"That's true," he agreed, "but our government makes all of these rules about these things, which makes them cost more than they would otherwise. Let's use education as an example."

"Okay."

"The way the system is set up, a huge amount of money goes into the school buildings, themselves, and there are a ton of rules and regulations which need to be met in order to legally open a school. Now, I grant that some of these rules and regulations are for the children's safety, but many of them are little more than overkill. And let's look at education, itself. Nowadays, teachers are paid just for showing up, not based on whether or not each child is learning something. I'd like to see a system where the children are given tests, and only when they pass the tests would the teachers be paid. Because let's face it: Our public education system has problems. If it doesn't, then why are so many parents doing home schooling or sending their children to private schools?"

I could see his point. I could also see that he'd given some serious thought to the matter. "You certainly have some interesting ideas," I said.

"So I've been told."

Just then, Colleen tapped me on the shoulder. "I'm sorry to interrupt, but are you ready to leave yet, Molly?"

I knew immediately from the look on her face that she was, and ready or not, I had to keep my end of the deal we'd made before coming, that if either one of us wanted to go home, the other would comply without any argument.

But why did she have to pick this moment to leave? I hadn't had a chance to tell Lars about my son yet, and given the things he'd said, I knew he had a right to know before we went out on that date we'd made. Sighing, I turned to Lars and introduced Colleen to him and vice versa.

"I'm sorry, Lars," I said. "I've really been enjoying our conversation, but. . . ."

He waved his hand to stop my explanation. "I understand."

I started to stand, and realized then that he hadn't asked for my number. Should I speak up and offer it to him?

I decided against it. After the way I'd boldly asked him so many questions, he'd probably changed his mind about our date, anyway, and I didn't want to put him on the spot.

"Aren't you going to give me your number before you go?" he asked then.

Immensely relieved, I tore out a deposit slip from my checkbook. "Here," I said. "It has both my address and phone number on it. Good night, Lars. It was a pleasure meeting you."

I knew it sounded trite, but I'd never meant it quite as much. I regretted leaving without saying more, but I reasoned that if he called, I'd still have the chance to tell him about my son before we actually went out.

"Me, too," he said, rising politely. "I'll see you, Molly."

Reluctantly, I walked away, wondering if Lars would leave, too, or if he'd find someone else to dance with or talk to. The hour was young, after all, comparatively speaking.

Outside, the minute we reached the car, Colleen began quizzing me about my evening. I enthusiastically recalled it for her in minute detail. Retelling my conversation with Lars only served to increase my feeling that the evening had been a momentous occasion in my life.

"I didn't know that guys like him even existed," Colleen remarked. "But he sounds a bit weird to me. Are you sure you want to go out with him?"

"More than anything. I'm just worried about what he'll think of Skyler. He made it pretty clear that he doesn't want kids in his life right now."

"Don't worry." She patted my arm. "Skyler's adorable. How could anyone resist him?"

"I hope you're right."

But my feelings of apprehension only grew as the weekend passed. I was euphoric about having met such a special man, but increasingly concerned that he'd turn away from me as soon as he learned that I had a child. After all, as far as he knew, I was an average person—clearly not nearly as intellectually curious as he was—so there was really no reason for him to accept my encumbered lifestyle.

The other niggling doubt that crept in had to do with the way I'd questioned him. I'd come on awfully strong, I realized now. At the time, Lars had seemed to laugh it off, but I wouldn't be surprised if he was already having second thoughts about dating someone who was so *obviously* looking for a long-term relationship.

Did he truly still want to take me to that movie? After all, he *had* asked me out before we'd even really sat down to talk.

I spent Sunday with my brother, and reiterated my meeting with Lars to him. He laughed at the story.

"There's no one else like you, Molly," he chuckled.

"But do you think I scared him away?"

"You'll find out soon enough. He didn't set a time for that movie date, did he?"

"No," I admitted. The thought had also crossed my mind. Had that omission been on purpose, or by accident?

"Then if he still wants to see you, he'll have to call first. And when he does, you'll have the opportunity to tell him about Skyler." Darren shrugged. "He'll either accept the fact, or he won't."

When the telephone rang Sunday night, I answered it, my heart in my throat.

"Hello?"

"Hello, Molly. It's Lars. I've been trying to reach you all day."

"Oh—I spent the day with my brother."

"Well, listen—I only have a minute. About the date we made for Friday night. . . ."

"It's okay," I said, already expecting him to bow out.

"Molly, I don't want to have to wait that long to see you. Are you free tomorrow night?"

"No, I'm not," I answered honestly, feeling immensely relieved—and intensely exhilarated! "There's a retirement party for someone at work. . . ."

"Oh," he said, sounding dejected.

Did he think I was making an excuse?

"I'm free Tuesday night, though," I added, hoping he'd be free also.

"Great, then. Would you like to go to dinner?"

As much as I wanted to see Lars, I made it a practice never to leave my son with the sitter more than one evening in a row. "Actually, I'd rather fix you dinner at my place. I make a terrific lasagna."

"Mmm. I love Italian. But are you sure it's not too much trouble?"

"No, it's no trouble at all. Would six-thirty work for you"

"That's perfect."

I took a deep breath. It was now or never. "Lars, there's something—"

"Deposit fifty cents, please," said the operator, interrupting the call.

"I have to go now, Molly. I'll see you Tuesday night."

The line disconnected.

Darn it! Now the situation was worse, rather than better. Lars was certainly in for a surprise when he came over. Even if I sent my son to the sitter's for the evening, it'd be obvious as soon as Lars walked in the door that a child lived with me.

Still, my obstinate streak told me that Lars needed to accept my son if we were ever going to have any kind of a relationship. And what better way for him to see what Skyler was like than to spend an evening in our home?

When the doorbell rang Tuesday evening, I wiped my damp hands on my apron, straightened my clothes, and opened the door.

Lars looked more handsome than I remembered. He wore an off-white, cable-knit sweater and gray slacks. From behind his back, he brought forth a small bouquet of flowers and handed them to me.

"Since I don't drink, I didn't think wine would be appropriate, so I brought flowers."

"They're lovely." I sniffed the rosebuds dreamily. On top of everything else, it seemed that Lars was romantic! I opened the door wider. "Come in."

"Dinner smells great. Is there anything I can do to help?"

"Mommy, who's that?" Skyler asked, toddling to my side before I could answer Lars.

Lars looked down at my towheaded son. "Hey, fella," he said. Then he looked up at me, his expression shuttered. I couldn't tell if he was annoyed or surprised, or both.

"I meant to tell you," I began, flustered. "But the opportunity just didn't come up. The operator interrupted the call, and. . . ." I shrugged.

"I hope you don't mind. . . ."

"Not at all."

"Well, then—dinner's almost ready. Why don't you follow me into the kitchen while I do the final preparations and put these flowers into a vase?"

I'd set the table before Lars arrived. After putting the flowers into water, I turned to see him frowning at the table.

"Is something wrong?" I asked, feeling my heart sink.

"I—I assumed we'd be eating alone."

My face started to burn miserably. "Do you mind if Skyler eats with us? I mean, I've never fed him separately."

"Do I have a choice?"

Although I was trembling inside, I kept my voice light and quipped, "Not if you want to eat my lasagna tonight."

Lars managed a sheepish grin. "Then my stomach rules."

Dinner was a rather tense affair. Skyler talked in what, to me, was clear, perfectly understandable speech, but Lars didn't understand a word he said, so I had to continually interpret for him. Also, since Skyler was used to having me all to himself, he tended to monopolize the conversation. I wasn't certain if Lars's silence was due to the fact that he was upset, quiet—or couldn't get a word in edgewise.

Finally, Lars set his fork down. "This isn't working out like I expected," he said quietly.

"No, I guess it isn't. I—I should've told you beforehand that I had a child."

He shook his head. "It's not that you're a mother. I've dated women with kids before, but they always had a sitter watch the child when we dated, and I guess I'm just not used to being around kids all that much. To tell you the truth, I feel like I'm being ignored."

"Look, Lars—Skyler's used to having me all to himself. He's only two years old, and he doesn't understand about being seen and not heard. I haven't raised him that way." I bit my lip, pondering the best way to lay it all on the line. Then I took a deep breath and spit it out. "I'm really attracted to you and fascinated by everything I've learned so far about you, Lars. I want to get to know you better, but in order for us to have any kind of relationship—whatever that may be—you have to accept my son as well as me, and be willing to spend time with both of us. I won't get involved with any man who doesn't understand this. After Skyler goes to bed, I'll focus all of my attention on you. But until then, you'll have to share me."

"I see. Are you giving me an ultimatum?"

"Yes, I guess I am."

"Let me think about this a minute."

Lars sat on the couch while I took Skyler into the bathroom to run his bath water.

Shoot. Why had I sabotaged the best thing to come my way in two years? Why had I been so darned obstinate? I could've sent Skyler to the sitter's. One evening wouldn't have made a difference in the scheme of things. And why had I been so darned truthful? I could've waited until Lars got to know me better before I scared him away.

Lars's deep voice behind me interrupted my thoughts as I knelt at the tub.

"What time does he go to bed?"

I turned to see him standing in the doorway, his expression pensive.

"Usually at eight, but I'll try to get him down tonight at seven-thirty if you'd like." I held my breath as I waited to see what he'd say next.

"I've decided to stay."

We were married a year later. THE END

HOT NIGHTS WITH THE NANNY

Ethan Garrett's home office was bigger than my apartment. In fact, his desk was bigger than my apartment. That made me very glad, probably for the first time in my life, that I wasn't exactly petite.

Of course, in my work, height was a definite advantage. Longer legs enabled me to outrun my little charges; longer arms enabled me to more easily snatch a giggling toddler squirming across a bed. And there was plenty of room inside my arms for lots of cuddles.

The day I interviewed for a position with Ethan Garrett, the first thing that struck me was the size of everything. The house, the room, the desk, even the man, were huge and untouchable.

The house was exquisitely furnished, some rooms in antiques, others in comfortable, contemporary decor—from what I could glimpse as one of the staff led me back to Mr. Garrett's office—but human warmth seemed in seriously short supply.

A mantle clock chimed as I sat, hands folded in my lap, while he read my résumé.

I didn't know what Garrett did, specifically. "Fingers in lots of pies," Mrs. Monroe, who ran the agency, had said. "Heavily invested . . . old, nineteenth century family money . . . travels a lot . . . needs someone reliable." And the man was desperate, she added, willing to pay top dollar for the right person.

Whether I was the "right" person or not remained to be seen. But I was relatively new in town, available, and not the type to be easily intimated by men like Ethan Garrett—or any other man, for that matter. My primary concern, as it had been for the four years in which I'd worked as a live-in nanny, was for the children—not their parents, or in this case, guardian.

I suppose desperation is a given when a bachelor suddenly finds himself saddled with a pair of children he's never laid eyes on before. And rich bachelors in such a position are apt to be generous—or so Mrs. Monroe assured me.

My usual employers back East had been the typical overextended, dual-income couples with one or two kids. After a few months, they inevitably decided they either couldn't afford a nanny, or were so wracked with guilt about shunting their kids off on a stranger, they decided to let me go. It never had anything to do with me, at least, as the letters of recommendation being shuffled in my prospective employer's hand attested.

Pale gray-green eyes bore into me from beneath a take-no-prisoners scowl. Mr. Rochester in *Jane Eyre* had nothing on this guy. Between the severely angled features, the haunting eyes, and the lost-in-time mansion, I wondered if I should be wearing a hoop skirt and a lace hair ribbon, instead of my standard navy blue, wash-and-wear, tailored jersey shirtdress.

I was considerably older than Jane Eyre, however. And I wasn't an orphan. My parents were both alive and well, enjoying themselves in a retirement community in Mexico.

"You don't drink?" Mr. Garrett boomed from across the desk. To my credit, I didn't jump. I could imagine how two small children might react, however.

"Never have."

An eyebrow lifted. *Well, don't believe me.* It's true, though. I never could stand the taste of alcohol.

"Or smoke?"

"No."

"No driving infractions?"

I shook my head.

"Health?"

"My last cold was in 1987, and I almost never get headaches—or cramps."

He coughed a little at that but recovered nicely. "Boyfriends?"

Now my eyebrow lifted. "Not at present, no."

A chilly glance darted in my direction. He rattled my résumé. "Why'd you move out West?"

"To be closer to my parents." I explained about Mexico.

He rubbed his chin. "Have you ever been married?"

My heart pounded. "My husband died four years ago," I said quietly.

Something that might have been compassion twitched in his eyes. "I'm sorry."

He went back to reading the letters of recommendation, giving me ample opportunity to study him. I couldn't quite peg his age, despite the liberal amount of gray streaking his dark brown hair and the character lines—in his case, "laugh lines" didn't seem to fit—around his mouth and eyes.

You know how some people look older than they are because of something that's happened to them in their past? I thought maybe that was the case with Mr. Garrett.

Even though he was in his own house, and it was barely nine A.M., he was dressed in full corporate regalia: gray pinstriped suit, white shirt, striped tie. I supposed he was on his way out and had squeezed in this interview beforehand.

I was impressed that he hadn't left the job to his secretary, a pleasant enough middle-aged woman whose domain was a small anteroom adjacent to the one I was in. She'd told him she'd hold his calls until we were through. I liked that.

"Why do you do this?" Mr. Garrett asked suddenly.

I blinked. "Do what?"

"Hire yourself out as a nanny."

He was hardly the first person to ask. I can't tell you how many people think it odd that someone would voluntarily take on someone else's children.

"Because I like kids and don't have any of my own."

"Why not?"

The question startled me. Outwardly, I didn't even flinch. Inside, however, anger at his impertinence flared.

"Because," I answered calmly, "my husband and I didn't have any." I lifted my chin. "But I'm not sure I think that line of questioning is germane to this interview."

A smile flashed across his mouth, but only for an instant. "I didn't mean to pry," Mr. Garrett said in a gruff voice. He leaned back in his leather desk chair, tapping his pen on the desktop.

"I don't know much about children in general, and nothing about my cousins in particular. But I do know, if I'm to be responsible for their well-being, then it's imperative their nanny be someone who can genuinely . . . care about them."

Something struck me as odd about the conversation. "I've always cared for and about my charges," I said carefully. "But it sounds to me as if you're expecting me to give the love they should be getting from someone closer, like . . . you."

He actually looked startled. Now I was the one being impertinent, I suppose. My mother always said my diplomacy skills left much to be desired. But Mr. Garrett didn't answer my comment—at least, not directly.

"Jared and Emily have just lost both their parents," he said quietly, frowning. "And I'm not around very much, I'm afraid. I agreed to see to their needs, but I can't change my lifestyle on their account, since it's that very lifestyle that enables me to provide for them."

I kept my mouth shut, for once.

After a pause, he went on. "Besides, I suspect what they miss most, right now, is a mother's comfort. Since I can't provide that, whomever I hire as a nanny will have to fill in that gap."

Oh, right—Mrs. Monroe had mentioned something about his confirmed bachelor status. Still, I couldn't help an inward sigh at the brooding some-woman-done-me-wrong-and-they're-all-the-same mindset.

Funny, I've never known a single woman who didn't keep trying to find her prince, no matter how many toads kept springing into her path. Yet if a man is burned once, he's scarred for life.

But I managed to keep those thoughts to myself. I did need this job, after all. And for a pair of children who'd just suffered a loss, maybe I could help them, draw on my own experience.

"I've never met a child I couldn't love," I said truthfully. "Although I will admit, some have been more of a challenge than others."

Mr. Garrett actually pressed his lips together, as if to keep from smiling. Jeez, Louise—what was with this guy? Had he been raised by ogres who'd threatened to beat him if he showed any emotion?

Actually, I later discovered that my employer had had a fairly normal childhood, if you can call being raised with every advantage normal. It was what happened later, much later, that had made him the way he was.

He asked me a few more questions, all of which were answered on the résumé or in the reference letters. Quizzing me, perhaps? He set the papers on the uncluttered desk, frowned yet again, then asked me when I might start.

I was glad Mrs. Monroe had warned me about his being desperate. Still, his handing over two children to someone he'd talked to for maybe ten minutes seemed a little precipitous.

"I take it you've interviewed other candidates?" I asked.

"As many as I need." That was a cagey reply if ever I heard one.

"I'd like to meet the children first, if you don't mind."

"I thought you said—"

"Not for my sake—for theirs. It's not fair to foist a new nanny on them without their having any idea of what's happening," I said.

His eyes narrowed a bit at that, then his lips curved up. It was almost a smile this time.

"Fine." He stood, towering over the desk. I have to admit, the idea of this imposing man cuddling and comforting a tiny child did seem rather preposterous.

He led me back through several rooms, to the marble foyer I'd entered earlier, then up the winding staircase to the second floor. He reiterated how important it was that the children's caregiver be the stability in their lives, since that was one thing he couldn't offer. I bit my tongue to keep from asking why.

He also explained that, for now, the children shared a bedroom. After they'd had time to adjust, they could have separate rooms. But for the immediate future, it seemed kinder to let them stay together. In fact, both nights since they'd come, the housekeeper said she'd found them cuddled together in the same bed, even though the room had a pair of twin beds.

His obvious concern, and perceptiveness, seemed at such odds with his aloofness. For a man with no children, he seemed to understand their needs a lot better than some of the parents I'd worked for. For a man who, on the surface, seemed determined to keep his distance, he also seemed determined to ensure his charges' emotional welfare.

I hadn't worked with so many different kinds of people for so long without learning probably more than I wanted to about human nature. But this guy wasn't fitting into any of the molds I'd thus far encountered in my career.

"They're how old?" I asked as we reached the top of the stairs.

"Jared's five, Emily's three," he replied, leading me down an endless corridor papered in an elegant white-on-white stripe, the honey-gold floor all but obliterated by a heavily patterned oriental rug.

I thought of how soon there'd be a grungy, amorphous gray stripe running the length of that white wall, and inwardly smiled.

"What happened?" I asked.

He stopped, crossing his arms. It was a protective gesture, I thought, chiding myself for reading too many psychology texts in college. In the distance, I heard the faint, protesting squeals of a child.

"The children's father was my first cousin. We'd seen each other a couple times as children, but not in the last thirty years or more. Ken and his wife were killed in that airplane crash in Bolivia last month."

I let out a soft moan. It had been a horrible crash, possibly terrorist-related. Hundreds had been killed, the cause yet to be determined.

"In any case, as I said, I hadn't seen Ken since we were kids. I didn't even know he was married, let alone that he had children. For some reason, it appeared I was the nearest relative they could find. And that took a month. The children were kept in foster care until they could find me."

I heard the thin thread of pain in his voice. The more he talked, the more I saw how thin his mask really was. This was not a cold man—only a hurting one.

"And you just accepted them?" The question popped out before I could catch it.

"What else could I do?" he asked, his gaze holding mine. "Leave them to the 'system'? They'd probably have been separated, you know. And it's not as if I can't afford to take care of them."

The words were calm, unemotional, logical. Yet I sensed there was more, a deeper reason for his generosity.

I pushed my luck. "Not many men in your position would do what you've done."

"I'm not like most men," was all he said.

He continued on down the hall, and I followed him to a large, bright room all in yellows and whites. A middle-aged maid in a gray uniform was struggling to get the tearful little girl dressed, while her brother sat cross-legged on the bed and quietly watched.

I immediately recognized the signs of stress in both children—her crankiness, his silence—and my heart ached for both of them. Love them? Not a problem.

"Emily? Jared?" Mr. Garrett called in a soft voice—no booming now.

Both little heads snapped around, both sets of eyes immediately latching onto me.

"This is Ms. Nelson," their guardian said. "She's come to take care of you."

He turned to me then. "I'll have my secretary draw up a contract while you get acquainted. If everything's satisfactory, would you be willing to start tomorrow?"

Minimum requirements as to salary, paid leave, and the like were pre-stipulated from the agency. My accepting the interview implied tacit agreement that, should the interview go well, I'd accept the job.

"Yes, that would be fine."

He touched my arm, just for a second, just enough to keep my attention. "I'm trusting you to give them what I can't." With that, he left the room. Instead of staying with me, easing the children through yet another change of guard, Mr. Garrett took off like a mutt being chased by the dogcatcher.

What was he afraid of, this kind-at-heart curmudgeon who clearly wanted the best for these two? Yes, obligation played a large part in his taking on his new role. Hiring someone to take full-time care of the children in a house already full of servants certainly should have tipped me off, but that was pretty common in wealthy families, anyway.

I'd worked in some of them, in fact; or known others who had. But never had I gotten quite the feeling of my employer's having just dumped his emotional responsibility on someone else.

Why was he so reluctant to become emotionally attached to his new wards? His excuse about being away a lot didn't cut it. I knew parents who had to travel on business who were still close and loving with their children. It took a bit of work, sure, but it could be done.

I decided the man had a screw loose.

For the children's sake, though, I quelled my confusion and irritation, instead slowly approaching the little girl. Wispy blonde hair that would undoubtedly go dark before much longer stuck out at all angles from her head as she gave me the once-over.

"Hi, honey," I said softly, crouching to her level. "I'm Isabel."

"Hi," came the equally soft reply.

I smiled, linking my hands over my knees. "What's your name?"

"Emily," she breathed.

"Oh, what a pretty name." I nodded toward the shirt in the exasperated maid's hands. "Is that what you're going to wear today?"

"No," she said. "It's stupid."

I glanced up at the maid, who rolled her eyes at me. I was tempted to dismiss her, but I hadn't been officially hired yet. I took the shirt from her, pretending to carefully inspect it.

"Looks nice to me," I said mildly. "Can you tell me why you don't like it?"

Out of the corner of my eye, I saw Jared slide off the bed and hesitantly approach us. I turned around to smile at him, noticing his shirt and jeans were at least a size too small.

"It's not hers," he told me. "At the place we stayed before we came here, they stoled all our clothes." He placed a hand on his little sister's shoulder. "It's okay, Emily. You can wear it. Go on."

"I want the butterfly shirt that Mommy gave me," she whined, her lower lip vibrating.

"I know," Jared said, patting her shoulder affectionately.

Tears welled in my eyes. In other circumstances, I probably would have found the child's adult manner amusing, but this little one had taken on adult airs because he thought he had to. I thought my heart would break.

I knew better than to suggest we try to find another butterfly shirt, since the shirt itself wasn't the issue. Losing the link to her mother was. And there was no replacing that.

Instead, suspecting the maid had chosen the shirt without soliciting any input from the child, I said, "Maybe you'd like to pick out something else. After all, it's kind of chilly this morning."

After a moment, Emily nodded. I let out a small sigh. She led me to the drawer where her things were, rifling through several shirts before picking one with a grinning teddy bear on it.

It was faded and had a small hole near the neckline, but right now, getting her dressed was the goal. New clothes would come soon enough, I was sure. As I slipped the shirt over her head, I talked softly to her, touching her hair and smiling, and gradually, I got a tiny smile in return.

Not to be left out, Jared tugged on my skirt. "I can make my bed," he announced.

"Really? That's terrific," I said, grinning. "Wanna show me?"

Of course, Emily, not to be outdone by her big brother, had to "show" me, too. As I watched, I sensed the maid come up behind me, her arms crossed.

"Poor things," she said quietly. "And then to have to come here."

I turned to look at her, but her gaze was fixed on the children, her mouth set.

After a minute, she held out her hand. "My name's Adele, by the way. Please say you'll stay."

I shook the woman's hand and nodded. "I think you can count on that."

Mr. Garrett had already left, his secretary, Connie, told me, but if I didn't mind waiting another ten minutes or so, she'd have the contracts ready for me to look over.

Contracts? Plural? I decided I'd heard wrong but said I'd be glad to hang around. With a smile, she pointed me to the coffeemaker, told me to help myself, and said I was free to wander around, if I liked.

With a mug of fresh-brewed coffee in my hands, I meandered from room to expansive room on the first floor, figuring that would be enough for one day. There'd be plenty of time for further exploration later. After a little while, I meandered back toward the office, to find there were indeed two contracts for my review.

Puzzled, I settled into a cozy leather chair in the outer office, sipping and reading. The first contract was fairly straightforward.

The salary was a bit over minimum, I'd have my own room and bath, the vacation and other amenities were pretty standard. A paragraph at the bottom indicated that either party could break the agreement at any time, with one week's notice, at which point I'd be given a month's severance and references, if warranted. That sounded fair enough.

Puzzled, I set the first one aside and scanned the second, quickly realizing that this one was more generous—far more generous. It was double the salary and paid leave, full medical and dental, a new car at my disposal, and the promise of a substantial bonus each year.

Stunned, I skimmed through the provisions, my eyes growing wider at each one, until I came to the final paragraph.

Should I accept this second offer, I had to guarantee I'd stay for a minimum of five years. Should my services be found unsatisfactory, my employer had the right to terminate the contract, as before, with one week's notice and a full month's severance. Otherwise, once I signed, I was definitely in this for the long haul.

There is one thing that always nags at the back of a nanny's mind: retirement. After all, by the time you're seventy, you're not really up to running after a two-year-old all day—or dealing with the volatile emotions of an adolescent.

But generally, nanny's salaries don't leave a whole lot for investing or saving. I quickly calculated how much I could sock away from this second offer. But I'd also be signing away my freedom.

However, although my mouth often got away from my brain at times, I wasn't fickle. I'd never been the one to leave my previous assignments; I'd been let go. When I made a commitment to a family, I fully intended to be there for as long as they needed me. I didn't need to sign away five years of my life to guarantee I'd stick around.

I would stay as long as the children needed and wanted me, money or no money. And I intended to tell Ethan Garrett just that, at my earliest opportunity.

He called me first. Or rather, he called Mrs. Monroe, demanding to know why I hadn't signed one of the contracts. I'd told her about them, and she agreed further discussion was in order.

I'd been sitting in my tiny apartment—I kept a lease on a studio apartment for the down times between jobs—trying to decide whether to go out scavenging for packing boxes or not, when he caught up with me. I could tell he wasn't amused.

"You forced me into a moral dilemma," I said.

"Oh?"

"I won't play coy and pretend I couldn't use the money, because I can." I looked around at my paltry furnishings and sighed. "More than you probably know. But I don't have to sign a contract for you to have my assurance I won't leave the children. I'm not like that."

Silence. "So if staying is no problem, why not sign the contract?"

"On principle, Mr. Garrett. You're *hiring* me, not *leasing* me. I'm not a car."

"So why not sign the first contract, if your principles are worth more than money?"

I'd had several hours to think about this. "Because I don't appreciate being manipulated, for one thing. And I dislike not being trusted even more."

I heard that clock chime faintly from his end of the line. "In other words," he said at last, "you won't sign either of them."

I hadn't actually gotten that far in my thoughts, nor were ultimatums my strong suit. "I didn't say that," I said after a moment. "I just needed some time to think, that's all. For the children's' sake, though, I'll sign."

"The second one?"

"The first."

"So you'll have your out?" His voice grated in my ears.

"So I'll have peace of mind, Mr. Garrett. I told you, I'm not going to just up and leave on a whim. I've never done that to any of my employers, and I don't intend to start now."

"Fine. The contract will be on my desk when you get here tomorrow morning."

I sighed, envisioning my retirement nest egg going up in a puff of smoke. "I'll be there at seven A.M. then, if that's all right."

"That will be perfect." Then, sounding relieved, he said, "And thank you."

When he got down off that darn high horse of his, he could actually sound quite human—and very . . . male. It occurred to me I'd never had an unmarried employer before.

"You're welcome, Mr. Garrett."

"I am leaving for Europe tonight. I'll be gone for at least two weeks," he told me. "Knowing you're here will be a major load off my mind."

"That's my job, sir," I said quietly, not particularly surprised that he hung up without saying anything else.

At seven-ten the next morning, the entire sum of my material possessions crammed into the back of my car, I quietly knocked on the front door of the mansion. The same maid I'd met the day before let me in with a smile, assuring me she'd see to having my things taken up to my room. She said that Mr. Garrett had left some paperwork for me on his secretary's desk.

I let out a groan of annoyance when I saw he'd left the second contract, not the first, until I noticed the little sticky note in the upper right hand corner. *See last page*, it said.

I turned to the last page. The five-year stipulation had been crossed out. I wasn't exactly sure what I'd just won, but I knew I'd won something. Grinning, I signed.

True to his word, Mr. Garrett wasn't around very much—at least, not at first. When he was in residence, he tended to eat his meals apart from the family, a practice I not only found odd, but downright rude.

True, the children and I—as well as the rest of the staff, who adored them—soon settled in as well as could be expected, considering the tragedy that had brought them there to begin with. Emily still cried a great deal and needed lots of cuddling, which I, or one of the staff, was only too glad to provide. And there were days when Jared barely doled out a dozen words.

But it had only been six weeks or so since their arrival, and I didn't see any signs to signal undue worry. They were eating and sleeping fairly well, and I made sure they had ample opportunity to talk about their parents as much as they wanted to, balanced with normal outings and activities—and lots and lots of laughter.

Then Mr. Garrett would return, and his standoffishness not only undermined everything I was doing to re-instill the children's' sense of security, but it was getting on my nerves as well. I knew that his chilliness was a front. This was not a mean or cold man. So why was he acting like this?

I'd been there maybe six weeks or so when I decided enough was enough. So one evening, after I'd tucked the little ones in and was officially off duty until the morning, I sought him out.

As usual, he was in his office, his desk lit up like a used car lot on an otherwise dark street. I knocked but didn't wait for a reply, just waltzed on in and plopped my booty in the plushly upholstered wing chair in front of his desk. I received a scowl for that.

"Come in, Ms. Nelson, and have a seat."

"Thank you." I leaned forward. "Just what is it you think you're doing?"

He leaned back, clearly nonplussed. Fall had set in with a vengeance over the weekend. He wore a heavily cabled turtleneck sweater nearly the same gray as the silver threading his hair. A few feet away, a small fire popped and periodically hissed behind an ornate fire screen, casting strange, undulating shadows throughout the room.

It was quite a contrast to my cozy, floral-wallpapered room or the gleaming, modern kitchen. At the moment, I would have much preferred to be in either place, but a nanny's gotta do what a nanny's gotta do.

"What exactly do you mean?" he finally asked.

"I mean, if you expect me to put the children's welfare first, then I consider it my duty to try to fix anything that, in my opinion, is standing in the way of their healing."

The scowl disintegrated into a glower. "I thought you said they were making excellent progress."

"They are, in many ways—in spite of your attitude."

I could hear my mother now: Isabel, that big mouth of yours is going to be your undoing one of these days, I swear.

"My. . . attitude," he repeated.

Underneath two sweaters, a shiver raced up my spine. But this guy was paying me reasonably big bucks to ensure his charges' happiness, so I figured I might as well give him his money's worth.

"Yes, your attitude. You act as if the children have some disease when you're here. Do you realize that? You never have meals with us. You only exchange the most cursory of greetings with the children when you accidentally run into us. You never come up to say goodnight or read them a story—"

He held up one hand. "That's what I pay you for."

"You pay me," I said with exasperated breath, "to take care of them in your absence. When you're here, I fully expect you to at least acknowledge them. Otherwise, why did you take them in to begin with?"

Something I knew I didn't like, even if I couldn't quite define it, flashed in his eyes as he leaned forward, his hands carefully folded in front of him.

"I'm fulfilling my duty to those children in every way I can. They're being fed, clothed, and housed, and more than adequate provision is being made for their emotional well-being. Whatever relationship I do or do not choose to have with them is, frankly, none of your business."

I stood then, leaning over the desk, my hands braced on the edge. "That's a crock, sir."

He stood as well, towering over me. Unfortunately, since I wasn't some quivery little governess from an eighteenth-century novel, but a grown, modern woman who'd been through her own version of hell, the gesture was lost on me.

"Perhaps you're forgetting how easily I can release you from your contract."

"Not at all. But you won't, and we both know that, so I think we can drop that angle, don't you?"

Our eyes locked. And yes, a sexual tension crackled between us. It was loneliness and frustration, I suppose, at least on my part. It had been so long since a man had paid me any sort of attention, it was easy to let my libido get carried away.

Of course, I had no idea what was going on in his head. He let out a sigh, then walked away from the desk, over to the fire.

"No. I'm not going to let you go," he agreed.

I breathed an inward sigh of relief, both from his words and from the collapse of whatever had been vibrating between us. But then, the conversation wasn't over yet. I joined him in front of the fire, my arms folded over my ribs.

"They know you don't love them," I said levelly. "And they assume your reluctance to be around them means you don't care about them."

I could sense his head turning toward me. "Then convince them otherwise. You know I care what happens to them, or else they wouldn't be here."

"For crying out loud, we're talking about a three- and five-year-old!" I said a brief prayer for grace and guidance when dealing with dense male creatures. "I didn't say you didn't care what happens to them. I said you didn't care *about* them. Big difference. Besides, words don't mean squat to small children. Actions do."

Now I shifted, facing him. "A smile, or a hug, or even sharing a meal with them means far more than my trying to explain your willingness to put them through college. All they know is that this big, scary man shows up from time to time, ignores them, then goes away again. Not exactly the best conditions for re-instilling confidence, you know."

I waited. Frustrated to near distraction, I pivoted on my heel and headed for the door.

"Ms. Nelson?"

I turned, my hand already on the doorknob. "Yes?" The word came out like a gunshot.

"I'm sorry I'm not measuring up," he said softly. "But my heart dried up some years ago, for reasons I have no intention of going into. I'm doing the best I can by Jared and Emily, but I can't give them something I don't have. And since I was the only person willing to take them on, we'll all just have to deal with what we've got, won't we?"

I walked back into the room, so angry I was shaking. "It's no skin off your back to act like a human being around them, Mr. Garrett—to sit at the same table with them, ask them about a picture they colored, or listen to Jared tell a riddle. I don't care if your heart is the size of a raisin, you can do that much at least." I was pleading, but I didn't care. After all, I wasn't begging for myself.

"They're sweet kids. And they want so desperately for things to be right again. Emily's too young to completely understand, but Jared knows he's never, ever going to see his Mommy and Daddy again. Can you imagine how he must be feeling, how much he aches, every single minute of his life? The last thing he needs is to think someone doesn't like him.

"So maybe you should give my idea a whirl. And who knows? Maybe their sweetness will rub off on you a little and start to reconstitute that dried-up heart of yours."

Before he could reply, I stomped out of the room, feeling both proud of myself and like a jerk at the same time. Because, if the anguished expression on that man's face was any indication, his heart wasn't dried up at all.

Sometimes, being a bully can pay off. My employer actually joined us for dinner the next evening. Okay, so he looked as though he'd rather face the Spanish Inquisition, but he was there.

The dining room was one of those grand things with crystal chandeliers and a table that seated at least twelve, so trying for an intimate family dinner was a challenge, to say the least. The kids and I usually ate in the breakfast room, but when word came His Majesty would be joining us in the dining room, I figured trying to change the venue might be pushing my luck just a bit.

Mrs. Murphy, the cook, and I decided to opt for something everyone was likely to eat, which meant something with tomato sauce. Tortellini won out, which turned out to be an inspiration, if I do say so. Even the little one could get it on her fork and more or less into her mouth—and mostly out of her hair—and they were fascinated enough with the meal to actually sit for more than five minutes.

Needless to say, however, they weren't quite sure what to make of the big meanie sitting at the head of the table; but since I blathered on about things in my usual manner, I guess they figured they were safe.

I wasn't sure I was, however. One advantage to my employer's unwillingness to engage in personal interaction was that this severely reduced opportunities for inappropriate male-female hormonal reactions.

Now, I may have been professional, but I was still alive, last time I checked. And far be it from me to deny being immune to the presence of in-your-face virility. So when I kept catching Mr. Garrett's glances throughout the meal, my skin tingled as much as the next healthy, sexually deprived female's.

Sure, I got plenty of hugs and kisses every day from my little charges, but my life wasn't exactly complete, if you know what I mean. And after that strange thing that had passed between us the night before . . . oh, brother.

Of course, what startled me so much was that, since James's death, I hadn't much thought about myself in that way. I hadn't really considered the possibility of allowing another man into my life.

Heaven knows, Ethan Garrett wasn't it. For one thing, he was my employer. And single or not, that was one self-imposed rule I never broke—ever. For another, I didn't think I was up to that big a challenge, frankly—not in this lifetime.

Still, it had been a long time since a man had been interested enough to stare, and I appreciated it.

However, the point of this little exercise was to get him closer to the children, not their nanny, so I found myself constantly swerving his attention back in that direction. I figured if I got one genuine, show-the-teeth smile out of the man, I would have accomplished my mission.

So I drew the little ones into a conversation, figuring they'd take it charmingly off track soon enough, and then I could just sit back and enjoy the show.

They made me proud. Emily decided to show off how she could count to twenty—even if she did miss a few crucial numbers—only to have her moment in the sun nearly usurped when Jared launched into a retelling of some video he'd watched that afternoon, complete with sound effects.

Eventually, I noticed Mr. Garrett actually paying attention to them, his features gradually softening. It was a start.

The next night, we repeated the dinner scene, although this time my employer suggested eating in the breakfast room, rather than the dining room. I suppose it was asking too much that the children be angels two nights in a row, however.

Emily got into a snit about the food touching on her plate—we're talking a single pea that strayed across her plate to snuggle against her five bites of chicken—and whereas Jared had been downright garrulous the night before, this evening he barely spoke.

Afterwards, I set them up in the den for their one short video before bath and bed, then returned to find Mr. Garrett still seated at the table, his lips curved into a soft smile. I don't think he saw me at first. I can't imagine he would have let me see that he'd let his guard down like that had he known I was there.

"I'm sorry," I said as I reentered.

He looked up at me, a puzzled expression crinkling his brow. He rang for the maid to clear the table—I'd finally gotten used to that by now—then sat back, his arms crossed.

"Whatever for?"

I stood behind my chair. "They weren't exactly models of decorum tonight."

He took a deep breath, then pushed his chair back, rose from the table. "They're children, Ms. Nelson. No one expects them to be perfect."

His attitude surprised me. He touched my arm, leading me out of the dining room to the den. We stood just outside the doorway, watching the children watch the video, and I was far too aware of Mr. Garrett's aftershave, the warmth radiating from his body.

I swallowed, forced my attention back to the children. They sat crossed-legged beside each other on the sofa in identical positions, chins propped in tiny hands.

"I thought, I mean I assumed—" I felt a blush warm my face.

"That I kept my distance because I didn't like children?"

I choked out an affirmative reply.

"Well, you were wrong," he said in a low voice.

We stood together, saying nothing for several seconds.

"After their baths . . . you said you read to them?" he asked.

"Yes, almost every night. It sets a comforting, quiet routine—"

"—eases them into bedtime without too many traumas," he finished.

I stared at the side of his face as he watched the children. And I knew. "Oh my God," I whispered. "You've done this before. You've had children."

He didn't answer. He didn't have to. Instead, he turned and walked away, his hands in his pockets.

"Okay." I was on the phone to Mrs. Monroe before eight the next morning. "What is there about Ethan Garrett I should know that you somehow forgot to tell me?"

The older woman sighed. "He made it a condition of employment that you not be told."

"That's unethical, not to mention potentially dangerous."

"I'll agree to the first part, although since I didn't think the second was a likelihood, I made a judgment call."

"To keep the truth from me?"

"To ensure that a client got the best person to meet his needs."

"Well, condition or no condition, if you don't tell me what you know, I'm walking," I said.

She had the nerve to laugh.

"Well, okay, so I wouldn't walk. But since he brought it up, how wrong could it be for you to tell me?"

Mrs. Monroe sighed again. "I don't know the details, frankly. It happened more than twelve years ago, before I came here myself. I only know Garrett's wife and two children—"

"*Wife? Two children?*"

"Well, what did you expect? You already figured out there'd been kids. Now don't interrupt me. Anyway, the wife and children were staying out at their cabin up in the mountains. They think one of the children—they were both under four, I gather—might have gotten hold of some matches, woken up in the middle of the night, and started playing with them in their bedroom.

"The smoke alarm malfunctioned, Mrs. Garrett didn't wake up right away, and Mr. Garrett was away. She couldn't save the children. She tried, heaven knows, but from what I gather, she died from her own burns later on. In all likelihood, the children were already gone by the time she got to them."

I held my hand to my mouth, tears blurring my vision. No wonder the man didn't want to get close to the children—or anyone else, for that matter.

But my understanding of the reasons for his withdrawal didn't mean I could accept them any better. The children still needed him. And now I knew he needed healing as much, if not even more, than they did—maybe even more than I had after James's death.

Besides, he'd accepted responsibility for the children's well-being, for at least as long as they were minors. I couldn't guarantee I'd be there for them forever, I now realized. Ironically, being with them and being around Mr. Garrett had awakened impulses and yearnings inside me that I'd thought buried forever since my husband's death.

I was only thirty-three, still young enough to have a family of my own, if I wanted. If the right man should come along—though how that might happen when I spent nearly all my time at this house—I saw no reason why I shouldn't get on with the life I now realized I'd put on hold for so long.

Because I'm basically stubborn and perverse, I saw no reason not to convince Mr. Garrett he had the same right: to get on with his life, put past sorrows and tragedies behind him.

I had no idea just how effective my powers of persuasion might be.

I didn't broach the subject for another week or so, deciding, for once in my life, to bide my time before opening my big mouth. During that week, I was glad to see he'd begun to warm up to the children on his own, although he still avoided any physical contact.

He even began to evidence a sense of humor, rusty though it clearly was, by telling an occasional joke or riddle at the dinner table. They were terrible, for the most part, but Jared, especially, thought they were hilarious, dissolving into peals of contagious laughter at every punch line.

With each explosion of childish giggles, I noticed my employer's face soften a little more. And so did my heart.

Let me set the record straight, though: At this point, maybe eight or so weeks after I'd come to work for Mr. Garrett, I wasn't in love with him or anything near it. Yes, I was attracted to him, and I felt for him, but I don't think any sort of romantic or sexual involvement even occurred to me. I mean, I guess I thought I had everything under control.

My employer had been making progress, but not enough. I wanted to see him bonded to the children. At the rate he was going, they'd be grown and gone before he was ready to read a book to them. And that just wouldn't do.

I found him that night, after a ten-minute search, standing outside on the stone patio off the dining room, seemingly oblivious to the bitter wind whipping across the property. Arms tightly folded across my middle, I crept into the November blast, holding my hair out of my face.

"News flash," I said through my chattering teeth. "It's winter—in the Rockies."

He turned to me, frowning, the frown suddenly melted into a genuine smile—a real smile, for me! A warning bell went off deep inside my brain, but did I heed it? No. I just barged on ahead, like the fool I was.

"I've always loved the cold," he said with a shrug. "And the wind. It airs out the brain."

"More like freezes it." I sucked in a frigid breath, then said, "I just thought you'd like to know that Emily cried bitterly for ten minutes because you wouldn't come say goodnight to her."

In the light spilling out from the French doors, I saw his jaw clench. "I'm sorry."

"So why don't you? How much would it cost you to tuck them in?" I turned to him. "To touch them?"

A gust of wind smacked into us. He merely slipped his hands into his pockets; I doubled over, trying to curl up as much as I could while still standing.

"I . . . can't," he said quietly.

"You mean you *won't*," I shot back. Freezing to death takes a real toll on my patience.

He didn't respond. I took a deep breath, then went for it. "Look. I know what happened to your wife and children. I know about the fire." Then I waited.

Silence stretched between us, punctuated by the wind soughing through the evergreens surrounding the house. I thought it curious that he didn't ask how I knew, almost as if he figured I'd eventually find out.

"Then if you know," he said, his voice barely audible over the wind, "you'll understand."

I was shivering so hard by now, I began to fear frostbite. But I knew to suggest changing our venue might mean losing the fragile momentum of the conversation. So I clamped my teeth together and pressed on.

"I understand, sure. But I do not accept it."

His eyes drilled into me. "Meaning?"

"Meaning . . . it's time you moved past all that and got on with your life, took a chance on loving someone again." I could hear my heart pound about a thousand times before he answered.

"Sometimes, the past doesn't let you move on, you know. Sometimes, the past is too much *with* you to do that."

Having passed into the numb stage, the cold no longer bothered me. I turned around, leaning back against the stone balustrade flanking the patio.

"No one's saying you have to forget your past," I said softly. "Just stop ignoring the promises of the present."

He looked at me again, his gaze questioning and hard. "Is that what you did when your husband died? Are you telling me you didn't go into child care as a substitute for what you lost?"

His words should have hurt. Maybe they didn't because of the cold, I don't know.

"Maybe I did. But I got over it."

He stepped closer. "You mean you'd be willing to love again?"

I still didn't catch on. "I doubt James would have wanted for me to live the rest of my life alone."

I don't know when he lifted his hand to my face, but suddenly, there it was. And there were those pale eyes, linked with mine, luminous in the faint light from the house.

"You've lost someone you loved," he said. "And it hurt." It wasn't a question.

"Terribly," I admitted, unable to tear my gaze away from his handsome face. "But I can't live the rest of my life in the shadow of that pain."

One eyebrow lifted. "Which is what you were doing?"

I nodded.

"And you don't think I should, either?"

"I don't think anyone should. It's not healthy."

A smile played over his lips, but it was a sad smile, one that sent my heart into a slow, dangerous spin, as our pasts rose from the depths of our souls, entwined for a moment, then vaporized, leaving something tender and new in their wake.

"I'm afraid," he said, his thumb stroking my cheek.

He was my employer. Even letting him touch me like this was inappropriate at best, if not unethical. But maybe the wind had frozen the part of my brain responsible for what little common sense I had. And four years is a long time to be lonely, to have gone without the feel of a man's hand on any part of my body, the feel of a man's lips on mine.

"Aren't we all?" I finally whispered back.

I felt like a character in a fairy tale, one who has to kiss a stone statue, only to have that statue spring to life from the embrace. I couldn't have imagined that hard, set mouth could be so warm and soft and pliant, that his touch could be so wonderfully tender—or that my body, frozen as a fish stick not ten seconds before, could thaw so instantaneously.

We were both breathing pretty hard when he lifted his mouth from mine. I lay my head on his chest.

"This isn't a good idea," I murmured.

"No," he agreed, then tucked a finger under my chin, lifting my face to look into my eyes. "Shall we end it right now?"

To my extreme consternation, my eyes filled with tears. "Heaven help me—no."

I honestly don't think anyone, including the children, knew of our affair. I never stayed in his room until morning, and we both took great pains to ensure that our outward relationship looked the same as it always had. We even still called each other by our last names, unless we were alone.

For six weeks, I lived the fairy tale, luxuriating not only in the warmth of having a man care for me again, but in the way Ethan finally began opening up to the children. It wasn't easy at first.

That first night Emily fell asleep, nestled against him as he read one of her favorite books to her, I saw the mixture of fear and awe flash across his features. But gradually, the fear left, replaced by a joy I know he hadn't let himself feel for many, many years.

The nights were filled with another kind of joy, the joy of rediscovery, of reawakening. Gradually, the joy blossomed into something deeper, and I realized I was in love again.

To be truthful, I wasn't even thinking in terms of marriage. After all, James and I had been together for two years, and sleeping together for more than a year, before we even started discussing it. I may be impulsive in some areas, but not when it comes to making lifetime commitments.

So at first, the subject's not coming up didn't faze me one way or the other. In fact, it took a casual comment from Jared, one day shortly before Christmas, to put the idea in my head.

We were decorating the biggest Christmas tree I'd ever seen—and the first the house had seen in more than ten years, according to the staff—when Jared asked why Ethan and I didn't get married, so we could be his Mommy and Daddy forever.

I nearly dropped the antique glass ornament I was about to hang. I did drop my jaw. And I probably turned as red as the cranberries we'd made into garlands for the tree.

"Oh, honey—I just work for Mr. Garrett. I can't marry him."

Jared gave me one of those grownups-can-be-so-dense looks. "Why not? Don't you like him?"

I longed to bury my face in the branches. "Of course I like him, sweetie. He's a very nice man—"

"I think you should get married, too," piped Emily at my knee. I looked down into those adorable blue eyes and sighed, grateful Ethan was out of town until the next day and couldn't be part of this delightful conversation. But I figured I'd better warn him, in any case, that the little darlings had shifted into serious matchmaking mode. I found it humorous at first.

But later that night, alone in my own bed, something kept nagging at me, a vague intuition that something was . . . off. James and I had been in our early twenties when we met. Life was one big unpredictability. Neither of us knew yet what we wanted from it, from ourselves, or from each other. Taking a couple of years to figure all that out made perfect sense.

But Ethan and I were mature adults. Our lives were fairly settled by that point. And then there were the children, who would certainly have been only too delighted to trade their nanny for a full-time mommy.

The more I thought about all this, the more confused I became. On the one hand, Ethan's not having assumed I'd become his wife, and thus ensure my permanence in his household, could be construed as a good thing. Why keep a nanny on payroll when you can simply marry her and not have to worry about SSI and federal income-tax withholding anymore?

On the other, I didn't like to think our sleeping together was quite as casual as it might have looked on the surface. Even at the beginning, I certainly cared about the man, and I'd been led to believe the feeling was mutual. Not that he'd uttered the "L" word yet, but then, neither had I. After only six weeks, it seemed a little precipitous.

After several sleepless hours, I finally convinced myself I was being paranoid. Of course it was too early to be thinking so seriously.

Then came the Christmas Day incident.

You see, I never questioned Ethan's comings and goings. His business dealings took him away a great deal, all over the world. We always knew where to reach him, and, especially in the last few weeks, he called us nearly every night. But when he said he had to be away on Christmas afternoon, I was stunned.

We were sitting on the living room floor, bicycle parts strewn all around us. I looked up at him, so handsome in a cranberry turtleneck sweater. I wanted badly to be alone with him, just as soon as we got that blasted bike together. His little bombshell kinda blew that idea all to pieces, however.

"Ethan! On Christmas! Why on earth can't you take the day off like the rest of the world?"

"It can't be helped, honey," he said, scowling at the instructions in front of him. He picked up a metal part and a wrench and set to work attaching it to the frame.

"Pardon me for being petulant, but of course it can be helped! For heaven's sake, what will my parents say?" Since I didn't want to leave Ethan or the children, I asked if he minded if I invited them to have Christmas with us. He'd readily agreed, and they were ensconced in the prettiest of the guest rooms upstairs, snoozing away, I hoped.

Ethan quelled whatever else I was about to say with a look that froze me. "I'm sorry," he said quietly. "I won't be gone long, though. I'll be back in plenty of time for dinner." Since we'd given the servants the holidays off, Mom and I were doing the honors. It'd be the first meal I'd ever cooked for him.

A strange, irrational fear leapt into my heart. I started to feel what I was afraid of was… jealousy. But of whom?

"Anyone" was my answer. After all, I only had his word that he hadn't been involved with anyone else since the tragedy. For all I knew, his whole "coldness" routine could have been an act. All those trips he took—he could have a mistress in any one of a dozen cities. And now he had one at home, too.

We finished putting the bike together in silence. When we were done, I headed toward the stairs and my own bedroom. Ethan's master suite was on the ground level, close to the swimming pool.

"Isabel?" he called after me. "Please don't be like this."

I turned, one hand on the banister. "I can't help it. I don't understand, and I'm even more confused why you can't tell me who it is you're seeing."

Why I expected him to open up, I have no idea. Hope springs eternal, I suppose. In any case, all he did was place his hand over mine and shake his head.

It was, without a doubt, the most miserable Christmas Eve I'd ever spent. I had a dreadful feeling things weren't going to get any better.

Another month passed before he put me out of my misery. Christmas went as well as could be expected. I concentrated on the children, on their effusive joy and excitement. They were well on their way to healing by then, and I was grateful for whatever part in that I'd been able to play.

If my parents suspected anything was amiss, they said nothing, for which I was immeasurably grateful. Ethan had to be gone for two weeks right after the holidays, after which I decided, after four months, to take some time off myself and think things through.

With the staff's help, I figured everyone would be perfectly capable of surviving for ten days or so, so I booked a room in a lovely old B&B

at a nearby ski resort, packed up a dozen novels, and went off for ten days of hedonistic bliss—eating, reading, sleeping, and the occasional walk along the snow-encrusted countryside.

When I returned, to many kisses and hugs from the children and audible sighs of relief from the staff, I'd made a decision.

I needed to know where Ethan's and my relationship was headed. I'd realized, after all those days of solitude, that I was too old to deal with a dead-end relationship. I loved the children, and I loved Ethan, but I had to love myself, too. If he wasn't ready for marriage right then, if he didn't want any more kids, I could deal with it—as long as I felt there was a future for us.

It turned out to be one confrontation too many.

I discovered Ethan preparing for yet another trip when I returned, and I realized, if I didn't get this out now, it might be a month or more before I got any satisfaction. I didn't think I could make it that long. I arranged for Adele to take the children into town to the newest cartoon movie, so Ethan and I could talk for ten minutes without interruption.

He gave me what I'm sure he thought was his usual smile when I walked into his office, waiting until I saw his secretary go to lunch.

"God, I've missed you, Isabel." I wanted so badly to believe him.

"Me, too." I noticed that he didn't exactly sweep me into his arms. I knew something was wrong, something serious. I didn't really want to find out what it was. But as tears welled in my eyes, I knew it would be far worse for me if I didn't.

I cleared my throat. "I need to know where we stand."

He was standing behind his desk, slipping several folders into his briefcase, an action which halted suddenly at my words.

"What do you mean?" he asked softly.

"Ethan, I've fallen in love with you. I think I'd like to spend the rest of my life with you. The look on your face is telling me I'm making an incredible ass of myself."

"No, no, Isabel." He swept around the desk and pulled me close, kissing the top of my head, then my face and my mouth, over and over and over.

"My sweet Isabel," he whispered, tucking my head under his chin.

"I never thought I'd feel this way again," I blubbered. "And I was so afraid you wouldn't feel the same way, that I was just a fling, that you wouldn't want to marry me—"

He only held me tighter. But he was shaking, I realized. Confused and worried, I lifted my head to see tears coursing down his cheeks.

"Ethan? Ethan, what—"

"You're the greatest blessing, and the greatest curse, to ever come into my life," he said, hurrying on before I could comment. "I never thought I'd ever love again, either. And I know you'll never believe how much I do—"

"Try me," I said, trying to lighten things up.

"I hadn't really expected things to go this way, honey. I truly didn't. But I can't marry you."

For several seconds, I heard nothing except my heart pounding. I recouped, remembering what I'd promised myself.

"If it's too soon, I'll understand, Ethan. I can wait—"

But he shook his head, taking my face in his hands. "It's not that I don't want to marry you. I can't. Isabel, I'm actually still married."

I'd never fainted in my life, but I came perilously close to it just then. Dizziness overwhelmed me. I clutched at Ethan's arms, my knees giving way as he lowered me into the armchair in front of his desk.

"Still?" I looked up at him, shaking my head. "But your wife, I thought she died in the fire."

His shoulders slumped, Ethan walked behind his desk and sank into his chair. He was effectively putting distance between us, I realized.

"So does everyone else," he said quietly, not looking at me. "She was raving when they found her, burns over forty percent of her body as she clutched our dead son in her arms. The burns healed. Plastic surgery left her more beautiful than ever. Her mind, however, did not." He covered his face with his hands for a second, then lowered them, still not looking at me.

"She's been institutionalized ever since, virtually catatonic, completely unaware of her surroundings. Most days, she has no idea who I am. Yet the doctors still feel there's hope, slim though it may be.

They think she may come out of it someday."

Finally, he turned those silvery eyes to mine, and I saw my own broken heart mirrored in them. I ached for all of us, at that moment. The anger wouldn't come until later.

"I couldn't bear the thought that maybe she might recover, only to discover her husband abandoned her. I loved Jane with all my heart, Isabel. I suppose I still do, on some level I can't even explain. So I'd kept myself safe, apart—until someone else's tragedy brought a pair of children into my life again."

It was a full minute before my brain functioned well enough for me to move. When I did rise, I felt as if I'd invaded someone else's body. I supposed I hoped I had, because I wasn't sure I could bear the heartache I felt.

"That's who you went to see on Christmas?" I finally asked.

He nodded. "Will you ever forgive me?"

Pain sliced through me with such force, I reeled for a second. "Hadn't you better ask Jared and Emily that instead?" I asked, then walked out of the room. He didn't follow me.

I made arrangements for my replacement while he was gone. Mrs. Monroe found a lovely middle-aged woman to take my place who'd just come off a long-term assignment with a family whose last child had recently left for college.

I know the children didn't understand, and my heart ached for them, but I couldn't stay in that house any longer. I did promise we'd see each other frequently, and in the last two years, I've kept that promise. I sense their growing away from me, however, and that's fine. It means they're continuing to heal.

I suppose I am, too. I learned a painful lesson about getting involved with someone I didn't know very well, and, although I won't let Ethan off the hook about not being honest with me, I take full responsibility for my impetuousness. I doubt I'll make that mistake again. In fact, I'm sure of it.

Ethan gave me an extremely generous bonus when I left, one I was sorely tempted to refuse, until my mother pointed out I could start my own agency with that much money, if I wanted to. I decided she was right, and I kept the money, opening a child-care agency specializing in children with special needs, both emotional and physical.

We have clients all over the country, even after such a short time in business. And, yes, I'm dating a little, from time to time. There's one guy in particular—but, as usual, I'm getting ahead of myself. It's still too soon to call. In any case, I'm doing okay, resurrecting a life out of the wreck I'd almost made of the one I had.

Sometimes, I think of that poor woman in an institution somewhere, mentally buried in a tragedy that wasn't her fault. I hope and pray she does come around one day, if for no other reason than to find out how very much she's been loved all these years. THE END

HOT FOR TEACHER
I played the dating game with a student's dad

Even having been a kindergarten teacher for five years, I still had never encountered a sadder case than little Elizabeth Plantagenet. She was a petite little girl with a mane of pale blond hair and big blue eyes you could practically fall into. As a teacher, I prided myself on understanding what made a child tick, but this one had me stumped. Something was going on in that kid's life that was hurting her so deeply that she was retreating into a shell. And I didn't know how to stop it.

It all came to a head one day when I found her sitting in a corner with her back to the room. Her head was down and she was rocking a doll in her arms, crying softly.

"Elizabeth, are you okay?" I asked softly, pulling her into my arms.

Turning, she buried her face in my shirt, soaking it with her heart-wrenching tears. Other children gathered around us, staring at little Elizabeth.

"Did Elizabeth get a boo-boo, Ms. Casey?" asked Kristen Thomas, a curly, red-haired child with a heart the size of Texas. Her eyes filled with tears as Elizabeth's tears renewed their ferocity.

"I don't know, Kristen, but why don't all of you go take your seats while Elizabeth and I go down to the nurse's office?"

"Yes, Ms. Casey," they murmured, and shuffled to their seats without their usual twenty reminders. Seeing a fellow classmate crying always made them sad and a little scared.

Stepping out into the hall with Elizabeth's hand in mine, we walked over to the next classroom and asked the teacher's assistant to take over my class while I took Elizabeth down to the nurse's office.

Nurse Krauss was an elderly woman with a stern face and a big heart. When Elizabeth and I came into her office, she dropped into a crouch and wrapped her arms around Elizabeth.

"What's wrong, Elizabeth?" she asked.

No answer.

"Does your tummy hurt?"

Although the movement was slight, we could tell she shook her head in a negative response.

"Does your head hurt?"

Again, the very smallest negative motion.

"Can you tell us what hurts, then?"

To our frustration, she shook her head again.

"Elizabeth, we can't help you if you don't tell us what hurts."

She stood with her chin touching her chest and a great, big tear welled up in her eye and slid down her cheek. My heart broke at her obvious distress. Gathering her into my arms, I hugged her, frowning and shrugging my shoulders at the nurse. After her tears quieted again, I set her back away from me and looked down into her face.

"Would you like me to call your mommy?" I asked.

The tears began all over again and the little girl began rocking back and forth on her heels. Pulling her back into my arms, I tried another tactic.

"How about your daddy? Would you like me to call him?"

Her rocking motion ceased and she looked up into my face and nodded.

"Nurse Krauss, would you please call Elizabeth's father?"

"I sure will, Ms. Casey. You two just stay put; I'll be right back," she said as she hurried from the room.

It was getting close to the end of the school day, but I knew the rest of my class would be all right with the competent teacher's assistant, Ms. Finch, so I sat in a chair holding Elizabeth and waiting for word from her father. I didn't have long to wait; Nurse Krauss soon returned with a determined smile on her face.

"Elizabeth, honey, we couldn't get a hold of your daddy, but the day-care van is outside and it's time for school to be over. Would you like for Ms. Casey to walk you out there and put you on the van?"

I stood up, placing Elizabeth on the floor, and ushered her out of the office, shooting a questioning look back at the nurse. She shrugged, giving me an apologetic look, as if to say, *We tried.*

I felt lousy putting that little girl on the van, knowing how distressed she'd been only minutes before, but what could I do? If I held her behind, there was no telling when her father would come to pick her up, especially because we'd been unsuccessful contacting him by phone.

After I waved her off, I marched back into the office and looked up the emergency information on Elizabeth Plantagenet, jotting her home phone number down. I could make a call to her house later that evening.

That done, I went back to my classroom to straighten up my desk for a clean start the next day. Gathering my purse, I lingered by Elizabeth's little desk, where her name was written on colorful paper and taped to the desktop. I couldn't get her melancholy face out of my mind.

What could make a five-year-old so sad that she'd break down in class?

That night, I dialed Elizabeth's home phone number several times, but only got an answering machine. I would've rather talked to her father, but I left a message on my third call. It was already past ten o'clock by then, and I was tired.

The next day, Elizabeth came to school as usual, but she didn't even look up when I smiled at her and told her good morning.

The way I looked at it, this situation could not continue. It wasn't natural for a child to be so depressed. Something must be very wrong at home.

After lunch, I took my class to the playground and watched as they ran, screamed, and played with wild abandon, just like typical kindergarten students. Looking around, I spotted Elizabeth climbing the monkey bars. When she reached the top, she just sat there, staring off into the distance.

My attention was momentarily distracted by a couple of boys fighting over a soccer ball, and I rushed to break it up. Minutes later, as I was turning back toward Elizabeth, I heard her scream.

My heart leaped to my throat when I saw that the spot where she'd been perched was empty and her fragile little body was lying deathly still on the ground below. Rushing to her, I knelt and checked her pulse and listened. She was breathing, thank goodness, and beginning to whimper.

"Elizabeth, are you okay, sweetie?" I asked, afraid to touch or move her. "Kristen, go get the nurse—quickly!" I ordered, returning my attention to the little girl lying in a moaning heap. "Elizabeth, can you hear me?"

"Yes, ma'am." I had to lean in close to hear her words.

"Are you hurt?"

"Yes, ma'am," she said, and sniffled.

"Can you turn over?"

Her little body lurched and she turned over, staring up at me with tears and blood running down her face. It appeared as though her chin had taken the brunt of the fall. There was a deep gash on it and a scrape above her left eye. Pulling the ever-present fresh tissue from my pocket, I pressed it gently to the bleeding gash on her chin.

"Ow!" she whimpered softly, flinching away from my hand.

"Elizabeth, darling, I need to put the tissue on it to stop the bleeding," I explained, gently placing the tissue back over the cut to staunch the flow of blood.

"Ms. Casey, I got here just as soon as I could."

A breathless Nurse Krauss squatted down next to Elizabeth, poking, prodding, and surveying the damage with a practiced eye.

"I think you'll live, little one. Just a cut and a scrape," she pronounced for the benefit of all the children gathered around fearing the worst, but mostly for Elizabeth.

"Should we move her?" I asked, hating to leave her lying in the dirt of the playground.

"Elizabeth, can you stand up?"

We watched as she sat up in the dirt, then, using my hand, pulled herself up to stand.

"Good girl! Now let's take you into the nurse's office where we can clean you up and call your father."

Calling to the other teacher supervising the playground, we took Elizabeth to the nurse's office and lifted her onto the examining table. Nurse Krauss went to work cleaning the wounds to get a better look at the damage while I held Elizabeth, speaking soothing words to her all the while.

When the cut and the scrape were cleaned, Nurse Krauss stood back, frowning. She turned her back to Elizabeth and whispered to me, "I think she'll need a stitch or two on that chin."

Poking her head out of her office, she called to the administrative staff in the front office. "Did you get a hold of Mr. Plantagenet, yet?"

"Not yet, but we're still trying," was the response.

"Well, leave a message that she was taken to the Children's Hospital emergency room and he's to meet us there."

"Will do," came the muffled response.

"I have to go to the hospital?" Elizabeth whispered, looking up at me with fear written in her big blue eyes.

"You need to have a doctor look at your chin, honey."

"Am I going to die?" she asked, a tear squeezing out of the corner of her eye, trailing down her face, followed by more as she wrapped her arms around my neck.

"Oh, of course not, sweetheart! Everything will be all right. Nurse Krauss will go with you and make sure that you're well taken care of."

"I want you to take me!" she cried, clinging to my neck as if clinging to a lifeline.

Looking over the top of her head at Nurse Krauss, I questioned her with my eyes.

"I don't see why not. I'll stay here in case we have any more casualties from the playground. You two go on to see the doctor."

Feeling the little girl relax instantly in my arms, I gathered the necessary consent forms and carried her out to my car. Strapping her in, I was careful not to bump the arm holding a piece of gauze to her chin.

It was only a short drive to the Children's Hospital, and we accomplished it without mishap. Elizabeth was afraid of the big building and held back, so I lifted her into my arms and carried her into the emergency room, sitting her on the counter next to me as I filled out the necessary paperwork and showed them copies of the consent forms.

Two hours and two stitches later, Elizabeth and I sat in the waiting room, waiting for her father to show up. It was well past time for school to be out, and I was well past angry with Mr. Plantagenet. How could he stay out of touch for so long that his daughter was stranded in a hospital emergency room, wondering if her daddy would ever show up to claim her? What kind of father was he? I was working myself up into a lather on the inside, while trying to maintain a calm and happy demeanor for Elizabeth.

She was asleep with her head in my lap when a tall, dark-haired man strode into the waiting room and looked around. Wearing dusty blue jeans and a light-blue chambray shirt, he must've been well over six feet tall. Scanning the room, he finally spotted us and headed in our direction, concern written all over his face.

Well, at least he has the decency to look concerned! I begrudged.

"Are you Mr. Plantagenet?" I asked, my voice a little too sharp.

"Yes, how's Elizabeth?" he asked, pushing the hair out of her eyes to inspect her face.

"She's fine, except for two stitches and one missing father." I suppose the long wait had worn on my nerves more than I'd expected; I sounded terse and angry, even to my own ears. And why shouldn't I?

As if reading my mind, he explained, "I'm sorry, but I was on a construction site and didn't get the message until just fifteen minutes ago. I got here as soon as I could."

It was then that he took his eyes off Elizabeth and looked up, giving me the full benefit of those gorgeous brown eyes of his. It was almost like being punched in the chest; suddenly, I couldn't breathe. I was glad when he looked back down at Elizabeth so that I could gulp air. I needed to clear my mind.

"Here, let me get her. I'm sure I've kept you long enough already."

Looking at his dusty shirt and jeans, I tightened my hold on

Elizabeth. "Maybe I should carry her out to your car. You look pretty dirty to be carrying her around."

"Thank you. My truck is just outside," he said graciously, unbending his body to stand at his full height. When I rose from the seat with Elizabeth in my arms, I felt positively dwarfed by him.

Elizabeth awoke just as we reached his truck.

"Daddy?" she said, recognizing the truck.

"Yes, darling, Daddy's here," he said, coming close to touch his hand to her cheek. "How's my little trooper?"

"I got two stitches, Daddy, and I only cried a little," she said proudly.

"That's my girl," he said, leaning over to kiss her forehead, mindful of her stitches.

My anger completely left me when I saw the love these two had for each other. I was certain then that if he'd gotten the message earlier, he would've been here immediately for his daughter. Climbing up into the truck, I placed Elizabeth on the seat and backed out, my left hip bumping into Mr. Plantagenet as I did. From where we'd touched, I felt an electric tingle run from the point of contact, all throughout my body, sending confusing messages to my brain to quit breathing, and then to breathe harder.

"Can we go to McDonald's?" Elizabeth asked with a pathetic look on her face.

I could see her father was completely wrapped around her little finger as he scanned her face and nodded with a slow grin. "Sure, honey, wherever you want is just fine with me," he said, tucking the seat belt around her in the front seat of the truck.

"Can Ms. Casey go with us?"

"Honey, she probably needs to get home to her own family. Don't you?" he asked, looking hopefully in my direction.

Before I could think about my response, I heard myself saying, "No, not really. I don't have a husband or children—unless you count my classroom."

"Then, it's settled." He held the door open for me and waved his hand with a flourish. "Hop in."

Not one who was usually prone to spontaneity, I was surprised to find myself "hopping in" without a second thought. There was just something irresistible about this gorgeous man and his sweet little girl.

The trip to the restaurant was quick, and Elizabeth's father was utterly charming, keeping up a running dialog the entire way. He had the two of us laughing about things that had happened on his construction site.

After a meal of hamburgers and French fries, I sat back with Elizabeth's father and together, we watched as Elizabeth played in the indoor playground. I found myself thinking: *We look like a family.* The very thought was enough to startle me out of my daydreaming.

"Elizabeth talks about you all the time and so far, I can see why. You have a genuine love for your students, don't you?" he remarked.

"Yes, I do, Mr. Plantagenet," I replied, blushing at the compliment.

"So, Ms. Casey, do you have another name besides Ms. Casey?"

"Lauren." I said, ducking my head and feeling suddenly self-conscious. I felt like he could read my mind.

"My name's Christian," he said, extending his hand across the empty wrappers on the food tray. "Nice to meet you, Lauren."

"Nice to meet you . . . Christian."

I couldn't help but think: *What a great name for such a hunky guy.*

"I want to thank you for taking such good care of Elizabeth. Not only today, but also every day. You seem to be the only stable thing in her life right now," he said, looking toward Elizabeth and smiling as she waved from her perch high up in the maze.

"I have to admit, I tried to call you last night several times. I'm concerned about her lately."

He turned his brown eyes back to me, frowning slightly. "What's up with Elizabeth?"

"That's what I'd like to know," I said, then relented and explained. "She doesn't play with the other children anymore; she sits quietly by herself, rocking a doll that we keep in the classroom. She's becoming more and more withdrawn. It just isn't natural for a little girl to be so quiet and sad."

Christian leaned his elbows on the table and rested his face in his hands. He didn't answer me for a few minutes, and then, running his hands through his hair, he sat back and looked at me.

"Elizabeth's mother walked out on us six months ago. One day, I thought we were just a happy family with the normal problems associated with everyday family life, and the next day, she was handing me divorce papers, giving me full custody of Elizabeth. We haven't seen her since."

Shocked and speechless, it took several seconds before I could put two thoughts together to make a sentence, and even then, it was just to repeat what he'd already said.

"You mean—Elizabeth hasn't seen her mother in six months?"

"Six months."

"No wonder she's so sad and withdrawn. Poor Elizabeth." I looked over at her, sliding down the slide, smiling and laughing—things she hadn't done at school in a long time. "But—how could a mother walk away from her own child?" I didn't realize I'd even spoken the words out loud until Christian responded.

"Having a child was my idea. Heather was always much more interested in herself than children. I guess I was just too blind to her nature to see her for what she really was until it was too late." He paused, staring off in Elizabeth's direction, but looking at the past, not the present. "I have to admit that it was mostly my fault—our breakup, I mean. I should've been a better judge of character and I should've been around enough to know when it was going sour. I've been so busy building up the business, I didn't spend enough time paying attention to my family, like I should have."

Reaching across the table, I covered his hand with mine. "You can't beat yourself up over the past. The main thing now is that you have a little girl who needs your love, as well as your time. She needs to know now that she hasn't lost both her parents."

"You're right, but I can't walk away from my work. I'm the sole owner of a small construction company. I have about a dozen or so people on the payroll, all depending on me to make it work."

His words left me cold. "Looks to me like you still don't have your priorities straight. If you don't mind, I'd like to go home now."

Gathering my purse, I rose from my chair and called to Elizabeth. It didn't take long to get back to my car, and then Christian Plantagenet drove out of my life.

Good, I thought, *who needs him, anyway?*

Trouble was, Elizabeth did. I sure hoped he'd figure that out soon, before he lost his daughter to heartbreak that couldn't be healed.

The spring semester of school was coming to an end and I was more than ready for the summer break. As always, the students got spring fever and their behavior went right downhill with it. I was constantly trying to think of different ways to keep their interest in what they were learning. The good thing was that Elizabeth seemed to be coming out of her shell a little more with each passing day.

It was two weeks before school let out when I received a message from the office to call Mr. Plantagenet about Elizabeth. His instructions were to call him after seven o'clock that evening. Curious, I waited until the appointed time and called their home phone number from my place.

"Mr. Plantagenet, this is Lauren Casey. You left a message for me to call you?"

"Lauren, I'm so glad you called back. I didn't think you would after our last conversation. Anyway, I just wanted you to know that I took your advice and hired some additional help, and I've been spending more time with Elizabeth. Actually, I'm really enjoying getting to know her better. We're quite good pals, now."

"I'm so glad to hear that. I have been noticing the difference in her lately. She's opening up and actually playing with the other kids on the playground again. I'm so glad for you two."

"Thanks, but that isn't exactly why I called."

"No?"

"No." He hesitated before plunging in. "I called because I wanted to know what you planned on doing this summer."

"What?"

"I know it's forward of me to ask, but what are you planning to do this summer?"

"Oh, nothing special. Why do you ask?"

"Well, I really didn't want Elizabeth to have to go to day care all summer long if I could help it."

"I'm sorry, Mr. Plantagenet, but I really don't understand what that has to do with me."

"Well, if you're not busy this summer, could you—uh, take care of Elizabeth? I'd pay you a salary and provide for any and all entertainment expenses. Please say yes—she really loves you and I feel comfortable when I know she's with you."

I sat in stunned silence. Never in my short career as a kindergarten teacher had I been asked to provide childcare for one of my students over the summer break. I didn't know quite how to react. Was it against the rules? I didn't know. Technically, after this semester was over, Elizabeth would no longer be my student, so I didn't think there'd be any conflict of interest.

What was I thinking? Obviously, I wasn't thinking, because the next thing out of my mouth was: "I'd love to take care of Elizabeth."

"Oh, thank goodness! You don't know how much this means to Elizabeth, and to me. It'll provide stability for a little longer, maybe just long enough to give her the time necessary to start feeling more acclimated to the way things are now."

We talked a little while longer, firming up starting dates and specifics about salary, and then I rang off and sat staring at the phone.

What on earth had I just committed to? I was about to spend the entire summer caring for one of my kindergarten students—whose father just happened to be one of the most gorgeous men I'd ever met. Was my motivation toward the welfare of the child, or toward my own interest in her father?

The question stopped me short. How could I, in good conscience, enter into this arrangement knowing darn well that I was more than a little attracted to Elizabeth's father?

On the other hand, I truly cared for Elizabeth and had taken a personal interest in her well-being. After all, what was not to like about that sweet little girl? It still baffled me that a woman could leave her behind—her own flesh and blood—and not look back. If I were

Elizabeth's mother, I knew I'd be there for her forever.

Pausing, I realized what I was thinking. I was about to go play Mommy For The Summer with one of my students. The more I thought about it, the more confused and distressed I became. Finally, I pulled my tennis shoes on and left the house to jog the doubts from my mind.

The end of the school year was marked by the graduation ceremony for the kindergarten students. Christian was there, beaming from ear to ear as he watched Elizabeth receive her diploma from the principal and a hug from me. We'd decided not to tell her about my taking care of her until after school let out.

After the ceremony, I agreed to meet Elizabeth and her father for supper at a nice Italian restaurant. Elizabeth was excited about the summer and no more school.

"Elizabeth, we have a surprise for you," Christian told her, looking across the table at me with a big grin on his face.

"A surprise? For me? May I have it, please?" Elizabeth couldn't sit still.

"It's not a present to be opened, silly. How would you like for Ms. Casey to watch you for the summer?"

"Really? Do you mean it?" Elizabeth's face lit up and she jumped into her daddy's arms, then ran to me, throwing her little arms around my neck. "I love you, Ms. Casey! I wish you were my mommy!"

Blushing, I shot a glance at Christian, but he looked away. His ex-wife had left him with scars that still needed to heal. But maybe Elizabeth's remark wasn't so far off base.

The first day of summer with Elizabeth was fun. I showed up at their door at eight in the morning and Christian promptly left for work. Elizabeth and I packed a bag with swimsuits and sandwiches and headed for the neighborhood pool. We spent a good portion of the day slathering sunscreen over our skin and splashing around with the other children. In the afternoon, when we came home, we rested for a little while and then read some books together.

Late that afternoon, Elizabeth got hungry and I fished around in the cabinets for something to cook for supper. Christian's cabinets were filled with quick-fix, ready-made meals—easy stuff that a single working dad could whip up at the end of a busy day. Nothing particularly appealed to me, though, so Elizabeth and I made a quick trip to the grocery store, loading up on fresh fruits and vegetables and food that I could cook to provide a balanced meal for my young charge and her busy father. When Christian came home around six, I grabbed my purse and left, calling over my shoulder that there was a plate warming in the oven for his supper.

The next day was very much like the first, only Christian asked me to join them for dinner that evening.

"Especially since you cooked it," he said. "You know, you're a great cook, Lauren, and I want you to know that I really appreciate what you've done, but you don't have to cook for us. That wasn't part of our deal."

"I don't mind. Really, it was no trouble at all."

"Well, at the very least, then, you should stay and eat with us—enjoy your own cooking."

And so, three weeks went by with me playing mommy during the day and eating dinner with Christian and Elizabeth each night. I was happy, but soon, I have to admit that I began to want . . . more.

And then Christian came home one night with a teenage girl.

"Lauren, this is Alicia. Alicia's going to baby-sit tonight, right, Elizabeth?" he said, as if they'd planned this all along.

"Right, Daddy!"

"Lauren, I know this is short notice, but would you like to go out with me tonight?"

My heart did a flip-flop and beat a fast tattoo against my chest. "Uh, well—I'll have to change first."

Laughing, he looked down at his dusty clothes. "I'll have to shower and change myself. But if you'll wait just a few minutes, it won't take me long."

True to his word, he was back downstairs in fifteen minutes, showered shaved, and smelling *great*. I kissed Elizabeth good night and went out the door with Christian. We went to my house, where I introduced him to my parents. They talked while I showered, put on fresh clothes, and applied a little mascara and lipstick. Before I knew it, we were alone in his car, headed for a quaint little seafood restaurant on the shore of the lake.

It was a glorious evening of laughter, conversation, and getting to know each other on a personal level—something that had been a little hard to achieve in the presence of a five-year-old. Christian was so warm and caring, I couldn't imagine that his ex-wife had truly left him, much less Elizabeth.

The evening was too short when he finally took me home, so we sat on my front porch and talked until midnight. When he finally got up to leave, he leaned down and kissed me gently.

"Thanks for all you've done, Lauren—not only for Elizabeth, but also for me."

I was on cloud nine, feeling all warm and tingly inside. That feeling lasted until four o'clock the next afternoon when the doorbell rang. Leaving Elizabeth at the kitchen table working on a puzzle, I opened the door to find a beautiful woman who bore a striking resemblance to Elizabeth standing outside.

"Hello, I'm Heather Plantagenet, Christian's wife." When I didn't respond, she added, "*Ex*-wife, I mean. Is Elizabeth home?"

"Ms. Casey, are we going to finish the puzzle?" Elizabeth came up behind me and peeked around my legs at the person standing outside.

"Mommy!"

Heather pushed through the door and bent down, holding her arms out to Elizabeth. "Aren't you going to give your mommy a big hug, baby?"

Before my eyes, I watched as Elizabeth instantly retreated back into her shell. Her eyes rounded with a haunted look as she stared up at her mother, the woman who'd abandoned her without so much as an explanation, or an apology. A single tear escaped the corner of her eye as she turned and ran upstairs to her room.

"What's wrong with her?" Heather looked at me accusingly.

"Her mother left her ten months ago, that's what's wrong with her," I said, my tone flat and unfriendly.

"Go get her. I want to see my daughter."

"I think it would be better if you wait until Christian gets home. Elizabeth's been through a lot and I'm sure he would want to have a say in this."

"I don't care what he has to say. I want to see Elizabeth." She started to walk around me to follow after Elizabeth, but I moved to block her path, planting my feet firmly.

"I'm sorry, but you'll have to come back when Christian is home."

When she realized I wasn't going to budge, she turned and left. With my knees shaking, I closed the door, locked it, and went to find Elizabeth. She was hiding in the far corner of her bedroom on the other side of her bed, clutching her doll and rocking back and forth, whimpering softly.

"Elizabeth? Are you okay, honey?"

No response.

I gathered her in my arms and brushed her hair back from her face. We sat there for a long time just holding each other before she finally looked up at me.

"I wish you were my mommy," she said softly, and buried her face in my shirt.

"I wish I were, too, Elizabeth. I wish I were, too."

Christian came home a little after six to find Elizabeth and me cooking a pot of chicken noodle soup. I'd always believed that chicken noodle soup was the cure-all for what ails you, and I was hoping it'd live up to that reputation. When Elizabeth didn't fly into his arms immediately, Christian looked at me curiously.

"What's wrong, Elizabeth? Don't you have a big hug for your dear old dad?"

Elizabeth hesitated, then ran to her father's arms, the tears beginning to fall even before she reached him. Lifting her up into his arms, Christian held her close, looking over her shoulder at me.

"What happened?" he asked softly, his face and voice filled with concern.

"Heather showed up here a couple of hours ago. She'll probably be back any minute now. I told her she'd have to talk to you before she could see Elizabeth."

Christian looked down at Elizabeth. "Did she see her?" he asked me.

All I could do was nod. The pain in his eyes just about knocked me to my knees. If ever a man had loved his daughter, it was Christian Plantagenet.

"Would you mind staying a little longer tonight, please, Lauren? Elizabeth might need you here when Heather comes back."

"You know I'd do anything for Elizabeth."

"Thanks, Lauren. That means so much to me. More than you know."

Heather showed up an hour later. I took Elizabeth up to her room before she could see her. We played a game of Old Maid and read a few books. It seemed like it was forever before Christian finally came upstairs. His face was pale and drawn. I went to him and put my arms around him. I would've taken his pain away from him if I could. Together, we put Elizabeth in bed for the night, tucking her in and kissing her forehead. When she was sound asleep, Christian and I went downstairs and sat in the living room together on the couch, just staring at the empty fireplace and not saying anything.

"She's gone," he said finally. "All she wanted was money. She didn't even really want to see Elizabeth; she just wanted to use her to get money out of me. Anyway, I called her bluff and she left. I don't think we'll be seeing her again anytime soon."

"Poor Elizabeth," I said, tears welling in my eyes. "She was devastated this afternoon."

"You know, when we were married, I felt like it was always all my fault that things just weren't working out—that maybe, if I could just be a better husband, Heather would be happier." Turning to me, his eyes full of realization, he continued, "Now, though, I know that it wasn't only me. Heather is a selfish, cruel person, totally unfit for family life and totally unsuited to being a mother.

"Lauren, you've helped me to see all that. You're kind, caring, and selfless. You would never harm a hair on Elizabeth's head, nor break her heart, or mine. I thought I'd never learn to love another, but you've shown me that somehow, I can love again."

My throat closed and I held my breath. No man had ever spoken to me of love before; I didn't know what to say. All I wanted to do was throw my arms around his neck and kiss him passionately, but I held back.

"Lauren, I know this is probably an awfully bad time to ask, but . . . will you marry me?"

I sat in stunned silence. This was what I'd been dreaming of my whole life, but there was something lingering that still bothered me.

"Christian, do you just want me to marry you so I can be a mommy for Elizabeth?"

It was Christian's turn to look shocked. "No, Lauren—oh, of course not, darling. I would never marry you just to make you the mother of my daughter. That would be as unfair to Elizabeth as it would be to you."

Slipping off the edge of the couch, Christian went down on one knee, kneeling before me, and lifted my hand in his. "Let me do this right," he said gently. Then, taking a deep breath, he looked into my eyes. "Lauren Casey, you are the most beautiful person I've ever met. Your beauty is not only on the outside, but also on the inside, where it really counts. You're a friend and a confidante and I want you to be everything to me for the rest of my life.

"Lauren, you and I are meant to be together and I have Elizabeth to thank for helping me to realize that. So will you marry me, Lauren? Please?"

"Please say yes, Ms. Casey," said a little voice from behind me in the hallway.

Turning around, we saw Elizabeth standing there, clutching her dolly. She ran into the room and stood in between Christian and me.

"Will you marry us, Ms. Casey?" she asked me.

"Oh, Elizabeth!" I said, hugging her to me. And then I looked over her shoulder at her father, and I held out my hand to him. He took it gladly. "Oh, Elizabeth, Christian—it's an offer I can't refuse," I said. "Yes, I'll marry you two!"

Christian gathered the two of us in his arms, bringing our little family together in one great, big, wonderful bear hug.

One year later, I became Elizabeth's mommy for good. THE END

TEMPTED BY A CONVICT—
IN LOVE WITH A COP
Horny For Handcuffs!

The front porch sagged just the way I remembered it. Shredded, dingy curtains hung in windows that may or may not have had any glass left in them. Under the tangle of weeds and blackcap vines that loved to reach out and draw blood from anyone, like me, unwise enough to still be wearing shorts on a mid-November afternoon, the rusting hulk of my father's cheap, riding lawn mower squatted like a monster waiting for one of the Three Billy Goats Gruff to trot unsuspectingly down the broken front walk.

I switched the key of my battered pickup to "Off," propped my chin in my hand, and stared pensively at what remained of the house I'd grown up in.

"What are you doing here, Tabitha Ingalls?" I asked myself for what had to be the hundredth time. The answer lay next to me on the front seat in the thick packet of papers that the lawyer had given me that morning.

I was back in town for many reasons, the most pressing of which was to settle the remaining debts left over from my parents' final years in the local nursing home. Alzheimer's had claimed my mother, while a series of strokes had left my alcoholic father unable to even hold a can of beer. They'd died a few weeks apart this past September, and with their passing, had dealt me one final kick in the teeth: They'd left me this house.

"Final expenses and death taxes aren't the problem," said the lawyer, Mr. Sandoval, a middle-aged man with curly red hair and a handlebar mustache. "Your folks had enough savings to pay their bills *and* Uncle Sam with a tidy bit left over for you." He cleared his throat, then began to fiddle with the folder in front of him. "The catch is, you have to live in their house for a year. I'm to dole out your money a little at a time, and if you make it through the full year, then you get the rest in a lump sum."

I couldn't believe it. I hadn't spoken to either of my parents since the night they'd thrown me out.

"Ungrateful tramp!" my mother had called after me as I'd limped away from the house, my ribs and face bruised and aching from yet another of their "tough love" talks.

When I'd tried to explain that I misbehaved because I felt neglected, what with my father's drinking, and the hours my mother slaved cleaning houses to keep him in beer, all I'd gotten was more slaps and kicks. Leaving had been a blessing because it forced me to put my bad-girl ways behind me and learn to earn a living for myself. And I had, getting married, earning my GED, and landing a job in a truck assembly plant up north. I'd been doing well until a strike at the plant, and my husband's subsequent death, had left me alone and with a wiped out savings account.

The nine months since Bill's death had been lonely and frightening. My husband had been ten years older than my twenty-four; a quiet man who, despite his plain appearance, had been a generous lover. Besides taming my wild side, Bill had been the one to insist that I complete high school, and go on to take some night college courses. He'd helped me to see that the reason I slept around as a teenager was because I believed all the hometown talk that I was a tramp, and worse. The greatest gift Bill had given me was love and belief in myself. But without him here today, I was finding it hard to face down the ghosts in my hometown.

Hot tears seeped out of my eyes. Since Bill had died, I'd discovered that grief was sneaky and merciless. Me, who'd been so tough that I never cried, not once, when taking a beating from my parents, would sob when thinking of my husband, dead these nine months. Still, the crying jags didn't come as often now, and in place of grief's rawness, there'd formed a restlessness that had been the main reason why I'd decided to take up Mr. Sandoval on his request to come back to Plotzburg.

The tapping on the driver's window startled me. Clutching the steering wheel with one hand, I used the other to scrub at my face. Then I looked out the window.

A broad, gray-uniformed chest with a shiny star pinned over the heart loomed outside my truck. My lip curled. When I'd been a teenager, the county cops had always been more than happy to believe my parents' stories over mine. While part of me understood that all cops weren't bad, I still retained a healthy mistrust of uniforms.

Muffled by the glass, a deep voice said, "Ma'am, are you all right?"

Slowly, I rolled down the window. "Yeah. Fine."

I drew back in my seat as he leaned over and looked inside. A trooper's hat covered his hair, while mirrored shades hid his eyes, but I knew he was doing an instinctive check for anything suspicious.

Good grief, I thought, *here I am in a battered truck with out-of-state plates, parked in a run-down part of town, in front of an isolated house, crying my eyes out. Of course he thinks something's wrong!*

"Ah," I ran my fingers through my hair, desperately wondering what one said to a suspicious cop to make him go away, "hi."

I could feel the intensity of his gaze through his mirrored lenses. "Ma'am, please step out of the truck."

Great, just great. Anger simmered inside of me that some things just never changed. I jerked at the door handle several times, biting back curses as the darn thing refused to open. Panting now, I said, "Officer, I'm sorry."

"Here." He brushed my hands aside, and with a well-placed hit to the outside lock, the driver's door swung open.

"Thanks," I said, swinging my bare legs around so I could hop out of the truck. The cop towered over my five-foot-three, a starched, polyester-clad tower of stern disapproval. Arms folded as much to stem a sudden bout of chills as to make me appear indifferent, I stepped aside and rested a hip against my truck.

The cop looked me up and down, spending what I thought was *way* too long staring at my legs.

"Do you have any identification?"

"Since when is sitting in a parked car a felony?"

In my previous experiences with county law enforcement, this was the point when the cop tired of my smart mouth and shoved me up against the hood of his patrol car. I waited, tensed, feeling guilty, for Bill had been so patient with my temper, and had helped me learn some caution.

Why then, wasn't I using it now?

"Ma'am," he said, with not a trace of irritation in his voice, "I'm just doing my job."

I closed my mouth with an audible "*pop.*" "Sure. It's inside."

At his nod, I reached for my purse and pulled out my license.

He studied the grainy picture. "Ms. Ingalls—"

"It's Mrs.."

One dark eyebrow rose above the rim of his glasses. "Excuse me. Mrs. Ingalls, are you new in town?"

I jerked a thumb over my shoulder. "I grew up in there."

His other eyebrow rose. "You don't say?"

"Yeah." Feeling testy, I pushed away from the truck until the toes of my dusty sneakers brushed the shiny tips of his black boots. "You got a problem with that?"

He didn't move away. "You planning to stay?"

"Yeah." Until that moment, I hadn't realized I'd made my decision. "I'll have the place fixed up in no time."

He shifted his gaze to the neglected front yard. "Looks like you might need some help."

"I do all right."

I could see myself reflected in his mirrored lenses—mussed hair, faded sweatshirt and cutoffs, ragged sneakers, my chin lifted in a stubborn pout.

One corner of his stern mouth lifted in a half-smile. "I'm sure you do, but if you change your mind—" He pulled a white card from his shirt pocket and held it out. "—give me a call. I've started a juvenile work program around here."

"And you thought that since I was a delinquent, I should know all about how a bad teenager's mind works."

I regretted the peevish words the instant they'd left my mouth. The cop paused, a muscle working in his cheek. "No, Mrs. Ingalls, I merely thought that the job of making this place fit to live in is just the kind of hard work that will tire out young bucks so they can't get into any more trouble."

Chastened, I looked down and fiddled with his business card in my hands. It read: *Ridge Cassidine, County Sheriff*. I couldn't place the name.

Quietly, I said, "I can't afford to pay anyone."

"You won't have to. The county will foot the bill, just as long as you provide supervision while one or more of the kids are here. And, if it helps, I'd be by a couple of times a day to check and make sure that things were all right."

I licked my lips, and kicked at a stone in the road. "I'd rather do it myself."

"I'd rather you didn't."

That made me look back at him. "You've got to be new around here."

He touched the brim of his hat. "Guilty."

Now that I was really looking at him, I noticed tiny lines along his cheeks that hinted of dimples—if he ever smiled, that was. His nose was slightly crooked, but no less appealing for it.

Too bad that his mouth looked more accustomed to issuing orders than making small talk. And, apparently, Sheriff Ridge Cassidine didn't pay attention to local weather forecasts, because he stood outside in mid-fifty-degree weather in his shirtsleeves, and not a goose bump in sight. His arms were tanned and dusted with dark, soft-looking hairs. Underneath, lay ridges of hard muscle.

I swallowed hard. Because of Bill's illness, it'd been over a year since I'd been with a man. I missed passion's furious desperation, and then, afterward, the closeness and sharing of quiet words and gentle touches.

Get a grip, I thought suddenly, scowling. I was lonely, sure, but so desperate that I needed to fantasize about a *cop?*

I thought not.

I fingered his business card. "I'll think about it."

"Good. Give me a call when you're ready to start."

"Yeah."

Pensive, I watched him get back into his patrol car and drive off. *Well, I thought, if this is ever going to work, I'll need some cash to buy basics—food, some linens, and lots and lots of cleaning supplies and trash bags.*

I sighed as I shoved the little white rectangle of paper into my shorts back pocket, then climbed back into my truck. The house sat there, all but mocking me out loud, as I peeled out and headed back into town to Mr. Sandoval's office. Now that I'd made my decision, I stared back at it and felt some of my resentment recede. After all, it was only a house. I was years older, and miles away from the skinny, frightened teenager who'd hitchhiked out of town with five dollars in her pocket.

No way would I let that place and its memories get the better of me ever again.

Mr. Sandoval handed over my first installment with a handshake and the caution to call him if I needed help. I couldn't conceal my surprise. Two people in one day offering me something apparently out of the goodness of their own hearts was *not* what I'd expected to find in my hometown.

My next stop was the local Wal-Mart. My heart fluttered a bit as I packed a cart overflowing with bargains, and headed toward the checkout aisles. The few familiar people I'd seen had nodded politely, then moved on to do their own business. I'd even helped a lost toddler find her mother, and received the kind of hearty thank you that I hadn't known existed until I left town.

So far, so good, I thought, taking my place in line and unloading my things onto the counter. Resting in my pocket, the wad of money I'd gotten from Mr. Sandoval brushed against my hip. I'd almost choked when he'd brought me my payment all in fifty-dollar bills! The people in front of me were all paying with tattered ones and fives.

I tried to reason with myself. *Hey, this is a national chain store; it's not like they never see anything over a twenty.* Still, my hopes fell as I recognized the cashier, a steel-haired older woman who'd once worked in the school cafeteria. Sour and often cruel, she and I had clashed more times than I cared to remember back when I was a troubled teen.

Taking a deep breath, I finished unloading my things and pushed my cart ahead. Muttering to herself, the cashier rang up my items and glanced at me with a hard expression on her face as the printed receipt grew longer and longer. Finished, she hit the total button, turned to me, and held out one grimy hand. I fished in my pocket and pulled out two crisp, fifty-dollar bills, more than enough to pay for my things.

Her mouth twisted as she grabbed the bills with one hand, and with her other, grabbed my arm in a painful grip. "Get the manager! Call the police!" she yelled at the top of her lungs.

"Hey!" I struggled to pull free, but the old bat only squeezed harder until I felt the bones in my wrist begin to grind together. "What's the matter with you?" I cried.

"Counterfeit!" She crumpled the money and dropped it on the floor. It crackled as she ground it beneath her sensibly shod foot. "If it's Tabitha Brewster, it gots to be funny money," she said with malicious triumph.

Embarrassment burned my cheeks as the other shoppers stared, pointing and whispering to one another. I heard snatches of: "Tabitha Brewster's back in town?"

"I thought she went to prison!"

"Once a bad apple, always a bad apple."

"What are you talking about?" I said to the cashier. "I got that money from Mr. Sandoval just a few hours ago."

"And why would he give trash like you money? You stole it, didn't you?" She tugged harder on my arm.

That time, I couldn't stop a cry of pain. The situation worsened as a herd of red-vested managers flooded from the front office. Their feet squeaked on the tile floor as they trotted along the aisle of cash registers.

"They'll fix you now," the old bat cackled. "Run you out so far you'll never show your face here again!"

I closed my eyes against the grinding pain in my wrist. My stomach lurched, and I felt faint.

"Miss Pruitt," said a familiar voice, "why don't you let me be the judge of whether or not something's against the law?"

The old bat shrilled, and then her painful grip on my wrist was gone. Dizzy, I sagged to my knees, panting, regretting letting down my guard. Nothing had changed; I would always be an outcast, the town bad girl.

And then, for the second time that day, I heard Sheriff Ridge Cassidine ask me, "Mrs. Ingalls, are you all right?"

His hands were warm on my arms as he helped me to my feet. I couldn't seem to stop shaking. My wrist throbbed, the skin around it red and already swelling. Tomorrow, I'd have a fine set of bruises.

"I—I'm okay."

"Do you want to press charges?"

I stared up at him, amazed. His glasses hung from his shirt pocket, and the banked anger in his chocolate-brown eyes floored me.

"Charges?" I squeaked.

"Battery, for one," he said over Miss Pruitt's and the manager's frantic protests. "Harassment, and I'm sure I can come up with a couple more."

I shook my head. "I—I just want to pay for my things and get out of here."

He turned his cold glare on the cashier. "Pick them up."

All but blubbering, her knees creaked as she hunkered down and scooped up the dirtied bills.

"Ring it up," the sheriff commanded.

"Now, just a minute," said one of the managers. "My cashier has reason to believe that she was handed a counterfeit bill."

"Got another one?" the sheriff asked me.

Wordlessly, I pulled out another fifty and handed it to the manager. He examined it closely.

"It's good."

"Did you hear that?" the sheriff said to the suddenly silent crowd. He turned his glare on the head manager. "Then if your cashier is ready to apologize to Mrs. Ingalls, here, we can call this case closed."

Miss Pruitt's face flushed a mottled red as the manager, Sheriff Cassidine, and the rest of the cashiers and store customers all turned and stared at her. Her mouth worked for several seconds before she said faintly, "Sorry."

The sheriff propelled me forward. "Mrs. Ingalls, after one of these nice people helps you put all your things in your truck, wait for me, please."

Numb, I followed one of the assistant managers as he pushed my cart out into the parking lot. Just as he finished putting the last bag in the back of my pickup, I heard the click of the sheriff's boots on the pavement behind me.

The assistant manager's Adam's apple bobbed as he scurried away with the empty cart.

Sheriff Cassidine reached for my wrist. "Let me see that."

"No." I pulled away from him, too rattled to take being touched by anyone—even if he *was* the sexiest sheriff south of the Mason-Dixon Line.

He held up both hands. "Settle down," he said in that calm, deep voice of his. "You don't strike me as the type to cry over a little bruise, so I'm betting it hurts pretty badly."

My wrist ached like the very devil, as a matter of fact, and I couldn't curl my fingers. "I'm fine."

"So you keep telling me."

"I bought a first-aid kit," I said, hoping to put him off.

"Smart lady, but I'm still not leaving until I get a look at your wrist." He moved a few steps closer.

I retreated, stiffening when my back hit the bed of my truck. "It's none of your business!"

"It is if I have to take an emergency call out at that sorry excuse for a house you're going to try and live in."

"I know," I said, my voice shaking with anger and pain, "you're just doing your job. But what you haven't thought of, Sheriff Cassidine, is that no one around here would lift a finger to dial 911 if they knew I was hurt!"

"Sondra Tasker did," he said, moving a few steps closer. "The mother of the lost little girl? She's the one who came and got me."

I swallowed hard, shaking even harder as he reached out and gently pushed my sweatshirt sleeve away from my injured wrist. His dark brows drew together as he used both hands to turn my arm this way and that. "So would Marty and Ann Sandoval. He told me a couple weeks ago that you might show up in town, and why you might be a tad skittish around police."

I found my voice. "I never knew Mr. Sandoval before."

"Well, he knew all about you. Seems not everybody believed your folks' stories."

"They didn't have to make them up."

"Maybe not. But from what I've heard, your parents also didn't take the time to try and help you."

I squeezed my eyes shut against a sudden flood of tears. Why did this have to happen now?

"Tabitha," I heard him say, "you're coming with me to the hospital."

I shook my head. "I'm fine—"

The touch of warm fingers on my chin made me open my eyes. His dark gaze was equal parts thoughtful and determined. "That's a mighty big chip on your shoulder, Mrs. Ingalls. Didn't you ever learn that it doesn't have to weigh so much?"

I sighed, tired, and recognizing defeat when all six-feet-two of it was staring me in the face. "What about my truck?"

"I'll have one of my deputies drive it over to the house tonight."

"But how am I going to get there?"

"You're not," he said, resting one of his large, warm hands at the small of my back as he guided me to his patrol car. "You'll stay with the Sandovals for tonight."

The next morning, with a good night's sleep and the comfort of two hearty meals resting in my stomach, the weight of a fiberglass cast around my wrist, I smothered a yawn as Mrs. Sandoval pulled up behind my pickup, parked neatly in front of my parent's vacant house.

No, I thought with a tiny spurt of pride. *I'm going to make it my house.*

Ann blew out a breath as she shifted her car into neutral, then took a look at the house. "My. I never thought about how much work was ahead of you. It's a horrid mess."

"I can do it," I said, stepping onto the concrete sidewalk. I paused and looked, then turned around to face her. "I haven't thanked you for taking me in last night. It was very kind of you."

Her smile made her eyes sparkle. I could see why Mr. Sandoval had fallen for her thirty years before, and why they continued to be a happy couple. "It was our pleasure, dear. Won't you let me come in and help?"

I bit my lip as I took in her pastel-blue, linen suit and matching pumps. Nevertheless, I knew her offer was sincere. "Maybe once I get the worst of the trash cleared out, I could use some advice on colors and stuff."

She beamed, reaching over to pat my hand. "I admire your gumption, dear. Marty or I will be by to check on you, and Ridge said he'd be sending over some of his boys to help."

Since when had that decision been made? I smiled tensely and waved as she drove off.

So, "Ridge" had made up his mind, had he? I looked at the piles of white plastic bags in my truck, imagining hauling them into the house with my bad wrist, and decided that he was probably right. Bill had been patient with me, letting me make up my own mind, even if I made mistakes along the way. Now, though, it seemed I had another sort to deal with—a take-charge kind of man. What bothered me most was that I didn't seem to mind.

I was proud of myself that I had hauled in most of the bags by the time Sheriff Ridge Cassidine pulled up in my driveway, an athletic-looking teenage boy occupying the patrol car's passenger seat. I couldn't see the sheriff's eyes again, but the way his mouth turned down in a scowl did my heart good as he watched me heft an armful of bags from the back of my truck.

"Didn't Ann tell you to wait?" he said, closing the patrol car door with what I thought sounded suspiciously like a slam.

I really didn't want Mrs. Sandoval to get in trouble with him. "I guess she did mention that you might be stopping by."

"You shouldn't be doing that," he said, taking the bags from me. "This is Charlie Eaton," the sheriff said with a nod to the teenager. "Charlie, this is Mrs. Ingalls."

"Hi," he said, brushing past the sheriff to lean against the side of my truck.

Under the pretense of a stretch, he flexed his chest and arm muscles for me. With his shaggy hair pulled back into a ponytail, his broad shoulders and bedroom eyes, Charlie was just the kind I'd have run with as a teenager.

Problem was, as an adult, I knew all too well that his easy charm was a mask. That he was trying to flirt with me in front of the sheriff made me feel disgusted, rather than pleased. I returned his brazen smile with a cool nod.

"I'm glad you're here, Charlie. I have a lot for you to do."

His smile faded.

I reached inside my truck bed and pulled out a brand-new rake and garden clippers. "Here," I said, handing them to Charlie along with some heavy-duty work gloves. "You can start with the yard."

His mouth tight, Charlie took the tools from me and lumbered off into the tangle of weeds and vines.

Behind me, I heard the sheriff whistle softly. "Nicely done."

"Thanks," I said, turning to face him again. "I've met plenty like him before."

The sheriff's gaze searched my face. "Be straight with me now. Think you can handle him?"

I smiled slightly and held up my wrist. "With one arm in a cast."

His sober expression didn't change. "In case you have any trouble, I want you to take this." He handed me a little black box, small enough to fit into my pocket. "It's a pager. Push the button on the top and I'll be here inside of five minutes."

I shook my head and tried to hand it back to him. "I won't need it."

The sheriff's hand was warm around mine as he gently guided my hand, and the pager, into my pocket. My fingers tingled, wanting to curl into his.

"Charlie's had a rough time at home, but he still has grand larceny and battery on his rap sheet. Before you, he's done well at odd jobs for some of the older folks around the county. He also thinks he's quite the ladies' man."

My mouth quirked. "I noticed."

He paused, that muscle jumping in his cheek. "Mrs. Ingalls, a man would have to be dead not to appreciate you."

My breath caught, and my heart pounded against my ribs. I opened my mouth to say something, but no words came out.

With a curt nod, Sheriff Cassidine pivoted on the heel of one polished boot and strode back to his patrol car. Wordlessly, I watched him start the engine and pull away.

What had just happened?

Had Sheriff Ridge Cassidine just made a pass at me?

Me?

The sheriff and me?

A giggle tickled the back of my throat. I clapped a hand over my mouth to keep it inside.

Feeling suddenly happier than I had in a long while, I grabbed a box of trash bags from the truck and headed into the house.

Charlie and I worked through lunch. I didn't have anything to eat besides some soft drinks, but we shared those in place of a meal. Charlie was a hard worker, clearing out the front yard down to the dirt by noon, then starting on the sides and back. At the end of the day when my stomach began to rumble uncomfortably, I was about to suggest to Charlie that he and I head out for some food when a familiar patrol car pulled up in front of the house.

Trash bags, discarded furniture, and neat piles of branches lined the sidewalk, testament to both Charlie's labors, and mine. I hadn't thought we'd made much of a dent until I saw the sheriff's face as he eased out of his car. A bucket of fried chicken under one tanned arm, he actually took off his mirrored sunglasses. His mouth hung open in awe. Feeling a bit sassy, I let a swagger wiggle my hips as I sauntered up to him.

"Better close your mouth, Sheriff, or you might end up with a fly in there."

His sharp lawman gaze measured the changes to the front yard, then lingered on the house. "Maybe you aren't such a nut, after all."

I narrowed my eyes. "And what's *that* supposed to mean?"

"I've lived here two years, and in all the times I've driven by this old place, never once did I think that it possessed even the *possibility* of looking nice under all that garbage."

I turned and looked with different eyes, and saw the freshly washed windows opened to let air circulate inside. Over the windows that were broken, Charlie had nailed plywood—not the most attractive option, but functional until I could replace the missing panes of glass. In front, I'd stripped the porch of its hide of rotting outdoor carpet and mildewed, sagging couch. I'd bought some plants yesterday, and now, several pots of gaily-colored fall flowers lined the porch railing, while baskets of ivy hung on either side of the front door. Through the opening, I could see the path I'd cleared across the wood floor to the kitchen, and off to either side, hints of the now clean rooms stripped of musty chairs, broken tables, and useless bric-a-brac.

"It's a start," I said, feeling proud of myself, and grateful to Charlie. "He," I said, jerking a thumb over my shoulder to where the whine of a grass trimmer in the backyard announced Charlie's presence, "has worked like ten men all day long."

"I told you so."

"So you did. How much longer does his sentence last?"

Sheriff Cassidine took off his hat, another surprise. I hadn't noticed at the store yesterday, but he had thick hair that, although cut short, tended to curl in the southern humidity. He caught me examining him, and hastily scrubbed his fingers over his hair, a sheepish expression on his face.

"Charlie has three weeks left."

I fell into step beside him as we walked around the side of the house. "And after that?"

The sheriff heaved a sigh. "His folks don't want anything more to do with him, but he has a grandmother in Gadslow who says she's got a job waiting for him."

I didn't like the worry lines creasing his face. "So, what's the problem?"

"Charlie's got real potential, but he needs someone to ride him hard for a couple of years and make sure that he stays clean."

I felt a shiver when I realized that was just what Bill had done for me. "And you don't think his grandma's up to it?"

"I don't know. I just don't know, and it eats at me."

Well, well, well. Under all that spit and polish beat a caring heart. Seems I was destined to say good-bye to some of my most cherished prejudices about cops. But was that so bad? And maybe I shouldn't resist the niggling little voice inside my head that kept saying, *Help him!*

"Uh," I said, clearing my throat, "I'm going to need help for a while. Could Charlie stay around after he's released?"

The sheriff gave me a level look. "Family court has already ruled that he's to go to Gadslow. There's nothing I can do."

"Maybe he just needs to make some of his own decisions," I said, thinking of the way Bill had handled me.

"He's too full of himself to think straight."

After a few hours with Charlie, I knew the sheriff was probably right about that. But part of me wanted to be contrary just because he was a cop. "And you breathing down his neck helps him learn to make the right choices in life?"

The sheriff's mouth hardened. "So, six hours with him makes you think you've got a better line on his character than I do, than the family court judge who's seen Charlie over twenty times? Oh, I forgot," he said, his voice hard with sarcasm, "you think that chip on your shoulder tips the scales for you."

I drew back, stung, but knowing I had no one but myself to blame. "You can leave, now."

The sheriff thrust the bucket of chicken into my hands and left.

For the next three weeks, Sheriff Cassidine dropped Charlie off each morning at eight, then picked him up after dinner, never stopping longer than it took for the teenager to slide into the front seat and slam the patrol car door.

Sad that I'd let a budding friendship turn sour, and not knowing what to do to mend it, I worked to ignore the little voice that said I should apologize. With Charlie's help, I re-seeded the lawn and replaced the cracked cement walk with new pavers. We raked the driveway clean of weeds and spread a layer of clean gravel over the top. We scraped paint and applied a new coat of white to the outside, then added new shutters around the windows. We replaced broken glass panes. Inside, we primed and painted all the walls and ceilings, and scrubbed the wood floors, because I didn't have enough money left over to sand and refinish just yet. Still, with the rag rugs I'd found at a garage sale placed strategically, none of the bare spots showed. All of the rooms were bare of furniture except for the kitchen, where I'd been able to salvage my parents' old table and chairs. For a bed, I slept on a mattress on the floor. Primitive, but clean. Then Marty and Ann Sandoval surprised me be dropping by with a gift of a small color TV. I couldn't stop the tears. Not since Bill had died had I had so many people just be nice to me.

And what had I done to the nicest one but turn him away with my arrogance?

And, too well, I did see the chinks in Charlie's charm. Still, he didn't try anything—not until the end of the three weeks, the very afternoon before he was due to be released.

I'd had him stop early so we could celebrate. I'd been to the store earlier for some steaks and an ice cream cake. I couldn't cook worth a darn, but I darn well wanted the kid to know that I appreciated all he'd done for me.

"You deserve this," I said, handing him a wrapped present.

He stared at me as if I'd suddenly grown a second head.

"What is this?"

"What does it look like? Open it." I gave his arm a nudge.

As if it contained a ticking bomb, Charlie peeled away the flowered paper and cautiously lifted the lid. His eyes widened.

"You got me clothes?"

"For when you move to Gadslow," I said, tugging off the lid of the gift box the rest of the way so he could see the new jeans and chambray work shirt. "You'll need something nice to wear when you're looking for a job."

His mouth twisted, and he tossed the box aside. I waited, not hurt, for I understood the kind of turmoil he was going through.

"I ain't goin' to my granny's."

"The family court judge says you have to."

"She's the same as my parents—always complainin' about my hair and my clothes."

"Have you tried listening?"

He stared. "Of everyone around here, I thought *you* might understand."

"Because I was a tramp?" I said coolly, pleased when a dull, red flush stained his face. "You're right, I do. And it's because I've been in your shoes, Charlie, that I'm telling you that you have to do what you're told and stay clean."

Charlie heaved to his feet, dragging me up with him.

"You're hurting me."

"The last thing I want to do is hurt you," he said. "I'm not a kid; I'm a man, Tabitha. Why won't you believe me?"

Then he leaned down and kissed me.

I held perfectly still, pressing my lips tightly closed to prevent him from deepening the kiss. I heard a frustrated moan rumble in his throat. He kissed me harder, then suddenly released me.

"What's wrong with you?"

Deliberately, I wiped my mouth with my sleeve. "Nothing's wrong with me."

"Don't you want it?"

"No," I said, letting my temper spike, "not from a snot-nosed jerk who can't tell when a woman doesn't want to be kissed."

"Excuse me. You must be waiting for Sheriff Perfect to tuck his tail between his legs and crawl back."

"My social life is none of your business, Charlie."

"Well, he's stuck on you," Charlie said with a sly sneer. "Always muttering under his breath about 'Widow Ingalls.' "

I tamped down the little thrill that tidbit brought, and tried another tack. "So, you think you're man enough for me?"

I let my hips sway as I walked slowly around him, looking him up and down like a rancher evaluating a prize bull. At first, he seemed pleased. But uneasiness crept into his eyes when my expression didn't soften.

"Have you changed your mind?"

"I just want to know what you think you can do for me."

"Huh?"

"If you think life with me or anyone else is going to be drinking beer and watching TV, then you can walk right now, Charlie. You've said yourself that there's nothing here for you."

He hung his head. "There isn't."

"Then get over it and move on," I said harshly. "Do you want to end up living in a cardboard box in some stinking alley? Then go right ahead and kiss off the chance your grandmama's giving you."

"But I told you about her."

"Your folks threw you out. Now you've been handed a gift-wrapped opportunity, and you want to argue about hair and clothes? Grow up, Charlie. Second chances don't happen often. Part of being a man is not only being able to see the gift in front of you, but having the sense to put your stubbornness aside and do what's right."

With a small huff, he kicked at a stray stone. "I guess I'm going, then."

Gently, I touched his arm. "I'll be there to see you off."

"No, you won't," said a familiar voice.

Stiff with surprise, I looked over my shoulder, freezing at the barely leashed anger simmering in Sheriff Cassidine's dark eyes.

How long had he been there, and how much had he seen?

Enough, that if his look were real flame, I'd have been a pitiful pile of ash by then.

"Is that a fact?" I said, feeling my own temper return. "I didn't know there were restrictions on waving good-bye at the bus station."

A muscle flexed in the sheriff's cheek. "Charlie has to leave tonight," he said in a quieter voice.

"Oh." I leaned over and picked up Charlie's present. "Will you wear them when you meet her?" I asked him.

"Yeah," he said with a sad grin. "Thanks for letting me stick around."

I held up my cast. "Couldn't have done it without you."

As he started to walk past me, I stopped him and gave him a hug. To my surprise, he hugged me back—nothing sexual, just a friendly clasp that let me know he'd learned at least one lesson.

Tears in my eyes, I gave him one last hug, and said, "Good-bye."

That was the last I heard from Charlie.

Two weeks later, after loading up on groceries and the rare luxury of a Christmas tree, my truck picked the time when I had perishable food in the back, and had been parked in a thirty-minute-limit zone for over two hours, to die in the center of town.

Nothing had been going well for me since Charlie had left. Sheriff Cassidine continued to avoid me. The Sandovals had invited me for Thanksgiving, and I'd gone, hoping to see a familiar patrol car in their driveway, all ready to apologize. My heart had felt hollow and lonely as I'd recited the Thanksgiving blessing that day.

Miss Pruitt and her cronies had made it their personal mission to follow after me like a herd of grim reapers whenever they spotted me in town. Today was no exception. I heard cackling off to my left, then smothered a groan when I saw four of the old biddies tittering and pointing at me from under the beauty parlor awning. It was Friday night, a quarter to five, and Bonita's Beauty Boutique was my only chance for a free phone call to Ann Sandoval. I *refused* to call the sheriff. Stiff with reluctance, I opened the driver's door, hopped out—and nearly collided with the sheriff where he stood, calmly writing me a ticket.

Unnerved, my first reaction was to let my hackles rise. But one look at Sheriff Ridge Cassidine's wide shoulders and dark, bedroom eyes made me take two steps back. I wanted so much more from him than friendship, but I knew I also had to make up for my mistakes.

"How much?" I asked him.

"Thirty dollars. Didn't you see the sign?"

"Yeah, but I guess I let time slip away from me." I held out my hand. "Where can I pay it?"

"The county clerk's office." He ripped the yellow form from his pad, but didn't extend his hand. Something simmered in his eyes.

I swallowed, unsure of just how much trouble I was in. Had I missed another sign? I looked over both shoulders, then back at the sheriff.

"What?"

The muscles in his cheeks twitched, and he crumpled the ticket in his hand. Miss Pruitt and her band of blackbirds began to titter.

"Dammit, Tabitha, I don't want to do this to you."

"It's okay," I said, trying to unfold his fingers and take the ticket from him. "I was wrong."

"So was I." His warm breath tickled my forehead. "Charlie's doing just fine with his granny. You were right to let him make his own decisions."

He wouldn't let me have the ticket. Instead, he dropped it and interlaced his fingers with mine. I sighed at the pleasure of feeling his skin against mine.

"And you were right that he needed a kick to set him off in the right direction. And you sure do know how to deliver a kick, Tabitha Ingalls."

The pride in his voice sent little sparks of pleasure racing across my skin. But I was worried, too.

"Just how much did you see that afternoon, Sheriff?"

To my surprise, Sheriff Ridge Cassidine set his ticket book on the hood of my truck, folded me in his arms, and kissed me—very thoroughly—right in front of Bonita's.

My knees wobbled, and I would have folded, but for the easy strength of his arms around me. Heat flushed my skin. Colors played behind my closed eyelids as the sheriff rocked my world with a kiss.

At last, he pulled away and examined me, nodding to himself.

"That'll do, Tabitha Ingalls."

"My," I said, and rested my head on the sheriff's chest, as I still felt dizzy. His heartbeat thudded quickly under my cheek, making me smile. "Sheriff, I do believe you've had practice kissing."

"So you think I'm man enough to know when a woman wants to be kissed?"

He'd seen more than I would have liked, but apparently, he didn't think worse of either Charlie or me for it. I looked up at him.

"I'd say you're man enough for any woman lucky enough to catch your eye."

Gently, he caressed my cheek. "You've caught mine, Tabitha."

And I was hopelessly in love, again. And, oh—this second chance wasn't going to get away from me.

Feeling sassy, I propped a hand on one hip. "Is that a proposition, Ridge?"

"How about a date, and then I'll proposition you?"

"I'd take some help with my truck, first."

"It's a deal."

We were married Christmas Day, and now we spend our free time on an addition to our little house, for the baby due this summer. THE END

WE WERE STRANGERS ON A SNOWY BUS TRIP. . .
Until the spirit of the season made us a family

For three years, I traveled home by bus for the Christmas holidays. My sister thought I was crazy to put myself through the emotions this trip caused. Dad offered to buy my plane ticket, not understanding that money wasn't the issue. The trip was my tribute to the sweet baby who was no longer mine, and I needed to make the journey in this way. Honoring her memory settled my soul and made me feel close to her in a way that I couldn't when I had to concentrate on driving.

Some said it was morbid to retrace the route to my hometown in the Rockies, to travel the same roads I'd traveled with her inside of me. But I relished the trip as a way of renewing my wavering belief that the choice I'd made was the right one.

In the middle of my sophomore year at a small midwestern college, I wasn't the right person to give her the best in life. Although I was sure of my love for her, I knew I couldn't provide her with a stable life. So I'd returned to the sanctuary of my parents' home for the last six weeks of my pregnancy.

Suddenly, the bus rattled through a pothole, and I was jostled from my reverie, taking a look outside. The afternoon sun shone weakly through low gray clouds that threatened snow before the night was over. The prairie grass was brown and matted, lying low as if hugging the ground for warmth.

The traffic alongside the bus had increased, which meant we were approaching another town. The repetition of short stops and cookie-cutter bus stations was soothing. I liked knowing that not too many miles farther along the road would be a well-lit, warm room where I could stretch my legs and buy a cup of cocoa.

Bus travel was as anonymous as I wanted it to be. I made the decision to either talk with my fellow passengers, or maintain my distance. On this particular trip, I was thankful that the bus wasn't too crowded, and for several hours, I enjoyed a whole seat to myself. Mostly, I was just glad that the other travelers were also going solo—military personnel, college students, and seniors—not families.

Christmas was always the hardest time of year for me. Seeing happy families enjoying each other chipped away at my belief that I'd done the right thing. I worried that her adoptive parents couldn't possibly love her as much as I did. That year, my baby would be almost two. To save my sanity, I'd been having to pretend that toddlers were invisible. At shopping malls, I kept my eyes straight ahead, not daring to let my gaze dip down to the huge eyes, rounded cheeks, and dimpled smiles beaming up at me from strollers and carriages everywhere.

After another short stop, at which I got off the bus momentarily to take advantage of the station's restrooms, my bus's departure was announced over the intercom, and I hurried back aboard. The bus creaked and moaned as it waddled away from the station. One more city left behind us.

Settling into my seat once again, I concentrated on the passing scenery through the window. Ten minutes passed in pleasant viewing before I heard the baby's first cry.

Someone with a small child must've boarded at the last city. Whenever I heard a baby's cry, my whole body went on alert, fighting my natural impulse to get close to that sound. The fussing sounds spun my thoughts back to the reason for my trek.

Three years before, I'd hoped for a quiet holiday spent in the loving atmosphere of family in my childhood home. My baby had had different ideas.

Content with the last-minute excitement of holiday baking and gift wrapping, I'd ignored the first labor twinges and promised myself that I'd put my feet up as soon as the next batch of cookies was done. But before I realized what was happening, Mama had taken one look at my hand bracing my lower back, bundled me into the car, and driven me to the local hospital. She'd stayed right by my side, whispering words of encouragement and telling me how proud she was of me. I'd clung to her words as tightly as I'd clung to her hand.

Not prepared for how the act of giving birth would touch my soul's most primal depths, I'd started wishing that I could keep the baby, that I'd find a way to make a life for us. But Mama brought me back to reality. From then on, I'd tried to believe that letting my baby be adopted was truly the best choice—for both of us.

For one fleeting moment at five minutes past midnight on December twenty-fourth, I'd seen my daughter's sweet face, and then she was gone. Gone forever.

Now, from behind me, the baby's cries grew louder, and I heard the low rumble of a man's soothing voice. I told myself not to turn around, not to make eye contact with the child. My cardinal rule was not to get involved with other people's children; I knew my heart wasn't strong enough.

But the cries tugged at my hardened mother's heart. I could see passengers with deepening frowns craning their necks to see what the problem was. Being inside the bus was more personal than being at the mall. Once those doors closed and the wheels started rolling, an intimate environment was created. As inhabitants of that special world, we couldn't truly separate ourselves from inevitably interacting with each other in some way or another.

I looked out the window, searching for anything of interest to distract me. If the child's father soothed it quickly enough, I'd be able to maintain my distance. And so I counted telephone poles, telling myself that if I reached one hundred and the baby was still fussing, then—and only then—I would go back and offer to help. Although I wasn't sure what exactly I thought I could do better than the child's father could. All I knew was that if the situation were reversed, I'd want someone to offer to help me.

And so I counted—ninety-eight, ninety-nine, one hundred.

And the baby's cries only grew louder, more high-pitched.

I knew then that I couldn't avoid the situation any longer, and my stomach knotted with nerves. I scooted to the aisle and glanced back. A small head covered with blond curls swung into the aisle and disappeared, cradled in a dark-haired man's arms.

Why did I feel compelled to help? What was drawing me to this baby—drawing me enough to make me put aside my rules about children?

As if he knew I was watching him, the man looked up suddenly and connected with my gaze. His eyes were the deepest blue I'd ever seen, but it was his look of mute appeal that went straight to my heart. Automatically, my legs propelled me toward the back of the bus. As I approached, I noticed that the seats around him were suddenly vacant.

Abreast of his seat, I spotted the baby, who seemed dwarfed by the big man's arms. She was older than I'd first thought—probably close to two years old.

About my daughter's age.

That thought sliced through me, and I sucked in a deep breath, resting a hand on the back of the seat to steady myself.

Could I do this?

Hesitating, I sat down across the aisle from him and smiled. "Hello, my name is Janet. Please don't think I'm trying to butt in, but I was just wondering if you might need a hand."

At the sound of my voice, the baby quieted, twisted around in his arms, and focused dark brown eyes on me. Clad in denim overalls and a pink turtleneck, snuggling against his chest, she stared at me, her breathing erratic with shuddering sobs.

At the instant change in the baby's demeanor, the man's eyes grew wide and he smiled, causing a dimple to wink in his left cheek. "What do you know? I think we should listen to the nice lady, don't you, sweetie?" He glanced at me. "Keep doing whatever it is you just did, Janet. It obviously works. I'm Rob, by the way . . . Rob Petrie."

I pulled my gaze from the little girl's. "Pleasure to meet you, Rob. And what's your daughter's name?"

"My niece. Her name is Grace."

"Grace," I repeated, liking the sound as I said it. "A pretty name for a very unhappy little lady." Instantly, I felt sorry for this man who, judging from the way he held her too tightly, obviously didn't have much experience with toddlers.

"She's got an ear infection, I'm afraid, and the doctor advised against making the trip by plane." He gazed down at the child fondly and brushed a tear from her cheek. "I thought that the bus would be quieter than the train. So, here we are."

Both of our tickets took us through Denver. We'd be sharing the same bus for at least another twelve hours, maybe enough time to become better acquainted.

Grace struggled to sit upright in his arms. Her eyes hadn't left my face since I'd sat down, and I discovered that I couldn't look away from her, either. She was a little beauty, all right. She didn't look much like her uncle, though, so maybe she took after her mother. The thought of who my own daughter favored flashed through my mind then suddenly, but I hastily pushed it back down deep inside of me.

"You know, she might actually feel better if she's seated upright." My suggestion was hesitant; I was wondering if I should be telling him what to do. After all, what did I know about taking care of a child? "My nephew, Devon, gets them, too. My sister, Claire, always props him up with extra pillows when he sleeps. Something about less pressure on the eardrum."

He nodded, adjusted Grace's position, and she snuggled her head on his shoulder. His large hand awkwardly patted her back, and immediately, her eyelids grew heavy.

"Does the trick every time," I whispered, smiling. "She's almost asleep." Relief shot through me, and I stood, ready to return to my seat.

"Janet!" His voice was quiet, but it held an unmistakable note of panic.

I stopped, quickly checking Grace's face, and then my gaze went to his. He was ruggedly handsome, his dark hair curling around his ears, and, judging by his jeans-clad legs jammed against the back of the seat ahead of him, well over six feet tall.

"Um, would you mind sitting back here with us? I'm a complete novice to this sort of thing, and more than willing to listen to any pointers you can offer."

Again, my stomach clenched. I'd thought I was done, that my foray into contact with children had ended. But one look at Grace's sweet face, and my resolve wavered. This was, after all, the perfect opportunity for me to test my abilities—a temporary interaction with a definite time constraint. Once the bus reached his or my destination, our association would be over for good.

"Let me get my things, and I'll be right back."

I quickly walked several rows forward, gathered my jacket, carry-on satchel, and the lightweight blanket I used for these trips. I returned and set my belongings on the adjacent seat. Then there seemed to be nothing to say.

"I really appreciate this," Rob said. "All I want right now is to get her safely to my parents' house."

"Where are her parents?"

He stiffened, and the baby moaned at his sudden movement. He automatically rubbed circles on her back, whispering quietly. I liked how natural his responses seemed. If he was indeed a rookie, at least his instincts were good.

"Look, if I'm being nosy, just tell me. I come from a big family in a small town. We're used to talking about everybody's business."

He angled his lean body, stretching one leg into the aisle, and rested his head against the seat. "My brother and his wife were killed last week in an automobile accident. Thank God, Grace wasn't with them. She was still at the daycare center, waiting to be picked up. They were on their way to get her."

"I'm so sorry for your loss." Immediately, I said a silent prayer that my two sisters and one brother were all happy and healthy.

He dipped his chin in acknowledgment. "Mom wanted to fly out to get her, but Dad's recovering from hip replacement surgery. I had vacation time due me, so I flew east to straighten out their affairs." He leaned his head back and closed his eyes for a moment.

For the first time, I noticed the lines of exhaustion around his eyes and mouth. I tried to imagine myself in a similar situation and knew that not living close to his brother's family had probably made Rob's worse. The poor child! How scared she must've been, and probably still was. The people she loved and trusted had disappeared, and now an inexperienced bachelor uncle was doing his best to take care of her needs.

Impulsively, I leaned over and tucked my blanket around the sleeping baby and tossed the rest over Rob's long legs. He'd fallen asleep, and his head nodded close to hers—dark waves almost touching golden curls. Outside, darkness was gathering, and I gazed out at the flickering lights of an unnamed city on the Kansas prairie. Soon, my eyelids drooped, as well.

"Janet."

A deep voice called my name, and I thought I was dreaming. I reached for my blanket, but my fingers came up empty. The jostling movement and monotonous purr of tires on wet pavement reminded me suddenly of where I was.

"Janet, you awake?" Rob spoke again.

I opened my eyes and turned my head slowly, wincing at the stiffness in my neck. "Barely."

"I need to. . . ." He jerked his head toward the back of the bus. "Can you hold Grace for a minute?"

My fingers yearned to touch her curls, my arms waited for her warm weight, but I panicked, doubting the wisdom of those thoughts. "Maybe you can lay her on the seat."

"Didn't you say that lying flat would hurt her ears more?"

"So, I did," I mumbled, momentarily frustrated because he was obviously a good listener. "Sure, pass her over." I sat up straighter and opened my arms to the sleeping girl. When Rob leaned close, I smelled musk, warm flannel, and a scent that was uniquely his—a masculine blend that sent shivers of awareness through me.

Grace arched her back at the movement and then snuggled her body to my chest. My senses were achingly overloaded by her closeness— warmth from where she'd cuddled with Rob, baby shampoo, and fresh, sweet skin. Instantaneous peace settled over my anxious heart, and I could do nothing but stare down at her innocent face. This child was single-handedly crumbling the aged stone wall around my heart.

When Rob returned, he held out his hands to take her from me.

"Oh, I don't mind holding her for a while." Even to my own ears, my voice sounded a bit shaky. "Stretch your legs a bit."

He leaned an elbow on the seat in front of me and arched his back. "Thanks. I had no idea that having a little one around can be so tiring. She's small, but demanding."

"It won't always be like that. The poor little thing's just trying to make sense of a senseless world."

"You're right. And I'm a poor substitute for the great mom that Molly was." His gaze flickered away to the window, and he swallowed hard before continuing. "Stupid drunk driver."

I reached out my hand and covered his, trying not to notice how solid he felt. "You're doing what needs to be done, Rob. And you're doing it with Grace's welfare in mind." I removed my hand and made a sweeping gesture. "Not everyone chooses to travel by bus these days."

He chuckled and sat back in his seat, smiling at me. "I appreciate your kind words. You sound like you've had practice calming people down. Is that talent connected to your job, by any chance?"

"Not really." I smiled. "I just finished my degree in education, actually. Now I'm facing a decision about teaching right away, or enrolling in a master's program."

"From the sound of your voice, I'd guess that further studies is not the favored option?"

I couldn't admit to him that my real reason for that stemmed from my not wanting to be responsible for other people's children, a feeling I'd thought would go away with enough time, but hadn't.

"Well, I'm tired of living the student life, except. . . ."

"That sounds like a big 'except.' "

"Last semester, my senior project got me interested in library science. If I focused on a master's in that, I could see my way toward extending my poverty lifestyle."

"Personally, I think that people should go after whatever interests them. After what I've experienced, I'll never tell anyone to delay their dreams."

His voice was filled with such sadness that I wasn't sure how to respond. This man intrigued me like no one else I'd met recently.

"What job did you leave to help your family?"

"I've been writing grants for my city's school district for the past two years." He looked at his hands, then back at me. "But what I'd really like to do is concentrate on my woodworking."

"You build things, like chairs and tables?"

He grinned. "No, I carve artistic pieces from chunks of wood using a lathe. So far, I've been doing it in my spare time, but my brother's death has changed my way of thinking. I realize now that we have no control over our time on this earth, and that we need to grab every moment we get and just enjoy it. I've decided I'm not going to waste my time any longer doing a job that I don't love."

For a moment, my mind flashed to my own indecision about which direction I'd take next. Rob's words resonated with something deep inside of me, and I knew suddenly that I would have to think a lot more about my choice.

Grace shifted in my arms then. I loved the feeling of her small, warm body snuggled close, so trusting and calming. I moved her higher up on my shoulder and gently patted her back.

Rob frowned and leaned forward. "Is she getting heavy?"

"Not too heavy," I quickly answered, wanting to keep her as long as I could, but not willing to tell him why. I never knew how people would react to a woman who'd given away her own child, so not many people outside of my immediate family knew about my daughter. "My nieces and nephews are all past this age, and holding her brings back fond memories for me."

The other passengers must've been asleep by then, because ours was the only conversation I could hear. The swaying movements of the bus, muted lighting, and the darkness outside the windows all combined to create a special, cozy, intimate world, and we talked in low voices, sharing our lives.

I learned that he lived in a mid-sized town in Washington, rode in a bicycle club, loved to read legal thrillers, and had a weakness for his mom's homemade shortbread. I shared with him my passion for quilting, my love of Celtic music, and the prize I'd won in the children's division at the county fair for my chocolate chip oatmeal cookies. Rob was easy to talk to. I surprised myself with how much I shared with this man whom I'd only known for less than three hours.

Then the bus slowed and turned off the highway. I peered out the window and saw blurry images.

"Rob, did you know that it's snowing?"

He leaned close and looked out my window. "By the looks of the road, it's been coming down for a while. I'm going to ask the driver what's up." He rose, swung into the aisle, and walked toward the front of the bus.

I couldn't resist a peek as his lean body moved away from me. His jeans accented long, muscular legs and narrow hips.

As the bus jerked to a stop at a red light, Grace stirred and raised her head, blinking sleepy eyes in my direction. A sinking feeling in my stomach hit. What if she panicked at waking in the arms of a stranger and started to fuss? What would I do? All my doubts about being around other people's children surfaced again suddenly, and I vowed to put distance between Rob and this sweet little girl and myself the first chance I got. What had I been thinking, sitting here and holding this sleeping girl, letting her baby scent and sounds wrap themselves around my heart? She sat up and looked around, then focused wide eyes on my face.

"Hello, Grace. Do you remember me?"

"Wady." She nodded, but her gaze moved, her eyes obviously searching for her uncle.

I lifted her in my arms and turned her toward the front of the bus. "Look, there's your uncle, Grace. Can you see him?"

Just then, Rob straightened from talking to the driver and started back toward us. He spotted Grace and raised his hand in a wave. Her chubby legs bounced in my lap, and she held her arms up for him.

"Want Wob!"

His last few steps were rushed, and with a wide grin on his face, he scooped her up into a tight hug. "Hey, Gracie girl, you're awake!"

Grace giggled and clamped her arms around his neck. Their affection for each other was obvious, and I was amazed at how naturally he seemed to handle her after only a week.

Rob lowered himself into his seat and set Grace in his lap. "The driver told me we're making an unscheduled stop to allow the snowplows to clear the highway ahead."

My first thought was of how the delay would affect my sister's picking me up at my destination. "Did the driver tell you how long the delay would be?"

"No, I don't think he knows, himself, really. I guess it all depends on how deep the snow is."

"Of course, you're right."

"Hungee, Wob," Grace piped up.

"Me, too, kiddo." He tapped her tiny nose with his fingertip, making her smile. "When we get to the station, we'll find some food."

"Want juice."

He reached under the seat, pulled out a backpack, and grabbed a bottle from the side pouch. "One request filled. Apple juice for the little lady."

Grace snuggled against his chest and happily drank her juice from the bottle, sucking noisily.

Rob looked over at me, noticing that my gaze was riveted to Grace, and gave me a sheepish look. "I know all the books say I should be encouraging her to use a cup, but I figure she's had enough changes in her young life for a while."

My gaze raised to his eyes and I smiled. "I think you're doing a wonderful job, Rob. She's obviously fond of you, and you're so gentle with her. Not everything follows a schedule in a book."

"Yeah, I'm amazed at how much she means to me." He ruffled her hair, his blue eyes softening as he gazed down at her in his arms. "Leaving her with my folks is going to be harder than I thought."

The bus squealed to a stop suddenly, and the driver stood to make the announcement about the delay. Right then and there, I silently vowed to use this stop to separate myself from Rob and Grace. Already, I felt a bond with the mismatched pair, and worried that I was becoming too attached to them. All around us, the other passengers gathered their belongings and disembarked.

"You coming?" Rob asked.

I peered under my seat, pretending to be looking for something. "I'll be along in a minute. My hairbrush must've fallen." Inwardly, I cursed myself for being a coward.

"Okay. See you inside, then."

He smiled and was gone.

I slowly gathered my things and dawdled until I was the last person off the bus. I don't know how I'd expected to keep my distance from them in the bus station of a small town in western Kansas. By the time I'd finished using the ladies' room, most of the other passengers had already staked out their areas. I bent over the drinking fountain, scanning the empty seats that were still available, hoping for one on the opposite side of the waiting area from where Rob and Grace already sat.

Out of the corner of my eye, I saw him waving at me. When I pretended not to see, he stood and called my name.

I was trapped.

As I reluctantly walked over to join them, I told myself that this togetherness was a good thing, that I'd learn to interact with a small child without experiencing the overwhelming regret I'd always felt in the past.

But why did this particular child have to come with such an attractive man attached?

Rob grinned and pointed when I finally stood before him. "We saved you a seat. Did you find your hairbrush?"

"Oh, yes. Thanks." I dumped my stuff on the floor and sat in the molded plastic chair beside him, looking around at the room. "There's not much to this station, is there?"

"You're right about that. Luckily, though, I spotted a vending machine when I first came in." He scooted to the edge of his seat. "Will you stay with Grace while I get us some snacks?"

"Sure. But here—let me give you some money."

"Oh, don't worry about it." He squatted in front of Grace's chair. "I'll be right back, honey. I'm just going over to that machine over there to get you some food. Okay?"

She nodded solemnly. I noticed that her gaze followed his every step across the room to the vending machine, and every step back to us. I tried to imagine what she was thinking. Was she worried that her uncle, the only constant in her upturned life, would now also disappear like her parents had? Suddenly, I remembered what Rob had said earlier about leaving her with his parents, and thought that no amount of explaining would take away her fear when that happened. Had Rob thought of that? Had he made plans for how to make that transition as smooth for Grace as he possibly could?

I stiffened at my thoughts and told myself that it was none of my business. By this time tomorrow, I'd be swept up into the holiday celebrations of my own boisterous family, and these few hours would've faded into nothing more than a pleasant, fleeting memory.

Rob stopped in front of me. "What's wrong, Janet? You have such a sad look on your face."

I pushed my gloomy thoughts away and forced a smile. "Oh, I was just thinking about how to let my sister know about the delay."

He sat down next to me. "Well, as soon as we know what the new arrival time is, you can borrow my cell phone. Now, for more important decisions." He held out his hands to me, filled with cellophane-wrapped snacks from the vending machine. "For our snacking pleasure, our choices are crackers and cheese, or crackers and peanut butter."

Grace held out her hand. "Cwackers and cheese!"

Rob quirked an eyebrow at her. "How do we ask, Gracie?"

"Pwease!"

"That's better, sweetie." He quickly unwrapped one end of the package and gave her two crackers. Then he leaned close, mischief dancing in his eyes. "I'm saving the good stuff for later. I've got candy bars hidden for when she falls asleep again."

"Ah, the privileges of adulthood." Rather than let the delay upset him, he was going to make it fun.

We nibbled our way through the dry cracker sandwiches, encouraging Grace to eat a couple more. Looking around, I noticed that several of the other passengers were engaged in conversation with people nearby or across from them. Suddenly, the waiting room had a congenial atmosphere about it.

"Janet, where do you think I should change her diaper?" Rob's brow was wrinkled into a frown as he glanced dubiously at the seats around us.

"Well, I saw a changing station in the women's rest room. Do you think she'll let me take her?" As soon as I spoke, I worried that he'd think I was being too forward.

"I don't know. But it's got to be better than out here." He grabbed the backpack and stood, picking her up, and started off across the waiting room. "You need a clean diaper, Gracie. Janet's going to take you into the ladies' room and change you. Will that be okay?"

I followed closely behind, admiring the way he stated the situation in a matter-of-fact tone. This man was a natural at fatherhood; I knew he'd make some lucky woman a great husband one day.

We stopped at the restroom door. Grace clutched Rob's arm tightly, looking anxiously at the two of us.

"There's a nice place for you to lay down while I change you, Grace, and then we'll come right back out to your uncle." I hoped my voice was calm and reassuring to her.

"That's right, sweetie. I'll wait right here by the door," Rob soothed gently.

Grace looked at me for a long moment, then held out her arms to me.

My heart filled with such joy at her gesture. I felt like I'd won a major victory. And in a sense, I had—I'd earned this small child's trust. At that moment, the walls around my heart that had kept me blocked off from babies and small children for so very long, were gone. They'd been knocked flat by this innocent little girl.

The diaper change was accomplished quickly, and the three of us were soon settled back in our chairs. Snow continued to fall outside, drifting along the edges of the windows. We talked quietly about nothing of importance. As the minutes stretched to hours, people walked the floor or visited the snack machine, sharing idle comments about our common experience of being stranded.

I stifled a yawn.

"Sleepy?" Rob whispered, trying not to disturb Grace, who was curled up in the seat next to him with her head nestled on his folded coat. "Why don't you lean against my shoulder and get some rest?" He slid his arm along the back of my chair.

I pulled my blanket from under my purse and tossed it over us. "Only if you promise to close your eyes, too."

Getting comfortable on the plastic chairs seemed impossible, and I doubted that I'd be able to sleep. But resting my cheek against Rob's warm chest and listening to his slow, even breathing was the perfect sedative. I was out in moments.

A little while later, a loud bang assaulted my ears, and I slowly came awake, aware that my arm was slung across Rob's stomach. His cheek rested against my head, his arm wrapped around my shoulders. I opened my eyes and saw an elderly woman staring intently at us. Looking around without moving my head, I realized that the waiting room was now very crowded. Maybe another bus had been forced to stop. Slowly, my gaze came back to the woman, who still stared.

"You have a lovely family," she said. "Treasure them."

I hesitated about correcting her wrong assumption, but, not wanting to wake Rob, I just mouthed the words, "Thank you."

Rob stiffened and stretched, letting out a low moan. I wondered if he'd heard the woman's words, too. I sat up gingerly, bracing a hand against my lower back. Turning to him, I was nervous about how intimately we'd been entwined just a few moments earlier.

"Did you sleep?"

"I must have. My arm's all tingly." He shook his arm and grimaced, his eyes widening as he looked around. "Wow. This room really filled up. I'll go check on the situation. Be right back." He patted my knee before standing and striding away.

I liked how he trusted me to watch out for Grace. I glanced over at her and saw that she was still asleep. My jacket had slipped off her legs and I straightened it. That's when I met the elderly woman's gaze again.

"Did your bus get stopped here, too?" I asked her. She nodded. "Snow was coming down real thick a couple hours ago. It's stopped now."

I turned my head and looked out the window. The sky was still overcast, but the clouds were higher and the far horizon had lightened with the coming dawn. Glancing at my watch, I was surprised to see that it was almost six o'clock in the morning. I really had slept longer than I'd thought.

I arched my back and reached my arms over my head, trying to work out the kinks. "These chairs aren't too comfortable."

The woman's eyes twinkled. "You looked real peaceful sleeping when I sat down. A good man always could put a smile on my face."

I opened my mouth to correct her, but spotted Rob headed in our direction.

He came over to me and said, "Our driver says the road's been cleared and we'll leave in about ten minutes. I just remembered about the candy bars. I could use a little something about now."

"So could I. What did you get?"

He looked at Grace, then back at me. "They're in my coat pocket."

I looked at her and giggled. "Maybe it's just as well. Chocolate's not the best choice for breakfast. Are there any more crackers?"

"Nope, I finished them off before I fell asleep." He leaned close to the window and looked outside. "Hey, there's a drive-through a couple of blocks away. What do you like on your hamburger?"

"Could you see if there's anything with eggs? And don't forget—"

"I know, milk for Grace." Hesitating, he glanced down at her. "Janet, will you. . . ."

I waved my hands in a shooing motion. "Go on, I'll watch her. Just hurry back so the bus doesn't leave you behind."

He scooped up my blanket, wrapped it around his shoulders, and jogged outside and down the street. I had to laugh at the silly image he made.

"That's a considerate man. You best hold on to him."

"Yes, he is." I hadn't taken my eyes off of Rob's retreating figure. But I knew I had to set this woman straight. "But he's not my man, and we're not a family. We met tonight on the bus and we're just making the best of this sudden change in our travel plans."

She shook her gray curls, a doubting look on her face. "That's not the impression I got from him. He looks at you like you're someone special."

Grace moaned, "Wob?"

I knelt down in front of her chair and rubbed her back, talking softly. My thoughts whirled with what the woman had said. Did Rob look at me with an emotion stronger than gratitude? We certainly worked well as a team, and had almost developed an understanding about what was needed.

So why was I listening to this stranger? Rob and I had separate lives and we'd be saying good-bye to each other within a few hours. So I concentrated on gentling Grace back to sleep, but she wasn't having it.

I sat in Rob's chair and brushed her tangled curls. "Uncle Rob went to get us breakfast. He'll be right back, sweetie."

She sat upright, her head swiveling in all directions. When she couldn't see Rob anywhere, her chin started to quiver.

The elderly woman seated across from us leaned forward in her chair. "Hello, sweetheart. And how old are you?"

Grace shrunk back from the well-intentioned woman and looked up at me, tears pooling in her eyes. "Wady?"

Poor thing! She was disoriented, and I was the only familiar face in the room. "I'm here, Grace. Shall we see if Uncle Rob is coming?" I held my arms out to her, and she scrambled into them.

I stood with her and moved toward the door. "Let's look through the window. Do you see all that white stuff on the ground? It's called snow."

I talked about anything and everything that I could see, hoping that the sound of my voice would keep her calm until Rob returned. With surprise, I realized that my natural response had been to figure out what would soothe her, and somehow, I'd succeeded.

Then an announcement came over the loudspeaker for passengers to Denver to start boarding. I glanced down the street and spotted Rob heading back. I pointed him out to his niece.

"Look, Grace, Uncle Rob is coming."

She pressed her nose up against the window, her eyes watching every step he took.

Rob swung the door open, cold air clinging to him, and stopped when he saw us waiting expectantly, a grin spreading across his handsome face.

"What a welcoming committee!"

Grace leaned away from me with her arms held up to him. "Unca Wob!"

Rob dropped the sack of food onto the nearest chair and reached for her. "Hey, punkin, you're awake!" He rubbed noses with her and she giggled. Cradling her head to his chest, he looked at me. "Is everything okay?"

I nodded, too overcome with emotion at the picture they made together to speak. How could he not see how much she needed him, that he was her family now? Immediately, I shoved my thoughts aside. "Our bus is boarding. We need to hurry."

I grabbed the sack and the blanket and hurried back to our seats. Maybe back on the bus, with the aisle between us, separating us, I'd be able to begin the separation process again. I tried hard not to think of the woman's comments about her impression of Rob's feelings.

But I couldn't help wondering—

Were the three of us like a family?

Why was I even listening to a stranger?

Within minutes, we'd settled into seats in about the middle of the bus, mine across the aisle from them. Rob distributed our breakfast sandwiches, and silence reigned as the three of us ate hungrily. Then the driver's radio crackled, and he held a short, muffled conversation.

"Folks, can I get your attention? We're going to board additional passengers from the other bus. Please stow your belongings under the seats and make room for as many people as possible."

Rob turned his head and looked at me. "Why don't you move over with us, Janet? Grace doesn't need a seat all to herself."

There was no argument I could give him. And, if I was honest with myself, I was glad he'd asked. I didn't really want to miss a minute of our remaining time together. People shuffled in, stowed their belongings, and soon, almost all the seats were filled. The driver thanked everyone for cooperating and announced that we should arrive in Denver by lunchtime, weather permitting.

I gasped and turned to Rob. "I forgot to call my sister."

He reached for his coat under the seat and pulled out a cell phone. "That's because we were too busy eating. Go ahead and use it first."

I looked at the phone in his hand, then back at him. "Instructions, please?"

He chuckled. "Tell me the number and I'll punch it in."

Within a few moments, I was relating the story of our storm delay to Claire. Before I hung up, I urged her to confirm my bus's arrival time before leaving the house. "I'm anxious to see you, too. 'Bye." I handed the phone back to Rob, suddenly saddened because our time together was waning.

He started to punch in his parents' number, and Grace wanted to play, too. I lifted her into my lap to give him more room and started a game of pat-a-cake with her. Her eyes lit up, and she played along. I tried not to listen, but I overheard Rob reassuring his parents that the two of them were fine.

"How's Dad? . . . If the weather turns, we'll grab a cab. I don't want you driving in the snow, Mom. Promise me? . . . See you soon." He dropped the phone back into his coat pocket and rubbed a hand over his face. "So, your sister's picking you up in Denver?"

I shook my head. "My stop is the one after Denver."

He started to say something, but Grace scrambled into his lap and demanded his attention. I told myself it was just as well that our destinations were different. Saying good-bye in the presence of our families would be awkward, at best. Ours was just a temporary alliance, after all, and I'd known all along that it would end.

For the next several hours, Grace occupied all of our time and attention. She was full of energy and had fun moving between our laps. Rob and I didn't share any more personal details, but several times, I found his intense gaze focused on me.

Outside, the storm had cleared, and blue skies filled the bus windows. The snow on the roadway had been melted by the morning sunshine.

"Want juice!" Grace demanded.

Rob searched through the backpack and held up an empty bottle. "Sorry, sweetie, but you drank it all. Anyway, we'll be there soon."

"No!" She started to whimper.

"I think this is where I come in." I kept my voice light, grabbed my satchel, and pulled out a half-full bottle of water. "She can finish this. My water is her water."

Rob turned a grateful smile my way. "Thanks, Janet."

My heart melted. Suddenly, I wished I could be two years old and demand to have what I wanted. I wanted Rob to smile at me like that, always.

Then the driver announced our bus's arrival at the Denver station in five minutes. Rob passed Grace to me so he could gather up their belongings.

I held her close as she finished her water, savoring the weight of her body pressed against my chest. It was hard to believe that I'd only known these two less than twenty-four hours. Suddenly, I was glad I'd impulsively introduced myself. I knew I'd always remember this bus trip with fondness.

Rob turned to me then, a serious look on his face. "There's so much I didn't say, Janet. How can I ever thank you for all your help?"

The brakes squealed, and the bus jerked to a stop.

"You just did. I've enjoyed sharing the ride with both of you." My throat tightened and I brushed my lips against Grace's curls. "You'll never know how much this has meant to me."

His gaze flickered to outside the window. "There're my folks."

I turned to look out. "Where?"

He leaned close, bringing his head close to mine. "By the benches. Dad's sitting in the wheelchair." The elderly gentleman slumped in his seat, his eyes closed. "Janet, they look so old. How are they ever going to manage with an energetic toddler?"

I immediately thought of my parents, and how their grandchildren kept them young at heart. "I've seen what my nieces and nephews do for my folks. You'll be surprised by the changes that take place once they're around her for a while."

He sat forward and looked out the window again, then stood. He reached for Grace and I lifted her up to him. He grabbed my hand and held on.

"Come meet my folks," he said.

I hesitated, uncertain of his intentions. "Rob, I shouldn't get off the bus. This isn't my stop."

"It'll only be for a second. Do it for Grace."

"For Grace?"

"Meeting you will take some of my parents' focus off of her."

He sounded so logical, and I had no argument. I followed as he led me down the aisle. As soon as we'd descended the steps, I tried to pull away, but he gripped me tighter. Maybe he was nervous about how this meeting would go.

In a moment, we were across the expanse of asphalt and I stood back from the exchange of hugs and exclamations of welcome. Then suddenly, Rob wrapped an arm around my shoulders and pulled me forward.

"Mom, Dad, I want you to meet Janet, who helped Grace and me on this trip. Janet, these are my parents, Howard and Judy. Hey, I don't even know your last name."

I extended my hand. "It's Vanvolkenburg, Janet Vanvolkenburg. Glad to meet you. Your son and granddaughter made great travelling companions."

Behind me, I heard the driver call for passengers to board. My gaze flew to Rob's, hoping for the strength to say good-bye before the tears that stung the backs of my eyes flowed.

"Well, good luck to you all. Thanks for breakfast, Rob." I swallowed hard against the lump in my throat. "'Bye, Grace."

She waved a hand. "'Bye, wady."

I waved and spun on my heels, quickly walking back to my seat in the bus. Calling myself all kinds of fool, I watched as they collected their luggage and moved slowly toward the parking lot. Rob turned once, raised a hand in my direction, and I waved back.

Thirty minutes later when the bus pulled into the Eagle Pass station, all signs of my recent tears were gone. I told myself that I should be happy for the experience of meeting Rob, but I couldn't help wishing for more time with him. Claire and Chloe, her youngest daughter, spotted me as soon as I stepped down from the bus, and I was instantly swept up into big hugs and the latest news of my family.

Arriving at Claire's house, more family greeted me, and there wasn't a single moment to myself for hours. As we cleared the table from dinner, Claire pulled me aside and asked me how the trip had been this year.

"You aren't as sad as you've been the past years," she observed.

"I know. I think this will be my last bus trip."

"Oh?"

My sister has the ability to put volumes of meaning in a single word. "I spent some time on the bus with a darling little girl, and I guess I just finally realized that parents aren't only created through giving birth. I'm finally at peace with my decision to let my baby be adopted."

"I don't understand." Claire was surprised. "Could you tell she was adopted?"

The phone rang once and was picked up in the other room.

"She'd recently lost her parents. I watched her uncle act as their stand-in, and he gave her everything she needed."

Claire's oldest, Matthew, stuck his head into the room. "Call for you, Aunt Janet. It's a Rob Petrie."

I sucked in my breath and reached a hand out to steady myself on the counter. How had he gotten this number?

"Thanks, Matthew. Claire, can I take it in Darren's office?"

"If I say yes, you're giving me details when you're done."

Suddenly, I felt carefree. Rob had called. "Sure. We'll talk later."

Carefully, I closed the door to the office and grabbed the phone. "Hello, Rob. How did you get my number here?"

"Remember, it was on my cell phone. I punched the number into memory."

"Well, it's certainly great to hear your voice. How are things going with Grace and your parents?" I settled into a chair and waited for his reply.

"I wish I could be positive. Everything's tentative. She's shy with them and clinging to me. Mom's giving her a bath right now, though, so I've got a ten-minute break. There're lots of breakable things in the house that Grace could accidentally knock over." He took a deep breath. "I miss you."

Hearing his words surprised me. I knew that we'd gotten along well, but I hadn't hoped for anything more. Then the words of the elderly woman in the station echoed through my thoughts.

"I miss you, too, Rob."

"Watching that bus drive away forced me to realize that we'd developed a special bond on that trip. I keep turning to ask your advice and you're not next to me. Tell me I'm not crazy, Janet."

I felt the first glimmerings of hope. "You're not crazy, Rob. I felt it, too, but I don't know where we go from here."

"We have to spend time together. Does your family do a Christmas Eve or a Christmas Day celebration?"

"Christmas Day. Why?"

His voice was confident. "Because you're spending Christmas Eve here, then. I'll pick you up and you should plan to spend the night."

"Wait, Rob. Won't your parents object to a stranger coming for the family holiday?" He was moving so fast, but I liked his confidence that what we felt for each other was real.

"Don't worry, I'll explain it to them." His voice grew husky suddenly. "I need you here because I value your opinion, and I have a big decision to make."

"What decision?"

"I don't think I can leave Grace with them. I want to raise her myself—maybe with your help, if things work out the way I'm hoping they will."

My heart stopped, then raced. He was offering me the opportunity to be a mom, and a chance at a real family. Before I could answer, I heard him laughing at someone in the background. His muffled voice said a few words, and then I made out my name.

"Grace wants to give you a good-night kiss," he told me. Next, I heard a loud smacking noise.

I couldn't believe how much I missed them. "Tell her night-night from me."

"I will. So, what do you think? Are you willing to see where this will lead?"

I felt like shouting, but I kept my voice calm. "Very willing. I like you, Rob, very much. I agree it seems sudden, but I trust what I feel."

That Christmas was three years ago. Rob and I were married on December twenty-ninth that year, and moved into a small house halfway between Denver and Eagle Pass. I have a part-time job at the city library, and Rob is happy working out of our garage, turning wooden objects into bowls and vases. Grace started school this fall, and she is thriving. Her younger brother, Jonah, will celebrate his first birthday soon. As the holidays approach each year, I still remember my first baby and send her and her parents loving thoughts. I've learned that families are created in more ways than we can possibly imagine, love and caring being the important factors.

Nowadays, when a bus drives by, Rob and I share a special look, ever grateful for that fateful, snowy trip. THE END

WHEN A SECRET ADMIRER GOES TOO FAR
Some women pack up and just walk away

"Hi, I'm Cassidy Roberts. I'd like to apply for a job," I said, glancing around the busy ranching supply store. It was the only place I hadn't already tried in Serendipity, and I needed the work.

"I don't know." Mr. Guthrie stood behind the counter, squinting his eyes at me. Starting from the tips of my faded sneakers, his gaze traveled upward to the top of my sandy hair. "You don't look like much, and this can be some pretty hefty work."

"Look, I've spent the last two years of my life at a truck stop, cooking, cleaning, and scrubbing for hundreds of people every day. I'm not afraid of hard work and I have a strong back."

"Still, I really need a man for the job."

"I tell you what: Give me a week and if I can't pull my weight, you let me know, and I'll leave, no argument."

"Weeelllllll. . . ."

I held my breath as he drew the word out for several seconds.

"I guess I can give you a try. Here's a broom; sweep up the hay and feed in the stockroom. If a customer shows up, help him load the feed into his truck."

"Yes, sir. Thank you, sir. You won't be sorry, Mr. Guthrie."

I grabbed the broom and practically ran in the direction of the stockroom, anxious to get out of sight before the man changed his mind.

Almost jumping for joy, I had the large stockroom clean and neat in practically no time at all, thanks to a lull in customer activity.

Hopefully, it would make a good impression on the owner. Because I really needed the job.

I was new to town, and the quaint charm of Serendipity gave me hope that this could become a home to me. My departure from the last town I'd lived in had been by necessity; I'd left practically in the middle of the night, leaving no forwarding address. The few friends I'd made wouldn't miss me for long with their busy lives and families to concentrate on. Not me. I was single, and, the way things were looking, I figured I might as well plan on staying that way forever.

I only hoped I'd left the object of my hasty departure behind at the truck stop where I'd worked.

For the past two months, I'd received letters accompanied by a single red rose left in different places where I was certain to find them. I'd found the first one on top of my purse under the counter behind the cash register.

Neatly handwritten, the note had read:

Dear Miss Cassidy,

I dream of the day when we'll be together forever.

Love, EK

I'd received one on Wednesday and Saturday of the first week, and again on Wednesday and Saturday of the second week. At first, I'd thought it was cute and kind of romantic. But then the notes had started getting more personal . . . and ugly.

Dear Miss Cassidy,

You really shouldn't wear your skirt so short. It gives men the wrong idea about you.

Love, EK

I remember looking around the restaurant that day for the author, tugging at the hem of my skirt and feeling very self-conscious. The next letter was more of a threatening nature.

Dear Miss Cassidy,

The men you smile at would never treat you as nicely as I will. Don't smile at them if you know what's good for you.

Love, EK

About that time, I started getting nervous. I brought one of the notes to a local police officer who frequented the truck stop, and asked him if there was anything he could do to stop the man from writing the letters. He told me that until there was a serious threat, there was nothing he could do. Well, needless to say, that didn't make me feel any better, and the letters continued.

I started receiving them at my house, and even in my locked car. It was really getting to me and I finally decided that since the police weren't doing anything, I would have to.

And so, I packed all my worldly goods into a rented truck and drove until I found a town that looked small and friendly, where everyone knew everyone else and I would be the only stranger. That's how I came to Serendipity, looking for peace and a place I could call home.

I used some of my meager savings to put a deposit on an old farmhouse about a mile outside of town. It was a fixer-upper, but the owner was going to let me rent to own. I didn't want to commit until I was sure I had a job, but I figured that if all went well, I'd be set with a new job, a new life, and no psychos around making me look over my shoulder every five seconds. In Serendipity, I felt like I could breathe for the first time in two months.

"Excuse me, could you help me find the sweet feed for horses?"

"Yes, sir," I said, setting the broom against the wall and, without turning to look at who I'd spoken to, hurrying down the aisle to the spot I'd committed to memory for sweet feed. Scooting a hand truck over next to the stack, I shoved one of the feedbags off the pile and onto the dolly.

"How many did you need?" I asked.

"Two, but I can get that," he said, reaching down to heft one of the fifty-pound bags of feed onto his shoulder as easily as if it were a sack of feathers.

"Sir, let me do that for you. . . ."

As I said the words, my gaze traveled up the sexiest pair of jeans, across a broad, masculine, chambray-covered chest, and into the most gorgeous pair of ice-blue eyes I'd ever seen. His hair was a dark brown, almost black, and his skin was tanned from many hours spent working under the sun. Confronted by the most beautiful specimen of male flesh I'd seen in a long, long time, all I could do was stand there with my mouth open and my heart refusing to beat.

"I'll just carry this out to my truck and come back for the other one."

His words jerked me out of my stupor and I looked in horror at him walking away with the bag of feed.

"Sir! Let me carry that for you."

"I wouldn't think of letting a pretty little thing like you heft a sack of feed for me."

"But, sir—that's my job," I said, looking around worriedly for Mr. Guthrie, hoping he wouldn't see me standing there, arguing with a customer. "This could severely damage my chances of keeping this position, sir."

"And letting you carry a big ol' bag of feed for me would seriously damage my pride," he retorted. Refusing to give up the bag, he was halfway across the feed room floor before I caught up to him.

"Please . . ."

Preparing to plead with the man, I caught a glimpse of Mr. Guthrie at the front of the store, turning in our direction. Before I could stop to think, I jerked the end of the bag off the man's shoulders. Gravity and fifty pounds of momentum worked against me, though, and I staggered backward under the weight of the heavy sack. The edge of another stack of similar bags of feed caught me behind my knees and I knew then that I was doomed.

Landing on my backside on the hard concrete floor, I had the wind thoroughly knocked out of me and the weight of the feed crushed my chest and stomach. I couldn't move, nor could I breathe. Peering around the tall, dark, and handsome stranger standing over me, I could see Mr. Guthrie rushing over, a frown marring his countenance.

"Help me, please," I gasped as soon as I could get sufficient wind in my lungs. Struggling to sit up, I waved my arms and legs futilely in the air like an inverted turtle, helpless and pathetically hopeless.

Rolling his eyes, but seeing my obvious distress, the hunky cowboy lifted the bag off my chest with one hand, extending his other hand to pull me to my feet.

"What's going on here?" Mr. Guthrie demanded, sweat popping out on his forehead, which he promptly mopped with a faded red bandana. "You need some help carrying the feed out, Cole?"

"No, I've got all the help I need right here," he said, smiling at me as I brushed the dust off my backside.

Holding my breath, I waited for him to tell Mr. Guthrie of my disastrous attempt to divest him of his burden. But instead of the expected criticism, I was shocked by his next words.

"Where'd you find such a nice addition to your staff, Rufus?"

The frown cleared from the old man's face, and he smiled. "Hired her today," he said, rocking back on his heels and taking all the credit for having the good sense to give me the chance I'd had to beg him for.

"Sure brightens up the place, if you ask me," Cole said, taking the last few steps to his pickup truck and tossing the bag in.

Suddenly remembering the other bag on the hand truck, I hurried to wheel it out to Cole's truck. Hefting it up to my waist, I could just get it halfway over the edge of the lowered tailgate. With a little more effort, I pushed and shoved until the bag was in the back of the truck right next to the other one. Stepping back, I admired my accomplishment and slapped my hands together. I could do this job, despite Mr. Cole Whatever-his-name-was. Feeling empowered, I walked away from the two men talking contentedly about the weather, cattle prices, and football.

Things were definitely looking up for me.

Later that evening, though, I wasn't so sure. My back ached, my feet were sore, and my car wouldn't start. Fortunately, it'd gotten me all the way out to my house before it decided to conk out. I just needed to figure out what to do with it before the next day, or I'd have to leave awfully early to walk all the way to work on time. Still, my phone wasn't hooked up yet, so all I could do was go to my nearest neighbor's house and ask to use their phone or jumper cables.

At least, that was the theory. Only, it was a good half of a mile to the next house. Knowing I might not find any help in the morning at the red-eyed hour of five-thirty, I bolstered my flagging spirits and set off at a brisk pace.

The December weather was much cooler than I'd expected for south Texas, and I was exhausted by the time I reached my destination. Standing on the porch of my new neighbor's house, I hesitated to knock. It was almost dark outside, and I hated making my first impression in my dirty, sweaty, forlorn state. But it could not be helped. I had to have assistance or I'd be faced with a long, exhausting walk to work the next day. And judging by the way my feet felt right then . . . well, suffice it to say, I wanted to leave that as my last option.

So, raising my hand resolutely, I knocked lightly. When there was no answer, I raised my hand again to knock louder, but before my knuckles met the door, it opened. My immediate reaction of relief sent a smile to my lips—

Until I looked into those ice-blue eyes and realized that the man standing in front of me was Mr. Cole Whatever-his-name-was from the fiasco at the feed store. The one I'd made a complete fool out of myself in front of earlier.

"Well, well, well," he said with a slow, sexy smile. "If it isn't the feed store lady. What brings you to my neck of the woods?"

Great. Just great. New to town and hoping to make this my home, I'd made my first impression with the county's best-looking man less than stellar, and now, I was about to prove my stupidity to him by asking for help with a cranky car. So much for being independent and standing on my own two feet!

"Actually, I'm your neighbor. Do you mind if I use your phone?" I asked.

"Don't mind at all," he replied, stepping back to allow me to enter the old frame house.

Curious, but not wanting to sound too curious, I asked, "Are you sure I won't be disturbing you or your family?" I thought that was a clever way of asking: Are you married? without sounding too obvious.

He smiled his slow, sexy smile again and my knees went weak. "No, ma'am, I'm not married . . . yet," he said, looking me over as if he were considering me as an offering.

Well, I certainly wasn't looking for a husband—even if he was the best thing I'd seen since sliced bread. Damn he was cute. Turning away from him, I looked around the interior of his home. It was a large, old farmhouse with high ceilings and big picture windows. The rooms were open and airy, sparsely, but tastefully, furnished. There was little in the way of decorative touches, but it was inviting and livable just the same, like a home should be.

"The phone is in the living room on the end table by the couch," he said from behind me.

I moved in the direction he indicated, his presence permeating the room, making it hard for me to concentrate on the purpose of my visit. "I also need a phone book, if you have one," I said, turning to look back at him. He was standing so close, I took an involuntary step backward and almost fell over the arm of the couch.

His hand shot out immediately to grab my arm, pulling me up quick against his chest to steady me. Pressed against him like that, I found it difficult to breathe and my head felt light. I put it down to hard physical labor and lack of food. Granted, it was something more, but I refused to let my thoughts go there.

Taking a deep breath, I inhaled the scent of him, all masculine and soapy-clean. My hands rested against the hard, muscled wall of his chest, and I stared at his neck through the opening in his shirt.

My gaze traveled upward. I realized that his lips were only inches away and they looked so . . . kissable. About that time, the corners of his mouth turned up, and I shot a glance to his eyes, where I saw a sparkle of humor. He was laughing at me.

Pushing hard against his chest, I sidestepped away from him, looking around with lifted brows. "Do you have a phone book?" I asked.

"Yes, ma'am. I certainly do." Rifling through the drawers of a nearby desk, he pulled out a thin phone book and handed it to me. "What in particular are you trying to find?"

"Do you know of a good auto mechanic around here?" I asked, flipping to the back of the book in the Yellow Pages.

"As a matter of fact, I know a very good auto mechanic. Why?"

I hated admitting to him that I needed help. He probably already thought that I was a disaster looking for a place to happen, based on our earlier experience at the feed store.

I shrugged. "My car won't start," I said with a sheepish grin.

"Why don't you let me have a look at it? Maybe it's something simple that can be fixed without having to take it into the shop."

"Oh, I couldn't impose on you; I've already interfered enough for one day."

"Hey, we're neighbors now, and what are neighbors for, but to help each other when they're in need? Besides, I'm pretty good with my hands."

I looked at his big, callused hands and thought about things other than cars that those hands would be good with. Shaking out of my errant thoughts, I smiled. "Okay. I'll take you up on that."

"Good," he said.

"Good," I repeated.

He stood a second longer as if I'd argue some more, then he smiled and turned toward the door.

Following him out, I got a good eyeful of a great tush in a sexy pair of jeans. Not a bad view. So what if I'd been driven from home by a scary secret admirer, landed on my can in front of my new boss and the most gorgeous hunk of male in the county—not to mention having my only means of transportation crap out on me? The day was not a total loss if I was going to get to watch as Cole Whatever-his-name-was leaned over the hood of my car. Life had its moments and I was not immune to them.

"You know, it occurs to me that we haven't been properly introduced. My name is Cassidy Roberts," I said, waiting for him to open the door to his pickup truck.

"I'm Cole Kittrick. It's mighty nice to meet you, neighbor."

Standing to the side, he held the door open while I climbed up into the truck. Settling into the seat, I thought about how nice it'd be, not to have to walk all the way back to my house.

"So, what brings you to our little town of Serendipity?" he asked, sliding in behind the wheel of the truck.

"I needed to get away," I replied without thinking.

He glanced sharply at me. "From the law?"

I chuckled. "No, not the law. From a man."

"Not your husband, I hope."

"No, I'm not married," I said, showing him the lack of a ring on my finger. "I had a secret admirer who left me creepy notes."

He frowned. "Must've been bad to cause you to leave. Why didn't you take it to the police?"

"I talked to an officer and he seemed to think that as long as I wasn't being threatened physically, there was nothing they could do."

"So you just up and moved?" His brow furrowed. "That's drastic."

"I didn't have any ties to the place, and I figured it wouldn't hurt to make a fresh start. So, here I am in Serendipity, hoping I can make a home for myself."

"Well, I, for one, am glad you're here. Like I told Mr. Guthrie, you brighten up the place."

"Thank you," I said, suddenly feeling a little shy from the unexpected compliment given in such close proximity. "And what about you?"

"What do you mean?"

"Have you ever lived anyplace else but here?"

"Nope. This is my home; I was born and raised here." He spread his arms wide and shrugged as he drove. "This place is a part of me. Always will be."

"What about family?"

"I have two brothers, a little sister, and both parents are alive and well. Never been married, although I came close once."

"What happened?"

"She decided the town was too small and she hightailed it out of here to the big city the night before our wedding." He shrugged and gave me half a grin.

"I'm sorry," I said softly, although guilty was the real emotion I was feeling. Guilty, because I was glad she'd ditched him. It meant he was available, and for this, I had another emotion emerging— anticipation.

"Don't be. It was a lucky escape, if you ask me."

"How'd you know it was living in the country that made her run?"

"We were at the wedding rehearsal when I told her that I never wanted to live in the city. She asked me if I wouldn't at least consider it someday, and when I said absolutely not, she turned a sickly shade of green."

"And that was the night she left," I finished.

He nodded. "And what about you? You don't look like a girl from a small town."

"I've never lived in a town as small as Serendipity. I've lived most of my life in the big city, but even though your neighbors are physically closer, you never really seem to get to know them. You're too busy beating the rush-hour traffic to and from work and the stress involved leaves you totally exhausted. I like a place where everyone knows everyone else. It's like one big, extended family."

Cole turned toward me and smiled, his eyes twinkling. "That's Serendipity. Everybody knows everybody else's business. You can't keep a secret around here to save your life. Still, I couldn't agree with you more about family. It's so obvious to me that when all else is lost, you still have family—be it immediate or extended. But I think it was more than living in the country that bothered Faith. It was obvious that she didn't really love me."

My heart turned flips in my chest, then lodged in my throat. This guy couldn't be real. He was everything a woman should want. Stealing a glance from beneath my lashes, I looked at him from the tips of his boots to the cowboy hat perched on his head. He was one-hundred-percent, pure, strutting, glorious male.

What's not to love? I wondered. The woman must've been blind, deaf, and an absolute idiot!

Cole chuckled and cast a rueful glance in my direction. I struggled not to drool and be too obvious in my attraction to him. After all, we'd only met that day, and he hadn't made anything even remotely near to a pass at me yet. How could I possibly tell if he even found me desirable?

"So, having been burned once, are you totally against all women now?"

Too late, I'd opened my mouth and asked exactly what I'd been wondering. Immediately, I cringed in the seat next to him, wishing I could take back what I'd said, strike it from the records, and eat the words if I could. I knew it was as bad as just outright asking if I could consider him as being on the marriage market or not.

Pulling into the yard of my house, he shifted the car into park and leaned toward me, his face only inches from mine.

"No, I am not against all women," he said, staring down at my mouth.

I licked my suddenly dry lips.

"A beautiful woman will always appeal," he said, lowering his mouth to mine, teasing me with a feather-light brush of his lips when I wanted so much more. So much that I wrapped my arms around his neck and pulled him closer, deepening the kiss.

One of Cole's hands rested on the small of my back, while the other slipped under the hem of my shirt, smoothing a path up my side to the elastic band of my bra.

I was a goner. His sensual onslaught made me want to jump right out of my skin, much less my clothes.

It was warm in that truck. No, warm wasn't the word for it. Raging inferno came closer to describing the spontaneous combustion triggered by that kiss. But when his fingers found and released the hooks on the back of my bra, a cool waft of air touched the heated skin of my back, having the effect of a bucket of cool water being poured over me.

Jerking away from him, I fumbled for the catch to my undergarment and hooked it back into place without looking at him. Straightening my blouse, I breathed deeply before turning to face him.

My gaze dropped before his. Which left me staring at the evidence of his arousal. I had done that? I was appalled from having teased him, but at the same time, I was feeling a strange sense of power. Wow. I had done that!

Realizing I was staring at an intimate part of his anatomy, my face burned.

"Cassidy, I'm sorry. I had no right to come on to you like that." Raking a hand through his hair, he looked out the front windshield. "I don't know what came over me." Then, tipping his head in my direction, he slanted a crooked grin at me. "No, I take that back. I've wanted to do that ever since I first saw you at the feed store. I couldn't help myself."

His confession left me feeling lighthearted and as giddy as a schoolgirl. "Perhaps we should see to my car, unless you'd rather I called a wrecker service," I said in a shy voice.

"You won't get a wrecker out here at this hour, so let's have a look and see if I can't figure out your problem."

It wasn't fifteen minutes later and some tightened spark plugs, that Cole had my car purring like a kitten.

"You're pretty good at that," I said as he dropped the hood over the engine. "You should own your own auto repair business."

Cole looked at me and rolled his eyes sheepishly.

"Don't tell me," I said, feeling even more foolish in front of him than when I'd been lying on the floor with a sack of feed on my chest. "You're the local auto mechanic, aren't you?"

"Guilty."

"How much do I owe you for your work?"

"Nothing," he said, wiping his hands on a rag he pulled from behind the seat in his truck. "It was just some loose spark plugs."

"Will you at least let me feed you supper? I haven't unpacked all the boxes yet, so it's a mess, and all I have to offer is from a can, but I make a mean canned stew." I knew I was babbling, but I didn't want the evening to end. This guy had found a way under my skin, and I liked it. Correction—I liked him.

"As a matter of fact, I love canned stew. I eat it all the time," he said with a grin, following me into the house.

Over dinner, and coffee, we kept it cool, avoiding any discussion of the kiss in the truck and sticking to safe topics. It was ten-thirty when we happened to look up at the kitchen clock simultaneously.

"Wow, it's that late already?" Cole said, jumping up from the table. "I have an early morning in the shop, as I'm sure you do at the feed store."

Following him to the door, there was so much more I wanted to say, but I settled on, "Thank you for fixing my car."

Turning to stand in the doorway, he lifted my chin with his finger and stared down into my eyes. "Believe me, it was my pleasure."

Leaning toward me, he captured my lips with his and kissed me gently, then turned to leave.

"Can I call you tomorrow?" he called through the window of his truck.

"Yes," I said, and then thought again. "I mean, no. My phone isn't hooked up yet."

"I'll see you tomorrow at the feed store, then."

"Hey, you're all right for a girl," Mr. Guthrie said, after I'd completed cleaning and reorganizing all the shelves of tack and animal medications. "This old place ain't never looked so good."

"Thanks, Mr. Guthrie." Looking over his shoulder, I could see Cole's truck pulling up in front of the store. "If you don't mind, I'd like to take my break now."

"You go right ahead. I can handle the register."

Slapping at the dust on the front of my jeans and chambray shirt, I shrugged. I hoped he didn't mind a girl who got dirty when she worked. Walking outside into the cool December day, I inhaled the crisp, clean air as Cole climbed out of his truck.

He smiled and walked toward me, taking my hand in his before he spoke. "Hi, gorgeous," he said, softly.

Suddenly shy, I answered back, "Hello yourself." This relationship was all so new. I'd only known him for a day, but already, it seemed like much longer.

"Would you have dinner with me at my house tonight? I'll cook," he said, a smile lifting the corners of his mouth, his eyes twinkling.

"What? You don't like canned stew anymore?" I asked, propping a fist on my hip and quirking an eyebrow.

"Oh, no, I love your canned stew. I just thought, since you've just moved here and you're still not unpacked, you could stand a break and to have someone else cook for you."

Smiling at his back-paddling, I nodded. "I'd love to have dinner with you, Cole. What time?"

"How's seven?"

"I'll want to stop by my place to shower and change first; can we make it seven-thirty?"

"That would be great," he said, leaning close as if he'd kiss me, but another customer drove into the parking lot before his lips made contact. Pulling back, he grimaced. "Later," he said, and, squeezing my hand, he turned and left.

Later. That one word held so much promise. I was flying on cloud nine all day long after he'd left. I worked hard and fast, completing each task in record time. By the end of the day, Mr. Guthrie was scratching his head.

"I just can't get over you, little girl. I don't have to wait a week to know when I've got a gold mine. You're hired for good, if you want the job still."

"I'd love it!" I said, throwing my arms around the big guy, hugging him in my enthusiasm.

Mr. Guthrie patted my back, then pushed me away, his face flushed and his countenance flustered. "Now, don't go getting all girly on me. Can't have the customers thinking something's going on between the hired help and me."

"Yes, sir," I said, snapping to attention and executing a sharp salute before relaxing into a grin. "Thanks, Mr. Guthrie. This job means the world to me."

I practically skipped out the door to my car. The giddy feeling of finally being accepted and the anticipation of dinner with a great guy had set me on top of the world.

Pulling into the driveway of my new home, I rushed up the front steps—and came to a dead stop, my heart plummeting into my stomach. A note and a rose were taped to my door.

With my hand shaking, I reached for the note and the seemingly innocent rose. Daring to look over my shoulder, I checked for shadowy figures in the darkness while I fumbled with my keys. Unlocking the door, I threw it open, practically falling through in my haste. Slamming the door closed, I shot home the bolt and ran around the house checking the locks on all the other doors and windows. Every light that could be turned on was on before I finally stopped, allowing my speeding heart to rest. It was then that I unfolded the paper and read the handwritten words.

Dear Cassidy,

I'm so glad I found you. I hope to be seeing a lot more of you soon.

Love, EK

Oh, God, he'd found me.

I sank onto the sofa and hugged a pillow to me, tears forming and coursing down my face. What did I have to do to get rid of this guy? It was so unfair! Just when I'd thought I was going to be okay, this had to happen. Perhaps I should call the sheriff.

Looking around, though, I suddenly remembered that I didn't have a phone yet. It would be another week before the local phone cooperative could get to my order.

The fragrant scent of the rose permeated the air in my living room, reminding me of my fear. Snatching it up, I tossed it into the trash and piled newspapers on top of it to stifle the smell.

Climbing the stairs to the second floor, I stripped out of my dirty clothes and took a quick shower. All of a sudden, I was physically exhausted. I pulled an oversized T-shirt over my head and lay down on the bed, crying myself to sleep.

Bang! Bang! Bang!

The sound startled me awake and I cowered under the covers for a moment before my head could clear and I recognized the sound as someone knocking on my door. Fear clutched my heart and I hesitated, not knowing what I should do.

Bang! Bang! Bang!

"Cassidy! It's me, Cole!"

An overwhelming sense of relief flooded my veins and I leapt from the bed, taking the steps two at a time. I struggled with the locks, then threw the door open, flying into Cole's arms, almost knocking him off his feet.

"Hey, hey! What's all this?" he asked, his arms coming around me as I burst into tears.

"He found me!" I cried into his shirt.

"Who found you?" he asked, attempting to disengage my arms from the death grip around his neck. Pushing me back, he smoothed the hair from my face and tilted my chin up. "Take a deep breath and tell me what happened."

"The secret admirer . . . he found me!" I said, a hiccup shaking my body.

Cole's face hardened and he looked around. "Where is he?"

"I don't know!" I wailed.

"Then how do you know he was here?" he asked, ushering me back into my house and closing the door behind us.

"The note and the rose," I said, leading the way to the table I'd laid the note on. Lifting the offensive scrap of paper between my fingertips, I handed it to him.

The scowl on Cole's face cleared and he gave me a sheepish grin. "Cassidy, this note is from me."

"From you?" I shook my head, not quite grasping his words. "But the rose . . . the initials. I don't understand. . . ."

Cole pulled me into his arms and rocked me, a gentle chuckle rumbling through his chest beneath my ear. "I put the note and the rose on the door." Holding the note under my nose, he continued, "See? It's signed CK."

Looking closely at the scrawling writing, I finally saw that it was a "C," not an "E," like I'd originally thought. But relief turned quickly into anger.

"How could you do that to me?" I stormed, pushing out of his embrace and pummeling his chest with my fists. "You scared the living daylights out of me!"

Grabbing my wrists, Cole halted my attack. "Look at me, Cassidy."

The quiet command in his voice got my attention and I tipped my head back to stare into his eyes.

"I wouldn't have done it if I'd known you'd react this way. I wouldn't do anything to hurt you," he said, running a hand along my cheek. "You scared the crap out of me when you didn't show up at seven-thirty. I imagined all kinds of things, from car wrecks to stalkers. I even thought you might've changed your mind about seeing me."

"Change my mind?" That was the most preposterous thing I'd heard yet. "No, I was just too scared to leave my house! Damn, what a mess." Suddenly feeling foolish, I turned and walked away from him. "You must think I'm a flake."

"A very beautiful flake," he said, walking up behind me to pull me back against his chest. "That guy really has you spooked, huh?"

"Yeah. But I shouldn't have overreacted."

"You had every right," he said, his lips brushing the sensitive skin behind my ear.

My blood stirred, picking up the pace until it was screaming through my veins, causing tingling reactions in multiple parts of my body. I turned in his embrace and, wrapping my arms around his neck, pulled his head down to mine.

"Hold me," I whispered.

Our lips connected and he deepened the kiss, pushing his tongue past my teeth to duel with my tongue. His hands slid lower, slipping under my nightshirt. He kneaded the flesh of my bottom, then roamed across the small of my back, and up my sides to my breasts. It felt sooooo good.

"Too many clothes," he said then, pulling the shirt over my head and tossing it onto the sofa. I stood in nothing but a skimpy pair of bikini panties, feeling incredibly sexy and excited.

My fingers hurried to work the buttons loose on his shirt, tugging it out of the waistband of his jeans and sliding it off his broad shoulders. My hands weaved through the coarse hairs on his chest, pinching the hard brown nipples.

With a breast in each hand and his lips pulling at one of them, Cole stopped and groaned. Before I knew what was happening, he'd swept me up into his arms and carried me up the flight of stairs to my bedroom, closing the door with his foot.

Every night for the next two weeks was the same. We ate dinner, either at his place or mine, and ended up making love into the wee hours. It was tiring, yet exhilarating. I'd never felt so cherished.

December flew by, and before I realized it, Christmas Eve was upon us. I was busily decorating a tree to surprise Cole. We'd spent time at his family's home with all his siblings and various cousins and in-laws that day. After the evening meal, he'd driven to a neighboring town to take his mother to visit his invalid grandmother in the nursing home, and had promised to be back by midnight to spend Christmas with me.

I was missing my parents and feeling a little melancholy, wishing that Cole would hurry back and chase away my loneliness. I'd called my mother and father earlier to wish them a merry Christmas, and the packages they'd sent had arrived in the mail a few days earlier, but the voices and the gifts weren't enough. I wanted to be held.

Sometime after ten, I fell asleep on the sofa while watching the news. I was startled awake by a knock on the door. Leaping to my feet, my happiness carrying me through the house to the door, I pushed back the bolt and flung the door wide.

"I'm so glad you're here—"

My words died in my throat as I stood in shock, staring at a strangely familiar man standing in the darkness of my porch. Stumbling backward over the threshold, I attempted to slam the door shut in his face, but a hand stopped it and forced it back open.

"Who are you?" I demanded, backing away from him.

"Don't you know me? You served me coffee every day for several months."

Suddenly feeling nauseous, I clutched the back of a chair, putting it between us.

"You're EK?" I asked, my voice barely a squeak.

"Bingo, Miss Cassidy. EK—Edward Krall," he said, moving closer until my back was up against the wall. Shoving the chair out of my hands, he grabbed a handful of my hair and lifted it to his nose, inhaling deeply. "You don't know how often I've dreamed of this."

"Get out," I said.

He ignored me, clenching the hair tighter, dragging my head back while his other hand rose to cup one of my breasts. "You're so beautiful . . . and much too good for that man you've been sleeping with."

That scared me even more. This man had been watching my house. He was crazy and I needed to get away before he hurt me.

And then another thought occurred to me. Cole was supposed to be here any minute. If I could just hold on until he arrived... But what would Edward do to Cole? He might hurt him, and I couldn't let that happen. So I had to warn him.

Just then, lights moved slowly down the driveway. Cole. Oh, thank God. Edward didn't notice because his back was to the windows. I knew it was up to me to distract him long enough for Cole to get out of his truck.

Edward's head moved closer to mine in a clumsy attempt to kiss me. The hand holding my hair was pulling so tightly that tears came to my eyes. When he was close enough, I lifted my knee fast and hard, catching him in the groin. The hand loosened in my hair as he doubled over in pain. I was free suddenly and racing out the door before he could regain his balance.

"Cole!" I screamed, launching myself into his arms.

"Wow! I guess you missed me," he said, chuckling in the dark.

"No, Cole—the secret admirer!" I struggled to catch my breath and pointed to the house. "He's in there!"

Grasping my shoulders, Cole shoved me toward his truck. "Get in there and lock the doors. If I'm not back in five minutes, go get the sheriff."

"No, Cole! I don't know if he has a gun!" I wailed, clutching his sleeve.

Cole pulled my hand loose, opened the door to his truck, and pushed me inside. "Stay put."

Obeying his command, I locked the doors and waited, peering through the windshield as Cole moved toward my front door. Rolling the window down enough to listen, I strained to hear what was going on. Minutes felt like hours, but after three long ones, Edward limped out of the house with his arm held twisted behind him by Cole.

"I've called the sheriff; he should be here shortly." Cole's words were punctuated by the sound of a siren screaming up the highway toward us.

When the sheriff had Edward safely handcuffed and tucked in the back of his car, I stood in the shelter of Cole's arms. Before the sheriff closed the door, I could hear Edward.

"He won't love you like I would have, Miss Cassidy."

"Thank God," I said, and turned to embrace Cole.

Arm in arm, we moved toward the house.

"Do you know what day this is?" he asked.

"Christmas Day?"

"Yeah, and the first day of the rest of our lives together, too." Pausing on the porch, he pulled me into his arms. "I love you, Cassidy."

"I love you, too, Cole," I said.

It was Christmas, and I'd finally come home. THE END

COFFEE, TEA—OR ME?
I served myself for dessert to my favorite customer!

"Mommy, Mommy!"

My heart stopped. Usually, I loved hearing my two-year-old daughter call to me, followed by her gurgly giggle, but not tonight.

How can Robbie do this to me? I thought as I turned around to face him.

"Now don't you go getting riled at me, sugar," he said in that southern drawl of his that had started rubbing my nerves raw somewhere between our first anniversary and his fourth straying into another woman's arms. Or was it his fifth? The count was up to ten by the time I finally got my divorce.

"Little Bit saw you when we was passing and wanted her mama. Ain't that right, Little Bit?" He gave his girlfriend a kiss on the cheek while our daughter, Amber, stretched her arms up to me.

My heart ached seeing the longing in my daughter's eyes, but I couldn't risk losing this job. I was refusing to take her, even though it required all my strength to keep my arms by my side.

"I'm working here, Robbie. This is your night to keep her." He'd fought long and hard with the judge for visitation rights, and convinced him that he not only really loved Amber, but would also do right by her as her father. Didn't a little girl need her father's love, after all? He'd even had me convinced.

I'd taken this waitressing job on the weekends to help boost my weekly salary earned at the credit union where I worked days. Robbie gave me only a pittance of support for Amber, and as a single mother, I needed all the extra money that I could earn. With our custody agreement, at least I didn't have to pay a baby-sitter on weekends. But lately, anytime it was Robbie's turn to watch Amber, he found some excuse to get out of it.

Tonight, his latest bimbo stood by his side, her eyes cast down. How long would it take before she saw his true colors, past all the good looks and counterfeit charm? Most women saw through Robbie after a few dates. For some reason beyond my comprehension, though, I hadn't woken up and smelled the coffee until after we were married. As it was, the only good that had ever come out of our temporary union was Amber.

"We got a problem here, Elodie?" the restaurant's manager, Mr. Hunnicutt, said in his "there-better-not-be-a-problem" voice.

"We just came in for a bite to eat," Robbie said as he switched Amber to his other side. "Miss Elodie, here, was going to get us an infant's seat. Wasn't you, Miss Elodie?" He emphasized the "Miss."

Mr. Hunnicutt took several menus from the hostess stand and proceeded to my area, where he seated Robbie and his latest squeeze. I got the infant's chair and placed Amber in the seat while Robbie scanned the menu.

"Can I get you anything?" I asked. Mr. Hunnicutt was still hovering in the background, so I treated them as though they were normal customers—customers I liked.

"What would you like, sweetie?" Robbie leaned over and reached for the slut's hand. I had to give her credit—when she casually moved out of his grasp.

You're not getting any tonight, Robbie, I thought, and hid my smile.

"Pick out something for the kid," he said, turning to me.

"She hasn't eaten?" I was furious. Here it was after eight o'clock, way past Amber's bedtime, and she hadn't even had her supper yet!

"No, she hasn't. She's been a real fusspot all day long. You got her so spoiled. . . ."

Crimson. That was the color swirling in front of my eyes, but I kept my temper. "I'll get her some macaroni and cheese. You want coffee?"

On my return with Amber's food, I grabbed a clean washcloth to wipe her hands. She wasn't particularly good with a fork and spoon yet, and she liked eating with her fingers. Who knew when Robbie had last washed her? If only that judge could see him now.

The next hour was difficult. Amber was overtired and cranky, but she did manage to eat most of her food, including the string beans. I had customers to take care of, though, and every time I went out of her sight, I could hear her whining and fussing. I was cleaning up one of my stations when a regular customer asked me a question. I was so tuned into my daughter that I didn't even hear what he said.

Automatically, I reached for the coffeepot.

"I've had my fill," he said, placing a hand over his cup immediately. I caught myself just in time before I poured the hot liquid on his hand.

"Did you want something else?" I asked, feeling embarrassed.

"Cute kid." He nodded his head in Amber's direction.

I smiled—the first since Robbie had come in. "Yes, she is."

"Yours?"

"Is it that obvious?"

He grinned. "I'd say she was cloned. She's going to be a beautiful girl when she grows up, just like her mama." With that, he got up, threw down a tip, and took his check up to the cashier.

What a nice thing to say, I thought as I cleared his table. I'd always believed that Amber got her good looks from her father. And this guy was a good tipper, too. He'd been a regular ever since I started working here more than a month ago, but I'd never paid much attention to him before. Ever since my divorce from Robbie, men hadn't ranked high on my list of interests. Now, though, I watched the tall, lean man walk to the register and decided that I'd try and be more sociable the next time he came in.

"You leaving soon?" Robbie asked me as I went back to check on Amber. She was listing to one side in the infant's seat, catching herself with a jolt, still trying hard not to fall asleep. I could tell she was exhausted, having gone way past her bedtime. I felt totally out of control. I wanted so much to be able to just take her away from Robbie, walk out, and never look back. Unfortunately, under the circumstances, it was nothing more than a fantasy.

"I'm not done till after ten. Why?"

"Because I got things to do, places to go, and this," he said, nodding in Amber's direction, "is really cramping my style."

"You're the one who insisted on joint custody."

"Well, Jenna don't much like kids."

"Who's Jenna?"

The woman next to him cleared her throat. For little more than a second, we made eye contact before she became fascinated with some spot on the Formica table.

"This kid business was never my idea," Robbie continued.

"No? Since when?" My voice rose as I placed my hands on my hips. Out of the corner of my eye, I noticed the customer at the register watching us. The last thing I needed right now was a scene that would draw more attention.

"Listen, sweetheart, you was the one who wanted to get knocked up. I just obliged." Robbie reached for Jenna's hand, and this time, she didn't pull away. "I can be real obliging, can't I, honey?" he said as he nuzzled her hand.

For one second, I closed my eyes and controlled the nausea that threatened.

My eyes flew open the moment Mr. Hunnicutt said, "We got a problem here, Elodie?" only inches away from my ear.

"No, sir." Hastily, I grabbed several empty cups from the table. "They were just leaving."

"I'll bring in her things," Robbie said as he got up and started for the door.

"What? I can't take her." I heard the panic in my voice as Robbie disappeared out the door with Jenna right behind him. Amber lay slumped over in her seat, unwilling to hold her head up any longer. I felt limp, unable to withstand the pressures that were piling up on me. I sank dejectedly into the booth.

Mr. Hunnicutt leaned over and breathed heavily by my ear. "I'm shorthanded, Elodie. You take off on me now and you can just kiss this job good-bye, you hear?"

"He'll be back," I said, unable to believe that Robbie would sabotage me again. I pulled Amber from her contorted position and held her tightly in my arms. "I'm taking my break. I still get one of those, don't

I?"

"Ten minutes. And you'd be better off spending the time calling someone to come get the kid." Mr. Hunnicutt started for the cash register, then made a quick return. "And you're paying his tab if he doesn't come back, you hear?"

I don't know how long I sat there, staring at the door while I slowly rocked Amber to sleep. I sensed Mr. Hunnicutt's disapproval, but I couldn't function. What was I going to do, after all? I couldn't afford to lose this job, and yet I had no one who could take care of Amber on such short notice. As much as I'd resented Robbie's insisting on joint custody, I'd come to rely on the times when he'd take her.

Robbie never returned. Instead, my former customer came in through the door pushing a stroller piled high with several bags. It took a moment before I recognized Amber's things. I stood up as he approached.

"Looks like she's conked out for the night. She can sleep in this, can't she?"

He removed the diaper bag and small suitcase and dropped the back of the stroller into a reclining position. Gingerly, I placed her in it so that she could stretch out.

"No customers in this corner," he said, and rolled her toward an empty table.

Mr. Hunnicutt quickly came over. "You're not leaving her there."

"No problem," my Good Samaritan said as he adjusted the stroller top to keep out the light. "I plan to stay right here and watch her." He sat down in one of the wooden-backed chairs and spread a newspaper across the table. "Could you bring me a cup of coffee, Elodie?"

My mind was a jumble. Could I trust this stranger? Still, what possible harm could come to my daughter in plain view of the few remaining customers? Especially since I'd be able to keep an eye on her myself.

For that matter—what other choice did I have?

I didn't wait for Mr. Hunnicutt's approval. In record time, I poured a cup and delivered it to my newest baby-sitter.

"What's your name?" I figured he knew mine from my nametag, and

I should know his, seeing as how he was doing me a personal favor.

He looked at me strangely for a moment before answering, "Mason."

"Thanks, Mason," I said before returning to my job.

I kept one eye on Amber while I worked and even figured out a few fast moves that I'd try if Mason decided to take her and run. Every tragic story I'd ever seen on the late news had me anxiously aware of how a child could disappear in an instant. Fortunately, my shift was completed without any further complications.

The moment I was through, I headed for the table. With a nod in my direction, Mason folded his newspaper, got up, paid for his coffee, and was out the door before I even had a chance to speak to him.

I left bewildered. Why hadn't he stuck around so I could thank him? Was he annoyed with me, or himself for having volunteered most of his evening away?

When I finally got home and into bed, sleep was a long time coming. I tossed and turned, wondering how I'd handle Robbie's latest maneuver. The divorce was supposed to rid him from my life so I wouldn't have to deal with his erratic behavior anymore.

Then my thoughts turned to the stranger who'd befriended me. Would Mason ever return to the restaurant so that I could thank him, or had tonight's events destroyed that possibility?

A week went by, and when Robbie didn't show up on Friday to pick up Amber, I didn't go into a panic. I'd already made arrangements with my mother to come over and watch her. Not that I wanted my mother to spend a great deal of time with my daughter. Mom hadn't done a particularly good job of raising me.

After my parents divorced when I was twelve, my mother decided that finding another mate was more important than taking care of a teenage daughter. Of course, I wasn't the easiest person to get along with. I hated every man she brought to the house to replace my dad. That's probably why I was such an easy target for Robbie—I wanted out of that house so much that I'd have gone off with anyone who'd offered me a roof over my head.

Now that my mom's remarried to a guy named Jasper who isn't half bad, she has a new attitude on life. She dotes on Amber, and I think in some ways, she's trying to make up for all of the bad times during my teens. Anyway, I sure do appreciate it when she's able to baby-sit for me.

"I brought over my own snacks," she said as I dressed in my small bedroom. I heard the refrigerator door open in the kitchen. "Everything you have is either something for Amber or healthy food. I don't know how on *earth* you're able to exist on salads."

"I'm sorry, Ma. You know I eat most of my meals at the restaurant. Want me to bring you home some pie? They make pretty good apple."

"Sounds great. And what do you want me to do if Robbie comes by? I can always ask Jasper to come over after he's finished bowling, if you think it could be a problem."

"It shouldn't be. Besides, he's supposed to watch her on weekends, so she can go with him." I flipped my overly long hair around so I could keep it in a neat French twist. "But if he comes too late after Amber's asleep, don't let him in. No sense in disturbing her. Just tell him he can pick her up in the morning."

"He's not the violent type, is he? You got anything handy so I can defend myself?"

I walked back into the large kitchen that also served as dining area and living room. Amber was on her little rocker, reading her newest storybook. She made up her own story in baby talk as she went from page to page. Mom would have to spend most of the night rereading the pages over and over again to keep her happy.

"No. I haven't seen him violent."

"Not even when he's drunk?"

I knew she was thinking about my father. "No. When Robbie drinks, he gets stupid. Most of his problems come from saying the wrong thing, actually. But if you can see he's been drinking, don't let him take Amber."

"I'm calling Jasper."

"Do what you want, Ma. I'll be home sometime after ten, unless we get a late crowd."

Although I kept an eye out, I hadn't seen Mason since he'd baby-sat for me the previous Friday. When he finally did show up that night, I wasn't quite sure how to act. He didn't give me any more than a nod to acknowledge my presence. So maybe he'd forgotten all about baby-sitting my daughter.

When I brought his coffee over, he took out a newspaper and spread it across the table. Hesitantly, I said, "I wanted to thank you for last Friday, but you disappeared before I could."

He looked up and smiled, showing off a hint of a dimple, and said, "No problem." He returned to his paper immediately, and I wondered what had happened recently in the news that could be so fascinating.

Well, since he showed no interest in pursuing the subject, I wasn't about to make him uncomfortable by gushing over his good deed. A half an hour later, I was handing him his check when in walked my ex. I sucked in my breath and tried to control my rising resentment.

"What? No baby this time?" Mason's voice, so close to my ear, shocked me back into functioning again.

"Um, no," I said as I hurriedly cleared his table. "She's with my mother."

He tucked his paper under his arm and headed for the cash register. As Robbie maneuvered toward me, he had to pass Mason, and I noticed how much space the man took up, forcing Robbie to sidestep to get out of his way. Robbie stopped, turned, and glared after the man, but Mason continued on as though he was totally unaware of his actions.

"Jerk," Robbie said as he plopped down in the same booth that Mason had just vacated. "Hey, sugar. Rustle me up some eggs the way I like them, will you? I don't have much time."

"You don't have to hurry. Amber's already in bed. Mom's watching her tonight."

"What are you talking. . . ." He slapped his forehead and ran his hand down over his face, momentarily pushing his perfect features into wrinkles. "Tonight's my night, huh?"

"Yes, tonight's your night. And tomorrow's your day and tomorrow night's your night again. Don't you remember? You wanted the weekends so you could help raise our daughter."

I'd started for the kitchen with an armload of dirty dishes when his hand came out and grabbed my arm.

Crash!

Silverware skittered under the table and broken glass mixed with the scraps of food on the floor. The heavy porcelain plate that hit the floor spun and vibrated loudly before finally coming to a rest. At least it didn't break.

Immediately, I crouched down to take care of the mess. That's when I saw a pair of worn cowboy boots stop by the table. I looked up just as a hand reached under my arm and pulled me to a standing position.

"Why don't you get a broom?" Mason said in a gentle voice. His face was expressionless, and the cold stare he directed at Robbie made me shudder. It didn't exactly delight my ex, either. Mr. Hunnicutt was headed for our table on the double.

"What's going on?" he asked.

"This gentleman accidentally knocked over the dishes and was just about to help Elodie pick them up. Weren't you?" The tone Mason used on Robbie could've brought a drill sergeant to attention.

"It was an accident," Robbie choked out, and immediately dropped to the floor, kneeling in French fries and ketchup. "But I'll help." Robbie had never been much of a fighter; he was probably afraid that someone would punch out his looks. But I was surprised to see how quickly he gave in to Mason.

I ran to get a broom and concentrated on breathing in and out, something I'd forgotten to do when the dishes went flying. I wasn't used to *anyone* coming to my aid, and I wasn't too sure that I liked it. Robbie might be compliant now, but I knew I'd hear about it later when Mason left.

And I did.

"What the—" Robbie sputtered when the mess was cleared away and Mason had gone. He plopped down in a seat and pounded the table with his fist. "He your new boyfriend or somethin'?"

"No, I—"

"I remember him. He's the guy that took Amber's stroller from me last Friday. You foolin' around? Because if you are, I'm tellin' my lawyer. You ain't no fit mother and the judge is gonna hear!"

"Oh, button it up, Robbie," I said, my hands on my hips. "Where do you get off saying I'm not fit? *You're* the one fooling around with anything in a skirt. And you're the one who's not living up to the agreement the judge handed down."

"You doing it with him?"

I shook my head in disgust and walked away from him. As I passed by Mr. Hunnicutt, I told him that I was taking my break.

Another rotten Friday. I doubted if I could handle any more.

Except for the few times when Robbie called to ask if I was sleeping around, the week went by without incident. I thought about Mason on several occasions, mostly wondering what was going on in his brain. Why had he been willing to butt heads with Robbie over those dishes? Why had he volunteered to watch Amber? Didn't he have a wife and kids of his own to care for? I really couldn't understand why he showed such interest in helping me, and yet, aside from when he ordered his meals, never spoke to me. Needless to say, by the time that third Friday came around, my interest was certainly aroused.

When Robbie came for Amber, he asked, "You seein' him tonight?"

Of course, I knew exactly who he was talking about when I answered, "Who?"

"Who? You know who. That guy that's sweet on you. That's who."

"No guy's sweet on me."

"Oh, no? Well, he tries pushin' me around again and I won't be so nice, you got me? Next time, I'll punch his lights out."

"There won't be any next time, Robbie," I said, trying to keep my voice low so my daughter wouldn't get upset. I sent her after her favorite stuffed toy so I could get a few things off my mind. "And you're not coming to the restaurant with Amber anymore. I spoke to my lawyer, and he says that if you're not fulfilling your end of the bargain, he'll take our case right back to the judge."

"Well, we'll just see about that. If I want to take my daughter to a restaurant, it's my business."

"Fine. Take her to one, if you like," I said, raising my voice. "Just don't take her to mine."

"Why? You wanna be alone with your latest lover?"

"Oh, get off it, will you? I don't even *know* the man. Furthermore, you've pretty much ruined it for me with other men."

I could see his little smile, and I knew where his thoughts were headed. Robbie still considered himself the answer to every woman's needs, the consummate lover.

I hurriedly continued, "I figure you're all pretty much the same—not worth the aggravation."

Amber came back then, and I gave her a kiss. She promised to be good, and I controlled my desire to pick her up and hold her forever. No matter how hard I tried, I just couldn't get used to her going off with her daddy.

Despite my remarks to Robbie, I looked forward to my shift that night. Maybe Mason would come in, and I'd have the opportunity to draw him into a conversation.

He certainly wasn't anything like my ex. I figured the man was a good five-to-ten years older than I was, and had probably seen more of life. He was clean cut, but he didn't have the dynamite looks that turn a lady's head. But then, I'd found out the hard way: Looks aren't worth a darn.

I saw Mason enter the restaurant near the end of my shift. I'd been watching for him all night, and I guess I smiled at him. Anyway, he stopped, backed against the door, and looked like he was about to take off for the parking lot.

Well, you can guess how that made me feel. Like I'd just sprouted horns and come down with a contagious disease. Quickly, I returned my attention to the booth in front of me and concentrated on removing an invisible spot from the Formica tabletop.

Out of the corner of my eye, I watched Mason waver. Finally, he decided to sit in a booth—but not one of mine. Since we weren't busy, I was able to finish up and head home early for a change. But I hesitated. What was with this guy? Why was he avoiding me? I couldn't go home until I knew.

Mason was finishing his coffee and reaching for his check when I plopped down across from him in his booth.

"How come," I asked, placing my arms on the table and leaning toward him, "you come on like gangbusters one minute, and dodge me the next?"

Without looking at me directly, he said, "I don't want to start anything."

I sat back. "Start what?"

He looked at me then with some very attractive, warm brown eyes. "Anything between you and me."

"Listen, mister," I said, getting to my feet, "I'm not interested in 'starting' anything with any man—now, or ever. So you can just rest easy and sit in my section without the fear of my throwing myself at you."

He didn't respond. Instead, he stared past me toward the restaurant's entrance. Instinctively, I felt the turbulence forming behind me.

"He's here, isn't he?" I asked in a soft whisper.

Mason got up and threw down a tip. "Yes." He started for the front, pushing me gently out of his way. When Robbie tried to move past him, Mason maneuvered so that he couldn't get by.

"Hey," Robbie said, and pushed Mason away from him.

"Is that an apology?"

"Apology for what? You pushed me first."

"Gentlemen, gentlemen," Mr. Hunnicutt said, rushing over. "Please take it outside. This is a family restaurant."

I hurried to the front, concerned—but not for the two lunkheads getting ready to brawl like juveniles. "Where's Amber?" I asked.

"Jenna's watching her."

"Where?"

"In the car."

"The car! She should be sleeping in her crib, Robbie!"

"That's what I want to talk to you about." He bumped his arm into Mason again.

I put a hand on Mason's shoulder to prevent him from retaliating.

"It's okay, Mason. I can take Amber home with me."

"You sure?"

I felt totally baffled by his attitude. If he didn't want anything to happen between us, why had he immersed himself in my problems again?

I nodded and turned my attention to Robbie. "I'm telling my lawyer. If you can't fulfill your end of the bargain, you won't get her on the weekends anymore."

Robbie turned to Mason, who still hadn't budged. "This conversation is private. You mind?"

Mason looked at me for confirmation, then went over to pay his check.

Robbie directed me toward a table and sat down facing me. "So you are seeing him," he stated as though it were fact.

"No, I'm not, and this conversation is about *you*, not me. Why isn't Amber at your place in bed where she belongs?"

"Because Jenna and me are getting' married." He paused for a moment to let that sink in. "We're headed for Vegas."

"Not with my daughter, you aren't!" That's all I could think of—my daughter's welfare. Robbie marrying a woman he knew less than a month had no significance for me except for how it would affect my daughter.

"That's why I'm here. I told you Jenna don't like kids. And . . . well . . . if we get married, I can't be taking Amber on the weekends no more."

I sat back as this revelation sunk in. Thank goodness for Jenna.

"So you're going to do this all legally—actually withdraw your joint custody plea?"

"Well, yeah—I mean, I got it all written down here." He pulled out a neatly typed, signed piece of paper with all the spelling correct— obviously not done by him. "I still wanna see Little Bit whenever I can, but it won't be so regular or overnight. I'm moving into Jenna's place, and she don't want any crib for the baby. You agree to that?"

"I'll take it up with my lawyer. As it is, you'll probably have to sign other papers. But, sure, you're her father; I'll try and arrange for you to see her whenever possible."

I felt all bubbly inside, thrilled that I'd no longer have to deal with Amber going away for the weekends. And I felt almost grateful toward Robbie for stepping out of our daughter's life, even though I couldn't understand how he could possibly do it. I knew I could never walk away from her, no matter how much I cared for another person.

The air in the parking lot was warm and humid with summer coming. Once I'd placed Amber in her car seat, I glanced around the parking lot, expecting to see Mason. I felt disappointed when I didn't, which was really silly of me. I didn't want to start anything between us any more than he did, and yet I couldn't help wishing. . . .

I started the car and headed home, calling myself all kinds of dumb names that included stupid, jerk, and idiot. After all, I finally had what I wanted—my daughter all to myself and my ex finally out of my hair.

So why on earth had another man started to look attractive to me? Stupid, stupid, stupid!

The whole summer went by and Mason never showed up again at the restaurant.

Robbie was true to his word, though, and I was finally granted full custody of Amber. He called a few times and came over to see her on her third birthday, but by the end of August, Jenna was pregnant. I wondered what her attitude toward children would be once she had her own.

I still checked every customer who came in through the door, expecting to see Mason again. When he finally did show, my heart took on an erratic pulse.

Once he sat in my section, I went over to his booth with the coffee pot.

"So, what kept you away so long?" I asked as I poured him a cup. "Working a cruise ship around Cape Horn or serving a prison term at the county jail?"

He looked up and grinned, showing off that dimple in his cheek. "Miss me, Elodie?"

Those warm, brown eyes . . . I'd dreamt about them for months. Of *course* I'd missed him.

"You kidding? With my busy schedule, I don't have *time* to miss anyone. Need a menu?"

He ordered a cheeseburger and spread out his newspaper. I was dismissed.

"How's your little girl?" he asked when I returned with his order. He folded his paper and placed it to one side.

"Fine. Amber's three now and starting nursery school. She can recite her ABC's." I paused for only a moment before asking, "So how's your wife and kids?"

I'd caught him off guard. For a moment, he merely stared at me.

"Fine," he said finally, and picked up his cheeseburger. I was dismissed again.

Usually, I ask a customer if he wants dessert, but I felt so depressed at learning that Mason had a wife and kids that I didn't want to speak to him again. Ridiculous. I mean, I didn't really *know* Mason at all, and he hadn't shown up for months. And, for all I knew, the guy really *could* have spent that time in jail. And yet here I was, moping, dropping his check on the table without even asking if he wanted some pie.

And we made darn good pie.

When Mason showed up the following Friday, I hoped he'd sit in someone else's section, but he took his usual booth.

"What can I get you tonight?" I asked as I poured his coffee.

"How about some conversation?"

"Sorry. It's not on the menu."

I'd spent the week calling myself stupid again for getting upset over him showing up, and I didn't need another week of depression. Besides, he was the one who'd said that he didn't want anything starting between us. And now that I knew he was married, I completely agreed.

"Isn't your shift almost over?"

"Yes. And then I go home to my daughter." I avoided eye contact. I wanted to steer clear of that mushy feeling I got when I looked into his eyes.

"I thought your ex takes her on the weekends."

"Not anymore. I have full custody." He hadn't touched his coffee. "You want something else?" When he didn't answer, I looked at him. Definitely the wrong move.

How could anyone make me crumble with a look—a stranger, no less?

"Yeah. Give me some pie. Whatever you have is fine."

As I headed back to the counter, I nearly bumped into Mr. Hunnicutt.

"The guy in my booth wants some pie, any kind. Can you have one of the other girls handle it? My shift is over and I have to get home so my baby-sitter can leave."

"Sure, Elodie."

Mr. Hunnicutt wasn't such a bad guy, after all.

I headed out the back way.

"So where's my pie?" my mother asked when I got home.

I smacked my hand against my forehead. "Oh, Ma, I forgot."

"That Mason show up again?"

"Yeah."

"Bad news, sweetie. You just got rid of one bad apple. You don't need another."

Her remark made me chuckle. "You're right, Ma," I said as I gave her a squeeze. We'd become friends over the summer, and I was finally learning to appreciate her wisdom, something I hadn't seen in my teenage years.

I dreaded the following Friday. Since Mason usually came in after nine, I considered asking one of the other waitresses to cover me for my last hour. Wouldn't you know it, though—we were shorthanded again, and I couldn't leave early.

Mason showed up close to ten. He didn't take a booth. Instead, he stood talking to Mr. Hunnicutt at the counter—and watching me. My nerves were so raw, I nearly spilled coffee on one of my regulars.

"Can we talk?" Mason asked when I had to pass by him. When I didn't answer, he continued, "And please don't pull that disappearing act again. I just have a few things to say. It won't take much time."

I nodded. "Meet me outside." I figured it would save me some humiliation if other people couldn't overhear our conversation.

A few minutes later when I came out to the parking lot, I found him leaning against a white pickup, his arms folded across his chest. He straightened as I approached and put his hands in his pockets.

"How's your wife and kids tonight?" I asked.

"My two boys are fine. I talked to them today, and according to them, my ex-wife's doing just fine, too. Thanks for asking."

"You're not married?" I placed my hand over my heart to still its wild beat.

"Haven't been for over five years." He pulled his hands out of his pockets as he walked over to stand by me. He started playing with a strand of hair that had come loose from my French twist, gently tucking it behind my ear.

Whenever had I grown nerve endings in my hair?

"My boys stay with her and her new husband most of the time. I get them for vacations and summers."

"So this summer. . . ."

"This summer we stayed at a cabin I have at the lake."

"Don't you work?"

"I'm a teacher. I have summers off."

"Oh." The word came out in a soft murmur, and then I couldn't think of anything else to say. It certainly explained why he hadn't been around.

"So, do you work all the time, or do you have days off?" he asked suddenly.

"I . . . why?"

"Because I'd like to ask you out—take you to a movie, a zoo—whatever."

"A date?"

"Yes."

"Now wait," I said, tapping the button on his shirt. "You said you didn't want to get involved with me. Dates can get you involved, you know."

He took in a deep breath and captured my hand in his. It felt warm...

and nice . . . and right.

"I said that because I wanted very much to get involved with you, but I was afraid it would complicate my life. Besides, I wasn't sure how you felt about your ex. I thought that maybe you wanted to get back with him."

I made a face and Mason laughed—a nice sound—one that I could really get accustomed to . . . grow to love.

"So now you want to complicate your life?"

When he nodded, I knew that Robbie hadn't spoiled me for men, after all. Mason was someone I'd enjoy getting to know, and this time, for all the right reasons. THE END

SEXY BUNS—AND HE'S NAKED IN MY KITCHEN!
What more could a woman possibly want?

"I can't tell you how much I appreciate you fitting me in," I said, leading the tall, muscular fellow down the narrow hallway to my kitchen. "Molly told me you were booked up till Christmas, so I really didn't expect you to make time for me this quickly."

"Happy to help." He rolled his shoulders. "Once I heard all the problems you were having around here—and well, once Molly explained your situation—it was just a matter of shuffling jobs around."

My situation.

His words scraped my senses like nails on a blackboard. I didn't want him feeling sorry for me . . . I didn't want anyone feeling sorry for me, for that matter. I felt I'd done a good job of getting on with my life since Tyler's death. Sure, some nights were long, but my thoughts were usually wrapped around our happy years—our teenage years—and not what we could have had.

"Well, thanks, Vinnie," I said, and flashed him the same smile I used with customers at work.

He was the handyman my cousin, Molly, and her all-thumbs husband couldn't live without. He was going to help me spruce up my tired little house for as long as my four thousand dollars held out.

"Like a lot of people," I went on, "I let things at home get away from me. Anyway, I guess suddenly, the negatives just outweighed the positives."

"I'll start with the walls," he said, and reached up to run his hand along an obvious crack.

I tried not to notice the display of hard muscles and tendons. I really tried.

"Spackling, fixing the holes, repairing the plaster. And then a new coat of paint."

"Sounds good. I'll leave you my work number."

"Work number? I didn't know you went back to work."

"I never quit." I fought the urge to put my hands on my hips. I was *not* some helpless little female—regardless of the way I'd let the house deteriorate. "I've been front desk manager at the Cedar Retreat Hotel for about five years now."

His gaze roamed over my face. I couldn't quite explain the warmth that heated my cheeks, or the swirl of nerves that rose from the pit of my stomach. But I felt the strong compulsion to elaborate on my independence, to let him know that I wasn't just Tyler's widow, or Keith Corsair's girlfriend. I was Jewel Eliot, and I had an identity of my own.

"I like working," I said. "And I'm hoping to transfer someday to another department to take on some new challenges and earn more money."

"Speaking of money, Molly told me you were paying with an insurance settlement."

Well, he certainly didn't beat around the bush!

"Yes, reimbursement from a car break-in, actually."

"Oh. I thought it had something to do with your late husband."

"I used his life insurance to pay off the mortgage." I opened my arms expansively. "This place may be a dump, but it's all mine."

Vinnie shrugged. "It won't be a dump when I'm finished with it."

"Well, I'm glad to hear it." I scribbled my work number on the pad next to the phone and walked out the door.

I didn't turn around. I didn't steal a peek in the windows as I pulled out of the driveway. But my house felt different with him in it. Warmer—more pleasant, somehow. And although I didn't plan to spend much time with the man himself, I couldn't shake the feeling that hiring Vinnie was the best thing I'd done for myself in a long while.

"Jewel, you're late," my boss said, and tapped his wristwatch.

"Sorry. The handyman started today, and I needed to show him around."

Keith Corsair had been my supervisor for as long as I'd been at the hotel, and my lover for the past three months. His long-standing marriage had dissolved when his wife pitched him out last summer, and now he divided his free time between his teenaged kids and me.

I'd been flattered when Keith suddenly asked me out. Although old enough to be my dad, he was distinguished looking and treated his employees fairly. We'd had some good times together, eating leisurely dinners at his favorite restaurants, watching movies back at my place, and snuggling up close.

Our sex life wasn't much to get excited about, but I'd come to believe that sex between adults didn't have the same molten fire as teenage backseat groping. And that the ladies' room talk of leisurely lovemaking and multiple orgasms was just that—talk. *No one* was having as much fun as they pretended.

"Well, all right." Keith patted me paternally. We made no secret of our romance, but we were careful to remain professional and discreet at work. "Just don't let it happen again, okay? We've been one clerk short for about fifteen minutes."

"Sorry," I said, and grimaced. "I'll be more careful."

We were swamped with checkouts that morning and I didn't get a break until lunchtime. Even then, in order to compensate for my lateness, I simply gobbled a bagel and returned to work.

"Phone's for you," my coworker, Elaine, said. "Someone named Vinnie."

My heartbeats hurtled into high gear. If I'd stopped to consider my reaction, I would've insisted that I expected bad news. Or, at least— expensive news. But in truth, a smile was tugging at the corners of my mouth when I picked up the phone.

"Sorry to bother you at work," came the deep voice over the line, "but we didn't get specific about the spackling. What kind of texture do you want? Smooth, or dimpled?"

I laughed out loud. "I haven't the slightest idea."

"You haven't?"

"Just do whatever is going to look the nicest."

"Nicest? Spackling isn't nice, Jewel."

"Well, neither is interrupting me at work with questions like these." As soon as the words were out of my mouth, I regretted them. "Vinnie," I said, and swallowed urgently, "I'm sorry. I didn't mean that."

"Hey, no problem."

The line went dead then—and so did something inside of me. Darn!

How could I have been so rude, so *insensitive?*

At the stroke of five, I grabbed my purse.

"Can you stick around for a drink?" Keith asked, and nudged me gently.

I was tempted. Sort of. But mostly, I felt like I needed to get home. To apologize again to Vinnie. And to pretend to care about the way he spackled.

His truck was still in front of my house when I drove up. Adrenaline raced through my veins as I rushed inside.

Vinnie's eyes were heavily hooded as he glanced down at me from the top of his ladder. "Do you like it? I finished spackling and went with a test wall of Navajo White. I wasn't sure if it was the shade you wanted, but I didn't want to bother you again at work."

"It's perfect. And Vinnie, about that phone call. . . ."

His gaze locked onto mine. "My mistake. I won't do it again."

"No," I said, and watched him climb down to my level. "I gave you the number. There was no excuse for me being so sharp with you."

"You're the customer. The customer's always right." His smile put another kick in my adrenaline rush.

"Anyway, I'm checking out of here, all right? See you tomorrow."

He turned to walk off.

I reached out to grab his arm, to stop him. But absolutely nothing of consequence came to mind to say. I realized I'd look like an absolute fool—worse than I did already.

"Okay," I managed. "See you, then."

The next morning, I greeted him with a pot of coffee, bacon, and pancakes. Although he walked in with a go-cup of java, he straddled a kitchenette chair and accepted a heaping plate of food.

"I'm surprised you have the fixings for a hot breakfast," he said between bites. "I thought single women just ate stuff like yogurt and fruit."

I did, but I wasn't going to let him get away with the sexist comment. "You're stereotyping." But then I remembered I was trying to make amends. "And, besides, my boyfriend likes a hearty breakfast, so I keep eggs and bacon around for him."

His fork froze midair. "Boyfriend?"

"Yeah, Keith. He's my boss, too. But we've been seeing each other outside of work for a few months now."

"Why isn't he helping you fix up the place, then?"

"I never asked." *And,* I continued silently, *he never offered.*

"I suppose he doesn't know a lug nut from a nail."

"I honestly don't know."

Vinnie frowned. "That answers my question."

I glanced at the clock. "Well, speaking of Keith, I don't want to be late two days in a row."

"No, don't want to keep the boss waiting. I mean, the boyfriend."

I could swear I'd heard a tinge of resentment in his tone. But that made no sense. Why would Vinnie care about what role Keith played in my life?

He moved to put his dishes in the sink. As he glanced out the kitchen window, I stole a couple of quick peeks at his tight, perfect derriere.

"Stop looking at my butt," he said suddenly.

My pulse went wild. "I'm not," I lied.

"You are now." He glanced over his shoulder at me.

"Of course I am *now*," I heard myself say, still staring. "And if you told me not to think about purple elephants, I'd do that, too."

Vinnie turned. His attractive backside against the counter, his smile was so vibrant that it touched his eyes. "Don't think about elephants at work today. Think about me."

"Whatever for?" I asked, hoping he didn't detect the catch in my voice.

He shrugged. "Why not?"

Elaine filled me in on the latest details about her upcoming wedding during a coffee break that day.

"It sounds like it's going to be perfect, Elaine. I'm so happy for you."

"Thanks. Invitations are going out next week, and of course, you'll be getting one. And Mr. Corsair, too." A shadow seemed to cross her face. "I hope you don't have a problem with this, but I'm inviting his wife. She's a family friend, remember—the one who got me hired here to begin with."

"Of course," I said, and smiled. "There's no tension between Mrs. Corsair and me. It's not like he's left her for me or anything."

Elaine matched my grin. But hers looked forced, somehow. Phony.

Keith asked me to dinner that evening and I couldn't think of a reason not to accept. So, I called Vinnie and told him to lock the place up when he was done.

"I'm going to be late," I told him.

"I hope he's taking you someplace nice, Jewel."

"I didn't say what I was doing or with whom, Vinnie."

"Well, you deserve the best," he said. "Just make sure you're getting it."

My thoughts reeled. I'd hired a handy man and gotten a guidance counselor in the mix!

"See you tomorrow, Vinnie."

"Yeah. What's for breakfast?"

"Probably cold cereal."

"Girl food."

"Hey, you can always eat before you come over."

He chuckled. "Better yet, I'll take care of breakfast. Just make sure the back door is open by seven, okay?"

I had a vision of him in tight jeans and my pink cooking apron . . . some morning stubble on his chin and cheeks from a hasty shave.

"It's a deal."

I must've kept smiling after I hung up because Keith moved in close.

"What's so amusing?" he asked, and slipped his arm around my shoulder.

I fought the urge to shrug his arm away, to stay in the moment. "Oh, the handyman's cooking me breakfast in the morning."

"Breakfast? What's his story?"

I explained how Vinnie worked for my cousin and numerous other people doing odd jobs.

"That's not what I meant, Jewel. What's his interest in you?"

I dismissed Keith's concern with a wave of my hand. "Oh, we're just friends. Actually, I think he feels sorry for me. The poor widow and all."

Keith frowned. "Just make sure he knows you aren't a *lonely* widow."

"I told him all about you." I put my hand inside his. I hadn't seen him jealous before. In truth, before his wife threw him out, I hadn't seen him so much as look *twice* at me. So it was sort of nice to see this display of affection now. Even if it *was* rather backhanded.

We ate at a local seafood restaurant and were waited on by his old friend. The two of them chatted about old times when both their kids were small. I smiled politely. Keith and I respected each other's pasts, which was one of the reasons why I felt we were well suited.

"I hope you didn't mind us going on and on like that," he said as we walked out. "She's my wife's friend, and I hadn't seen her in awhile."

I shook my head. But as he took my arm, I thought about how many people Keith seemed to know in our city. He ran into friends and acquaintances at least half the time we were together. Clearly, he was a guy who got out a lot.

But that night, he was too tired to stay out. We kissed good-bye in the hotel parking lot and went our separate ways. When I got home, plastic tarps and the odor of fresh paint brought to mind a completely different male, and I found myself anticipating the morning's home-cooked breakfast.

I was waiting in my hunter green jumpsuit when Vinnie rapped on the door at seven. The waistline of the jumpsuit was loose enough that

I figured I could get away with a big breakfast. Plus, Keith had once told me that the color was flattering on me. Since Vinnie was going to the trouble of cooking for me, I'd felt compelled to make an effort with my appearance.

He was in his usual jeans and a T-shirt. Form-fitting, while not particularly tight. Work-splattered, while not dirty. And eye-catching, if not downright *sexy*.

He deposited two Styrofoam takeout containers and a quart-sized Thermos on my kitchen table. "Eggs Benedict," he said. "And French toast. A meal fit for a king."

I crossed my arms in front of my chest. "I thought you were cooking."

"I don't cook."

"But you're a handyman! You're supposed to be able to do anything!"

"I pick and choose my skills. Cooking doesn't happen to be one of them." He popped a lid and a delicious aroma swirled up toward me. "Are you gonna eat or complain?"

I pulled out the seat across from him. "It smells wonderful." I let out a little sigh. "Thank you."

"You're welcome." He poured coffee into two mugs. "And you look great, by the way. I hope Mr. Boss Boyfriend appreciates it."

"He's going to be away at an all-day meeting."

Vinnie smiled. It was a terrific smile, one I didn't seem to tire of seeing. "Then you must've dressed for me."

I opened my mouth to deny it, but no words came out.

"I dressed for you, too," he went on, still grinning. "This is my very best work T-shirt, with far fewer stains and wear-and-tear than the others."

I managed a grin, but I wasn't sure how I'd be able to maintain my composure if he kept talking about his body . . . his magnificent body.

"So," I said, and stirred creamer into my coffee, "are you from around here?"

His tone grew somber as he discussed moving to our city with his family back in high school. "Both my brothers ultimately went back to Canada. They give me a hard time about staying here, like I'm too chicken to make a big change. Truth is, though, that I like it here. My business is doing well. For a while, I even thought I was putting down roots and getting married."

"I'm sorry."

"Oh, don't be. All she did was nag, nag, nag." He smiled. "When we found out she wasn't pregnant, after all, I don't know which one of us was more relieved. We broke off the engagement and never saw each other again."

A myriad of memories sprang to life. The glory days when Tyler was our high school's quarterback and I was his front-seat girl. The joyful toasts by his parents and mine at the wedding they'd orchestrated and paid for. And then the years of make-believe, emptiness, and regret. Until the fated night when my drunken, disillusioned husband had lost control of his car.

"People shouldn't marry for anything less than love." I grabbed Vinnie's gaze and held it. "Just because people say you look good together or you're perfect for each other doesn't mean you've got what it takes to make it. Situations change, interests change, people change. Only those who are truly in love can weather the storms and keep a marriage alive."

His gaze intensified. "It sounds like you're speaking from experience."

"Unfortunately, yes. I'm not the broken-hearted widow some people think me to be. But don't misunderstand—I still grieve for him in my own way. I just wish we'd gotten divorced after that first year and gone on to be friends."

A tense silence enveloped the room.

"Your boss is the man you've been looking for then?" Vinnie looked soulfully into my eyes. "He gives you everything your husband didn't?"

I shifted in my chair, conscious of some undefined energy radiating between us. "Keith is kind and attentive."

"That's not what I asked."

"Well, that's all I'm going to tell you." Irritation hummed along my nerve endings. Wasn't it enough that I'd shared intimate details of my marriage? "I'm not the kiss-and-tell type, okay?"

He stood. "Fair enough. Listen, I'm going to start work on your kitchen cabinets today. Sand them down, replace the hardware. Do you want them painted or varnished?"

I was momentarily taken aback. But Vinnie was right to bring the conversation back to business. Because that's all that really connected us, anyway. "Varnish."

"High gloss or satin finish?"

I checked my watch. "Look, I've got to get going. Do whatever you want. Better yet, I'll come home on my lunch hour. We can talk about it then."

"Will you have something special for me?"

"I'm stuffed from breakfast. How can you be thinking of food again already?"

"Who said I was thinking of food?"

A vaguely sensuous light seemed to pass between us, one I wasn't prepared to acknowledge, much less deal with. My heart did a crazy flip-flop and I headed out the door before I responded with something I'd live to regret.

My cousin, Molly, telephoned later, and I took the call in Keith's office.

"How's it going with the handyman? Are you happy with him?"

"Sure. Except for the fact that he can't cook." I laughed, and when she didn't respond, I added: "Just a joke."

"How do you know he can't cook?"

"He told me over breakfast."

"Breakfast?"

"I made it yesterday, and he brought takeout today. We ended up having a long conversation, actually—about his ex-girlfriend and my marriage, of all things."

Molly seemed to hesitate. "Are we talking about the same Vinnie LaGree? The one who quietly does his work, and then slips out? I think you've gotten to know him better in two days than I have in two *years!*"

Joy bubbled inside of me, although I couldn't quite explain why.

Outside, at the front desk, Elaine was chatting with a former coworker, Cindi.

"Good to see you," I said to her in passing, and cooed over her adorable baby.

"Is Mr. Corsair back in his office?" Cindi asked. "I'd like to say hello."

"Sorry, Keith's out for the day," I told her.

"You call him Keith now?" Cindi shot a glance at Elaine. "Has something changed around here?"

I shrugged. "He and I have been dating for a few months, actually. It's no secret."

"You mean his wife's nightmare actually came *true?*" Cindi laughed and cupped her hand over her mouth. "Oops!"

"What?"

Elaine's lips were pulled taut into a thin, straight line. "Oh, rumor had it that Mrs. Corsair was jealous of you, Jewel. Especially after your husband passed away. She thought that you and Mr. Corsair might have something going on."

"What? That's not true! And why haven't I ever heard about this before?"

"I guess people were just being careful," Elaine said, and shot Cindi a look.

My thoughts circled back to the times when Keith had mentioned his wife. I knew that she had a hot temper and had thrown him out of the house. But he'd never made mention of her feelings toward me.

After Cindi left, I tried to pump Elaine for more information, specifically about whether employees at the hotel thought that I'd wrecked Keith's marriage. She assured me that no one did. But then she added something that stayed in my brain all afternoon.

"It *does* seem strange, though, that he put the moves on you the moment she chucked him out," Elaine said. "As if he really was in love with you all along. Or just trying *really* hard to hurt his wife."

My thoughts went awhirl. Only I knew what Keith was like in the heat of passion, when he looked into my eyes, when he reached for me. He was gentle, and often eager. But in no way was it an expression of love.

Anger began to churn within me.

Was Keith using me?

So when he called later to check on things, I told him that I needed to see him. At my place, six o'clock.

He agreed readily, if not warily.

He either had to do some serious explaining, I decided as I replaced the receiver, or I had some serious reassessing on my hands.

"You take an awfully late lunch."

Vinnie was standing on a tarp in the middle of my kitchen floor that evening, his T-shirt wrapped turban-like around his head. The skin from his taut belly to his sparkling eyes was exposed and primed for my eyes.

"Sorry. I got busy and couldn't get away."

"Well, I went with the high gloss."

"Fine." My gaze bounced around the room, looking everywhere but at him. I liked what I saw a little too much.

"What's with the turban?"

"I forgot my favorite painting hat. And I'd rather get varnish on a shirt that I can soak or throw away than in my hair."

I don't know what came over me, but I couldn't resist a gentle tease. "A little vain, are we?"

A smile skimmed his lips. He moved toward me then, wet paintbrush in the air. "Let's just see how *you* feel with some of this in your hair."

I took a few steps backward, laughing. "Okay, okay, I get your point."

"You do, huh?"

I bumped into the washer and watched in breathless anticipation as Vinnie closed the distance between us.

"I'll tell you what, Jewel," he said, his voice so close that I could almost feel its rumble, his body so close that I could almost feel its heat, "I'll let you off the hook if you go pick me up another can of this varnish."

I nodded in exaggeration, pretending to be scared. "Okay, okay," I mimicked.

He laughed and retreated, leaving me with swirls of disappointment.

"The store closes at six, so you'd better hurry."

Six. Keith.

"My boyfriend's due then."

"You'll be back in plenty of time."

"Okay. But if he shows up, just tell him to wait."

I headed out, knowing the drive would do me good. I needed to gear up for this showdown with Keith, and Vinnie was too much of a distraction. It seemed like whenever Vinnie and I were in the same room, my pulse went wild and my thoughts went *crazy*. There was no reasoning with my reaction, no remedy for what ailed me—nothing but a clean break.

I tried to center my thoughts on Keith to rev up my resentment and indignation at his using me. But when I returned and saw him standing on my lawn, I felt mostly sadness. Regardless of what went down, our romance was over. I'd let this sweet, but passive, relationship go on too long. Much the way I'd done with my marriage. Things had to change in my life, and now was as good a time as any!

"There's a naked man in your kitchen," Keith charged when I got out of the car.

"He's not naked. He's just using his shirt as a hat."

"He's naked."

"He's naked?" I looked at the kitchen windows, but couldn't see a thing.

Darn it.

"Is this what you called me over for, Jewel? To rub your affair in my face?"

"No. There's no affair. He's just my handyman." I felt my eyes squint in concentration. "I wanted to ask you about your wife and why she was so jealous of me all these years."

The anger drained from Keith's face.

"And why is it," I went on thinking aloud, "that we usually run into people you know on our dates? Do you *purposely* take me to the places where your wife's friends hang out?"

"Okay," he began in a clipped, deliberate tone. "I admit I asked you out the first few times to get her goat. I was thinking it would ignite her jealousy and she'd insist I come home. But friend after friend has reported to her about seeing us together, and she's still going ahead with the divorce proceedings."

My mouth hung open.

"And I've started to care for you, Jewel," he said, and attempted a smile. "I mean, maybe my wife really knew what was best all along."

Conflicting feelings vied for dominance, but my voice remained calm. "What's best is being with someone you love, Keith. Someone who loves you back. And that's not us. We both know it."

He was silent for several seconds. Then: "No, I guess it's not," he said, and exhaled loudly. "Well, I'm going to go now. Let's talk more about this tomorrow."

"This," I said, "and maybe about arranging a transfer for me to another department."

"That's probably a good idea."

He turned and walked to his car. I watched for a moment, but then my gaze immediately swept back to the kitchen windows.

Was Vinnie really *naked* in there?

"Uh, Vinnie?" I said loudly, and hovered in the doorway. "Are you there?"

"Yeah, I'm here."

"Are you . . . uh . . . dressed?"

"Why don't you come in and find out?"

I reminded myself that it was my own house, after all, my own doorway that I was hesitating in.

"Oh, for Pete's sake," I said, and took a couple of bold steps.

Vinnie was standing in the same sexy and silly outfit he'd been wearing when I left. "I just saw Mr. Boss Boyfriend drive off. I hope nothing's wrong."

I put the varnish on the table. "No. For the first time in a long time, everything is just fine. We broke up, and I'm going to transfer to another department, and I think it's time to pop open a beer and celebrate."

"Open one for me, too, then." He put down his paintbrush and pulled the turban from his head. His sweat-soaked hair stood up at odd angles, but he still looked like a calendar-worthy hunk. "That's the best news I've had all week."

"I thought things were going well. You're doing a great job here."

"On the house, yeah."

I handed him his beer, letting my gaze linger with his.

"But I was failing miserably with you."

I arched a brow.

"Look, I have more customers than I can handle. But as a favor to Molly, I promised to meet with her widowed cousin." His eyes lit up. "I got one long look at you and no one else existed. So I lied and said I could start immediately."

That weird flutter returned to my chest.

"Turned out you had a boyfriend. But you didn't seem all that crazy about him. So I thought I'd keep trying. And until you stood me up for lunch today, I thought I might actually be making progress."

"I didn't stand you up. I got busy." I grimaced. "And forgot to call. I'm sorry."

"Well, I figured I was going to have to do something drastic. Tell you how I felt, or learn to cook or something. Then you said your boyfriend was coming by, and I had an idea."

"To paint with your clothes off?"

Vinnie grinned boldly. "I figured you'd tell him afterward that I was just some nut you barely knew. If you had a good thing going, you'd laugh it off together and there'd be no harm done. But if things *weren't* going so good . . . well, my intention was to make things worse."

"He could've punched your lights out."

"Part of the gamble, I guess."

"You'd get beat up for me?"

"Well, I'd have gotten a few good hits in, myself."

I laughed. Was this guy for real? And where had he been all my life?

"What if I'd come back from the store before he got here? And walked in on you in the nude?"

"Then I'd just have to hope that you liked what you saw."

"You're incredible!"

"Well, I put my jeans back on, didn't I?"

I laughed, feeling blissfully, happily alive. And something else was stirring inside me, too. A long forgotten ache. . . .

"Okay, Jewel, I'm going to put my cards on the table. I'm crazy about you. And if I didn't go out on a limb to make you notice me, I'd never forgive myself."

"Oh, I've noticed you, all right. I've been fighting these feelings for *days*, Vinnie. . . ." My body moved toward his with a will of its own.

"Tell me about those feelings," he said huskily, and with the tip of his finger, lifted my chin to his face. "Better yet," he whispered. "Show me."

My heart lurched madly as Vinnie's lips closed over mine. I threw my arms around his bare chest and returned his kiss with a passion, a fervor, I hadn't felt since my teenaged years.

I was in love. I was in lust. With a man who wanted me as much as I wanted him. And, best of all, from his mere kiss, I knew he had the power to take me to places I hadn't been in a long, long time. Maybe to places I'd never been before.

There was about to be a naked man in my kitchen—again.

And in my bedroom every night from now on.

I was sure of it. THE END

I WOKE UP HUNGOVER—
AND MARRIED!
Remind me to drink again!

When I woke up in bed next to Ronnie on that beautiful June morning, I didn't even know his name. I looked at his handsome face, his dark hair and rugged build, and thought:

What have I done?

Ronnie yawned and let out a gross gurgling sound.

"Yuck," I muttered as I slipped quickly out of bed.

He moved his arm across my lap as I tried to stand up. I noticed he was wearing a gold band on his finger.

"Oh, great," I muttered, putting my feet on the floor. "He's married, too."

I grabbed my dress and handbag from a chair and hurried into the bathroom. I moaned when I saw my face—blotchy, gray, and puffy. My hair looked like some wild, ratty pile of yarn. I turned on the cold-water tap in the small motel bathroom, and, to my horror, as I splashed water on my face—

I saw a gold ring on my finger, too!

"What in the world?"

I gasped, pulling at the ring, but it was jammed tightly on my finger. Physically, I felt horrible. I remembered drinking *way* too much the night before at Genevieve's wedding—but the rest of the night was a blur.

How in heaven's name, I wondered, *did I end up here with a man whose name I do not know, wearing a ring just like the one he has on his finger?*

I took off my dress—wondering, as I did, where my underwear

was—and got into the shower. The steamy spray felt wonderful against my face and body and slowly, as I turned and scrubbed my body with the small bar of complimentary soap, I began to feel human again.

I dried off and put my dress back on. It felt old and dirty, and it smelled of smoke. I ran a small brush from my bag through my hair, but I didn't bother with any makeup. I felt like my very life depended on my getting out of that room fast and finding a way back to my car and home.

I opened the door to peek out—and nearly collided with the stranger.

"Oh, hello," he said cheerfully. "I was just brewing some of this horrible coffee the motel offers. Let's have some and then go to the coffee shop for breakfast. What do you say?"

He kissed me tenderly on the forehead and turned away to the coffee, whistling happily. I walked past him and spotted my underwear, stockings, and shoes in a clump at the bottom of the bed. I blushed fiercely, horrified at the intimacy they implied. I rushed over to pick them up, and then I scurried back to the bathroom and locked myself inside.

"Coffee's almost ready," he called, as, with a shudder, I stood pressed behind the door, wondering how I was ever going to get out of the situation.

I got fully dressed, took a deep breath, and then, gritting my teeth, I forced a smile on my face and opened the door. He was waiting for me, looking fresh—and quite handsome, actually—holding a cup of coffee out to me.

"Do you take anything in it, Nora, my sweet?" he asked, kissing me again on the cheek.

"No, black is good," I said, sinking down onto the bed and sipping the hot, bitter brew.

He came over and sat down next to me, caressing my leg. "Well," he said. "Here we are—married."

I coughed and spat some of the coffee down the front of me. I swore as I stood up to dab at it with a tissue from the table. When I turned to look at him, he gave me a deep smile.

"Are you okay?"

I sank down on the bed next to him, putting my coffee cup on the nightstand. "Look, I have to say this," I said, my voice dry and strangled-sounding. "I don't remember a thing after Genevieve's wedding. You and I—we—got married?"

He laughed. "I was pretty lit, too, but, yes, we did. I sobered up before I drove us here, though. You slept or hummed to the car radio most of the ride. Here we are, though, in Las Vegas, and, yes, we two are wed."

I let out a groan and fell back onto the bed. "I will never drink again," I vowed.

"Oh, well," he chuckled, "it could be worse. You could be a dog and I could be a dork. Neither one of us got rooked in the looks department."

I sat up. "How can you be so casual about *marriage?*" I wailed. "At least you know my *name!*"

He reached out and took me in his arms. He had big, strong arms, yet his touch was gentle. I was too stunned to resist; besides, his arms felt wonderful wrapped around me.

"My name is Dex Henderson," he whispered. "You are Mrs. Henderson, as of last night. It's nobody's fault—not yours, not mine. We got drunk and we got a little nuts, that's all. I'm not usually so impulsive, but the moment I saw you I thought, 'There's my angel.' "

"Oh, come on!" I said, pushing away from him. "You don't believe in love at first sight or anything so silly, do you?"

Dex shrugged. "I don't know. I just know that when I saw you, my heart started beating like a big, old bass drum, and it hasn't stopped since."

I sat down on a chair and looked at Dex, who still sat on the edge of the bed, watching me like a hopeful little boy. "So, we're in Vegas?" I asked.

He gave a soft laugh. "You really don't remember last night at all, do you?"

I put my head in my hands and felt the stabs of the headache I'd been trying to ignore. "No, I don't," I moaned softly. I looked up at him.

"I want you to know—I'm not a heavy drinker. I guess Genevieve's wedding and the way my life's been going set me up to do something stupid. I never dreamed I would go this far, though. It just isn't like me." I looked at him and sighed. "Just see what happens, though. You put your reserve aside for one night, and you end up married in a town a hundred miles from home with a man whose name you don't even know." I shook my head in despair.

"Hey," he said, coming over and rubbing the back of my neck. "This doesn't have to be permanent if you don't want it to be." He knelt down beside me and took my face in his wide, soft hands. "I wish you could remember some of last night, though. Boy, were we gangbusters together in bed!"

I blushed, and felt horribly embarrassed. "Oh, please," I whispered. However, memories of the night before were starting to come back to me. I looked into his soft, brown eyes and confessed in a whisper, "I am starting to remember that part, though. It was good."

Our eyes locked for a moment, and I had an impulse to draw him close to me. I couldn't believe my own feelings, but he seemed to know what I was thinking. I smiled at him, he smiled at me, and then, suddenly, we were kissing.

"Oh, heck," I whispered, as he joined me on the bed.

"Relax, baby," he crooned. "It's legal."

We ate breakfast later, and I felt oddly refreshed.

"I can't imagine why I'm in such a good mood," I said to Dex. "I've just made the biggest mistake of my life and I can't wait to taste the eggs. That's being an adult, isn't it?"

Dex took my hands in his and caressed my fingers with his own. "Maybe you're just relaxed."

"I cannot argue with you on that point," I said, and raised my water glass in a little toast. He beamed a big, broad smile like he'd just won a blue ribbon.

"We're very good together," he said softly, rubbing my leg.

"Unfortunately," I said, moving my leg away, "life isn't all about sex."

"Are you sure about that?" he asked, squinting his eyes and revealing attractive laugh lines on his tanned face.

"Tell me what happened last night," I said, nervously folding my napkin. "I can remember dancing and laughing, and then it's all a blur."

Dex told me about dancing with me, and then us kissing passionately, and then us leaving together. "I didn't want to drive until I was sober, so we went for coffee, but you had another drink," he said with an indulgent smile. "Then we both just decided to head for Vegas. And, when we got here, we thought we might as well get married. That's about the whole story."

"It just isn't like me," I said, leaning my head back against the booth and closing my eyes. "I can't *imagine* what came over me."

Dex raised his eyebrows teasingly, but didn't reply.

"Where did we get these rings?" I asked, looking down at my finger.

"Oh, the wedding chapel had everything. We were good to go."

The waitress brought our breakfast order then, and after she left, Dex continued, "We bought them, along with the license, and as I recall, a little veil for you to wear on your head. I still say we should have had pictures taken, but you didn't want to wait."

I stopped eating. "I did *not* wear a veil!"

"Yeah," he said, chuckling deeply. "You did. Then, on the way to the motel, you pitched it out the window and yelled, 'I'm a married woman and I am in love!' "

"Oh, dear," I managed to croak out.

"Now you're starting to remember, aren't you?" he asked with that slight, wonderful grin of his.

I nodded ruefully. "What are we going to do now?" I asked, sipping my coffee.

Dex leaned back into the booth, his huge shoulders resting against the red vinyl. He looked wonderful; I couldn't take my eyes off him.

He looked at me like he could read my mind. "Why don't we stay a few days?" he suggested. "We're here now; we can see some shows, gamble a little—why don't we?"

My inclination, borne of a sense of caution I'd learned the hard way over the last few years, was to say no, let's get back home and get this over with. Besides, I was not the impulsive type by any means. I always had to have a plan of action—that's how I lived my life, and how I felt some control.

But I looked at him and remembered the loneliness that waited for me back home. His invitation, incautious and impulsive though it was, was too tantalizing for me to resist. I just *couldn't* resist. I looked at him and saw that lazy smile on his face; I felt his hand, back again, rubbing my leg, and all I could do was whisper and nod.

Dex paid the check and we walked out together. "We'll have to get some clothes," I murmured. "You know—some essentials and a change or two, just a few things."

"You won't need much," he whispered into my ear as he squeezed my hand.

I gulped and let him lead me, willingly, back to our motel room.

Las Vegas was wonderful. We even won a little money, despite the fact that we also spent a lot. Dex paid for everything, refusing to let me pay at all.

"I have credit cards, too," I protested.

But he said, "I'm an old-fashioned kind of husband. I think I ought to be the one to pay."

I liked his sense of humor, and the gentle way he treated me. I also loved the physical storm we created in bed; truth was, I had never felt such a physical rapport with a man—ever. And Dex seemed to know exactly what to do to excite me, and just how to do it.

We did get to know one another a bit in between our lovemaking sessions. I learned that Dex owned a trucking company back home, and that he actually went out on the road himself on occasion. I told him about my work with after-school programs in the city. We discussed our likes and dislikes in music, movies, and that sort of thing, and, finally, we got around to discussing our past love lives.

"I was married once before," he told me. "It only lasted two years. I never felt I knew my wife and when she got to know me, she left." He gave a little laugh, but I sensed the hurt behind the laughter.

I told him about my relationships with men. "I dated a lot, and then

I found one guy I really wanted to marry," I told him as we sat in a casino in a relatively quiet corner bar. "I thought he was the answer to my lifelong dreams, not to mention all of my prayers. We had the whole wedding planned, and then the day before, just as we were leaving for the rehearsal, he took me aside and started to sob. 'I can't do this,' he told me."

I stopped talking for a moment because the memory still hurt me so. Dex reached over and gently touched my cheek with his hand. I gave a little forced laugh and said, "I didn't even know what he was talking about. I thought he didn't want any dinner." Even though I tried to joke about it, the tears still came to my eyes. Dex reached for me and I nuzzled down into his warm arms.

After a few moments, I sat back up and said, "To make a long story short, he didn't love me, and he just couldn't stand the thought of being married to me." I put on a brave smile and gave a little shrug of my shoulders, hopefully to show that it didn't matter all that much anymore. Dex stared at me.

"Was there something wrong with him?" he asked.

"No, he just didn't love me."

"He must've been crazy," Dex said firmly. "You're beautiful and fun and smart. The guy must've been nuts. I'd give anything to be married to someone like you."

The moment he said the words, we both looked at one another and burst out laughing.

"Oh, I guess I am," Dex said. Then he bent and kissed me, and that's all it took.

"Let's go," we both whispered fervently at exactly the same time.

On our way home from Vegas, Dex and I talked about what we wanted from life.

"I guess I want to be happy," he said, stretching out his muscular arms on the steering wheel of the car. He looked over at me. "I guess everyone wants that, though, right?"

I nodded. "I think so. It's just that finding out *how* to be happy is harder than it sounds."

"What about kids? I own my own home, but it's empty with just me living in it. As it is, I'm hardly ever home. I think it'd be nice to have a house full of kids."

I looked at him and said, "Kids?" He looked at me quickly and saw the alarm on my face.

"What? You don't like kids?"

"That's not the point. It's just that, when you mentioned kids, I realized that I'm not on any kind of birth control. How about you?"

He turned his head quickly back to the road. "No, no—I didn't bring anything with me, and I guess I just assumed . . . well, you know—that you were okay that way."

"Oh, dear God," I moaned, and leaned my head back against the seat. "*Now* what have we done? This is getting worse and worse!"

He reached over and patted my hand. "Hey, it's nobody's fault. Let's not panic. We may be fine."

"But what if we're not?" I practically wailed.

Dex straightened up his shoulders and grinned. "Well, then, I guess we'll have a kid."

I sat back and stared out at the highway slipping by. The enormity of what I had allowed to happen to me finally began to sink in. I started to tremble all over. "You certainly have a nonchalant attitude about things, Dex. I mean, a baby is probably the biggest deal in a man or woman's life—or, at least, it should be! And we haven't even really talked about what we're going to do about our marriage!"

He looked at me. "Oh, hell, I don't think a kid is nothing," he said in a surprised tone. "What are you saying?"

He turned the car onto an exit ramp and, without explanation, he drove on silently. I assumed we were stopping for gas, but instead, he pulled up to an ice cream stand.

"I think we need to celebrate the possibility of a baby before we grind out and destroy all the possible joy a baby would bring to the world."

His words and actions astonished me. "You sound like a greeting card," I snapped at him. "We have to act like *adults*, Dex, not kids."

"Still," he said in his unflappably cheerful voice, "ice cream never hurts. What's your pleasure? Chocolate chip, or caramel pecan?"

I watched him walk, almost dancing a jig, up to the ice cream stand. His cheerful outlook amazed me, but his personality set off warning signs in my mind. I was so into planning and organizing, I couldn't help thinking that maybe Dex had some very serious problems. He certainly wasn't like me at *all*.

We sat and ate ice cream together in the car under a huge, shady tree near the stand. Surprisingly, the sensation and taste of the cold sweetness actually lifted my spirits.

"You're right," I said finally, dabbing at my chin with my napkin. "Let's just wait and see what happens with the baby and all. I'm probably worrying for nothing, anyway. I mean, what are the chances?"

Dex leaned over and kissed me, licking my lips with his tongue. "Yeah, what are the chances?" he whispered.

I was a lot calmer as we neared home. Smiling, I turned to Dex and said, "I wish I were more like you, you know. I wish I could take life as it comes, but I guess I've lived long enough in this crazy world to always expect the worst to happen, so planning ahead gives me some sense of security and control. But, you—you seem to always hope for the best."

Dex shrugged. "I think the truth is just that I live each day as it comes. I just want to be happy." He smiled and cleared his throat. "Anyway, we're almost to my house. Why don't you just stay over tonight? It's nothing fancy; I have to warn you ahead of time: I've never really completely moved in. But, so what? I've only lived there for five years!" he said with a chuckle.

I couldn't imagine living anywhere without getting things organized and comfortable as soon as possible, but I didn't comment. Dex continued, "Anyway, tomorrow's Sunday, so we can take it easy for another day. How about it? We still haven't really decided what to do about the fact that we're legally married."

I sighed. "I guess I could stay at your place—but only if we stop at a drugstore and get some . . . well, you-know-what."

"More ice cream?" he teased.

"You know what I mean, Dex. Some protection," I said, feeling very young, and very foolish all of a sudden.

He laughed. "I have some at home, honestly, I'm really not a careless man; I just wasn't expecting you to come into my life that lovely night."

"For a simple guy, you can sure be eloquent," I said, inching closer to him on the front seat. "And you really seem like such a nice guy. So, what is it that you're hiding, Dex? There must be *something* wrong with you."

Dex's face went all serious for just a second. Then he smiled and said, "Well, I have to admit that there *is* something. . . ."

I steeled myself for news that he had a wife, or a live-in girlfriend, or some such awful secret that would spoil everything. "What is it?" I asked warily.

"I really do like Wayne Newton," he said. "I lied to you back in Vegas."

I burst into laughter, and felt wonderful. As we pulled into his driveway, I could hardly wait to get inside his perfectly ordinary-looking, split-level home. Dex's bedroom was the first room I really wanted to see—

And that is precisely where he led me.

When we woke up the next morning, I looked around and realized that Dex hadn't been exaggerating about his house being disordered. There were two empty bedrooms stacked with boxes and assorted items; there was a bathroom that only needed tiling to finish it up, and the kitchen was a disaster with old appliances and damaged cabinets.

I held my tongue about the disorder, even though it bothered me. Instead, I said, "Well, your house definitely has that *not*-lived-in look."

Dex laughed. "I'll get around to it someday. I'm just not here much, as I said, but I like the house and the neighborhood."

"I should think so," I said. "It's a lovely house with great potential."

"Like me," he said, brushing his lips on mine.

Dex poured me a cup of coffee and brushed his hand across mine as he did so. I looked up at him and our eyes met, and then locked.

"How do you take it?" he asked, referring to the coffee, but not moving his eyes from mine an inch.

I gently pushed the coffee cup aside and said, "Why not surprise me?"

He set the cup down and led me back to bed.

Later, we ate breakfast and chatted about everything but what to do about our marriage. There seemed to be a mutual reluctance between us to take on that topic.

"I should go back home this afternoon," I told him finally. "I need to get ready for work. I can't imagine the mess I'll go back to—I dread it. Whenever I leave, the whole place goes crazy."

"How crazy can it get when you're working with kids? They don't need a lot of rules, do they?"

"Spoken like a man who makes his living far from the world of children. Rules are what keep the whole program going . . . and I seem to be the only one capable of enforcing them, or even acknowledging them." I shook my head and took a bite of my muffin.

Dex's eyes were twinkling as he looked at me. "You're quite the worrier, aren't you?"

"Yes, well, I do like to have *some* idea of what's going on in my life and work." I didn't like having to defend myself to Dex, so I decided to bring up our marriage, despite my earlier reluctance to mention it. "What are we going to do?" I asked, trying to avoid his eyes. "You know—about this marriage business?"

"Business?" Dex said, leaning back in his chair and showing off his mouthwatering physique in the best light. "Is it a business?"

"You know what I mean," I said, desperately looking away from him so I could keep focused on the topic at hand.

"Well," he said, standing up and walking to my chair. He started kneading my neck, and the feel of his warm hands sent me swooning like a teenager. "I think we should just wait and see what develops."

I turned around quickly and his hands dropped free of me. "You mean—a baby?" I asked in a strangled voice.

Dex took my hand and pulled me up next to him. I leaned into him as if it was the most natural thing in the world, because that is how it felt. He held me in his arms and stroked my back.

"Yeah, a baby," he said. "Don't you think we'd better wait to be sure that isn't a part of the picture?"

"Yes," I said breathlessly.

As he leaned down to kiss me, despite my determination not to, I forgot all about the future, the past, and cared only about the moment. And that moment was blissful, and I wanted it to last forever.

Dex and I established a kind of routine in the weeks following our marriage. We saw each other every day he was in town, sometimes at his house, but most often at mine. I couldn't stand the disorder in his house, and he refused to let me organize it for him.

"We'll get after it one of these days," he would say with a disinterested yawn.

He did seem to enjoy the cozy comforts of my clean house, however. Try as I might, though, I couldn't get him into the habit of picking up his clothes where he'd left them, or even noticing when he tracked in dirt from outside.

Back at work, I took out my frustrations with Dex on my coworkers. I was even more dynamic than I'd been before about rules and structure until one day, my assistant, Rosie, said, "Egad, Nora, back off a little! I always thought being married would do you good, but now, I know better!"

I was insulted and angry at first by her words, but then I thought about it and realized that Rosie was my friend. She was giving me fair warning that I needed to indeed back off our staff—and I did, but only a little.

Meanwhile, my physical attraction to Dex only intensified. But his impulsive nature and ho-hum attitude about life in general were slowly driving me mad. I told myself that I should be grateful for his good qualities. After all, he was never mean—not in the least bit—nor was he sullen or pouty. He ran his business well, and his workers loved him. But he was so sloppy sometimes with details, and so vague about plans that I just *knew* he had to change or something awful would happen.

On the other hand, Dex never criticized me for being so finicky about details. "We really need to make some plans," I would whisper to him sometimes after one of our miraculous lovemaking sessions.

"Yeah," he would murmur, "let's go dancing tonight."

In despair, I would try again and again to make him more grounded. But Dex resisted with the force of a stubborn child. In the end, I always gave in to his way of thinking because—and I had to admit it—Dex made life *fun*.

About six weeks later, I began to suspect that I might actually, indeed, be pregnant. I didn't mention my suspicions to Dex; he appeared to have put all thoughts of a baby aside, and I didn't want to remind him if it wasn't true.

Still, I went in for the examination, trying to be hopeful that I just had a virus or a bug—but reality hit hard when the doctor told me, with a beaming smile, "Congratulations, Mrs. Henderson. You're going to be a mommy."

I was not happy. It wasn't the baby—I liked babies well enough—but suddenly, Dex and I had to face some hard truths. And I was not convinced that Dex would even settle down long enough to even *think* about what we should do.

So as far as I was concerned, there were only two options: We could keep the baby and raise it together, or we could end our marriage—or what we called a marriage—and bring up our baby living apart. I was not going to give this baby up, that I knew.

I drove over to Dex's business. The office was bustling with activity that day, but Dex stopped working with a big grin on his face when he saw me come in.

"Hey, nice surprise," he said, putting down his pencil and getting up from his desk. "Why aren't you working?"

I asked him if he could take a break and come for a short ride with me. He gave me a big, pleased smile and I knew he thought I was stealing him away to make love. I drove us to a park nearby and pulled up next to a shaded grove of trees by the river. Then I turned to him with a sigh.

"What's wrong?" he asked, looking suddenly alarmed. "Is there something wrong?"

"I just got some news from the doctor," I said quietly.

Instantly, his face changed from worried, to immensely pleased. "The baby!" he cried, smacking his forehead. "Are we having a baby?"

"Oh, Dex," I said in exasperation, "what are we going to do?"

He tried to pull me close, but I resisted him—for once. He let go of me.

"Why do we have to do anything? We're married; we get along. Why don't we just see what happens? This baby is nobody's fault, but it wanted to be born, obviously, so here it comes. I'm very happy, aren't you?"

"What about our living arrangements?" I persisted, trying to keep the irritation out of my voice. "My place isn't big enough, and your house, well—I couldn't bring a baby there."

Dex looked a little hurt. "No, I guess not the way it is," he agreed. "So why don't we just decide what to do when the baby comes? There's time enough. We don't have to decide today." He reached for me again and I pushed him away.

"Stop it," I snapped at him. He pulled back from me as if I'd burned him. His face went red and then I saw his eyes turn cold.

"I guess I'm not really the kind of guy you ever wanted to marry, much less have a child with," he said. "My place is a mess, my life is a disaster, and I'm a loser in your eyes."

"No," I said. I reached my arms out to him and he came to me. "Oh, Dex—that is so not true! I'm just afraid and shocked that it's really true about the baby. How will we ever manage?"

"Do you love me?" he asked, taking my face in his large hands.

I looked into his eyes; they were warm again, and filled with tenderness. "Yes, Dex. I love you—despite myself, sometimes."

"Well, you know I love you, too," he said, "and after all, isn't that what really matters?"

I wasn't at all convinced, but I didn't want to spoil the moment, and I didn't want to hurt him or make him angry again. "I think I'll go home for a week or so," I told him. "I think I'd like to see my mom."

"I can't get away right now."

"It's all right. I think I need to see her by myself, anyway."

"Absolutely, my love," he said. "No problem. But I'll miss you."

As I drove the fifty miles to see my mother, my mind raced with all the ways I could tell her what I was facing without actually having to face her with the whole truth. But when I saw her there, standing out on her porch, excitedly waving at me and waiting for me to get out of the car, I knew I would tell her everything just the way it had happened. There was no way I could ever lie to my mother.

It was good to be home again in that clean, cool, big house I'd lived in for so many years. I missed Dad, and I knew that Mom did, too. He'd died so suddenly that it'd caught us all off guard. I asked Mom about my three brothers and their families, and she passed on the news as we sipped some tea together.

"Now," she said, pushing a strand of her graying hair from her forehead, "what's up with you?"

I looked at her and felt my cheeks redden. "How did you know I have a problem?" I asked.

"I didn't," she said. "But I knew something was on your mind when you called and said you wanted to come home. So tell me what it is, Nora."

I talked fast and kept my head down low. I told her everything that had happened between Dex and me. I didn't miss her shocked gasp when I told her about my waking up married to a stranger. But when I came to the part about my being pregnant, I didn't hear anything from her for a very long moment. I looked up finally, and there were tears in her eyes.

"Well," she said, "it's not the way I always dreamed of hearing about a wedding and baby from you, but Dex sounds like a wonderful man, and your eyes tell me how much you love him. So? What do you want to do?"

"That's just the problem, Mom; I don't *know* what to do." I stood up and walked around the kitchen with my fists clenched. "I mean, he *is* a good guy—I know he is. But he is so, well—he's almost like a *child*, really. He never lets anything bother him. Even when I told him about the baby, it was like I'd told him we were getting a new car! He loves the idea, but I have a feeling he's never really *thought* about what it would mean, I mean—a real, live, little person coming into the world and depending on us."

Mom let me talk a while, and then she asked, "Doesn't Dex own and run a successful business, though? Doesn't he have a home? It certainly *sounds* like he takes care of his responsibilities—maybe just not the way *you* would go about it."

"But, Mom—he hasn't even *really* moved into his house yet, and he's lived there for *years*. What does that tell you?"

Mom shrugged. "Maybe it just doesn't feel like home to him yet."

I stopped pacing and looked at her. "Well, *my* place doesn't feel like home to him for long, either! He comments on how pretty and clean it is there, and then he promptly gets so restless that we have to go out! I swear, he isn't housebroken!"

Mom laughed and motioned for me to sit down. I slid into my chair and took a sip of tea.

"Let me tell you something," she said with a sigh. "Did you know that when your father proposed to me, I almost said no because I thought he was so socially inept?"

"*Daddy?* But—he was the life of the party! He *loved* having people over, and he was the biggest jokester in the world!"

Mom smiled. "Yes, he was, here at home, but when we were out of the house, around people he didn't know, he always clammed up and begged me to leave almost the moment we got anywhere. He never did change, really. But I got used to it."

"Well, that isn't Dex's problem," I said, almost sulkily. "He *loves* people."

"What is it about you, do you think, that Dex would like to change?" Mom asked quietly. "I know Dad always wished that I liked music and theater more than I do."

I stared at her. "Well, if I *need* to change, all he has to do is tell me," I snapped.

Mom didn't answer; she just looked at me and waited. I finally bowed my head and muttered, "Okay; I get your point. Nobody and nothing in life is perfect—including me."

Mom got up and came over to where I sat. She hugged me and

kissed my forehead. "Ah, and that is the mystery and the joy of life and love. How easy and how boring it would be to be in love with someone perfect and live in a perfect world. That isn't the way life works, darling. But I promise you—if you two are in love and you're right for each other—despite the fact that life isn't perfect and neither are either of you—you *can* be perfectly happy together."

Her words made sense to me. I sighed and said, "I'm glad I'm home and away from Dex for a while. I can think better when he's not around."

I stayed for ten days, and it was a good thing for me. I visited with my family and had long talks with Mom about everything, including more about Dex. I took long walks alone, and by the time it was time for me to go back to Dex, I couldn't wait to see him. I knew then how much I wanted to keep him in my life, and how much I wanted him to be a part of our baby's life, too.

On the drive back home, I got very excited, thinking about Dex and how much I wanted to be with him. When I got home, I called him immediately at work. He wasn't in, a man told me, and they didn't expect him back for a few days.

I was dumbfounded. Dex had promised he would call me at my mother's house if he was going to take a truck run, but I hadn't heard from him at all, except for a message he'd left on Mom's answering machine one day.

Dex called me from his house a few days later. He sounded odd, evasive, and tired.

"Where did you go?" I asked him. "I thought you were going to call me at Mom's."

"Oh, I've been around. I've just been busy."

"Busy?" I asked. I was bewildered. But I decided to drop the subject because I was so eager to see him. "Let's get together tonight for dinner," I suggested. "I have so much to tell you. I can cook here, or at your place. . . ."

"No!" he said in a loud voice.

"No?"

"No, Nora—no. It's just that—no, it isn't a good idea," he said.

"Let's go out somewhere."

"Is something wrong?" I asked, feeling the first rush of real doubt about Dex come over me. "You haven't changed your mind about the baby and me, have you?"

"No, absolutely not," he said. But he was talking in a strange tone of voice, like maybe someone was listening to him.

"Is someone there with you?" I asked. "I thought I heard voices."

"No—who would be here?" he asked with a nervous laugh. I was certain I detected a note of panic in his voice.

"Should I come over?" I pressed, growing more and more apprehensive about how he was sounding.

"No!" he said loudly. "I mean—no, don't do that. I'll come and get you and we'll have a nice dinner out somewhere."

I dressed and put on my makeup carefully. I wanted to look good for Dex. I wore a low-cut, pink top that he liked, with some jeans that were very soon going to be snug on me. An hour later, when I heard him at the door, I ran eagerly to open it. He kissed me hard and I kissed him back.

"Oh, I have missed you!" I said, snuggling as close to him as I could get.

"Me, too," he whispered, picking me up in his arms and hurrying us to the bedroom.

We ate dinner about two hours later in an Italian restaurant that we both loved. After we'd ordered, I took Dex's hands in mine.

"It just keeps getting better and better between us, doesn't it?" I asked.

Dex was staring off into space. I waited for him to answer me, but he didn't.

"Don't you agree with me?" I asked him.

He turned his head to look at me; he seemed dazed and confused. "Oh, yeah, sure I do," he said, taking a big drink from his water glass. "I think that's absolutely right."

"What did I say, Dex?" I asked him, feeling hurt, and a little angry.

"What?" he asked, blinking like he'd just been awakened from a deep sleep.

I dropped his hand hard on the table and sat back in the booth. The waiter brought our food then, and Dex's attentions seemed instantly riveted on the bread and pasta before him.

"Haven't you eaten today?" I asked him. He was wolfing down his food like he was starved.

He swallowed hard, and then gave a little chuckle. "I guess I hadn't, now that you mention it," he said, taking another big bite of his bread.

I started to eat, little nibbles of the food, waiting for Dex to pay attention to me, like he usually did, but he continued to just eat and stare off into space.

With a sigh, I leaned forward and touched his hair at the sides, his dark curls.

"Wait till I get you home again," I told him. "I'll get your attention again, I promise."

"I can't stay over tonight," he gulped.

He actually looked a little frightened then—and a *lot* guilty. My stomach lurched and a sense of queasiness came over me so strongly that I grabbed my napkin and put it to my mouth. It wasn't morning sickness from the baby—I had a mild case of that and knew the difference. This was panic.

I tried to stay calm, but inside, I was a mass of nerves. I could tell then, by the way Dex was acting, that something was different between us. What I feared was that, flighty as he was, he'd simply lost all interest in the baby and me in the short time I'd been at Mom's. I couldn't bear to think of it actually being true.

He looked at me with concern. "Are you sick?" he asked. The old familiar tenderness was back in his voice, and I relaxed a little.

"No, no," I said. "I just get really emotional sometimes. I mean, it isn't like you to turn down an offer of lovemaking," I continued, feeling desperate and horrible. "Maybe a pregnant lady just doesn't turn you on."

"You don't even *look* pregnant," he said, trying to comfort me.

But his words, for some reason, were like a fist to my stomach. I put on a brave smile.

"Then I guess I can consider myself warned that when I *do* look pregnant, you may lose interest. So I should prepare myself, right?"

"Huh?" His eyes widened in disbelief. "When did I say that?"

I didn't answer him then because I was sniveling into my napkin in between little sobs that sounded like hiccups. Oh, how I *hated* the loss of control being pregnant brought on with all of my hormones clashing around and making me act so crazy!

"I'd better get you home," Dex said gently. His words made me feel better until he added, "I've got a lot to do tonight."

On the drive home, I tried once again to reestablish the security and safety I'd always found in Dex's company.

"You know, that talk with my mom really did me good," I told him in a soft voice. "I don't want this marriage to end because of the baby, Dex; I want it to begin—really begin."

Dex looked at me as he turned into my driveway. "Sure, sure," he said in the most maddeningly distracted voice. "I know what you mean."

He walked me to the door, but he refused to even come in for a few moments. "I have to go," he said urgently, gently removing my arms from around his shoulders. "It's nobody's fault, Nora; I just have to go."

I stood there and watched him drive away, and I guess that was about the lowest point of my entire life. I had so taken for granted that I would get to call the shots in our marriage—that I would decide whether we stayed together or not—that the shock of Dex pulling out—and I was sure, suddenly, that that was precisely what he was doing—was more than I could bear.

I cried for a long time, and then I finally decided to call my mother. She wasn't home; I got her answering machine. I hung up without saying anything because I was suddenly unable to speak; I was crying again, great whooping, sorrowful sobs.

I expected to hear from Dex the next day, for sure. He always called and checked in. I decided in advance that I would just be firm and tell him that we really needed to talk.

When he hadn't called by midafternoon, I swallowed my pride

and called his cell phone. All I got was his answering service; it was Sunday, so there was no point, I knew, in going over to his business to try to find him.

And so I paced the floor all day, and every time the phone rang, I raced to it, but it was never Dex. I tried his cell phone again, with no luck. I took a long bath and tried to watch some television, but I couldn't concentrate.

Finally, I got dressed, hating myself for what I planned to do, but realizing that I'd go crazy not knowing where Dex was. So if it meant I had to track him down in my car, I would do it.

I drove by some of the places where I knew Dex liked to go and socialize. I didn't see his car anywhere. It occurred to me then that he might be at some woman's house, and that I would never be able to find him.

Finally, in desperation, I drove over to where he lived. I didn't really expect him to be home, but I wanted to be sure. I approached his street slowly, and then I turned off my headlights as I neared the loop where his house sat back from the street.

I didn't see his car, but a truck was parked in the driveway, and it looked like someone was home. I stopped the car a distance from the house and stared at the place I'd once thought was so "rustic" and uninhabitable. Now, suddenly, I wanted to be inside there so badly. I wanted to be with Dex.

I could see a dim light shining in the back of the house in one of the empty bedrooms. Thoughts swirled through my mind—thoughts of Dex in the arms of some new woman, lying in "our" bed, with the pale light from that back room shining on their ecstatic faces.

Suddenly, I was filled with such outrage, jealousy, and pain that I couldn't stand it one more minute. I yanked the car door open and ran to Dex's front door. I started pounding on it with both fists.

"Dex!" I shouted. "I know you're in there! Open the door. I have a right. I have a *right!*"

I could hear the sound of movement in the house, and then several lights went on. I backed away from the door, suddenly overcome with feelings of shame and embarrassment. I had turned to run away, when the door opened, and Dex stood before me. Behind him, I saw a woman with dark hair. She was wearing coveralls, and staring at me with big, frightened eyes.

Rushing down the stairs, I only wanted to get to my car. But Dex was close behind me. He grabbed my arm and pulled me to him. His hair was messy and his clothes were dirty, flecked with paint and what looked like tar.

"What are you doing here?" he demanded. But his touch was gentle as he held on tightly to me.

"Oh—it's nobody's fault, Dex," I sputtered between tears. "You just don't love me anymore! The baby and I got boring, so you picked a new toy to play with!" I gestured wildly in the direction of the doorway, where the woman still stood and stared at us.

"Toy?" Dex asked. Then he looked at the house and saw the woman, too. "Who—Rhoda?" He started to laugh, and then said softly, "She works for me; she's one of my drivers. She's just helping me out with something."

"How convenient," I sniffed.

"Nora, what is *wrong* with you?" he asked, cupping my face in his hands.

"What's wrong is that you don't want me anymore, or the baby. You act as if you hardly *know* me!"

Dex dropped his head, but held onto my arms. "Oh, Nora," he said, "I didn't realize that's what you thought. Come with me."

I was shaking all over, but I followed his lead. We walked to the house, and when we got inside, I gasped.

The whole inside had changed. The kitchen was totally changed, with brand-new cabinets, flooring, and appliances. The living room's walls were freshly painted, and there was new carpeting throughout the house.

"I didn't want you to see it until it was finished," Dex explained. "I wanted it all to be done. But that's not important now. Follow me."

All this time, the woman trailed behind us, holding some kind of tool in her hand and smiling. Dex opened the door to one of the empty bedrooms and I gasped. The room had been transformed into a nursery. The walls were painted yellow and blue, and papered with little animals, with matching drapes at the windows. New French doors opened out onto a lovely little terrace that was also brand-new. The wall-to-wall carpeting in the nursery was a wonderfully bright blue.

"You—you did all this?" I finally managed to ask.

"Yes," Dex said, looking pleased. But then he turned to me and said, "Was I wrong again? Should I have told you? I just can't seem to do anything right with you, Nora, and I want to please you so much."

"But—when did you start it?" I asked, still so shocked that I could barely speak.

"As soon as we found out that the baby was coming. I knew we needed a home."

"I think I'll go now," Rhoda said from the doorway.

Dex turned and waved to her. "Oh, right—thanks, Rho. We'll get the rest of that tiling done in the bathroom soon. Thanks for all your help." Then he turned to me. "Rhoda's a good friend who just happens to be great at this kind of work. But there was nothing else going on, Nora."

"I should go and apologize to her," I sniffled as I pressed my face against Dex's paint-smelling shirt. "I didn't even introduce myself. She must think I'm crazy to yell at you the way I did."

"It's okay. I think she gets the picture," he said with a tender smile.

I looked up at Dex then—at this beautiful man who'd come into my life so suddenly, so unexpectedly, and realized how supremely lucky I was.

"The house is beautiful," I whispered to him. "I can't believe you've been working so hard to do all this."

"It's all your fault," he said with a grin. "You inspire me."

"I just want you to love me," I told him. "I want you to love our baby, too."

"That I do," he said. "I already do."

He took my hand then and led me to "our" room.

"I haven't changed anything in here yet," he said gruffly, as though he was a little embarrassed. "It seemed good this way."

"Then let's leave it just the way it is," I sighed, pulling him down with me onto the bed. "It *is* good this way, after all."

Much later, as I lay in his arms, Dex whispered in my ear, "I think I'm happy, Nora. How about you?"

"Perfectly," I answered. "Perfectly happy." THE END